The Sound

&

The Echoes

Valerie Flying Her Albatross

Dew Pellucid

~~~~~~~~~~~

The Sound

&

The Echoes

~~~~~~~~~~~

Art by Andy Simmons

Echoland Publications
TheSoundAndTheEchoes.com

Illustrations by Andy Simmons
ANS-Graphics.com

ISBN-13:
978-1478305187

Manufactured in the United States of America
August, 2012

To Blue,

Without you this book would still be a manuscript.

Table of Contents

Illustrations

Dew Pellucid

Dear Un-Pellucid Reader,

Far, far away, in a land few Sounds have ever seen, stands the palace of Agám Kaffú. Not a palace of marble and silks, you understand. Nothing like those over-gilded palaces of the Sound realm. No, in the Land of the Echoes the palace glitters like a frozen snowflake in the early light of morning. And it looks like one too.

The walls are carved from gleaming ice that never melts, and the floors look like silent ponds you can walk on. Yes, you'll find curtains and tapestries to rival the finest woven art of the Taj Mahal or Buckingham Palace, but here they look like waterfalls sown together, foaming and splashing but never, never flowing away.

It's so many decades since my father took me to see it, that magnificent palace on Iceberg Mountain. Or is it centuries? Even the chandeliers resembled frozen bubbles, I remember. And the pillars looked like towering mounds of snowflakes. But if *you* were to see it, un-pellucid reader that you are, you wouldn't notice the waterfall curtains or the ice cube walls. No, for you the things that would stagger belief would be alive. Trees, people, dogs... Because, you see, in the Echo realm, every living thing is see-through.

Not entirely see-through, you understand. Not invisible... well, not everyone... not all the time. But I'm getting ahead of myself. You'll have to find it out in the proper way, turning page after page in this strange story of a Sound, a boy, who was hunted by

3

those terrifying demons of darkness known as the Fate Sealers and their oracle masters, the Fortune Tellers.

But did it really all happen, you might wonder? Certainly, in the Echo realm, that is.

But is the Echo realm real?

Ah! That is the fortune-changing question you'll have to answer for yourself.

Yours Obscurely,

Dew Pellucid

The Crystal Ball Clock

The Mysterious Reappearance

Will Cleary sat in the dark listening to the howling wind.

It was an old, familiar sound that reminded Will of his nightmares, where creatures he could not see were shrieking through the holes in his bedroom walls. The creatures were a dream, but the holes and room were real and so the nightmares felt real. Will used to try and plug them, the holes. But the old cabin he and his parents lived in was falling apart with age, and Will had long since given up.

Only one precious object was beautiful in Will's ugly room and he held it, cool between his hands. It was a crystal ball that glowed faintly like a strange basketball made of shimmering glass. There were numbers inside, falling through a bright mist, the big ones like snowflakes, the small ones like rain in slow-motion. At the moment the number eight was the biggest, and it hovered beside the smaller forty-one, with a tiny two raining down on the right, then three, four, five… It was eight forty-one in the morning according to the crystal ball clock, the start of a new day. But the falling numbers that disappeared in the fog made it seem as if time was raining out of existence.

The crystal ball clock was the first thing Will Cleary remembered from childhood. That and his nightmares.

The pale light of the shimmering crystal ball blinded Will to everything else in his cold, dark bedroom. But he could still see, a little past him, almost hovering in the blackness, the face of his white wolf with her dark-rimmed yellow eyes that seemed to see into his soul.

"'Cause I had the nightmare again," said Will, as if the wolf had asked a question. "Not going back to sleep to have it again... and again and again. Anyway, almost time. Look."

Will held the crystal ball out to the wolf, and in her yellow eyes two crystal ball reflections appeared with silent, falling numbers.

Then, in a moment, there was something else.

Inside the crystal ball a miniature boy appeared, looking tall and lanky, with long gangly legs and glasses. The falling seconds bounced off his curly brown hair, and the large hour and minutes hovered over him like a cloud. But the boy inside the crystal ball never noticed.

"He's here," said Will to the wolf.

In a flash Will was dashing downstairs. The floorboards groaned under him, and the front door whined as he tore it open, as if it would fall off. But it didn't, and there was the boy from the crystal ball clock standing on the creaky doorstep, looking real and full-sized and very pleased with himself.

"You found it?" asked Will.

"In the museum library," said the boy, waving a greeting at the wolf. "It's all about—"

"Wait, Ben... Outside."

"Outside...? As in sit and chat? It's freezing, if you haven't noticed."

"I've noticed," said Will, leading the way to a snowy porch bench.

The morning was still black and ominous, as if the winter wind had blown the sunrise off the ledge of the horizon. But Will had brought the crystal ball clock with him, and it cast its pale white light between him and Ben as they sat down. Then Ben pulled out a slab of white marble from his coat.

"I thought you were bringing a book?" Will frowned.

"It is a book."

"But it looks—"

"Like a gravestone, I know. Lots of gravestones, actually."

With trembling hands, Ben turned the strange book over to reveal the title: *Disappeared without a Trace?* It was printed where the names of the dead were usually carved in cemeteries.

The white wolf turned to look at Will and Ben, as if something had startled her. Then she took to pacing the porch, back and forth, back and forth, her yellow eyes peering at the dark snowy garden where the leafless trees were swaying in the wind like dancing skeletons.

9

But Will didn't notice his pet. *"Disappeared Without a Trace..."* he read the title aloud, as a dark hiding place ripped open in his mind.

It was that secret place where Will tucked his most painful thoughts of his twin sister, Emmy—the sister he couldn't remember because she disappeared ten years ago when they were only two. Emmy was the reason Will's parents had let their home fall apart. She was the reason they had almost gone mad with sorrow. And now she was the reason why he and Ben had to sit outside, shivering in the cold, just to keep their conversation secret. For any talk of Emmy always ended in insane rescue plans and false hope.

"You found the proof?" Will gasped. "Emmy's dead."

"No, Will." Ben's pale eyes glittered by the light of the crystal ball clock. "You don't understand. It's just the opposite. You're in the book. You disappeared just like Emmy. But you came back. And if you came back, you know what that means?"

But Will had expected to hear something quite different. An end to the mystery, not more infuriating false hope.

"Don't you start, Ben!" snapped Will. "My Mom's out there on the pond—looking for Emmy! She's been doing that for *ten years*! My Dad hasn't stopped looking for clues either. The last thing they need is you telling them *I* know the secret to bringing Emmy back."

"But if it's true?"

"Ben, Emmy drowned! Unless she's a mermaid, she's not coming back."

"So why didn't they find her body?" insisted Ben.

"Because—"

But that was the fatal question no one could answer.

For a moment Will listened to his old home creaking and groaning in the wind, until he could face the disappointment of another impossible idea. For Ben had to be wrong.

"Don't you think my parents would have told me if I disappeared like Emmy?" said Will quietly.

"Perhaps we should have," answered a quiet voice from the wild, snowy garden. And an old man with a young face ambled tiredly up the broken porch steps into the pale light of the crystal ball clock.

"Dad!" Will jumped back, startled. "Thought you were in the library."

Mr. Cleary bent to shake Ben's hand in greeting, and in the light of the crystal ball clock Mr. Cleary looked more like Will's older brother than his father—with blond, tousled hair that looked like straw and a small, thin body that resembled a scarecrow dressed in old clothes. Even Mr. Cleary's eyes were a lot like Will's; large, melancholy brown eyes that spoke of a sad heart.

"Came across this idea in Dew Pellucid's manuscript," Mr. Cleary said sadly, puffing on a large pipe. "Secret passage in the pond... False scent, I'm afraid. But this?" Mr. Cleary frowned at the strange gravestone book. "New clues to Emmy?"

"Yes," said Ben eagerly.

"No," said Will flatly. He could feel himself getting angry.

Not a make-your-blood-boil sort of angry, but a hopeless, helpless, falling-into-a-dark-hole anger that leaves you feeling cold and bitter.

"What now?" said Will sharply. "Think I disappeared like Emmy? Think I can remember how to bring her back?" Suddenly Will felt as if all these years his parents had been blaming him for something he couldn't even remember.

"That's just it," said Mr. Cleary softly; while Ben fidgeted with embarrassment, and the wolf seemed to raise her eyebrows at Will in disapproval. "We knew you'd think that," explained Mr. Clearly. "So we never told you, Mom and I. But how could you possibly remember anything, Will? You were barely two. It happened on Christmas, you see. On your birthdays. You and Emmy disappeared together. Well... we think you were together. We'll never know for sure."

"Because you can't remember, right?" said Ben, rifling through the gravestone book. "Every page here's about someone who disappeared. Hundreds of people, but especially kids. And no one remembers *how* they disappeared. Not one witness."

"What does the book say about me?" asked Will grudgingly, dreading something terrible, a horrible reason why his sister died, but he had managed to return alive.

"Finally!" said Ben. And he dropped the strange, heavy book in Will's lap.

But as Will started reading the page Ben had bookmarked for him, he realized that his disappearance was clouded in as much mystery as his sister's. And yet, the story of his return was no

12

mystery at all.

"My pets brought me back?" mumbled Will in disbelief.

"Yes, a week after you disappeared," said Mr. Cleary, his face shrouded in pipe smoke. "We were there, Mom and I. Saw everything. How strange... So hard to believe. One minute the pond was frozen, the next the center was melting. And then you popped out, riding a wolf... with a falcon circling over you. You kept calling out the animals' names: 'Deá, Damian... Deá, Damian...' in your cute toddler's voice. That's how we knew what to call them.

"Mom never let the hole in the pond freeze over since then," added Mr. Cleary. "Kept it defrosted with buckets until I had the water heater installed. One day Emmy will follow you home, and we will be ready, Will. We will be ready."

Mr. Cleary sighed and whispered to himself, "Ah, Emmy.... alone, alone, all, all alone... alone on a wide, wide sea."

In the same moment, the shadow of a bird circling in the bleak black sky fell over Mr. Cleary's features, making him look almost faceless. Soon the dark, speckled bird came to a landing on the wolf's white back, and the two animals stared long at each other as if exchanging wordless greetings.

In the back of Will's mind he could hear his father and Ben still talking, but he stopped listening. He was watching the falcon and the wolf, wondering what other secrets his pets could reveal if they could talk. Or if he could read their minds the way they sometimes seemed to read his. Then, his thoughts still mingling hope with curiosity, Will bent over the gravestone book again and read the

13

rest of his story.

William Cleary was naked at the time of his reappearance, but his body was covered in a strange glowing plant. No such plant is known to grow anywhere on earth. Despite extensive laboratory testing, it remains unknown why the plant glows at times but not at others. One unsubstantiated theory postulates that a chemical reaction results when the plant comes in contact with a yet unidentified type of gas.

"Dad?" Will looked up. "Was I covered in a plant? A glowing plant, when I came out of the pond?"

Smoke billowed from Mr. Cleary's face, swirling in the wind.

"Why, yes..." Mr. Cleary nodded. "A beautiful shade of luminous green. Stopped glowing after a day or two, then started again from time to time. Last month, in fact. Glowed for me and Deá when I went to water the plant... down in the cellar. Would you like to see it?"

Will caught sight of Ben nodding so hard his head seemed about to pop off. And breathlessly, Will nodded too. He had no idea his home even had a cellar, and he wondered what else he might find there.

Mr. Cleary led the way into the cobwebbed, windswept house, past mountains of moldy books in the living room and stacks of filthy pots in the kitchen. Will's crystal ball clock lit their way behind a moth-eaten curtain at the back of the dank laundry room, then down a dark, dusty stairway that creaked ominously. At the bottom, Mr. Cleary pulled on a dangling, filthy cord and an overhead light came on with a click.

Will gazed in wonder at the musty, windowless cellar. All the walls were lined with iron shelves from floor to ceiling, and every shelf was crammed with chests and boxes, piles of paper and shapeless bundles that gave no hint of what they hid inside. It was all covered in a thick layer of frosted dust and cobwebs, like a crypt that had been closed for centuries. But even down here, Will could hear his old home creaking and moaning in the winter wind blowing outside.

"You kept the plant in the dark?" wondered Ben.

"It likes the dark," said Mr. Cleary, wiping cobwebs off a manuscript he found on a bottom shelf by the stairs. *"Warts and Witchcraft in the Middle Ages."* Mr. Cleary sighed with fond remembrance. "I was twelve when I wrote it. Emmy's age... and yours, of course, Will. Well, we didn't come here for that."

Patting his son's shoulder affectionately, Mr. Cleary reached behind an old wicker chest labeled *Our Memory Box* and withdrew a jar of leaves floating in water. "Not glowing, I'm afraid," he said, securing a lid over the jar.

But at that moment veins of luminescent green began to spread all through the stringy plant, up its stalks and down its leaves, which started to drift to and fro as if an invisible teaspoon were swirling the water. Soon the whole jar was glowing like a lantern between Mr. Cleary's fingers, casting an eerie light on the wolf's white fur as she pushed past Will, the dark, speckled falcon still

15

perched on her back.

Spellbound, no one spoke—until the distant honk of a car shattered the silence.

Inside the crystal ball clock Will was still hugging to his side, the miniature hologram of Ben had disappeared. But now a tiny purple minivan emerged in its place, with a shadowy figure waving hello behind the steering wheel. The hour and minute numbers of the clock hung above the car, and the seconds bounced off the roof and vanished in the mist at the bottom of the crystal ball.

"My Mom," said Ben, already rushing off. "Promised I wouldn't make her wait...."

"Take it!" Mr. Cleary nodded at his son.

Will stuffed the glowing jar in his coat pocket and followed Ben to the front door of his creaking home, the wolf and falcon at his heels.

"Bring the gravestone book to school tomorrow," shouted Ben, rushing to the real-life purple minivan parked before the house, its headlights slashing the early morning darkness. "And the plant!"

With a farewell honk the car sped away, and Will was left alone, wind gusting in his face, shaking snow showers from the treetops overhead.

Inside the crystal ball clock a tiny boy with strawy hair had replaced the fading car. It was Will, and in the smaller version of his face Will could see all the confusion he was feeling. Glowing leaves and reappearance acts, he thought desperately. What next? Talking pets? And suddenly Will heard a strange girl's voice answering, as if someone was hearing his thoughts.

"Yes, you're quite right. It's time we had a good long chat, Will."

Will snapped his head back. There was no one there! No one except Deá, the wolf, curled on the porch bench, watching him with her dark-rimmed yellow eyes.

"Yes! So let's get on with it!" agreed a young man's voice.

Will looked around, baffled. Only Damian, the falcon, was there, perched on the rail, fluttering his speckled wings.

"Who's there?" cried Will.

"Don't be an idiot!" the young man's voice replied.

Will swiveled—and caught the falcon rolling his eyes at him.

"We have a lot to tell you," said the bird impatiently, while the wolf jumped off the porch bench and gestured with her paw.

"Maybe you should sit down first," she said kindly, and Will could have sworn that his white wolf was smiling at him.

We're Not Dead

The See-Through People

At long last, the sunrise was unfurling in the sky with skeletal fingers of faded gray and pink. It was a cold, bleak December morning in Alaska, a place so far north on planet Earth that if there were such things as popsicle people, they could live there quite comfortably.

Will shivered from the cold, but mostly from amazement, and watched the wolf and falcon watching him. For ten years they had been perfectly normal pets... well, except for being wild animals that seemed to read his thoughts... But the wolf and falcon never plunged into a sudden conversation, not even to wish Will happy birthday when his parents had been too busy looking for Emmy.

"You— can— talk—?" Will blurted out finally, but it sounded more like coughs than words.

"I know it's a bit of a shock," said the wolf, nodding kindly, "but there's a perfectly logical explanation."

Will sunk on the broken porch steps, too stupefied to speak. The crystal ball clock slid from his hand and rolled to the bottom of the stairs, and inside it Will's miniature hologram swiveled a few times then sat down too.

"Less and less promising," muttered the falcon, shaking his head.

Then, to the sound of Mr. Cleary humming a sad tune somewhere behind the open front door, the majestic bird spread his speckled dark wings and flew away.

"We'd better talk in the privacy of the forest," suggested the wolf. "Leave the clock here. It won't work out there. But bring two shovels... and don't forget the Waterweed."

Pointing her paw at the glowing jar peeking from Will's pocket, the wolf promised to explain everything soon. Then she galloped off down the gloomy, snowy path leading to the frozen pond.

Will followed, stopping only to pick up the shovels from a rusty garden shed. As he rounded the pond he waved to the thin white figure tugging a black hose across the ice. *Emmy...* Will thought desperately, *always Emmy...* And he stopped hoping that his mother might notice him for a change and wave back. Up ahead, the wolf leapt into the snowy forest behind the pond and Will rushed after her.

"Where are you?" Will cried into the silence of the tree trunks, which echoed his voice back at him.

Suddenly Will saw his pets.

The wolf and the falcon were lying in the snow not far from Will. They looked dead without any reason to be dead. There was no blood, no weapon, only the fresh snow that was starting to bury the animals as the wind shook the treetops. Without realizing it, Will dropped the shovels and dashed forward, the pit of his stomach turning to stone.

"No!" Will cried, falling in the snow beside his pets.

He started shaking them, first the wolf, then the falcon. "You can't be dead," he said desperately. "Deá, Damian. Wake up. It's not funny. Wake up! Wake up!"

"We're not dead." Will suddenly heard Damian's voice—but the sound came from above.

Will looked up.

A boy of about sixteen was standing not far from Will. The boy's skin, proud face and curly hair were as dark as coffee. His eyes were darker still, and they glittered with intelligence. He wore shimmering black clothes, and everything about him was see-through, so that Will could see a snowy tree showing right through the boy's face. It felt like looking through a brown-glassed window.

"Who are you?" marveled Will.

"I'm Damian," answered the boy, in Damian's voice. "And this is Deá."

The see-through boy stepped aside, and a beautiful girl of about fifteen emerged from behind the same tree. Her skin was as white as the snow at her feet, and her shimmering clothes were as white as her skin. Her long hair and large gray eyes were both so pale that for a moment Will thought she was made entirely of mist— like the mist inside his crystal ball clock—especially since the girl, like the boy, was see-through.

23

The two strange beings exchanged radiant smiles, as if they hadn't seen each other in years and were trying to make up for lost time. Then the pale girl turned to Will.

"The Waterweed… in your pocket," she said, in Deá's voice. "It stopped glowing after I left you. Did you notice?"

Will shook his head, as if in a daze.

"Well, it did," said the girl. "But now it's glowing again. Look." She waited for Will to numbly pull out the jar of luminous leaves from his coat pocket. "Told you. Glowing. We're *still* Deá and Damian, Will—but now you're seeing us in our true forms."

As if the girl had slapped his face, Will's sense of reality came back to him.

"My pets." Will shot to his feet. "What d'you do to them? Bring them back. Bring my wolf and falcon back to life."

"We can't," said the girl sadly, daylight glittering on her beautiful white face like sunshine on a lake. "They're dead, Will. They've been dead for ten years."

"That's a lie!" Will dug his fingernails into his fists. "They were talking to me just a few minutes ago!"

The dark boy chuckled. "Animals can't talk," he said dryly.

"Mine could!"

"Yes… Because they weren't animals at all. Look—" the boy lost his smile "—I know it's a shock for you, Will. And I wish we had time to discuss this comfortably over milk and cookies—"

"—Oh, how stupid of me!" Will rolled his eyes furiously. "Obviously, my pets just turned into Snow White and the black

24

dwarf. No mystery here."

The dark boy's eyes flashed. He was far from a dwarf, but the insult made him stand up even taller. He took a deep breath, as if to keep his anger in check, and tossed back his shimmering black cape. The cloth looked like tar trapped in an hourglass, flowing slowly down from his shoulders to his feet.

"The ceiling in your bedroom leaks," said the boy. "You keep a bucket on the floor."

Will gasped. "You've been to my room—?"

"—Yesterday," the boy ignored the interruption, "I stuffed a sock in the new hole under your window. To stop the wind."

"How—?"

The girl giggled. Her long hair fluttered as she moved; her dress shimmered like melted diamonds. "Haven't you ever wondered why your wolf was a vegetarian—?"

"—Or why your falcon went with you everywhere, even to school?" The boy kicked snow off his black boots impatiently. "Did you think I enjoyed sitting on the hood of the school bus like an overgrown ornament? Or on the windowsill of your classrooms... watching over you... with all those stupid pigeons cooing at me? Still don't believe us? All right, ask me something only Damian could know."

Will felt dazed. How could these see-through strangers know so much about him? Who were they? *What* were they?

"All right..." Will muttered, glancing down at his dead pets. "All right..." He fought back the sadness that confused him. And

25

then Will's gaze fell on the falcon's wing, where an old scar showed white between the dark, speckled feathers. And that gave Will an idea.

"When did Damian meet our school nurse?" Will asked casually.

The dark boy chuckled. "Very sneaky, Will. You know very well I never met Nurse Bell... or Tinker Bell as the students like to call her because she's so short. The day I cut my wing when the school bus hit a lamppost, you snuck me into the school infirmary when no one was there. Ben kept watch outside. And you covered me in bandages until I looked like a bird in a straitjacket. Thank you for that, by the way."

Will blinked, astonished. He and Ben had never told anyone about this.

"Now, ask *me* something," said the pale girl, almost singing the words.

Will looked at his motionless wolf, wishing he could bend down and wake her with a hug. Instead, he forced himself to think of another trick question.

"What did Deá bring up to my room on my last birthday?"

The girl's large gray eyes grew hazy as she searched her memory. At last she smiled.

"Not on your birthday. Last spring. When you were sick, and your Dad was away on a book tour. I brought you a sandwich. And you were amazed because you thought—"

"—That my Mom made me something to eat for the first

26

time ever." Will nodded eagerly. "I forgot all about it, Deá. I thought—"

Will shut his mouth abruptly.

"You called me Deá!" The girl clapped her misty hands soundlessly. "You believe us! You believe us at last!"

Will swallowed hard. Impossible, he thought. And yet he knew that this was the truth, no matter how strange.

*   *   *

"It's about time," sighed Damian, and he walked away, his lucent cape drifting behind him like dark, black fog. He stopped to pick up the two shovels Will had dropped in the snow.

"We have to bury our animal selves," said Damian quietly, and he started digging beneath the shadow of a stately cedar.

A deep silence fell over the three of them, and the sound of the wind grew loud above the trees. Will couldn't believe it was happening. He couldn't believe that he would never see his wolf and falcon alive again. But he felt stupid, because they weren't really dead.

To stop the tears stinging his eyes, Will picked up the second shovel and cleared away a circle of frost a few feet from Damian. Deá came to stand between them, and suddenly Will noticed crystal drops falling at Deá's feet, like beautifully polished hail.

Will looked up, a little shyly because the see-through girl was so beautiful, and he saw that Deá was crying frozen teardrops.

"What kind of people are you?" asked Will, starting to dig the second grave to keep himself from staring at the girl.

27

Damian's shovel struck the frozen ground with a clang. "First, promise you'll never repeat what we tell you," he said sharply

"Promise? Why?" asked Will suspiciously.

Damian's glance darted anxiously to Deá. "A small matter of risking our lives."

Will's shovel froze in midair. "Your lives..." He still felt protective towards Deá and Damian, even if they weren't his pets anymore. "All right, I promise. I won't even tell Ben."

"Good," snapped Damian. "Unless you want your best friend to die because of you."

"Die? Because of me? What d'you mean?"

But Damian shook his dark head infuriatingly. "No more questions. Dig. Shut up. Then I'll explain."

"You can't just say something like that and tell me to shut up," Will snapped back.

"I can if you want to get anything more out of me."

"Damian!" Deá stomped her shimmering white boot, though it made no sound nor raised any snow drift.

Damian started digging furiously, his shovel banging against the frozen ground. Will expected Deá to take over explaining everything, which would have been a relief, but the girl seemed happy just to watch Damian and see what he would do next.

"Deá and I come from another realm," the dark boy said finally.

"From outer space?" Will nodded. Finally things were starting to make sense.

But Damian raised a haughty eyebrow. "I said from another realm, not another planet! Just dig and listen." He waited for Will to obey.

"Beneath the North Pole…" the boy resumed, "…and areas down to the 50° North latitude. Underground, I mean… there are other lands. Places a lot like here. There's light, for example. Trees, mountains, lakes." Damian kept digging, and his breath was coming in gasps. "There are animals too. And people. Cities, villages… Deá and I come from one of these lands. We… everyone who lives there… we're called …ekos."

Will wasn't sure he heard right. "You're Geckos?" he asked, not trying to be funny. It was just that Deá and Damian had lived in a wolf and falcon for so long, and he had no idea what else they could do.

Damian smiled wryly, his coffee eyes glinting with amusement. "Not Geckos, you idiot. Echoes! As in a sound and an echo."

Will smiled in embarrassment, and it didn't help to hear Deá giggling beside him.

"Have you ever looked in a mirror and wondered if your reflection was actually another person?" the girl asked.

Will took a moment to consider his answer, and he kept digging, ignoring a stinging blister forming in his palm. "You mean alive?" he asked finally.

"Poor Will." Deá giggled again. "This is all going to sound really strange."

"Stranger than you two living in my pets?" Will muttered, more to himself than anyone.

"'Fraid so," said Deá, without giggling this time. "Like nothing you've ever heard before. Though maybe you've seen it... some of it... in your nightmares...?"

But Will had never seen the creatures shrieking in his nightmares. He always seemed to wake up a second before the walls of his room cracked open in the dream.

"They're real... those things in my nightmares?" he stammered.

"Oh! They're real," said Damian. And he wasn't smiling anymore.

"They're Echoes," said Deá. "Like us."

"But *what* are you?" asked Will.

"Think of the beginning of an Echo as a bubble of air," said Deá, "or gas, actually."

"Gas?" Without thinking, Will scrunched his nose like a kid making a silly joke.

"Oh! How hilarious," snapped Damian, driving his shovel harder at the ground.

"There's more to life on earth than you realize, Will," Deá went on explaining. "Every time something in your world comes to life, gas is released into the air. It happens at the same time. Two forms of life come into existence together. A Sound and an Echo. And the Echo is made of gas. But it's not ordinary gas. This gas is *alive.* It's a living being. And it looks like a *reflection.*"

30

"Of what?" asked Will, finally starting to begin to understand.

"Of whatever released the living gas into the air. If the gas came to life when a flower began to grow, then the gas-being will look exactly like the flower. And it will grow like the flower, open up its petals, bloom... just like the flower. If the gas came to life when a tree sprouted, then the gas-being will be a tree. And if the gas came to life when a human was born..."

"Then the gas being will be a human," said Will, hardly noticing the pile of snow the wind had just dropped on his head. "And you and Damian are reflections? Gas-beings, I mean."

"Echoes." Deá nodded. "And we come from the realm of the Echoes. The place where all reflections live."

"So this is the Sound realm?" said Will, not really digging anymore. "I mean, that's what you call us... me?" And suddenly a thought blazed through Will's mind, the way a flashlight beam can suddenly light up a doorway. "Hold on!" he added. "That means *I* have an Echo. A reflection of me. A gas-being that looks just like—"

But before Will could ask if his nightmares had something to do with his reflection... and if Emmy's disappearance was also connected to it... Before Will could ask any of it, he suddenly noticed a deep, dark grave gaping in the snow where Damian had been digging.

The dark boy was gone. As Will turned around to look for him, he spotted Damian standing with his back to him and Deá, the Echo's shimmering black cape billowing like a storm. A moment later Damian turned, and Will saw that he was carrying the body of the white wolf with the speckled falcon resting on her chest.

As Damian drew near, Will saw a muscle pulsing in the Echo's dark, see-through cheek, as if he was clenching his jaw. Will looked away, feeling intimidated by this brooding boy that was probably just a few years older than he was, but who looked so much like a warrior.

It was Deá who moved toward Damian first, reaching her see-through misty hand to comb away a cluster of fur from the wolf's tail. She gave it to Will, who was suddenly feeling the tears pricking his eyes again. He looked at the ground to keep Damian from seeing him crying, and saw the Echo's dark hand extending a speckled feather to him without a sound.

Then the funeral just happened, without any of them telling the other what to do. They lowered the pets into the deep grave Damian had dug, and Will realized that Damian was just trying to keep him busy before, making Will dig a second grave to stop him asking questions. It was clear the wolf and falcon belonged together in a single grave.

Looking down into the grave, Will thought of his crystal ball clock and the falling numbers that rained inside it and disappeared as if Time was dying. He tucked away the fur and feather without taking his eyes off the dark hole where his childhood pets where lying, as if this was all some nightmare Will was trapped in. Except that it wasn't a nightmare. It was worse. It was real.

And then a swirling feeling of drowning came over Will, as if the grave was some deep, dark pond calling him to plunge inside. And Will wanted to, because up here where he stood in the cold light of day Will felt as if his heart would break and rain down like the disappearing numbers in the crystal ball clock. Just as the days and years of Will's life had rained down, every new day washing away the hope that Emmy would ever return. She couldn't return, Will knew that. No more than Deá and Damian could. His pets, not the Echoes… Will meant his pets… But his pets had been the Echoes….

Will shook his head. A haze of tears was blinding him. He started pacing the frozen forest floor that crackled under his feet as if threatening to collapse. He tried to think of more questions to ask the strangers who used to be his favorite beings in the whole world. He looked at the Echoes and thought, *Deá and Damian aren't dead. Only their bodies are different.* And then, like a lightning bolt flashing through a dark night, a question shot through Will's sadness and confusion.

"How long did you live inside my wolf and falcon?" Will asked breathlessly.

Damian was already shoveling earth back into the open grave. He looked up, smiling mirthlessly with his see-through, coffee lips, like some strange coca cola ice sculpture.

"Ten years," he said, with that ironic curve of his lips to one side. "And before you start showing off your brilliant mathematical deductions, let me explain something. I wasn't six years old when I entered the falcon, and Deá wasn't five. We were the same age we are today. An Echo living in a Sound doesn't age."

33

"Doesn't age? You mean… you live forever?"

Damian shook his head. "An Echo living inside a Sound weakens gradually and eventually will die. You can actually see how weak Deá and I are… just look at the transparency of our skin. Normally, we shouldn't be more see-through than our clothes. Now, help me finish! There's a lot more you need to hear, Will, and we're running out of time."

The Echoes, Deá and Damian

The Secrets of the Crystillery

Damian led the way deeper into the forest, away from Will's mother who could still be seen through the snowy trees, standing in the middle of the frozen pond, putting on a black diving suit that glistened in the morning sun.

"Don't forget this," Deá said to Will, and she slipped the glowing jar of Waterweed into his coat pocket and turned to follow Damian. "Coming?" she glanced back at Will.

Will memorized the spot where his pets were buried and walked away, feeling for the ball of fur and feather in his pocket.

"Is this where you got your clothes?" Will asked, seeing Damian picking up a shimmering black bag behind the tree he and Deá had first appeared by.

"Yes," said Deá.

"Where d'it come from?"

"Your Echo left it for us."

"My Echo—?" Will was stunned. His Echo had been there? When? Why? Will's mind no longer groped for questions; they were flying at him like darts.

37

"Not here!" snapped Damian, before Will could ask any of them.

Gradually the forest grew thick and dark. The trees, which had looked like snowy triangles before, were so crowded here that very little snow made it past their thick, green branches. Many shadows fell on the brown, frozen ground. There were no bird sounds or wind. No sounds at all. The forest looked eerie and evil, like a place where bad things could happen if you didn't watch out.

At last Damian stopped and signaled for them to sit beneath a heavy veil of icy branches. Then, without a sound, the Echo opened his shimmering bag and pulled out a glittering object.

For a second Will thought he was looking at a huge sapphire about as big as Damian's palm. But then Will realized that the top of the strange blue stone was round and perfectly smooth, like a polished dome. And it was see-through, so Will could look inside and see blue waves ebbing and flowing like a miniature sea.

Suddenly three glittering things burst through the waves, and at first Will thought they were tiny fish. But the glittering things were star-shaped, and in a moment Will realized that they were gems. The first was red like a ruby, the next blue like a sapphire, and the last yellow like a yellowish sort of diamond. Twinkling on the waves, the stones looked like magical fireflies.

"This is a Crystillery," said Damian, and he started rocking the blue dome between his dark, see-through palms.

The blue waves grew stormier and stormier and soon they were frothing. And maybe that's why it seemed to Will that the starry stones were twinkling brighter and brighter.

"We're going to use the Crystillery to look back at the day you and Emmy disappeared," said Damian.

"How?" gasped Will, enchanted by a string of silver bubbles that suddenly floated up between the twinkling stones.

"The Crystillery can read memories," said Deá, her pale gray eyes twinkling too.

"And thoughts," added Damian darkly. "Reach inside your back pocket, Will."

"My pocket? Why—?"

But suddenly Will remembered something brushing against him in the cellar that morning when he, Ben and his Dad were looking at the glowing green Waterweed.

"Right pocket," added Damian, though he really didn't need to.

Already Will was pulling out the photograph of a beautiful woman seated cross-legged on a green lawn, blowing soap bubbles. Will didn't have to ask how the photograph got there. The falcon must have slipped it in Will's pocket as the bird perched on the wolf's white back.

"On the ground," said Damian, and Will set the photograph down and had barely snatched his hand away before the Echo lowered the Crystillery over the smiling woman's face.

Instantly the waves inside the blue dome parted, and a terrible whirlpool sucked them away. The red, blue and yellow stones clashed together and sparked like fire, then they too disappeared. And in their place rose the woman from the photograph, only now she looked alive and real, as if the Crystillery was some tiny television screen.

The woman floated up to the top of the dome, and the green grass and her pink dress looked more and more real as the blue dome slowly turned as clear as glass, then clearer still, until it looked like it wasn't there at all.

No bigger than a thumb, the woman seemed as if she was standing with her feet in her world and her head in Will's, and when she laughed and blew bubbles Will waited to see the bubbles drifting up at him. But they never did, though the woman's voice rose up like a splash of summer in the dreary, dark forest where her mouth kept blowing air into the soap bubble wand. And there were other voices rising behind her, the giggles of little children and a hiccuppy sort of laugh Will recognized at once.

"My Dad…"

"Yes," said Deá softly.

"Who is she?" wondered Will, suddenly thinking that he recognized the woman, now that her eyes started sparkling like diamonds with rainclouds trapped inside them. Which was strange, because Will never knew anyone with eyes like that.

"This photograph was taken on Christmas morning… ten years ago," said Deá, her words sounding like steps taken cautiously over thin ice.

"The day Emmy and I disappeared?" asked Will, frowning.

"Yes… You see, Will." Deá sighed. "That's what your

mother used to look like… back then."

It took these words a long time to begin making sense to Will, and when they did Will felt as if his world was turning upside down.

"That's… my Mom?" Will shook his head, staring at the beautiful, happy woman.

He had never seen his mother laughing. He had never seen her in a pink dress or in a garden. Only on the pond or on the way back from it, with her hair dripping and her skinny body trapped in a black diving suit.

"But she looks like a completely different person," said Will, shaking his head.

"She was—"

A shriek rose from the Crystillery and silenced them.

The miniature woman was suddenly screaming, eye's wide with horror, staring at something behind Will.

Will twisted back in a panic, but there was nothing there except trees and shadows.

"It's in her world, not ours," said Damian, and Will twisted back to face the screaming woman that was supposed to be his mother.

"Inside! Take the kids inside!" Will heard his father's voice shouting from the blue dome, only Will couldn't see him there. "Lock the—"

But suddenly the voices stopped as if someone had turned off a radio. In a second, the woman turned see-through and faded away.

The dome turned blue again, and the water inside it returned with the red, blue and yellow stars floating over the waves like twinkling fish.

"Turn it back on!" yelled Will breathlessly.

"We're not expert Crystillery readers," said Deá, shaking her head. "We don't know how to see anymore."

"There's another way," said Damian.

"What way?" Do it!" Will couldn't stop shaking.

"*You* know what happened next." Damian stared at Will, as if his coffee eyes were trying to read something in Will's face. "*You* were there. *You* were one of the kids we heard laughing."

"Me?"

"Ten years ago. The day you and Emmy disappeared."

"I was two years old! I can't remember." But as Will said this, he suddenly felt nauseous and terrified, as if something terrible was starting to happen.

"You're remembering something…" cried Deá. And from the corner of his eye, Will saw her turning and crying, "Quick, Damian!"

A split second later Will felt the chilly bottom of the Crystillery slamming into his forehead, and the forest around him disappeared.

Will could feel the cool crystal of the dome softening against his head like a clammy mouth. Then it started to suck him. Images, memories, feelings flashed through Will's head like insane streaks of light. They had voices, and they shouted and laughed and talked at him in a mad jumble of a thousand days mixed together. Will tried to raise an arm to knock the squeezing pain away, but he couldn't remember how to move a muscle.

"Enough! Damian, stop!" Will heard a girl yelling far, far away.

Then the squeezing disappeared, and the storm in Will's head vanished. He heard the girl asking if he was all right. He opened his eyes and saw the world in fuzzy doubles. Two Damians were saying, "Don't worry, you won't stay cross-eyed forever."

Will shook his head to stop the buzzing in his ears and heard himself asking, "Did it work?"

"Yes," said two Deás—but they were merging into one already.

Once again Damian rocked the Crystillery, stirring the blue waves into a storm of silver bubbles. Soon the surface of the dome turned invisible, and a circle of dark fog rose up to stand where the laughing woman had been.

Will heard his mother screaming again, but he couldn't see her in the Crystillery as before. "Take the kids inside! Lock the door!" Will heard his father shouting in the blue dome. And suddenly the circle of dark fog turned, and Will realized that he was looking at two see-through creatures.

The strange beings inside the Crystillery looked like dark smoke. But they were men. Men whose faces were masks of terror. Their eyes were dark, bottomless holes with no pupil or any sign of life. Their toothless mouths gaped as if screaming, silent screams. They were thinner than any human Will had ever seen, with chests that looked like extra-long ribcages, and arms that reached down to their feet, as if the horrifying men had been starved and stretched on torture racks for years. As Will thought this, he realized that the gray skin of the creatures sagged off their skeletal shapes like dirty gray robes, and this drooping skin was the only clothes they were wearing.

Will heard his mother scream again and children wailing. The dark skeletal men laughed at this, in high pitched screeches, and their sagging lips swung from side to side like grotesque pendulums. One of them reached beneath his sagging skin and brought out a luminous horn, like that of a ram only made from ice. Wrapping its swinging lips around the wide end, the creature filled its lungs until the thin chest looked like a balloon in the middle of the endlessly long body. Then the creature blew into the horn and a shower of icy needles fired out the other end.

"Watch out!" shouted Will, flinching back.

But nothing had happened in his world. The nightmare was happening in the Crystillery-world alone. For there Will suddenly saw the woman in the pink dress again, and she was running away with two toddlers wailing in her arms.

The shower of ice hit her head from behind and she fell forward on the green lawn, her pink dress specked with blood. A sagging gray arm swept before her to grab the toddlers hurled into the air. In seconds the icy shards coated the woman's head until it looked like a bowling ball of prickly ice. And where the ball rested Will saw a second ball of ice on the green lawn, this one attached to the shoulders of a man.

Will didn't realize that he was shaking, until something terribly cold hugged him tightly. It was Deá, shaking a little too.

"I'm so sorry, Will," she whispered in his ear, her cold breath feeling like a freezer. "I'm so, so sorry."

Will saw Deá wiping frozen tears, as Damian wiped the Crystillery with his shimmering cape and slipped the blue dome back inside the black bag. The visions in the Crystillery were gone… the visions that were memories from Will's childhood, from the day he saw what happened to Emmy.

"What were those… *things*?" Will gasped. He didn't add that the shrieks of the creatures were the same shrieks he had always heard in his nightmares, when creatures he could not see would scream through the holes in his bedroom walls.

Damian's face was rigid and full of pain. "They're called Fate Sealers."

"Fake what?" stammered Will.

"Fate. Sealers. They are… or, more precisely, they once were… Echoes. Now they are tortured creatures that live only to inflict pain and misery. Ask me one day what turns an Echo into a Fate Sealer," added Damian. "But not today. Not today."

Will wasn't sure if Damian was being impatient again or showing the first sign of compassion.

"What did they do to my parents?" Will forced himself to ask.

"They froze their brains," said Damian, speaking softly.

45

"That's how Fate Sealers attack."

"But my parents didn't die."

"Brain Freeze doesn't kill. It just wipes off chunks of memory."

"So that's why they couldn't remember anything..." Will thought not only of his parents but of all the witnesses Ben had read about in the gravestone book. So many kids disappearing, and no one remembering how it happened. "Is it painful?" Will asked. "The Brain Freeze?"

"I'm told it is," said Damian, the muscle in his dark see-through cheek pulsing tensely.

No one spoke for a while, not even Damian to remind them that they were running out of time. In the distance something hummed over the dark forest. It was the water heater by Will's house, the one his dad had installed to keep the center of the pond melted in winter. Will thought about his mother and the woman in the Crystillery, and how they were supposed to be the same person. Then for the first time in his life, Will didn't feel sad that his mother never noticed him. He felt sorry for her instead.

"There's a reason," Damian spoke again, "why Deá and I revealed ourselves to you today. After keeping our identities secret for ten years. We were sent here to guard you from the Fate Sealers."

"Guard me?" asked Will. "Who sent you?"

"For the last ten years," Damian went on, ignoring the question, "Deá watched over you by night, staying awake in the corner of your bedroom. I guarded you by day, going with you

46

everywhere you went."

"Why? Why are Fate Sealers after me?"

Deá laid her hand on Will's knee; it felt like ice. "Just listen, Will. Damian will tell you everything we know."

"In less than three weeks," Damian continued, "you'll turn thirteen. That changes everything. We can't protect you here anymore. It's time you came with us down into the Echo realm."

"What?!" Will jumped to his feet and scratched his face on a branch. "Are you *insane?*" he asked, not noticing. "D'you know what'll happen to my parents if I disappeared too?"

Damian rose also and held his hand out to Deá. A tree trunk showed through his dark body, making the Echo look scaly.

"We know where Emmy is," said Damian. "She's alive, and we want—"

"—No, no, *no!*" Will shook his head in frustration. "The Fate Sealers took Emmy. The Crystillery showed us. She's dead. How many times do I have to tell everybody. Emmy drowned."

"Then why are you alive?" asked Deá. "Your Dad told you… you disappeared too. But you came back. Why?"

"That's different. I—"

"—Do you or don't you want to know what happened?" said Damian, in a whisper that cut into Will like a knife.

"You were never this annoying as a bird," muttered Will.

Deá giggled.

"You were never this inquisitive when I was a bird," said Damian. He raised a dark eyebrow and curved his lips in that wry smile Will was starting to recognize.

Will smiled back. "I want to know," he admitted.

"Good," said Damian, but not smugly. "A party of the King's loyal servants caught up with the Fate Sealer who kidnapped you. You were saved. It was decided that Deá and I should take you home and stay with you, to guard you."

"And Emmy?" asked Will

"The Fate Sealer who kidnapped her got away. The search for Emily Cleary continued for years. In the end, she was found when she was already seven years old… far too old by Echo law to return to the Sound realm."

Will hardly dared to breathe. "Where was she found?" he muttered.

"In…" Damian's coffee eyes narrowed and his lips tightened. He seemed to be fighting himself to keep talking. "In Shadowpain," he said at last. "The dungeons of the Fate Sealers. She's the only human to survive captivity in the hands of those monsters for so many years."

Will felt sick. He kicked the frozen ground with his foot to stop himself screaming that this can't be happening. Emmy can't be alive, not after living with creatures like that for…

"Years?" Will asked, still shaking his head in disbelief.

"Yes," said Damian.

A frozen teardrop fell out of Deá's eye.

"Where is she now?" asked Will. He couldn't believe he was having this conversation. Emmy was alive! His parents were right after all!

But Damian's words were drowned by a scream.

It came soaring over the thick, dark trees, piercing the cold air, echoing from far away. It was the same cry Will was used to hearing on stormy nights when his mother would mistake the wail of the wind for the cry of a little girl and rush out into the rain in search of Emmy.

In a flash Will was on his feet.

He darted away, past tree trunks and falling shards of ice, retracing his steps back to the forest's edge. A dark shape flashed past him; Damian moving at a speed no Sound could match. Branches slapped Will's frozen cheeks, blinding him for seconds at a time. As the forest grew less thick, whiter and whiter trees seemed to dash forward to meet Will. Light streamed through their snowy branches, everything streaking between them in a confusing smear.

And then, suddenly, Will slammed into a wall of ice where no wall existed, only a see-through mist. And out of this mist rose a terrible face, its eyes hollow, its sagging, swinging lips curled around the wide edge of a luminous horn.

A Fate Sealer!

Will's mind spun in a whirl of terror. In a moment, icy needles were shooting into his eyes, his cheeks, his mouth... And through the never-ending pain Will thought he saw Deá's see-through body bending over him like an umbrella trying to stop the rain—but then she melted away and everything went black.

49

The Fate Sealers

The Most Precious Coin
In the Land

It was night outside when Will woke up, shivering badly. To his amazement there was no ceiling over his head or a bed under him. No! He was staring up at the constellation Cassiopeia, his initial W written in starlight. And under him stretched the hard, frozen pond he knew so well. The pond with the hole melted at the center.

Suddenly Will heard a whisper, very near him.

"How can we… just leave him? What if he can't… remember… anything?"

Will tried to move. But his body was too frozen, and in his head pain exploded like fireworks of ice.

"It's not working anymore, Deá," answered a firm voice. "You're losing a lot of blood. I'll try another bandage. But if I don't get you real help…."

The speaker broke off. But after a moment, Will heard him again.

"The Brain Freeze didn't last long enough. Will's memory

isn't erased, I'm sure of it. Not permanently anyway. He lost consciousness twelve hours ago. Soon he'll wake up. Then we'll see."

Will tried to move again, and now the pain in his head felt like rain, not ice. So he dared to turn his head a little more.

And then Will saw a boy, dark as the night, crouching quite near him. At the boy's feet lay a girl that looked as pale as the crescent moon shining over her. How strange that both the boy and the girl looked as if they were made from colored water that was a little see-through.

"Woo are yoo?" Will hooted, realizing that his tongue felt disgustingly fuzzy and numb.

The dark boy turned and very slowly asked, "You don't remember me?"

"Nwo," answered Will thickly, though he wondered why the see-through stranger seemed so perplexingly familiar.

"Roll your tongue in your mouth. It will help," said the boy. He pulled out a small blue dome from his pocket and rose to his feet. "Remember this?" he asked, holding the dome over Will's face, until Will spotted three star-shaped stones inside, glowing faintly like fireflies.

Will shook his head, then flinched from the pain.

The strange, see-through boy promised Will he would soon feel better. Then he dashed sideways in a blur of speed that made him disappear into the night for a moment then reappear by a large block of ice.

"Can you see her?" asked the Boy.

Will turned his head a little more. But what he saw seemed impossible. Inside the ice he thought he saw a human being.

Suddenly the dark boy raised his arm and slammed the blue dome into the block of ice on the top right side. Cracks appeared as the ice there shattered, and the boy cleared the broken shards away, until what seemed impossible to Will a moment ago became terribly real.

Inside the block of ice, Will saw a face with eyes shut tight, and a screaming mouth that made no sound.

"Mom!" Will recognized the face in horror.

In a flash, memories shot into Will's mind like scenes from a horror movie. A scream of terror— A rain of icy needles— A sagging face with dark black holes for eyes—

"A Fate Sealer!" Will screamed.

"Do you remember me now?" asked the see-through boy.

"Yes, Damian," said Will.

And with the whirlpool of memories flooding Will's mind came a terrible longing to see his pets again. The falcon had always gone with him everywhere, and at night the wolf had always been there. But now Will would never see them again. And missing his pets felt as if someone was drilling a hole in his heart.

"Come, I'll help you up," said Damian. And he grabbed Will's wrists with his cold, Echo hands and pulled Will to his feet. "Give it a few seconds. Your head will stop spinning, I promise."

With everything a blur, Will looked around, wishing at least that his crystal ball clock were here with him. It always cheered him up after a nightmare.

"What time is it?" asked Will, shaking off Damian's icy hands.

"About four A.M. It's Monday morning. Sure you're all right?"

"I'm fine. Monday morning? How long was I—?" But suddenly Will gasped as his roving glance fell on Deá.

The beautiful Echo girl he remembered from the forest was lying motionless on the frozen pond. Her eyes were closed, her face and hands looked almost invisible, and her body was so thin and frail that she might have been a puddle of moon drops, if the moon could trickle down to earth.

"She's dying," muttered Damian helplessly.

Will noticed white liquid oozing from Deá's bandaged neck. Echo blood, he realized. "How?"

"Fate Sealer… He slashed her throat."

"She bent over me." Will remembered. "She protected me."

"I'm taking her to the Echo realm," said Damian, lifting Deá so gently in his arms that she seemed to float up like a cloud. "I have to, Will. She wouldn't approve, leaving now after guarding you for ten years, I know she wouldn't. But I can't let her die."

For the first time Will saw fear in the proud Echo's face. "I'll be okay," Will said, because he felt he should say that. But he knew it wasn't true.

"You won't," said Damian, as if he could read Will's mind.

"Not if you stay here."

Damian gestured for Will to follow him, as the Echo walked away with Deá lying limply in his arms, her see-through head resting on Damian's shoulder. To Will it seemed that an invisible hand was erasing Deá's beautiful face out of existence and that soon she would disappear.

"By now they know in Shadowpain," said Damian. "They always know." As if looking for something, the Echo scanned the distant dark shore. "Fate Sealer messenger ravens are everywhere. You've been lucky, Will. The attack on you failed yesterday. But the Fate Sealers will make sure it doesn't fail again. You have four… maybe five hours before more Fate Sealers get here."

"I can't leave my Mom like that," said Will, glancing back at the frozen figure lying on the ice, screaming a silent scream.

"Use hot water to defrost her," said Damian.

The Echo stopped by the melted hole in the pond where a long green hose, left forgotten on the ice, was pouring steaming water into the hole, keeping it from freezing over.

"But melt your mother slowly," added Damian. "You have to go slow, Will, you understand? If you rush, your Mother could break… like glass. But if you're careful, she'll wake up without remembering anything. Not even the pain. Your father might, though. His brain was only partially frozen, like yours. I left him in the house."

Drops of Deá's pale blood trickled through Damian's dark fingers and fell into the hole at the Echo's feet, where dark water rippled.

"Can't let her die…" Damian muttered to himself, looking down at Deá.

"I'll be fine," said Will, trying to sound convincing. "After my parents wake up, we'll leave together."

"No!" said Damian, and suddenly his voice was sharp. "They'll find you. Fate Sealers never give up. Never!"

Looking torn, Damian shook his head, stared at Will and shook his head again. But finally the Echo seemed to make up his mind what to do.

"Take my Crystillery," he said, turning his back to Will. "That's right, lift my cape. It's in my back pocket. Found it?"

Damian's dark shimmering clothes felt like warm Jell-O between Will's fingers. "Yes," said Will, pulling the cold blue dome out.

"Do you remember the chest in the cellar, back home?" asked Damian. "The one the Waterweed was hidden behind?"

Will nodded. "*Our Memory Box.*"

"That's right. There's a coin hidden in the lining of the box. D'you understand?"

"Memory Box. Coin. Got it!" Will held the Crystillery tightly with both hands. "And this is for?"

"I don't have time to explain," said Damian. "You'll have to read the coin's memory with the Crystillery. Just copy what you saw me doing in the forest."

Will nodded and so did Damian, as if fighting to convince

himself that Will will be okay.

"You won't be alone," added Damian, as if answering his own troubled thoughts. "He'll help you, I'm sure he will. Just take the coin to school—"

"School?" asked Will, amazed. "My school?"

Will glanced back at his mother, wondering how soon he and his Dad could get her away from here. How could he possibly go to school now?

But Damian just kept on talking, as if he didn't hear Will at all. He told Will the name of the person he should see at school, the only person who could help him now. And Will might have heard the name despite talking at the same time, if only Deá had not suddenly groaned.

After that it was too late to ask Damian to repeat the name again, because the Echoes splashed into the pond and disappeared.

*　　　*　　　*

Will was alone. The night seemed suddenly darker. And in every shadow, every whisper of the wind, Will imagined a Fate Sealer swooping down on him like a giant bird of prey. It was like being trapped in one of his nightmares, except that now Will couldn't wake up.

Lifting the hot water hose, he started defrosting his mother. Just a trickle at a time or she would break like glass... A human being breaking like an ice sculpture.... Will worked in slow-motion like a gardener watering the most delicate plant in the world. And every time the cold wind bit into the back of his neck, Will jumped, terrified. But he never dropped the hose. He never stopped watering his mother back to life.

Hours later, or was it years? Mr. Cleary came running across the moonlit frozen pond. He remembered nothing, and Will just let his father believe that his mother had fallen into the hole in the icy pond without wearing her diving suit.

"I'll stay behind in case Emmy comes back," said Will, as he and his father laid Mrs. Cleary on the backseat of their beat up old station wagon. Then Will's father sped away to the hospital, and Will raced for the safety of his ramshackle home.

At the bottom of the porch stairs, it waited for Will, his glowing crystal ball clock. Only yesterday Will had left the clock there to go chasing his wolf into the forest. So much had changed in a day! Now peering into the clock's mist, Will saw a miniature hologram of himself, just as yesterday he had seen Ben's hologram inside.

Holding the crystal ball clock before him, Will walked up to the front door of his home. There, too, a crystal ball waited for him. Only this crystal ball was a doorknocker that looked like a giant pearl hanging in the middle of the weathered front door. With every step Will took, the pearly knocker glowed brighter—while inside the glowing crystal ball clock held between Will's hands, the head of Will's tiny hologram grew bigger and bigger as if a lens was zooming in on him.

Will sighed with relief. This meant that the camera inside the doorknocker was working fine. Anyone nearing his home would be filmed by the doorknocker and converted into a hologram inside the clock. So long as Will kept the crystal ball clock before him, he would see any approaching Fate Sealers. He would have a few seconds' warning. Though what good that would do him, he wasn't sure.

Holding the glowing clock with both hands, Will lit his way through his cobwebbed home down into the musty cellar. When Will found the chest labeled *Our Memory Box*, he remembered the jar of Waterweed that had been hidden behind the chest yesterday but was now tucked in his coat pocket. Waterweed only glowed when Echoes were near, so Will pulled the jar out quickly to see if the leaves were luminous. But the plant drifting in the water looked like dull, ordinary seaweed. Will was safe, for now. And his parents were far away and safe too. It was time to look for Damian's coin.

Will sat on the dusty cellar floor with the Memory Box before him, the clock on his right and the sleeping Waterweed on his left. Then he pulled the lid of the chest back—and forgot all about Damian's coin.

Will felt as if a time machine was sucking him into the past.

The chest was brimming with photographs. Ordinary photographs that stay still and never speak. But Will had Damian's Crystillery, and when he swirled it the way Damian had in the forest, everything in the photographs came to life. Faces smiled at Will across the years. He watched his happy parents celebrating birthday parties and opening presents, hanging holiday decorations and playing in the park on those normal sunny days that used to be—

before Emmy disappeared. Before Will's home started crumbling. Before his parents went mad with grief.

Laughing with the photographs felt more real than life had ever felt, and Will forgot where he was or what he was supposed to do. Until his fingers struck something knobby under the lining at the bottom of the chest. In Will's hand the Crystillery suddenly turned black like a giant drop of tar. Then, like sounds rising from a radio, Will heard muffled voices coming from the Crystillery.

"You say Will doesn't even know this crumbling hovel of a house has a cellar?" asked an old voice.

"I made sure he doesn't," answered someone younger.

"You sure you can't keep the coin?" asked a third voice, a girl's.

"'Fraid not," answered the first voice. "What if I'm murdered? The likelihood increases daily."

Suddenly the world inside the Crystillery changed.

Darkness and light mingled in a jostling mess and the voices stopped. The Crystillery looked like a tiny swamp in Will's hand, brewing with slow, lazy waves. Until, in a flash, the swamp turned into a face.

It was an old face that stared at Will through the Crystillery as if seeing him. And Will stared back in amazement, recognizing the man but just not understanding. What was *he* doing in the Crystillery? He was just a teacher from Will's school. His new chemistry teacher. The terror-of-the-lab sort of teacher. Mr. Drinkwater to his face but Frankenstein behind his back. What was he—?

"Your Majesty," said Drinkwater, his wrinkled face hovering in Will's hand as if talking directly to him. "Not a palace maybe, but safe. Even Fate Sealers won't find you here."

"I agree," said the younger voice, and now Will recognized the sound immediately. It was Damian.

In a moment Deá spoke too. Will saw her as his old chemistry teacher drew back. Only Deá wasn't in her Echo form but still looking like a wolf.

"I hope we're doing the right thing," she said softly, looking directly at Will through the Crystillery, with her white, pointy ears actually peeking out of the blue dome.

"No one else will know," said Damian reassuringly. And, in a moment, Will saw him fluttering in his falcon form and landing on the wolf's white back.

Standing behind them, Drinkwater didn't even blink to hear a wolf and falcon speaking. He raised a beautiful golden dagger in the air, then the world inside the Crystillery became a haze of colors and everything turned black and disappeared.

Feeling trapped in a dream, Will clawed at the lining of the chest until the tear he could see in it ripped open. A blob of dry, chewed-up purple bubble gum rolled out, followed by a coin that looked like water trapped in a circle of polished blue ice.

*   *   *

An hour later Will rushed into his school, casting a final glance at the dark parking lot where a yellow bus was driving away.

Still no Fate Sealers, thought Will with a sigh of relief. Even so, the ride to school had felt like a bad dream. Everyone on the bus had quizzed Will about his falcon's disappearance, and his best friend, Ben, sulked the whole time because Will didn't want to talk. Which, of course, was the opposite from the truth. Will was dying to talk. But how could he? His secrets were too dangerous. If Will revealed them to his best friend, Fate Sealers might try to kill Ben too.

"Where are you going?" Ben asked for the fifth time, following Will into the school. But Will slipped away down the side corridor leading to the Chemistry lab, still giving Ben the silent treatment.

Will found his chemistry teacher, Mr. Drinkwater, standing in the doorway of the laboratory. He was looking wrinkled and ill-tempered as usual, dressed in the same shabby purple outfit he never seemed to wash: a faded fuchsia shirt with a zippered pocket, a sagging plum-colored cardigan (it too with a zippered pocket), and a pair of violet pants with faded knees. Drinkwater's round-rimmed glasses wobbled on his nose where masking tape patched them together. And a bubble of purple gum erupted out of his mouth and exploded in a loud pop.

"Pests!" Drinkwater bellowed at the students banging locker doors in the corridor. "Curse your foul noises, you tone-deaf brutes!"

Then Drinkwater noticed Will, and his scowl deepened.

"What a vision you make this morning, Mr. Cleary." Drinkwater chuckled. "A new fashion statement?"

In the dark school bus windows Will had caught a glimpse of

64

his reflection. The Brain Freeze had given his complexion the color of vomit, and his strawy hair looked electrified. He didn't care, not about that. He stopped beside Drinkwater and said flatly, "A Fate Sealer tried to kill me."

In a flash, Drinkwater's scowl disappeared.

"In here," he barked.

Mr. Drinkwater shunted Will through the laboratory door, past shiny metal tables, test tubes and microscopes. Students stopped doing their homework to stare as Will was propelled forward like a science experiment about to explode at any minute.

"In here!" Drinkwater swung open an office door at the back of the lab, and in a moment it slammed shut behind them.

"Ouch!" Will hit his head on a rusty birdcage hung at the entrance. It was strange that the dove sleeping inside didn't wake.

Beyond the cage, shelves lined the narrow room Will and Drinkwater had entered. They were crowded with creepy, slimy things that floated in glass jars, and a few floating eyes even seemed to follow Will as Drinkwater still pushed him forward.

"Well, sit boy. Sit!"

Drinkwater finally stopped at the end of the room and pushed Will into a creaking chair. Then he sighed his way into the seat opposite and leaned his elbow tiredly on a lopsided desk, where precariously high piles of paper were defying gravity.

"So what makes you think I can defend you against Fate Sealers?" asked Drinkwater, reaching for a teapot behind the tallest mound of papers, which was marked with the sign, *Exams, F*, at the top.

Will cleared his throat, feeling scared but not of Frankenstein. After the Fate Sealers, a mad science teacher was unimpressive.

"Damian wanted me to talk to someone at school," said Will, as Drinkwater stretched a steaming teacup to him. "No, thank you. Not thirsty. I think Damian meant you, Mr. Drinkwater," Will rushed on. "I saw you with my wolf and falcon. I think you were hiding this." And Will took out the coin he found in the Memory Box.

It was a strange coin, very small but rather thick, and more beautiful than any coin Will had ever seen. Clearly Echo-made, it was slightly see-through and seemed carved out of polished blue ice. Except that it couldn't really be ice, since it was warm to the touch.

The engravings on the coin felt perfectly solid under Will's fingers, and yet they looked like flowing water. One side was covered with strange, curly letters, the other with the bust of a boy— a boy with a sparkling crown on his head and a face that looked a lot like Will's.

"Is this my Echo?" asked Will—but before the words were out of his mouth, Drinkwater snatched the coin out of Will's hand.

"What in Fortune's name?!" the old teacher bellowed. His eyes flashed insanely behind his taped glasses. "Are you a suicidal maniac? What do you think you're doing? Have some arsenic with your tea and be done." And again Drinkwater shoved the teacup at Will, who didn't dare refuse this time.

But just then, the old wrinkled teacher deflated as if someone had stuck a pin in him.

"Damian, you say?" he asked, blinking in confusion. "Damian sent you to me? Ah…" Drinkwater nodded his head sadly. "Then Deá was hurt very badly, right? You don't have to answer, I know it. There can be no other explanation. Damian would never leave you otherwise."

Drinkwater sighed but smiled at Will at the same time, and his face wrinkled in a thousand places. Suddenly he looked like a perfectly nice old man with bad taste in clothes. Nothing about Drinkwater seemed mad or even weird. He just looked tired, terribly tired.

"Well, drink your tea. Go on, it's not poisoned," said Drinkwater, and he dropped six lumps of sugar in Will's steaming cup and offered him a teaspoon. "Stir it well, your body needs the sugar."

Indeed, Will suddenly felt famished, and despite the arsenic comment before he took a sip from the sweet amber liquid, and the scent of the tea made his stomach growl.

"And eat," said Drinkwater, unveiling a box of crystal ball cookies in seven different colors. "Didn't bring you here to listen to your stomach."

For a second Will wondered if Frankenstein had concocted the cookies in his lab. But looking at the old man, Will couldn't remember him as Frankenstein, the science teacher from hell. It was as if that other person was just an act, and now Will was talking to the real Drinkwater.

"Why did you get so upset about the coin, Mr. Drinkwater?" Will asked, biting into an orange crystal ball that spilled delicious peach filling into his mouth.

Looking thoughtful, Drinkwater leaned back in his creaking chair and blew a purple bubble with his gum. After it exploded softly, he asked, "You saw me hiding the coin, how?"

"Damian gave me his Crystillery."

"Gave you his Crystillery...?" Once more Drinkwater sighed, as if he was seeing a sad story unfolding in his mind. "No choice, I suppose. Blurry Memory, was it?"

"What?"

"Me? Did I look fuzzy? Things all smeared? You know, blurry Memory when you read the coin with the Crystillery."

"Oh, yes. Kind of." Will bit into his third crystal ball cookie, a blue one this time, feeling so hungry it was hard to be polite and eat slowly.

"Thought so. Memory Crossing!"

Drinkwater fished a purple velvet bag from the zippered pocket of his frayed purple cardigan and asked, "Kept the coin on the floor, by any chance?"

"It was in the Memory Box," said Will, crumbs flying out of his mouth.

"Chest and coin, you see," explained Drinkwater. He tossed away his purple bubble gum into a garbage bin by his chair. "Memory Crossing. Now, watch carefully, Mr. Cleary," he added. "And keep eating. Surely you can look and chew at the same time."

Drinkwater smiled kindly, and Will smiled back and watched.

Withdrawing a Crystillery from the purple velvet bag, Drinkwater swirled the blue dome gently in his wrinkled hand until the water in the Crystillery became wavy. Then three glittering stones suddenly floated up and crashed together, shooting red, blue and yellow fireworks into the air above the blue dome.

"Wow!" Will gasped.

"Wait till you see the rest," said Drinkwater, winking at Will.

Drinkwater rested the ice-blue coin on his faded purple pants and lowered the Crystillery over it.

And suddenly the glittering, starry stones arranged themselves in a line. Then, like a finger drawing in the sand, the stones began to draw a crown on the waves rolling inside the Crystillery. The crown was no bigger than a walnut but it looked real, made of gold with sparkling jewels.

"Takes years of training to master a Crystillery," said Drinkwater, lovingly rolling the blue dome in his palm. "It's a hobby of mine. As for you, young Mr. Clearly, when you know so little about Crystillery Reading, all you can expect to see is the most recent, complex Memory."

"What do you mean?" asked Will between cookies, staring at the line of stones drawing something new on the waves of the Crystillery, a long pointy object that soon turned into a metal sword no bigger than a toothpick.

"What do I mean by recent and complex?" said Drinkwater. "Well, if you tried to read the coin now, what would you see?

Remember: *recent* and *complex*."

Will shrugged uncertainly. "You put the coin on your leg, that's the last thing that happened to it."

"That would be a recent Memory, yes," said Drinkwater encouragingly, like a patient teacher. "But not a complex Memory. The Crystillery will look for a Memory with several variables: sounds, colors, motion."

"Maybe the Memory of me taking the coin on the bus?"

"Yes, that's a possibility. But, of course, you'll be limited by perspective."

"You mean, 'cause the coin was in my pocket?" asked Will. "I wouldn't be able to see anything? Only hear?"

"Very good." Drinkwater smiled, looking impressed. And Will felt a surge of pride.

"Luckily, I am skilled at both Target Acquisition and Perspective Control," said Drinkwater, winking at Will again. "We'll be seeing the Memory I want you to see. The way I want you to see it."

Will bent closer, watching a gold dagger replace the metal sword as the finger of starry stones kept drawing on the waves.

"You mean the real Memory of the coin?" Will asked eagerly.

"The important Memory, yes. Ready?"

All at once, the glittering stones crashed again and the sword disappeared. The waves in the Crystillery turned into a terrible whirlpool, and the ruby, sapphire and yellow diamond went round

70

and round in circles until they were sucked under the water. And then the Crystillery seemed to turn into a window in the wall of someone's mansion.

Will found himself looking at a candlelit white chamber that was so small it could fit inside the blue dome resting on Drinkwater's palm. There was a man in the room, a see-through man lying in a bed that looked like a fluffy snow ball with tiny snowflake pillows and a puddle for a blanket.

"No, don't!" Drinkwater warned, as Will reached his hand in fascination to the hologram bed. "You'll mix your Memories with the coin's."

"But is it real?" asked Will

"The room?"

"No, I know the room isn't. I mean, the bed. What's it made of?"

"Echo fabrics. Wonderful things... Feel warm to Sound hands. Cool to Echoes. Shhhh... Watch and listen."

Two see-through men entered the miniature chamber that seemed to float on Drinkwater's hand. As they walked, their robes flowed down their bodies like shimmering water. They looked as if they were only half inside the Crystillery, with their heads sticking out into Drinkwater's office. They came to kneel on either side of the snowy bed, and Will noticed that both were armed, the first with a gold dagger, the second with an iron sword. The men's backs were turned to Will and Drinkwater, but as each spoke he bowed his head to the man in the bed, and so Will could tell who was talking.

"Can Your Majesty speak?" asked the Echo with the gold dagger, a little too loudly.

"And hear, as well," answered the old Echo in the bed, his voice as faint as a sigh.

"Alas!" said the Echo with the iron sword. "Death shows no mercy. Better to have seen you die in battle, My Liege, than by this slow suffering."

"But if suffer, suffer in comfort." The ill King lying in the bed chuckled dryly, and his face turned even more see-through against his snowflake pillow. "But enough with insincerities!" he snarled in a moment. "You have not come to visit a dying man. You wish to learn which of you shall be King hereafter."

Wheezing painfully, the old King turned his see-through head to look up at the Echo with the gold dagger.

"Stephen, our brother," he spoke faintly, though majestically, in the manner reserved for royalty, using *we* when he really meant *I*. "Should we anoint you King in our place, the royal coffers will glitter from floor to ceiling. But the people of this land shall die of hunger!"

The waterfall blanket rippled as the old King slammed his fist down, as if passing sentence on the Echo kneeling beside him.

"John, our warrior brother…" The King now looked up at the Echo with the iron sword. "Should you become King after our death, no ocean or mountain shall stem the tide of your armies. But the women of this land shall lose their sons, theirs brothers and fathers! And with them, all happiness and hope."

72

Coughing and wheezing more painfully still, the King's face turned so transparent that Will had to lean closer to still see him, which was strange because the snowflake pillow showed straight through the King's face, as if he were a man with a giant snowflake for a head.

"We shall not leave so meager a gift to our people," hissed the dying King. And once more he slammed his angry fist down on his watery blanket, which rippled as if a stone had been cast into a pond. "Let Fate decide between you—this King shall not!" he added bitterly and reached under his pillow.

Between see-through fingers that barely showed at all, the King held out a small ice-blue coin and tossed it high into the air. The coin shot straight out of the candlelit chamber into Drinkwater's neon-lit office, twisted in the air then fell back again into the Crystillery.

The old King cried, "Name your selections ere the coin lands—or forfeit your claims forever!"

"WORDS!" shouted the Echo with the gold dagger.

"KING!" shouted the Echo with the iron sword.

The coin landed on the old King's forehead, but he did not stir. For the old King was dead.

Will couldn't make out which side the coin had landed on, but the kneeling men seemed in no doubt.

The Echo with the gold dagger jumped up. Then, for a second, Will thought he was seeing things, for the Echo turned entirely invisible. Not his clothes, just his body. His watery robe

73

floated on thin air as if enchanted. A sleeve moved as the robe made its way around the bed. Then the gold dagger rose up by itself behind the back of the man with the iron sword, who was still kneeling to kiss the hand of the dead King.

"Watch out!" shouted Will, forgetting it was all a Memory.

But already the Echo with the iron sword whooshed up in such a daze of motion that Will didn't see it beginning or ending. There was only a terrible shriek of pain that forced Will to stop his ears with his hands. Then the Echo with the gold dagger grew visible again in all but his right hand, which dropped on the carpet of the candlelit chamber, a milky white liquid oozing from it.

"Echo blood," Will whispered in horror.

"We shall not kill you for this, brother," said the Echo with the iron sword, now kissing the ice-blue coin that had won him a kingdom. "You shall live—if you kneel before your new King."

The Echo with the gold dagger fell to his knees in submission, and Will could see his burning eyes and twisted mouth looking straight at him through the Crystillery.

"My Liege," he snarled. Then he mouthed the silent, vengeful promise, "For now!"

*　　*　　*

The candlelit chamber turned into a giant soap bubble, floated up over the Crystillery and popped in midair.

"My favorite finale," chuckled Drinkwater, but his smile faded almost at once. "So what do you think?" He turned to Will.

"He became invisible, that Echo," Will said the first thing

that came into his head.

"Yes, some Echoes can," said Drinkwater, polishing his Crystillery with its purple cover. The starry stones now glowed quietly inside the blue dome like tiny lanterns.

"Then this *really* happened?" wondered Will.

"Oh, yes! Two hundred and fifty years ago, to be precise. What we just saw is a story every Echo knows. It is the story of the Royal Shekel."

"Sh...ekel? What's that?"

"Think of it as a Dollar, in Echo currency. Amazing, isn't it?" With his crooked fingers that looked so old, Drinkwater held up the ice-blue coin to the neon light buzzing on the ceiling of his office. "Just an ordinary Shekel, like a million others," he said thoughtfully. "But this one decided who would be King. The Echoes never forgot that."

"It's still just a coin, isn't it?" said Will.

"Not to the Echoes, it isn't," said Drinkwater, his faded eyes flashing suddenly behind his taped glasses. "You have to understand one thing about the Echoes. I've never known a more superstitious people. They believe Fortune rules their lives. And they have good cause to think it too," Drinkwater added to himself.

"How do you mean?" asked Will, confused.

"It's simple, really," Drinkwater explained. "Since Fortune made her wish known through this coin, the Echoes expect every king to possess it. As proof that Fortune is on his side. People have died trying to steal this simple, small coin. No king has ever been without it. Because a king without the Royal Shekel will not remain King for long."

"But then—" Will frowned. "How did *you* end up with the coin, Mr. Drinkwater? You're not a king... are you?"

"No," said Drinkwater, tucking his Crystillery away. "I'm not a king. But one day, I very much hope your Echo will be. Which brings us back to who you are, William Cleary. And why you must stay alive. You understand now, don't you?"

"Not everything," said Will, understanding very little.

"Agám Kaffú," continued Drinkwater, "that's the Echo land stretching beneath Alaska."

"You mean, Deá and Damian's home," said Will. And in his heart something started to ache a little, and not just because he missed his pets, but because he realized how much he was hoping Damian would manage to save Deá.

"Yes, Deá and Damian's home. That land is not a Republic like the United States. People there don't get to vote on who will lead them. Agám Kaffú is ruled by a King. And, what's crucial to you personally, Mr. Cleary... the next in line to the throne is the Prince."

"My Echo."

"Precisely."

"But if Echoes look like their Sounds...?" wondered Will.

"They do." Drinkwater nodded.

"But I'm the smallest kid in class," said Will reluctantly. "I look like a scarecrow. Which means my Echo looks like a

76

scarecrow, right? So how can he be a Prince?"

"Nevertheless," said Drinkwater, turning the ice-blue coin to show Will the engraving of the crowned boy's head. "This may be the Prince's distant ancestor, but the Cleary family resemblance is striking... the untamed hair, the thin features... But what you look like and how great you are rarely go hand in hand. Otherwise, we'd have no trouble judging good men from bad, now would we?"

"So that's why Fate Sealers are after me?" said Will with a sigh. "Because of my Echo." It was all starting to make sense. But then again... it wasn't. "But Why?" added Will. "I mean, if I live here and my Echo lives in... Agá..."

"Agám Kaffú."

"Right. Then why are Fate Sealers coming after me here... in the Sound realm? What's in it for the Echoes?"

"Ah!" Drinkwater nodded as if at last they were getting to the heart of the matter.

But at that moment the school bell rang, signaling the start of first period.

Drinkwater slipped the Royal Shekel in the zippered pocket of his purple shirt.

"Time to become Frankenstein again," he said, fishing a stick of gum from the same pocket before zipping it closed. "Come see me after last period," he added, already sounding irritable. "And I don't have to warn you about leaving the school, do I? Fate Sealers won't hunt you in here. Too many witnesses. But, never doubt it! If you go outside, the Fate Sealers will find you. And they will freeze your brain. And drag you down into Shadowpain. No two ways about it."

And Drinkwater blew his bubble gum into a purple bubble that exploded in a loud pop.

A Coin Like Any Other

Every Echo Has to Die

It was the longest day of Will's life, but when the dismissal bell finally rattled through the school, Will rushed out to his locker, where he found his best friend, Ben, fighting a losing battle with the mess in the locker next door.

"And stay in—" Ben kicked the door shut "—side!" But the locker burst open to an avalanche of books. "Ouch!"

"You okay?" asked Will, as a text book crashed into Ben's face.

Ben turned, rubbing his nose. "Oh, it's you. Talking to me again, are you?"

"I never stopped talking to you," said Will, feeling guilty for keeping his friend in the dark all day. But how could Will drag Ben into his troubles? How could he risk his best friend's life?

"Then I must be going deaf," said Ben, rolling his eyes. "'Cause I didn't hear a word you said about what happened to Damian. Or the glowing plant. Or the gravestone book. But that's okay. Just explain everything again. I'm listening."

"For the hundredth time, nothing happened," said Will,

trying to sound annoyed.

"For the ten-thousandth time, I don't believe you!"

"I can't help what you believe, Ben." Will shrugged. "So can you just listen for a second. I want to tell you something. Important."

"What?" Ben couldn't help looking curious.

Will took a deep breath. "Ben... In case I end up disappearing like my sister..."

"Oh! No you don't!" Ben slammed his locker door as a pile of gaming magazines catapulted out. "I knew it! I knew it!" He beamed at Will a second later, as if nothing happened. "You *are* in trouble, aren't you? I want to help."

Will chuckled and pretended nothing was wrong, just as he had done all day. "Just *if,* Ben. If I disappear. Or get kidnapped by aliens or something."

"Well, what?" Ben scowled.

"I want you to have my stuff."

"Your stuff?" asked Ben, now leaning his whole weight on his locker door as things inside kept thudding in total collapse. "Does it sound like I need more stuff? What's going on, Will? And don't talk to me about aliens."

Will shook his head. "For the last time. Nothing. Nothing's going on."

"Then why are you keeping your locker door closed like that?" asked Ben suspiciously. "What are you doing back there?"

"Nothing!" Will pulled out his gym suit, with the gravestone book now wrapped inside it. "Just feel like going jogging, if that's okay."

"Jogging? Now?"

But Will pulled out his coat in silence, then slammed his locker door and stomped off.

And from behind Will probably did look fed up, though he had to close his eyes and visualize the sagging, horrifying face of a Fate Sealer to stop himself turning back and telling his best friend everything.

*   *   *

The rows of shiny metal tables were empty when Will entered the white chemistry lab, and no one sat behind them. But on the teacher's podium, Will spotted Drinkwater wiping his wide metal table from the sticky orange remnants of a science experiment gone wrong. Even the old man's faded purple clothes looked a little orange for a change.

"That one's safe," said Drinkwater, pointing to the only chair on the podium that still had a seat. "Take your coat off and get comfortable, Mr. Cleary."

Will knew better than to ask what happened here. Drinkwater wasn't known as Frankenstein, the-terror-of-the-lab, for nothing.

Will sat down and looked up to the sound of something buzzing overhead. It was a strange streak of light going round and round in a circle just below the white ceiling.

"My pet," explained Drinkwater, tossing away a soggy mound of orange paper towels. "Flit's the name."

Suddenly the streak slowed down, and Will saw that it was

actually a bird, only no kind of bird Will had ever seen before, because the feathers on the bird's wings shimmered like the insides of oyster shells.

"But… Isn't he see-through?" wondered Will.

"She," corrected Drinkwater. "And, yes, Flit's an Echo. Lives inside a Sound over there, most of the time."

Drinkwater pointed at the corner window where the rusty birdcage from his office now stood on a tall, metal stool, the cage door open. Will saw a sleeping dove perched inside the cage, the same dove that didn't wake up when Will bumped into the cage that morning.

"Strange how Echoes can live inside dead Sounds, don't you think?" said Drinkwater.

"Dead sounds…" Disturbing was nearer how Will felt. Especially as it occurred to Will that if Echoes like Deá and Damian, or like this bird, could live inside dead animals, they could probably live inside dead humans too.

"Shall we have some tea as we talk? It's been a long day," said Drinkwater, wiping off the last splotch of orange slime.

Sinking in his comfy teacher's armchair, Drinkwater opened the cupboard behind his metal table and pulled out a teapot and two cups, which he soon filled to the brim with a steaming amber liquid.

"So, where were we earlier?" the old teacher asked, pushing a cup over to Will's side of the table.

"You were going to tell me why Fate Sealers are after me," said Will eagerly.

"Well, that's perfectly straightforward," said Drinkwater. And he leaned back in his creaking armchair, until he looked as if he would summersault backwards off the podium and take his chair with him.

"You'll fall," warned Will, jumping up.

"What? Oh! The chair? Perfectly safe." Drinkwater chuckled. "We're both in mortal danger, Mr. Cleary. But not from killer chairs. Look outside." The old teacher pointed at the window. "Students are getting on the school buses. Soon there won't be any witnesses left around the school. No one except you and me. And then the Fate Sealers will come inside. And find us. So we don't have a lot of time. You've heard of the Law of Death?"

Will shook his head, suddenly feeling colder than before.

"No, I don't suppose you have," said Drinkwater. "Then I'd better tell you." But the old teacher started sipping his tea until his glasses fogged up.

"Mr. Drinkwater…?" said Will. He could see anger and fear mingling in his old teacher's face, and for a moment Will wished he didn't have to hear whatever Drinkwater had to tell him. But wishing couldn't change facts.

"Please, Mr. Drinkwater," said Will, "I need to know why Fate Sealers are after me."

"Because…" Drinkwater sighed. "In Agám Kaffú … that's the Echo—"

"—Land, yes, I remember."

"In Agám Kaffú Echoes tend to die. No, not die."

85

Drinkwater's voice grew bitter. "Echoes are murdered... when their time comes."

"Murdered?"

"When a Sound dies, his Echo is executed," said Drinkwater coldly. "That's just the way of things."

"You mean if I die, my Echo... the Prince will have to die?" asked Will, horrified.

"Just the way of things," repeated Drinkwater bitterly.

"But why?"

"Remember the Memory of the Royal Shekel? The Echo who *didn't* win the coin toss? The one with the gold dagger? It was all his idea."

Drinkwater glanced thoughtfully up at the Echo bird still streaking circles of light under the ceiling.

"It's always been a superstition with the Echoes," Drinkwater explained. "They've always believed that when a Sound dies his Echo is destined to die soon after. The life of a Sound and his Echo begins together, it should end together. That sort of rubbish.

"Then two hundred and fifty years ago, Stephen V convinced his brother, the King, to turn the superstition into law. The Law of Death. After that, Stephen sent a Fate Sealer to murder the King's Sound, and then the King had to die. Of course, Stephen got what he wanted. He became King instead. But he was no fool. He changed the Law of Death to exclude himself and all future kings, so no one could get rid of him the way he got rid of his brother."

Looking up again, Drinkwater smiled to see his bird slowing

down. "Ready for some tea, Flit?" he asked, as if the old man was in the habit of talking to his bird. And shaking off his gloom, Drinkwater rose with his teacup.

Overhead the see-through bird twittered then flew into the open cage by the window.

Will watched the bird hovering in a shimmering smear before the dead dove. Then, suddenly, like water getting sucked through a straw, the Echo disappeared through the beak of the Sound.

"Did it just...?" Will shuddered, watching the white dove waking up.

"Yes, Flit just entered the dead Sound. It's as easy as that," said Drinkwater, stepping off the teacher's podium and heading for the cage by the window.

Will unwrapped the gravestone book from his gym suit and rushed after his teacher. "So all the people who disappeared," Will asked, "everyone in this book... They all—"

"Yes." Drinkwater sighed, glancing back at the gravestone book as if he already knew everything about it. "All kidnapped by Fate Sealers hired to murder an Echo."

"Then... they're all dead? All of them?" Will blinked in shock.

"Quite the reverse." Drinkwater slipped his arm inside the birdcage. "Many Sounds were rescued. Your sister, in fact. Though in her case it took four years, I believe."

"Five," muttered Will, watching the white dove hopping up on Drinkwater's sleeve.

"Yes. Another tragedy." Drinkwater nodded. "But then, tragic things happen all the time in Agám Kaffú. That's what comes of taking away a person's right to his own life."

"But how do the Echoes find out when a Sound dies anyway?" asked Will, looking nervously out the window.

The last bus was speeding away and the winter sun was setting behind the forest on the other side of the school road. Just for once Will wished the winter days in Alaska weren't so short.

"Not so close to the window," snarled Drinkwater, shoving Will into the corner behind the birdcage. "Keep your wits about you, Mr. Cleary. There's no second chance, if you don't. And that reminds me. There's something I've been meaning to ask you. You said Damian gave you his Crystillery."

"Yes."

"Let me see it!"

Will rushed back to the shiny metal table to fetch the Crystillery from his coat pocket.

"Turn it over," ordered Drinkwater, when Will returned. Then the old teacher scowled and his face wrinkled in a thousand places. "As I thought. *Not* Damian's Crystillery," muttered Drinkwater.

"But Damian gave it to me," said Will, staring at the flat bottom of the blue dome, where something was carved.

"Nevertheless. Take a closer look at this emblem," said Drinkwater.

Will raised the Crystillery until he could make out the

frightful face of a Fate Sealer etched into the blue crystal.

"This Crystillery belonged to a Fate Sealer," explained Drinkwater. "Probably the one who tried to kidnap you."

"The one Deá protected me from?"

"Or the one Damian must have killed to save you both."

Drinkwater tipped his teacup so the dove perched on his sleeve could drink.

"You must understand, Mr. Cleary," he went on explaining. "Only three types of people are permitted to own Crystilleries. The Fate Sealers, if you can call them people. The King and his close advisors... in their case this emblem would be a crown. And then there's the third group... which brings us back to your question."

"You mean, this group has something to do with how Echoes find out when a Sound dies?" asked Will.

"Precisely." Drinkwater's faded eyes looked so sad behind his taped glasses. "They are the ones that spy on the Sounds. And when a sound dies, they..."

"They kill the Echo?" Will could hardly believe that anything so twisted could be real.

"They kill the Echo." Drinkwater nodded slowly.

"So what are they called? Death Sealers?" asked Will bitterly.

"An apt name, Mr. Cleary. But, no. They call themselves Fortune Tellers. Their emblem is a crystal ball. And they don't just spy on the Sounds. The Fortune Tellers copy each death. They make sure every Echo dies in the *exact same way as his Sound*. As if this was Fortune's wish all along. "

The dead dove with the Echo inside it was tapping its beak on the teacup as it drank. The noise echoed through the empty Chemistry lab. It made Will think of a ticking time-bomb.

"They'll never leave me alone." Will sighed, feeling all hope draining from his heart. "Not until I'm dead."

"Or until the false King is dead," said Drinkwater, tilting the teacup to stop the tapping.

"The false King?" asked Will, bewildered. "Who's he?"

"Do you have an uncle by any chance? Someone short? Ugly?"

Will nodded. "My Dad's brother. Half-brother, really. What's he got to do with it?"

"His Echo is the King of Agám Kaffú now. The *false* King," snarled Drinkwater, as if he hated that King with all his heart.

"But if my Echo's the Prince, shouldn't my father's Echo be the King?" wondered Will.

"He should. And he was! Until his half-brother murdered him four months ago."

"Murdered him…" Will gasped. The story of the Echoes kept getting worse and worse. "So now the false King is trying to murder the Prince—by killing me. Is that it?"

"In a nutshell. Only the false King doesn't have much time. He can only remain king until the Prince becomes old enough to take the throne. That will happen when the Prince turns thirteen."

"You mean on my birthday…" Will blinked in shock.

"In two and half weeks." Drinkwater nodded.

*　　*　　*

Withdrawing a fistful of sunflower seeds from his pocket, Drinkwater filled the empty teacup, and the dead dove with the Echo inside it jumped on the rim of the cup and dug in with her beak.

"There is a silver lining to all this," said Drinkwater, smiling down at his pet. "Isn't she lovely?"

"Best looking dead bird I've ever seen... A silver lining?" asked Will skeptically.

"Aren't you forgetting something?" said Drinkwater. "The false King doesn't have the Royal Shekel."

"Yes. So?"

"So, there's a ceremony in Agám Kaffú called Melech Emet... True King," explained Drinkwater, still smiling at his pet as if the sight of a bird eating seeds was a miracle. "During this ceremony a King must show the Royal Shekel to the people with a Crystillery. To prove that Fortune is on his side, you understand. Without Melech Emet a King will lose his throne very quickly. The false King knows that. Which is why he won't rest until he finds the Royal shekel."

Absently Drinkwater patted the zippered pocket of his frayed purple shirt. Will could see a rectangular outline in the fabric, his teacher's pack of purple gum. Will remembered seeing Drinkwater unzip the pocket that morning, take a piece of gum out and drop the Royal Shekel in.

"No..." Drinkwater shook his head thoughtfully. "Until the

false King gets his greedy hands on the Royal Shekel, he won't dare to kill the Prince. Or you, Mr. Cleary. After all, the false King believes in Fortune with all his rotten heart. And She may not approve... not without the coin. No... That fat fool will wait, I'm sure of it."

"Then let's hide the royal Shekel somewhere no one will find it," said Will, staring at the purple pocket eagerly.

"Leave that to me," said Drinkwater. "Right now, that see-through coin is the only thing keeping you alive. The only thing. But it won't stop the Fate Sealers. The false King may not dare to kill you, but he is evidently only too happy to have you kidnapped. And if his Fate Sealers find you and the Royal Shekel together... Unthinkable! There's more than just your life at stake. Remember that."

Will closed his eyes in frustration. The only thing keeping him alive was hidden an old man's pocket. Why, he thought desperately, why did he let Drinkwater take the coin?

"I know there's a lot at stake," said Will in a moment. "But I know I can hide the Royal Shekel without getting caught."

"You?" Drinkwater looked horrified. "Haven't you heard anything I said?"

"But the forest behind my home," Will insisted. "I know it by heart. If I hide the coin there..."

"In the perfect hiding place?" asked Drinkwater, glaring at Will behind his taped glasses.

"Yes," snapped Will.

"There is no such thing, don't you understand?"

"Why? You hid the coin in the Memory Box. That worked until Damian told me about it. Why won't you trust me? It's my problem. It's my life."

"It's the Prince's life, too. You can't hide the coin, case closed."

"No! No it isn't," Will shot back. "Tell me why, Mr. Drinkwater? Tell me why I'm not good enough to hide the coin, but I'm good enough to die because of it?"

"Look, Will," said Drinkwater, and for the first time he patted Will on the shoulder affectionately and didn't call him Mr. Cleary. "You're incredibly brave for your age. For any age, by Fortune. But bravery isn't always enough. Think about it. What if the Fate Sealers torture you for information?"

What if they torture *you*, thought Will. But he said nothing more. He could read the cold truth in Drinkwater's faded eyes. His old teacher would never give up the Royal Shekel. If Will wanted it, he would have to steal it.

"Leave it to you?" said Will.

"Leave it to me." Drinkwater nodded, patting his pocket once more.

Will didn't need more proof. The coin was there! But Will had no idea how to get it. After all, how could he expect to get away with unzipping the pocket and sticking his hand in it, if Drinkwater was still wearing the shirt?

"By Fortune!" Drinkwater cried out suddenly, staring out the window in amazement. "A welcome sight for sore eyes! She's well again! She's well and she's back. They came back."

Will stuck his head out carefully to look out the window too.

"Oh! Look, boy. Look!" Drinkwater pushed Will closer to the window, after warning him to keep away before.

In the gathering twilight of the late afternoon Will saw no more students in the parking lot. But on the snow-covered sidewalk leading away from the school, a few students were walking. And a little behind them stood a tall girl dressed in a shimmering white jumpsuit and a cape that glittered like sunshine on a lake as it fluttered in the wind.

"Deá?" Will gasped, looking in amazement from the girl to the large white dog padding beside her. Or was it an arctic wolf? Will couldn't really tell from that distance.

"You have to go, Mr. Cleary," said Drinkwater urgently. "Now! Immediately!"

Suddenly Will caught a flash of light from the corner of his eye. He flinched from the window, spotting Drinkwater's pet zooming toward him. The next second, the Echo living inside a dead Sound crashed into the windowpane, missing Will's nose by an inch.

"Quick!" Drinkwater caught his swooning bird but kept talking to Will. "Not safe for Deá out there. Get your things! Where's your coat?"

"But she was dying yesterday..." stammered Will, staring out the window again. Something didn't feel right. Or maybe it was just that Will couldn't decide who Deá really was: The girl or the dog that looked like a wolf.

"Dying, yes." Drinkwater nodded. "Not dead. She came back for you. What loyalty! And Damian's armed and ready in the forest, if I know my old friend. It's time, Will. Go! They'll keep you safe."

Will tucked the gravestone book in his belt and rushed back to the metal table to get his coat. And all the while his old teacher talked to him in a rush of words.

"Go with Deá and Damian. Go to the Echo realm. Find your Echo. Help him become King. Before your birthdays. It has to be before you turn thirteen. Then your Echo will send you back here. With your sister. Who knows... in two and a half weeks your life could be happy, Will. Your family could be whole again. You have a choice about it. By Fortune, there is luck in that!"

Will was by the window again, his mind a blur. Drinkwater's promises sounded insanely, absurdly, too good to be true. Two and a half weeks, and Will could have a normal life? He didn't even know what a normal life was.

Will pushed his strawy hair back, thinking hard. Fate Sealers were definitely after him! He didn't know Drinkwater long enough to trust him. But he trusted Deá and Damian—and they wanted to take him to the Echo realm. It was the right thing to do. Will just wished it didn't terrify him so much.

"This isn't the time for daydreaming!" urged Drinkwater.

"My parents—" A tornado of excitement and fear twisted in Will's chest. "—Can you give them a message, Mr. Drinkwater? Tell them I'll come back. As soon as I can."

"Yes, yes... Now, go! Out the window. We're on the first floor. It's quite safe."

Comically Drinkwater tried to open the window, but the dove was wiggling in his fist and sunflower seeds kept spilling from the teacup in his other hand.

"Oh, damn and blast that silly bird!" Drinkwater reached for the birdcage.

"No, wait!" Will slammed the cage door shut. "I'll do it."

And in a flash Will opened the window himself.

"Good luck," said Drinkwater in farewell.

But Will turned back, away from the cold, snowy world waiting for him past the window.

"Can I have some gum for the road?" he asked, looking at Drinkwater's zippered pocket.

"Gum? Why you foolish..." But kindness washed over Drinkwater's wrinkled face and he nodded. "Yes, of course. To steady your nerves."

"I can get it!" said Will quickly, before Drinkwater could free his hands.

Moving almost as fast as Flit could fly, Will unzipped Drinkwater's pocket and fished out the purple packet of gum—and as he did so, he flexed his fingers tightly so the flat, round object he was pinning to the shiny foil would not slip back inside the pocket.

"Take it all," said Drinkwater kindly, "just close the pocket. Zip it all the way. Now go! Before Fate Sealers spot you. Go! And may Fortune be with you!"

Will hoisted himself on the window sill, looked down for a second to judge the height, then jumped down onto a snowy garden patch, still hearing his old teacher calling after him. "See you again in two and half weeks... Good Fortune to you..."

But the cold wind blew away the sound as Will ran over the snow-covered lawn toward the girl and white dog walking on the sidewalk by the forest's edge.

And all the while, Will's hand was clutching the shiny packet of gum and the Royal Shekel held fast under his thumb—the only thing keeping him alive.

Like a Ghost Through the Trees

The Coldest Sleep of All

It was not yet four in the afternoon and already the lazy Alaskan winter sun was setting, filling the world with shadows.

Will dashed past a small group of students, who shouted after him, "Where's your falcon?" and "Bird killer". The girl in the shimmering clothes on the other side of the street turned to see what was happening, and her cape drifted behind her like a cloud. While the white dog suddenly galloped away from her side, heading toward the school.

Will stopped beside the girl who was supposed to be Deá. And it was then that he realized something was very wrong.

"You're not see-through…" Will panted, fighting to catch his breath after running so fast.

"William Cleary?" Deá croaked back. She sounded like an electric toad.

"Your voice…" gasped Will. He stared at the white scarf encircling Deá's neck, wondering just how badly she was injured by the Fate Sealer on the pond by his home.

"Just a cold." The girl sniffed the air as if she had a runny nose; though Will had the crazy idea that Deá was picking up his scent.

Again the girl croaked, "William Cleary?" As if she wasn't sure who he was, and her forehead wrinkled like the forehead of a much older person.

Then, suddenly, the girl raised her arm, and a black raven flew out of the darkening sky and landed on her wrist. Will was amazed to see that it was an Echo, a see-through bird. And beside it, Deá just didn't look like an Echo herself.

"You're not see-through," said Will again—but his voice was drowned by a scream.

He twisted back and saw the students pointing at the school and shrieking in horror.

In the gathering twilight, the white dog was galloping back towards Will and Deá. Its white face and mane looked stained with something dark. And behind the beast, a man dressed all in purple was flailing his arms and staggering across the slushy parking lot like a zombie from a bad horror movie. A second later, the man collapsed.

"Mr. Drinkwater…" shouted Will.

Will couldn't understand what his teacher was doing outside. Did he jump out the window? But why?

The students ran off to see what their mad science teacher was up to this time, and Will dashed after them. He could hear girls shrieking up ahead as the dog galloped past them. Suddenly a boy screamed, "Blood! It's covered in blood!"

Will stopped in his tracks.

The dog stopped too. For an instant. Then it charged at Will again.

And all at once Will knew, knew with a shudder of terror, what happened to Drinkwater—and that if he didn't race back to Deá for protection, the gory beast would attack him next.

"Deá, your dog!" Will screamed.

But the girl in the shimmering white clothes was running away into the dark, snowy forest behind the parking lot.

Will raced after her, his heart pounding, his feet slipping on the frozen grass. He shot through the trees, shoving branches out of his way. Snow showers blinded him. Ice crackled under his feet. Before long he found himself in a shadow-filled clearing with Deá standing at the center, laughing grotesquely, her head thrown back. Behind Will something growled. He twisted back and saw the dog leaping to a stop so close to him that Will could smell the blood on the beast's fur.

Then, in a flash of fear, it hit Will—the memory of Drinkwater's bird, the Echo who lived inside a sound. How could he have been so stupid? A trap! He had walked straight into a trap!

"You look like a Sound, because you *are* a Sound," Will gasped at Deá, fear stifling his voice. "A *dead* Sound."

"Very dead." Deá stopped laughing and stepped closer to Will, her pale eyes sinking into her pretty face and turning black.

Will darted his eyes from the girl to the dog, seeing no hope of escape from the dim, frozen forest.

"You're *Deá's* dead Sound," he muttered. "That's why you look ten years older. Deá didn't age inside my wolf. But her Sound did."

"Deá's twin, actually. But you catch on, at last," croaked the girl.

Will shuddered. "You have an Echo inside you?"

"Not just any old Echo. A FATE SEALERRRRRR...."

Before the chilling, raspy screech faded, the beautiful young girl collapsed, and through her screaming mouth a see-through being poured out like gray vomit. It spiraled higher and higher until Will saw the tallest, thinnest person in the world, as if the Fate Sealer was a skeleton coated in sagging, filthy flesh with a mask of terror for a face.

"Go! Deliver the message that Drinkwater is dead," the Fate Sealer croaked triumphantly, stuffing a rolled sheet of paper in the raven's beak.

The black bird spread its see-through wings and flew away over the snowy treetops, disappearing in the darkening afternoon.

Chuckling in gasps, the Fate Sealer locked his hollow eyes on Will, eyes that were filled with a spinning, terrifying blackness. The creature reached beneath his sagging gray arm and pulled out a beautiful luminous horn, like a ram's horn made of pearl. And when the Fate Sealer blew into the horn, a storm of horizontal hail shot out like a thousand needles streaking through the shadowy forest to shatter at Will's feet.

"Think I missed?" The Fate Sealer rippled with laughter.

"Think again!"

Will looked down at his clothes.

Silvery cobwebs of ice were spreading up his shoes into his pants at a terrifying speed. Like crackling rivers of ice, the cobwebs reached over Will's knees and raced for his coat, spreading numbness through his body, as if he were turning to stone.

Will remembered the Royal Shekel in a panic—the only thing keeping him alive! And it was in his pocket! Desperately, he looked around for a hiding place. Two... three steps, and he could reach that hollow stump over to his left and pretend to trip, just long enough to slip the coin under the snow.

Using his hands to force his frozen legs forward, Will tried to move. But from the corner of his eye he saw that it was hopeless. Already the ferocious dog was leaping through the air. A second later, the breath was knocked out of Will's lungs and he crashed face down in the snow. And the weight of the dog settled over him like a giant paperweight.

The next second Will felt a cold presence rising into the air above him. He guessed that another Fate Sealer was leaving the body of a Sound, because the dog's head flopped lifelessly on his ear, trickling saliva... or was it Drinkwater's blood? And all Will could do was lie in the snow, feeling too cold and too terrified to move. While before him the Fate Sealer stood grinning, his sagging gray lips swinging from side to side like waterfalls of sewage.

"You take too long to dress, Valerian," croaked the creature, tucking his beautiful luminous horn under the waves of his rippling skin. "Tell me what you found out!"

"After you free my niece, not a moment before, I swear it!" vowed a beautiful voice quite near Will's ear.

With a flash of hope, Will realized that the second Echo was not a Fate Sealer after all! For such a voice couldn't belong to a monster. And yet, monster or not—while still inside the dog, that Echo killed Drinkwater.

"You will tell me everything I want to know, make no mistake," croaked the Fate Sealer, the darkness in his eyes spinning wildly.

"First this," said the beautiful voice cryptically.

And soon the Echo talking at Will's side stepped forward into Will's line of sight.

He was an old Echo, skinny but for his protruding belly. He walked toward the Fate Sealer, looking tall, proud and fearless, dressed in a tight-fitting gray suit of shimmering Echo fabric. And in his hand, the Echo held a small blood-red crossbow ornamented with golden, twirling lines that glittered even in the dim forest.

"Who said the rotten heart of a Fate Sealer was good for nothing?" asked the old Echo bitterly, though even in bitterness his voice was beautiful.

"You wouldn't dare—" screeched the Fate Sealer.

In the black whirlpools of the creature's eyes Will suddenly saw green pupils pulsing like the slits of cat eyes.

"Oh, yes, I would!" vowed the old Echo.

A second later the blood-red crossbow shuddered in the old

106

Echo's hand. Something streaked away from it, like a blur of light. And in the next instant Will saw an arrow stuck in the Fate Sealer's chest where his heart might be.

"NOOOOOOOOOOOOOOOO!" screeched the creature in a terrifying roar that shook snow off the trees.

Will stopped his ears with his frozen hands and watched, horrified.

White spirals were pouring out around the arrow like smoke. The forest filled with a nauseating stench. More spirals leaked from the screaming mouth, hollow eyes and dark nostrils. As if the creature was melting from every hole, the Fate Sealer evaporated until nothing remained of his folds of wobbling flesh but a few ribbons of drifting, putrid smoke and a faint, dying wail of agony.

After that, a terrible silence fell on the dim, frozen forest.

*   *   *

Almost at once, Will felt warmer beneath the fur of the dead dog. He shook the heavy animal off, grabbed a broken branch and jumped to his feet. The last strips of daylight had fled the frosty forest. Only the Echo in the tight gray clothes shimmered a little in the faint moonlight like a poisonous, eerie brew.

"You killed Mr. Drinkwater!" snarled Will, clutching the branch like a club.

Very slowly the Echo turned. For the first time Will saw the old man's thin, see-through face and pale, twinkling green eyes. For some reason, which Will couldn't understand, this old Echo reminded him of his father, though there was really no resemblance

107

at all.

"You killed Mr. Drinkwater," Will snarled again, to shake off the feeling.

"I didn't kill him," said the Echo sadly, with a beautiful, caressing voice. "Wounded him only. Had no choice. He was coming to warn you. We didn't know if you expected to see Deá as a girl or a wolf, you see. So we came as both. Well, near enough... a Siberian Husky could pass for a wolf from a distance. But Drinkwater must have guessed..."

"So you attacked him." Will shivered, clutching the branch even more tightly. The Echo seemed so gentle but at the same time terrible, like a snake coiled to look like a harmless rope. And Will couldn't make up his mind if to trust or fear the stranger who had just saved his life.

"Drinkwater had to be stopped, William, believe me," said the Echo gently, walking toward the spot where the Fate Sealer had died. "No need to look so surprised at my knowing who you are," added the old Echo in his beguiling voice.

He paused to pick up the luminous horn dropped by the Fate Sealer and explained.

"All Echoes are named after their Sounds, officially at least. And I know your Echo well. So tell me—" The old Echo reached for the blood-red arrow lying in a murky puddle where the Fate Sealer had melted away. "How much did Drinkwater tell you about the Royal Shekel?"

Will's heart pounded a warning in his chest. "The Royal...

what?" he asked, squeezing the tree branch like a lifeline in a raging river.

"Oh, very good!" The Echo smiled coldly. "But not good enough, I'm afraid."

Resting his blood-red crossbow over his lumpy belly, the Echo rearmed his weapon, as if his hands alone couldn't manage the task. "I wish there was another way," he said softly and shrugged.

"Let me guess, you don't have a choice," snarled Will, making himself angry on purpose, to stop himself feeling so scared.

Inclining his gaunt head in agreement, the gray Echo raised the crossbow and took aim at Will's head. In the moonlight, Will could see the old man closing one eye to better his aim.

Desperately, Will wanted to close his eyes in terror. But he forced himself to look at the man who was going to kill him. Look him in the eye with all the defiance he could muster.

Suddenly a rustle burst through the silent forest.

Will snapped his head to his left.

Where before there had been only dimness, now a black figure stood, shimmering in the faint moonlight with a black crossbow gleaming in its dark hands. See-through hands, Will realized, seeing snow showing straight through the fist that was griping the black weapon so tightly.

"Damian..." Will gasped.

"What's going on here?" asked Damian, darting his glance from Will's branch to the crossbow gleaming in the old Echo's hand.

At once, the gray Echo pocketed his weapon and smiled, his

teeth sparkling white.

"Damian? Damian Black?" he said, his beautiful voice full of surprise. "It is you, isn't it? Ten years... and still guarding the Prince's Sound?"

"He still needs guarding, Valerian," said Damian suspiciously.

"Indeed," agreed Valerian in all earnestness. "Which is why we shouldn't stay here. I just killed a Fate Sealer to stop him killing William."

The old Echo pulled out the Fate Sealer's luminous horn from his shimmering gray belt and waved it as proof at Damian, who was still watching him narrowly, his black crossbow aimed to kill.

"Fate Sealers always come in twos, as you know," added Valerian. "The second one may be lurking nearby. We should go. Follow me, I'll light our way."

The old Echo hurried deep into the dim forest, holding the Fate Sealer's horn before him like a lantern.

Damian turned anxiously to Will. "By Fortune, are you all right?"

Will tossed the branch aside with an unconvincing chuckle. He never imagined relief could be so overwhelming.

"Happy to see you," said Will, trying to breathe normally again. "Real happy. Where's Deá?"

"Still in the Echo realm. Healing slowly," said Damian. "Don't worry, she'll make it. What about you? Can you walk?"

"Think so."

"Here, lean on me."

Damian wrapped his cold arm around Will's shoulder and started leading them after the thin gray Echo moving like a ghost through the snowy trees up ahead.

"No, wait." Will refused to move. "You don't understand. Valeri... whatever his name is... he was going to shoot me."

"Valerian shot the Fate Sealer," said Damian, unimpressed. "That's what you saw. It's dark. Now, come—"

"No. I know what I saw."

"Forget about Valerian," insisted Damian. "I know him, he'd never attack an unarmed person. Now, tell me—" Damian lowered his voice "—what about the coin? Did you do what I told you? Did you get it to Drinkwater?"

"Drinkwater's dead," hissed Will, shaking Damian off. "Valerian attacked him. An unarmed person."

The old Echo must have backtracked his steps, for suddenly there he was, by the tree on the right, near enough to catch every whisper.

"Not dead," the old Echo corrected Will in his mesmerizing voice. "Wounded. As I already explained. Though William doesn't seem to believe me.... I had no choice," the old Echo added and shrugged.

For an instant a moonbeam set his pale green eyes on fire.

"The Fate Sealers kidnapped my niece," he explained. "My dead brother's only child. She and her mother have no one but me left in the world. I cannot let them down. I have to buy Valerie's freedom. I have no choice." Again the old man shrugged with that cold manner of his that seemed to wash him of any blame.

"There is always a choice," said Damian quietly. "How much will it cost?"

"To free Valerie? Not much," answered the old Echo, as his pale eyes slid to watch Will. "Only the Royal Shekel."

Will's heart missed a beat.

"The Royal Shekel?" said Damian, and for a moment Will felt his friend's cold Echo hand gripping his shoulder tensely. "Is that all?"

Then Damian glanced around them with his crossbow aimed at the dark trees up ahead.

"We'd better hurry," he added. "Before the second Fate Sealer appears."

They started walking, Will leaning against Damian's icy body, his legs still feeling numb with cold. Valerian walked in the lead, lighting the way with the Fate Sealer's horn. Over the crunch of their feet on the frozen ice, Will heard an owl hooting and the wind shaking snow from the treetops.

"How is Deá, by the way?" asked Valerian, without turning to face them, his voice once more balmy and calm. "I understand she was injured. Did you know a Fate Sealer read her memory? How unimaginative of Drinkwater to choose a cellar as a hiding place."

Will stiffened, knowing exactly which memory Valerian was talking about.

"Hiding place?" asked Damian, faking indifference.

"Oh! Come now, Damian," said Valerian softly. "We both know I'm talking about the Royal Shekel. I was in the cellar earlier... went to verify the memory for myself. There is no doubt. The coin had been there. Until William took it away."

Suddenly Valerian whirled to face Will, with his blood-red crossbow once more in his hand and aimed at Will's forehead.

"I saw you in my Crystillery," he said in his soft voice, as if casting a spell. "I Saw you take the coin. Where's the Royal Shekel, William? For Fortune's sake... for the sake of a little, helpless girl— tellllllll meeeee..."

"NO!" Damian thrust Will back, and his black crossbow struck the blood-red crossbow with a clang. The moonlight glinted off the still weapons. For a moment it seemed to Will that both Echoes would shoot.

"Stop it," Will pleaded.

But Damian only stepped protectively before Will.

"I'll come with you into Shadowpain, Valerian," said Damian. "I'll help you rescue your niece... or at least try. But don't ask Will to sacrifice himself. The Royal Shekel is the only thing keeping him alive—and our Prince."

"I... I..." Valerian stammered, and in his pale green eyes Will saw something changing.

"I understand," Damian whispered back.

"It's just that Valerie is so young...."

"That may work in our favor," said Damian gently, coaxing the old Echo forward. "A Brain Freeze helped heal Emmy Cleary

113

after her release from Shadowpain. A young mind can recover from horrors no adult mind could withstand."

Will followed, still leaning on Damian, his strength slowly returning. He didn't know Emmy's Brain had been frozen, and anger bubbled inside him—anger for the normal life he and his parents never had; and anger for his twin sister that suffered worse than any of them. He was sick of the Echoes, the way they treated Sounds like something to kick out of the way. No! Worse! Like something to torture, so they could kick an Echo out of their way. Will was even sick of the way Damian kept protecting him like a helpless little boy. Everyone was trying to take control of his life. But it was his life. His!

Valerian raised his left hand, and Will noticed for the first time that it gleamed oddly in the moonlight.

"I have this plastic ornament to make up for the hand the false King cut off," said the old Echo bitterly. "But it is not a hand. And never will be. Pain and suffering leave a shadow in their wake."

Suddenly, Valerian stiffened.

"What was that—?" he hissed, lighting a cluster of dark trees to their left. "Not see-through," he sighed with relief, as a black raven fluttered away, cackling. "Still, we'd better hurry. Where do you plan to hide the boy, Damian?"

"You're coming with me, right?" Damian nodded his question at Will. "To the Echo realm?"

Will nodded back, gritting his teeth. "Can't sit around waiting for Fate Sealers to come get me, can I?"

"No! No, he can't come," interrupted Valerian, once again shining the luminous horn before them like a giant flashlight. "Fate Sealers are guarding the Passage Well in case the Royal Shekel turns up."

"A Sound won't make it through?" asked Damian.

"Not a chance. Not unless…"

"Yes?" asked Will, a knot of tension twisting in his stomach.

"Unless, William…" Valerian glanced back, his pale eyes looking like glass marbles. "Unless that Sound is as cold as an Echo. Which means… as cold as a corpse."

"Are you saying I have to die first?" snapped Will, stopping still in anger.

"Not die… sleep," said the old Echo.

"You can't, Valerian!" said Damian, shaking his head. "If you're talking about Cold Sleep, the answer is no! This kid's been through a Brain Freeze already. He's not going through a Cold Sleep on top of it."

"Don't you think it's up to me?" demanded Will. "I know you're trying to protect me, Damian. But I'm not two anymore. I can make up my own mind."

"Not about this, you can't," said Damian flatly. "It's bigger than you. If you die, my Prince dies. And the last ten years of my life are wasted. Besides," Damian muttered to himself, "Deá will kill me. No Cold Sleep."

"Then, I ask again," said Valerian gently. "Where do you plan to hide the boy, Damian?"

"In the Echo realm. I'll manage."

"How?"

But Damian kept silent.

"If you're thinking of using a different Passage Well, forget it," said Valerian, and his beautiful voice sounded desperately worried. "More than a thousand Fate Sealers were sent out this morning."

"There are Wells on other continents," said Damian.

"And by the time you get there, they will be guarded too."

Suddenly Valerian locked his pale eyes on Will, as if Damian wasn't there anymore.

"Cold Sleep is the only way, young man," he said earnestly. "You don't have to trust me on faith. I have just as much interest in keeping you alive as Damian. I will try to rescue my niece from Shadowpain. But if I fail... and I probably will... I'll need you to tell me what you did with the Royal Shekel. No, don't answer me now. First, let's get you out of danger."

It struck Will suddenly, the realization why Valerian reminded him of his father, though the Echo looked so different. It was the way Valerian smelled of cherry tobacco even though he wasn't smoking a pipe. It was the scent of home. A cold, ramshackle home with holes in the walls and dark memories. It reminded Will of what he had to do. And why.

"What is this... Cold Sleep exactly?" asked Will.

"A gradual freezing of a Sound's body," said Valerian, his voice as soft as a lullaby. "Until a cold sleep comes over every organ, even the brain."

"You mean like a Brain Freeze?"

"More gradual."

"More painful," Damian corrected, his features looking stern in the pale light of the luminous horn. "And you won't forget the memory either," Damian added, slapping his icy hand on Will's shoulder. "You'll become as cold as I am. And slip into a deep Cold Sleep. You may not wake for days, weeks... We don't know exactly. It hasn't been tried enough times."

"But those who did it, woke up... eventually?" asked Will.

"Certainly." A frozen twig snapped under Valerian's shimmering gray boot.

"All two of them," Damian clarified.

Will swallowed hard. "And when they woke up... they were fine?"

"No!" said Damian, his dark cheeks pulsing tensely. "The first one died. The second is still in a wheelchair. I can't let you do it, Will. I can't let you take the risk."

"Thought you only wanted to keep me alive because of the prince." Will smiled at Damian, and all the tension between him and his faithful Echo friend just melted as if it had never happened at all.

"Doesn't look like we have too many options," said Will.

"It's my fault. I shouldn't have left you this morning," said Damian bitterly.

"You had even less options then," said Will, thinking of Deá bleeding in Damian's arms.

Thoughtfully, Will turned his back on the Echoes and started pacing back and worth. An icy branch crunched under his feet, and he wondered if his skin will become as brittle if he agreed to be frozen.

"You can't stay here," Will heard Valerian's beautiful voice at his back. "Think of your parents. The Fate Sealers are not acting on their own. They're working for the false King. If that villain is blackmailing me with a ten-year-old girl, do you think he would hesitate to blackmail you with your mother and father? Do you want to see them dragged into Shadowpain? Isn't it enough one member of your family almost—?"

But Damian must have silenced Valerian, for the forest grew so quiet suddenly that Will could hear his own breathing and realized that he was gasping from fear—deep fear that felt like someone gnawing at his chest from the inside. But it didn't matter. Will knew what he had to do.

"I'll go. On one condition," said Will, turning to face the Echoes again.

"Excellent," said Valerian.

"What is it?" Damian sighed.

Will took a deep breath. "I want to meet my Echo. I want to help him become King. Then Emmy can come home with me, right?"

"By all means." Valerian's pale eyes glittered with impatience.

Damian looked worried. "Things will change if the Prince

118

takes the throne. But a meeting? Both of you together in one room? It's risky. But…" Suddenly Damian chuckled. "You know what? Our Prince is as stubborn as his Sound. He'll probably want to meet you too, Will. I'll arrange a meeting."

"Thanks," said Will quietly.

"Excellent, excellent." Valerian clapped the luminous horn with finality, beaming at Will. "Then you'd better get on with it. Your clothes, take everything off."

"What? Why?" Will glanced at Damian for support.

"It's a good idea," agreed Damian.

"Why?" asked Will again. He couldn't help blushing at the thought of his skinny body. A naked scarecrow! Did he have to be humiliated on top of everything else?

"Because whatever you have on will be destroyed in the freezing," explained Valerian gently. "Your buttons, the fabric, anything you might have in your pockets…"

"What will happen to them?" asked Will.

"They will all simply crumble."

Will wondered what would keep him from crumbling.

"You can leave your things with Damian," said Valerian, more gently still. Then he coughed and added, sounding far too casual, "*Do* you have anything in your pockets?"

Wouldn't you like to know, thought Will. But he said nothing as he walked away to remove his clothes behind a tree; first his coat, making sure the Crystillery and Waterweed didn't fall out of his pockets, then his shirt, shoes, socks and pants. He folded everything and placed the gravestone book on top. His underwear he kept on. They could crumble for all he cared, he wasn't taking them off.

Shivering in the moonlight, Will cast a parting glance at the feather and ball of fur left to him from his dead pets. Then he slipped these cherished keepsakes back inside a pocket of his pants.

Then only one thing remained to be done. Glancing back cautiously, Will took the Royal Shekel out of his pocket. Somehow he had to slip the coin to Damian without Valerian noticing. But how?

And suddenly a whole new idea struck Will.

Drinkwater had said that the false King wouldn't dare to kill the Prince or his Sound before he got his hands on the Royal Shekel. So what if Will destroyed the coin? But without anyone knowing! The hunt for the Royal Shekel would go on. And Will and the Prince would be safe… or at least in less danger.

Without hesitation Will rolled the slightly see-through blue coin in snow, until a small ball was formed. Then he put the ball in his mouth and swallowed, wondering why Drinkwater hadn't thought of destroying the Royal Shekel in secret.

Will felt immense relief as he stretched down on the snow, naked but for his underwear.

"I'm rrready," he shouted, fighting to stop shivering.

Damian and Valerian rounded the tree, the luminous horn casting an eerie glow on their faces. Damian looked anxious, Valerian impatient.

"Don't ffforget to bbbring my ssstuff," Will shivered at

Damian. Somehow knowing that his things would wait for him on the other side made crossing into the Echo realm less frightening.

Damian nodded. "I'll just leave the Waterweed behind. You won't need it in the Echo realm. It always glows there."

Will's heart was pounding like a wrecking ball against his chest. All I have to do is help the Prince take the throne, he reminded himself. How hard can that be?

"Will you send Drinkwater a message?" Valerian asked Damian. "Tell him the boy has passed safely into Agám Kaffú?"

Damian nodded and leaned in the snow beside Will, his face stern with worry.

"And mmmy ppparents..." Will blurted out with effort, his teeth chattering painfully. "Drinkwwwater pppromised."

"Then he'll keep his promise," Damian assured Will, "as soon as he's well enough. Now try to relax. Valerian's going to freeze you with the Ice Loom. This will hurt, Will. But it won't take... too long."

Valerian towered over Will and Damian. His face contorted painfully as he struggled to wrap his lips around the wide end of the glowing horn, a horn designed for the sagging lips of Fate Sealers. The light of the horn shone eerily through the old Echo's see-through mouth, turning Valerian's whole head into a freakish lantern.

"Close your eyes, Will," said Damian, "or you'll go blind."

Like a lump of fear, the Royal Shekel slipped down Will's throat as his eyelids drifted shut, enveloping him in darkness and the pounding of his heart. A sense of impending doom crept over Will. Placing the Prince on the throne suddenly seemed as hopeless as his desperate wish to feel warm again. After all, the false King was bound to put up a fight. And what could two boys hope to achieve against an army of Fate Sealers?

But the time for hesitation was past. Already Will was drowning in a wave of ice. He felt as if his body would break free of his skin. Except that he had no skin anymore. Only a suit of armor, which was shrinking tighter and tighter, until he could barely breathe. And when the pressure turned to pain and the ice burned like fire, Will's ears filled with the sound of cracking bones, and he knew that he was dying—because no one could suffer such agony for more than a second.

So why was the second stretching on and on and on....?

The Orphanage

The Orphanage
Of Castaway Children

Time seemed to have frozen long, long ago.

Will floated like a block of ice on an endless dark sea, nothing around him but a dark, dark night. In his mind he heard his father's voice echoing like a giant bat with wings of darkness. And the words were painfully familiar, lines from a poem Will's father always quoted when thinking of Emmy.

"Alone, alone, all, all alone
Alone on a wide, wide sea!"

So cold, so dark, so empty.... Will started counting how many times he heard his father's voice, and the word *"Alone"* seemed to echo through the whole wide world that wasn't there.

"Alone, all, all alone..."

Will counted and counted and the numbers piled high in his mind, until he reached nine thousand nine hundred ninety nine and gave up and started counting all over again. Then again, and again, staring up into the void of blackness. Floating, floating... frozen in a

Cold Sleep nightmare.

*   *   *

At last, Will woke up with a gasp, like a diver coming up for air from the bottom of the sea.

Blinking his burning eyes open, Will remembered why he was asleep and where he should be, and he blinked and blinked, expecting to see see-through people and strange glowing plants. But all Will did see was his own face staring down at him, looking delicate and pretty and enveloped in fog.

"My Echo…?" Will wondered, and he started to cough. His throat was burning as if the words had cut him on the way out.

The face turned and shouted, "Nurse Flight! Nurse Flight! He's awake. He's awake finally."

And again the face looked down at Will, and Will wondered if he imagined that this person who looked just like him actually sounded like a girl. But then, suddenly, it hit Will, as if he had known who she was all along, though he still couldn't believe it. Not after all those years.

"You're not—?"

"Yes. Emmy," said the girl, fog drifting from her mouth. Her brown eyes twinkled with happiness, but the way their oval shape slanted down in the corners kept her eyes looking melancholy, as Will's always did, and his father's. "Your twin!" added Emmy, as if she didn't think Will understood.

Will stared up at his sister, speechless. What was he supposed to say to someone who came back from the dead? Nice to

126

meet you? How lame was that?! Will shook his head, bewildered, and the smile faded from Emmy's lips.

"You don't know who I am?" muttered Emmy, her long straw-colored hair slipping across her face to hide a falling tear. "Mom and Dad never talked about me…?"

Will could only laugh bitterly, a shallow, stabbing laugh. "Talk about you?" he whispered, his throat still so sore. "They never talked about anything else!"

"Mom and Dad? Really?" Emmy stared at Will again, her eyes bright with tears of joy. "They talked about me? They missed me?"

"They were miserable without you." Will smiled sadly, realizing that fog was drifting from his mouth too. "Happy?"

Emmy nodded, her smile too wide for speaking, and Will stared at her, mesmerized by the sight of his own face on another person. But soon Will's eyes spotted other strange things, and he looked around and caught his first glimpse of the Echo realm.

It was a cold place, as cold as a fridge—that much Will had realized from the fog drifting out of his and Emmy's mouths as they talked. Nothing unusual about that, though. In Alaska people's icy breath often ballooned from their mouths like speech bubbles without words inside them. But the room, the little of it Will could see, was like nothing he had ever seen before.

For starters, Will was lying in what looked like a snow heap, slightly see-through snow in fact. But the heap felt warm and dry like a cozy bed. And indeed it had railing sticking at its sides as in the beds of toddlers or sick people in hospitals. Except that here the railing was not made of wood or metal but ice, gleaming warm ice, like the Royal Shekel Will had swallowed in the forest. Even the septic smell hovering on the cold air was hospital-like. But the shimmering floor was checkered blue-and-green like a strange chess board of square puddles, and the ceiling was made of rough stones as ancient looking as the walls of a medieval fortress.

As if all this wasn't strange enough, a curtain that looked like a waterfall of algae cascaded around Will's snow heap, obscuring the rest of the room. Drifting on the curtain, like the reflection of the moon on a lake, was a crystal ball. It was enormous, and yet it looked just like Will's crystal ball clock and the crystal ball knocker on the front door of his home.

Suddenly a small woman blustered through the green waterfall curtain. Her spiky red hair quivered like a strange bird's nest caught in a storm, and her glistening white coat flapped around her short legs like a small blizzard.

"Nurse Flight to the rescue," she huffed in a billow of vaporized breath.

An instant later, she grabbed Will's arms, kicked off his gleaming blankets and pulled him to his feet.

"Exercise Time!" the little nurse twittered, her voice so high-pitched that she sounded like an enraged hamster. "No, no! Crystal my foot! But you don't understand!" She shook her spikey hair at Will. "Don't sit. Stand! And stretch! Don't want you ending up in a wheelchair like my last Cold Sleep patient, now do we? Come on, pull those knees up! Elbows to your sides!"

Will's body felt like something that didn't belong to him, a plank of wood washed up on a frozen shore. For one terrifying second, he wondered if his underwear had crumbled in the Cold Sleep. Then Will saw that someone (he preferred not to wonder who) had dressed him in white pants and a sweater, which felt soft and warm but glistened like ice in sunshine.

Between his flailing arms, Will caught snatches of something embroidered on his sweater, some sort of crest. After a moment he realized what it was: a glittering white fortress with the words *Cast* floating over it like a cloud, and *Away* encircling its bottom like a moat. Since Emmy was likewise glistening, though in a white skirt instead of pants, Will guessed that this was some kind of uniform.

"Keep it up!" the enraged hamster insisted. "And stretch, and bend, and one, and two…"

Will swayed drunkenly, trying to keep his balance through all this exercise. A stinging vapor, like ammonia, was making his eyes water, but he couldn't figure out where it was coming from. And through the tears he noticed that his sister wasn't smiling anymore.

"What's wrong—?" Will asked.

But Nurse Flight cut him off. "He's ready," she chirped at Emmy. Then she turned to Will again.

"I'll be right back. You keep moving, you hear me? By all the flying crystal balls! You'd better keep moving! Understand?" And the little woman blustered through the waterfall curtain and disappeared.

Will glanced at Emmy again. She looked ready to strangle him.

"You could look more happy to see me," said Will, letting his heavy arms drop by his sides. No matter what Nurse Flight ordered; he was too tired to move.

"Happy?" Emmy exploded, spewing smoky vapors like a dragon. "What for? That my brother's a total idiot."

"Excuse me?" Will blinked in shock.

"How could you just volunteer to come here?" demanded Emmy. "Don't you know the Echoes will never let you leave? Now we're both stuck here! What possessed you?"

"How about I didn't want Fate Sealers dragging Mom and Dad into Shadowpain?" Will drawled sluggishly. For some reason he sounded like a tape recorder playing at low speed. He had sounded like that from the moment he woke up, he realized. "And what's wrong with my voice?"

But, at the mention of the Fate Sealers, Emmy had deflated like a stabbed balloon. Will watched his sister's melancholy eyes blinking back tears, and he wished he hadn't mentioned Shadowpain. How could he have been so thoughtless? Emmy spent five years in the dungeons of the Fate Sealers…

"Standing idol?" Nurse Flight blustered through the waterfall curtain again, her spiky red hair quivering more than ever. "Oh! My flying crystal balls!" She stopped to stare at Will in horror. "This won't do! Won't do, I tell you. Stretch, young man! You've got to stretch. No time to waste."

And once again Will was feeling like an out of control circus clown, his glistening white uniform flailing in every direction as the nurse pulled him hither and thither.

"Got the contact lenses," he heard the Nurse chirping past his swinging arms. "Final touch. Not a bad disguise, by Fortune."

"He looks like a blimp." Will caught a fuzzy glimpse of Emmy nodding. "Nothing like me."

Then a sudden wave of nausea washed over Will, and he didn't hear anything anymore.

Will's stomach lurched, and a second later he was vomiting on the shimmering blue-and-green floor and on his glistening white shoes. After that, everything felt different. Will became so weak and dizzy, as if he was moving in slow-motion as he fell back on the bed... Or was the opposite happening? Was the world starting to move at fast-forward speed, because everything was suddenly too quick to make sense?

First, something round and hard stuck to the roof of Will's mouth. Through the blur of confusion Will knew it was the Royal Shekel. Slowly, Will dragged his arm forward and took the coin out while pretending to wipe his mouth on a sheet that looked like snowflakes sown together. Across from him Emmy zoomed out of sight past the waterfall-curtain, and the little nurse whizzed across the watery floor, wiping the vomit with a blanket that looked like a sparkling puddle.

"This is too much! Too much, I say!" Will heard the nurse twittering.

And suddenly a little brown dog appeared out of nowhere and started feasting on the leftover vomit.

"That dog'll eat anything," said a boy, who popped through the waterfall curtain after the dog. And maybe Will was imaging it, for it was all so confusing, but the boy's face was all wrong. His lower lip looked as swollen as a second chin, and his right eye was as puffed and bruised as a baboon's backside.

Nurse Flight ordered the dog back in an icy cage the boy was carrying. Then she rushed away past the green curtain, disappearing like Emmy. The strange boy waved goodbye at the little woman's back, then he grinned at Will before pouring him a glass of water, which seemed like a nice thing to do. Until the boy decided to turn the glass upside over Will's head.

"Hey—" Will ducked in slow-motion. But instead of water, two ice cubes tumbled down Will's nose. Will stared up at the boy in stupefied confusion. "How d'ya—?"

"Turn water into ice? Don't bother asking," declared the strange boy, his swollen lip hula dancing as he spoke. "A magician never reveals his tricks."

Amazingly, the boy blew his frosty breath into the shape of a magician's hat, before he bowed gallantly in his glistening white uniform and introduced himself.

"Peter Patrick Peterson. Tongue twister by name, magician by fame. And this gorgeous dog—" the boy pointed at the brindled mutt barking in the icy cage "—is Poudini. Houdini with a P. Named after the greatest magician ever. And after me, P for Peter Patrick

Peterson. Get it?"

Will smiled, not to be rude, but in his mind a thousand worries were jostling. The Cold Sleep hadn't destroyed the Royal Shekel. It was glistening between his stiff fingers as if nothing had happened to it at all. The only thing keeping him alive was still in one piece, and Will had brought it into the Echo realm, the land where Fate Sealers lived.

Slowly, though finally not so slowly as before, Will slipped the coin into the glistening pocket of his white pants, trying to think of something dismissive to say to the strange boy staring at him curiously, like someone about to start asking questions. Lots of them.

But suddenly Nurse Flight and Emmy were back at Will's side, and the little nurse shoved a mirror in Will's hand and held out a small box to him with two tiny blue disks inside.

"Contact lenses," she explained. "The crowning glory of your fortunerific disguise."

And then, all at once, as if someone had applied the brakes to the entire dizzying world, Will felt the merry-go-round of faces, voices and shimmering white fabrics screeching to a grinding halt.

Will stared into the mirror.

But what he saw staring back at him wasn't his own reflection. It was more like looking at a zombie version of himself.

The nostrils were the size of olives. The cheeks looked like gray tomatoes, and the nose like an even grayer pickle. Between the puffy buns of skin the eyes showed like slits. And now Will saw that

133

the hand he was holding the mirror with was gray too and twice its normal size, as if someone had puffed it full of air. The rest of him was equally bloated, Will realized, as if he had put on one hundred pounds overnight. He looked like a human buoy bobbing on the shimmering blue-green floor.

"Cold Sleep, that's all it is, young man," said the nurse matter-of-factly, poking one of his puffy brown eyes with a blue contact lens. "You'll look like your normal self again in no time. Six months at most... probably two." She poked his other eye.

"The hair was my idea." Will heard Emmy, and he realized where the scent of ammonia was coming from. His once yellow strawy hair was now bright red and spiked like some weird picket fence. He saw where the inspiration came from. Nurse Flight's head looked scarily familiar.

"The painkiller was mine," added the little nurse, as she forced a small lustrous box into Will's puffy gray hand. "Always thought it was a bit of a problem, painkillers that leave you sounding like a moron. This time, we couldn't have wished for anything better." Nurse Flight's gray eyes twinkled like raindrops in sunlight. "Take three a day. No!" she reconsidered, "Five. Five should do the trick. You'll soon forget you ever had a normal voice."

"Terrific," muttered Will, hearing himself sounding nothing like himself.

"So who are you?" asked the strange boy with the tongue twister name, blowing another magician's hat before his bruised face. "And what's with the baby elephant disguise?"

134

"His name is Fredrick Fingeldy," answered a voice that made Will's heart leap. And Damian emerged through the cascading green curtain, looking so tall and handsome in his shimmering black clothes and cape that Will managed to feel even more hideous than before.

*   *   *

A short time later, Peter Patrick Peterson left with his brindled mutt, Poudini, barking in the icy cage. Emmy lingered only to warn Will that in public she will have to pretend she didn't know him and say things she didn't really mean. Hugging him goodbye without explaining why she had to leave, Will's long lost sister rushed off with Nurse Flight at her side. And then, when Will and Damian were finally alone, the Echo sat on the edge of the snow heap bed and explained to Will where he was.

This was the Orphanage of Castaway Children, a refuge in the Echo realm for kids who were kidnapped by Fate Sealers. Both Sounds and Echoes were welcome here; for Echoes, too, were sometimes hunted down by Fate Sealers. The Orphanage was a sanctuary, a home and a school; though Will would not have to attend classes until after Christmas break, two weeks from now... if he was still in the Echo realm by then.

How long was Will asleep? For four days. And did he have to look like a fat, gray midget? Yes, because no one must see who Will really looked like. No one must guess that Will was the Prince's Sound.

Everything about Will's identity had to remain a secret, his name too. As a surrogate name, Damian suggested Fredrick Fingeldy. Will's disguise would benefit from an amusing name, Damian said. But, more importantly, it was a real name of a boy who died tragically many years ago, though Damian would not say how, except that the death was a secret.

"Memorize Fredrick's short life story in the gravestone book," Damian concluded, no cold breath escaping his mouth. "Then destroy the page. No one must see the photo of little Freddy. He was dark-skinned, like me. Nothing like you. Understand?"

"*I'm* nothing like me," muttered Will.

"A good thing," said Damian. "Though it won't be easy for you, I know. You'll need a friend at the Orphanage," added Damian. "I talked to Emmy yesterday, when I dropped by to see how you were doing. She said you can trust Peter... the boy who just left."

"Yes, we met." Will nodded. "He can blow a magician's hat with his cold breath. Is that supposed to be helpful against Fate Sealers?"

Damian chuckled and handed Will a glistening black bag. "Maybe this will cheer you up. It's all here," added Damian, as Will peeked inside. "All your stuff. Except the Waterweed. You'll find plenty around here."

"Won't fit me now," said Will in his slow, medicated voice, dumping his old clothes on the snowflake blanket. Lifting his folded Jeans, Will found the tuft of wolf's fur and the falcon's speckled feather. The memory of his pets didn't make Will sad anymore, not with Damian beside him. Still, he shoved these childhood mementos

136

in the glistening black bag, then added the gravestone book too.

Damian clapped his see-through hands soundlessly on his thighs and rose from the snow heap bed.

"We should get going," he said, still no cold breath escaping his Echo lips.

Will slipped his Crystillery in the gleaming white pocket of his Orphanage uniform and rose too. "Is it always this cold here?" he asked, shivering.

"Not everywhere," answered the Echo. "Sound rooms are heated. But the temperatures in shared rooms are better suited to the bodies of Echoes than Sounds. Follow me," he added, parting the waterfall curtain.

There was no one in the room beyond. Walking fast, Damian led the way between two rows of empty snow heap beds with icy railing at their sides and cascading waterfall curtains half open around them. Will watched the shimmering blue-and-green checkered floor quivering beneath Damian's feet, like a lake after a pebble is thrown inside. It looked as if Damian was walking on water.

"You won't always feel this cold," said Damian, smiling back at Will. "Your uniform… It's supposed to get warmer the longer you wear it."

"I think it's starting to," Will realized, noticing pleasant warmth spreading over his stomach.

"Good," Damian nodded, still leading the way between the rows of empty beds half hidden by waterfall curtains.

Will couldn't stop staring at the curtains, for everyone had a huge crystal ball floating at its center. Some were all folded up where the curtain was drawn away from the bed. Others were hovering on the side as if they had the power to move along the shimmering green fabric. The crystal balls reminded Will of disembodied eyes, and he felt as if they were watching him, though he saw no signs of life inside them. Still, Will lowered his voice and drew close to Damian's cold ear.

"What about the Prince? Did you arrange a meeting?" Will asked.

"Sure have," said Damian, grinning as if remembering something amusing. "I was right. Your Echo was just as adamant about meeting you. Danger or no danger."

Damian stopped by a massive door that seemed carved from ice, turned the crystal ball knob at the center and led the way outside. "All clear," he said, peeking through the door. "Let's go."

Will found himself in a drafty stone corridor which was so narrow, at first Will thought the walls were closing in on him like clapping hands. But it was only a delusion caused by the fact that the walls were curving. On both sides of the narrow stone passage, windows in the shape of large crystal balls lined the walls, making the thin corridor feel like a walkway in the sky; because though the windows on the left looked into the room Will had just left, those on the right stood high over a glittering, icy garden with a blue, blue sky overhead.

It was an amazing garden like nothing Will had ever seen.

Everything was covered in snow and glittering ice, the winding paths, the clusters of trees and what looked like mazes. And here and there blue fountains splashed and a river meandered between them, though the water didn't look like water at all but like a stream of sapphires. And strangest of all was how see-through everything looked, trees showing through trees, the river showing through heaps of snow. It was all like a daydream, half imagination, half reality. But Will knew that it was real, and for a moment he forgot all his troubles and gaped in startled wonder at this fantastic Echo garden.

Then he realized that he was falling behind, and he rushed after Damian who was talking again in whispers.

"Sorry, didn't hear," Will whispered back.

"On the ground floor of the fortress," repeated Damian, and Will noticed the blue sky showing through the Echo's dark see-through face. "At the back of the Sound kitchen... there's a giant fireplace. The only fireplace with real fire in the whole Orphanage. Meals for Sounds are cooked in it, baked in it. Anyway, the mantelpiece there is made of shimmering crystal ball stones. One of them, on the top right, is chipped in the corner. I want you to find that stone... then push it up... then down... then up again. Got that?"

"Up, down, up." Will nodded.

"The fireplace will slide away from the wall."

"A secret passage?" asked Will breathlessly. "Is that—?"

But Will's swollen thighs tripped him and he fell against a crystal ball window, the breath knocked out of him.

"You'll get used to looking like this... being like this," said Damian, steadying Will again with his cold Echo hands.

"I look like something Frankenstein cooked up in his lab," muttered Will, and the memory of what happened to his Chemistry teacher, Mr. Drinkwater, only made Will feel worse.

"That's why you need Peter, you understand? You need a friend here. Someone who'll help you find the secret room behind the fireplace."

"The secret room," repeated Will, forcing his mind to focus on the reason he was here.

"The Prince will be waiting for you there. Tomorrow."

Will spread his legs a little to avoid losing his balance as he started walking beside Damian again. It made Will sway oddly, like someone walking on the deck of a ship in a storm. But it kept Will's thighs from knocking. "When tomorrow?" he asked.

"Midnight. You'll have to find the fireplace by then."

"I'll find it."

"First floor... Sound kitchen."

"I'll find it! Promise."

Damian nodded, but his dark forehead creased with lines of worry.

Will looked outside again, not at the garden this time but at the walls of the Orphanage of Castaway Children.

He was in a great fortress, he realized, with walls that curved around the glittering garden to enclose it in a circle, like a giant alabaster ring. Will saw the long, curving line of crystal ball windows on the bottom floor. So many windows... so many rooms... Which were the windows of the Sound kitchen, he wondered. He glanced at the Orphanage Crest on his glistening sweater; it didn't do justice to the real fortress.

"Built to shelter its inhabitants," said Damian, following Will's gaze. "The Orphanage is a giant wall."

"With guard towers?" Will saw shimmering turrets and an icy parapet—though, strangely, no guards.

"Yes. All of it built in a circle."

"To keep Fate Sealers out?" Will guessed, but Damian frowned and didn't answer.

They walked on, and Will realized that even the ordinary flagstones under his feet were rippling slightly in Echo fashion. High overhead lustrous crystal ball chandeliers drooped down like enormous pearl necklaces.

Through the windows on his left, Will saw strange rooms that resembled icy caves, with unbelievable bunk beds that looked like flowing water frozen in time, and blankets and pillows that might have been layers of see-through snow. It was all bizarre and beautiful but, also, chillingly, eerily deserted... There wasn't a soul in sight.

"Where is everyone?" Will whispered nervously, suppressing a shudder that was more than a shiver from the cold.

Damian pointed at the glittering white garden, and Will spotted two tall walls of icy ivy far below on the right. They looked like frozen waterfalls standing side by side, and through their see-through surface Will thought he saw the shadowy backs of people, but it was all too faint to make out clearly.

"That's the back of the bleachers," explained Damian. "The whole Orphanage is there. Waiting to welcome the new Castaways with a Pet Selection Ceremony. I know…" Damian nodded gravely. "Would have been better not to draw attention to you. But it wasn't up to us. It's a tradition."

"You mean the whole Orphanage's there… waiting for me?" Will looked down miserably at his bloated body and gray hands. He preferred to forget what his face looked like, but he couldn't. How could he face the whole Orphanage looking like this? "I can't," he stammered. "Just can't."

"You have to. Everyone at the Orphanage has a pet," explained Damian. "You'll have to choose one at the ceremony. Don't attract attention to yourself… well, not more than you can help, okay? Choose something unimpressive. A rabbit or a hamster will do nicely."

Will chuckled at the impossibility of keeping a low profile when you look like a walking blimp, but Damian ignored him and kept walking, and Will forced his heavy legs to wobble on down the interminable corridor.

At long last a landing appeared, and they headed down an enclosed stone staircase that felt like the inside of a giant nautilus shell. It spiraled downward and out of sight, enveloping them in the echoes of Will's heavy footsteps and the pale light of two crystal ball handrails that hung in festoons on the wall at waist height.

"The Crystillery I gave you, you brought it?" asked Damian in a hushed voice, his shadow falling on the spiraling wall before them.

Will nodded and took out the blue dome from his pocket. He was about to give it back to Damian when he noticed something strange.

"That's not the same Crystillery," he said, confused. "The one you gave me before... That one had a Fate Sealer symbol, here." Will pointed at the emblem etched into the back of the blue dome. "Now it's a crystal ball."

Damian missed a step and steadied himself with the luminous crystal ball handrail.

"Do you know about Fortune Tellers?" Damian muttered under his breath.

Will nodded, remembering what his Chemistry teacher told him about the Echoes who copied the death of Sounds exactly. "Mr. Drinkwater told me," said Will, his upper lip curling in disgust.

Damian kept walking, staring at his feet, the spiraling stairs showing through his shimmering black boots. "I took the other Crystillery back," he said in a moment, "because it wasn't safe for you to have it."

"Why not?" wondered Will.

In his usual way Damian ignored the interruption. "This Crystillery is mine," he said. "I'd like you to keep it." Damian stopped and pressed his dark, see-through hands over the blue dome still resting in Will's palm. "Just keep it hidden. You're not supposed to—"

"I know," Will cut in. "Only the King's advisors, Fate Sealers and Fortune Tellers can have a Crystillery. So how did you get one, Damian?"

"Let's just say it was mine..." said the Echo, almost in a whisper, "...a long time ago."

"A Fortune Teller's Crystillery was yours?" insisted Will, his medicated voice making him sound infuriatingly stupid.

Damian just started to walk again, faster than before.

"But Fortune Tellers are murderers." Will rushed after Damian. "They kill an Echo after his Sound dies."

"You've learned a lot about the Echoes." Damian sighed. "Perhaps Drinkwater should have also mentioned that I used to be..." But Damian broke off.

"What? A Fortune Teller?"

To Will's horror, Damian nodded.

Will flinched back, shaking his head in amazement. He knocked into the spiraling wall. The Crystillery slipped from his puffy hand and tumbled away down the steep, stone stairs, chips of blue crystal flying after it.

"For Fortune's Sake!" snarled Damian, and he tore after the Crystillery at a speed no Sound could match.

Within seconds Damian was back, the Crystillery unbroken in his see-through hand. He stopped on the stair below Will, and they looked into each other's eyes.

"Sometimes a Sound is born dead," said Damian, the nautilus

staircase showing through his head. "A stillborn, they call it. But when his Echo is born alive, then... and only then... the Law of Death permits an Echo to outlive his Sound. But there's a catch. It is believed that Fortune spared the life of the infant Echo for a purpose. And so the child is raised to be Fortune's servant. He is raised to become a Fortune Teller."

"Is that what happened to you?" asked Will, fighting not to shiver with Damian's cold body so close to his.

"That part wasn't up to me," said Damian. "But when I turned fifteen, I escaped. And I took Deá with me... Yes—" Damian answered Will's gasp "—Deá was a Fortune Teller too. The girl who couldn't hurt a fly.... We can't always choose what happens to us," added Damian, "but we can choose what to do about it. I want you to have my Crystillery, Will. My way of saying thank-you."

"For what?" said Will, suddenly feeling a sense of hope and defiance, as if what Damian could do, he could do too.

"For choosing to come here... to help your Echo."

"I didn't have a choice." Will shrugged. But for the first time he felt that he probably did, just that the option of hiding or running away wasn't something he was willing to do.

"There's always a choice," said Damian, as if he could hear Will's thoughts. "My Crystillery is yours." He pressed the blue dome back into Will's puffy palm. "Take good care of it."

"I chipped it," Will realized sadly.

"Take's more than a chip to destroy a Crystillery. Kind of like people." Damian smiled.

Thank you, thought Will, *for everything*. But before he could say it aloud, the Echo answered his thoughts again.

"You're welcome."

"How do you do that?" asked Will. "Hear my thoughts like that?"

Damian chuckled and his coffee eyes twinkled. "No," he shook his head at Will's wondering gaze. "Echoes can't read minds. But when you get to know someone very well, you can read their expressions. Pay attention. It will happen to you too."

They didn't speak again until they reached another landing several floors below and stepped into a cold crystal ball windowed corridor. It looked identical to the one they had just left, except for the wide icy doorway at the end of the corridor and the glittering white garden showing through it. There, on the doorstep, stood the first two people Will had seen in this strange, icy fortress.

* * *

Will recognized Deá even before she rushed over to hug him, her white cape fluttering and shimmering behind her like sunshine on a windy lake. For a moment Will stood frozen in place, remembering the horror of a Fate Sealer pouring out of Deá's pale mouth in the dark forest behind his school. Then he remembered what Damian said about the Sounds of Fortune Tellers dying at childbirth, and what the Fate Sealer said in the forest about Deá's sister—

"You've got a twin, like me…" will realized.

Deá let go of him, smiling. "How did you know?" But she

forgot her question and giggled, looking as sparklingly beautiful as ever. Only the glistening bandage around her neck gave any indication that she nearly bled to death a few days ago. "You're well, you made it…" She giggled again, letting off no vapor like Damian, and Will guessed that Echoes never did.

"You made it too." Will beamed at Deá. "Thanks for saving me."

Deá hugged Will again, a cold, bone-chilling hug that made Will forget all his troubles for a second. But then, over Deá's shoulder, Will glimpsed the second person standing on the doorstep, and the sight sent a different sort of chill down his spine.

She was a slightly see-through girl dressed in a glistening Orphanage uniform. Her enormous blue eyes were lost in deep dark circles, and her short black hair was a jagged mess, as if she had given herself a haircut without looking in a mirror. She looked deeply unhappy, and, muttering under her breath, she kept twirling an enormous sapphire ring around her thumb.

"Is that Valerie Valerian?" asked Damian, his voice full of pity.

"Her uncle rescued her from Shadowpain," said Deá, taking Valerie by the hand as they headed outside into the snowy, glistening garden. "Rescued her in just four days. From Shadowpain… in four days." Deá shook her head sadly, watching Valerie muttering to herself. "But look what it did to her, poor thing."

"You can rescue someone from Shadowpain in four days?" asked Will in amazement, watching Valerie also but thinking of his sister. Why did Emmy have to wait five years to be rescued?

"Valerian must have found his niece before she was dragged into the dungeons," said Damian, pointing the way they should go. Up ahead, the snowy path forked between a row of icy trees glistening in the sun.

"Didn't you go with him?" asked Will, remembering how desperate Valerian had been in the forest; how he didn't believe he could rescue Valerie even with Damian's help.

Damian shook his head. "I offered to go with him, if we brought you here first. But Valerian wouldn't wait. We parted after crossing the Passage Well. I told him he was crazy to go alone. Thankfully, he ignored me, the brave fool."

They fell silent, except for Valerie who kept muttering to herself and twirling her enormous blue ring. Will wondered if she would have to go through a Brain Freeze, like Emmy, to wipe off all her memories from Shadowpain.

Gradually the snowy path widened before them, and soon they were walking in a sparkling garden with the alabaster fortress rising high all around them. It was the half frozen garden Will had seen through the crystal ball windows of the orphanage; a garden that felt magical, because everything that was alive in it was a little see-through.

Through a line of see-through trees Will could see a river streaming in the distance. It made it seem as if the lucent branches of the trees had blue water running inside them. A cluster of half-snowy bushes on Will's left looked more like green windows than plants.

Will peered straight through them at a field of icy flowers and snow heaps.

On his right, something even more enchanting caught Will's eye. Inside tall, fragrant white roses Will spotted miniature water fountains, trails and snow heaps. But these were really just far-off spots in the garden, which showed straight through the see-through petals of the flowers.

Soon they rounded a line of fruit trees and came upon a garden of topiaries, frozen trees that were trimmed down into the shapes of icy fairies and fawns that looked so real Will expected them to jump off their perch at any moment.

A strange whisper of falling water filled the garden, as if the trees and flowers were breathing secrets at each other. The sound mingled with the hum of a distant crowd carried on a fresh, cold breeze. Will looked up as an Echo bird fluttered overhead, its white wings shimmering in the sun; an Echo sun that was ten times bigger than the sun back in the Sound realm. It looked like a velvet ball of flames floating in an upside down lagoon.

"But we're underground," gasped Will. "Aren't we?"

"It's Echo made," explained Damian. "The sun, the sky. The moon and stars at night. The weather… Everything that doesn't exist underground, but has to exist if anyone's going to live there, Echoes make it all."

Will looked and looked, enchanted. Nothing was ever this beautiful in the Sound realm. It was hard to believe that any of it was real, and the fuzzy focus of looking through solid plants and people as if they were made of ice or fog or colored glass just made it all seem more unbelievable.

"Oh, I almost forgot," said Deá, glancing back at Will. "Drinkwater's here. He's still weak from his injury. But he said he wanted to talk to you right away. Right away! I hope nothing's wrong..."

Like a beautiful dream that suddenly twists into a nightmare, reality seemed to change before Will's eyes. He forgot all about the glittering garden and remembered all his troubles instead. The Royal Shekel felt so heavy in the glistening white pocket of his Orphanage uniform. If only the Cold Sleep had destroyed it.... But Will would have to try again. Maybe melt the coin in the fireplace Damian talked about, the only one with real fire in the whole Orphanage.

Will could see Deá and Damian staring at him curiously— Deá and Damian who used to be Fortune Tellers. Would they agree to help him destroy the Royal Shekel? Will couldn't be sure. Deá and Damian weren't his pets anymore. They were Echoes. Their loyalties would be divided. How could Will trust them with his secret?

"Everything's fine," Will lied, but he spoke so quietly that his words were almost lost in the growing hum of voices filling the snowy garden.

Still walking, they were nearing the two walls of cascading ivy Will had seen from the fortress windows. Like mighty waterfalls they streamed down from the blue, blue sky, and Will felt sick at seeing all the shadowy backs of people jostling on the other side of

150

the see-through bleachers, talking in a roaring babble of voices. Even Valerie's mutterings were drowned. Until, suddenly, she screamed in terror—

For one second, Will saw Valerie's slight, see-through fingers drawing a trembling circle on the air, as if she was trying to ward off something evil. Then past her shivering figure, the shadow between the icy bleachers started to move. Something was there, something dark that rippled out into the sunlight like a human being emerging from a swamp.

"They're everywhere," Will heard Deá muttering in bewildered sorrow, as she pulled Valerie protectively behind her white shimmering cape.

"Just draw a crystal ball on the air, like Valerie," said Damian softly at Will's side.

And then, with sickening horror, Will realized what they were all seeing.

A Fate Sealer slinked out into the bright daylight, a smile rippling his sagging lips. In the creature's hollow eyes, the darkness was swirling as he stared at Will. Then he blinked once, as if not believing his eyes. But in the next instant the Fate Sealer swept forward in a terrifying whirl of dropping flesh and long curving fingernails that clawed at the air as if wishing to tear it to shreds.

"Vomit face," the Fate Sealer screeched so loudly that Will had to stop his ears with his hands.

"Stand aside, Fate Sealer," ordered Damian, shoving Will behind his back. "They're waiting for us. At the ceremony. Stand aside!"

The Fate Sealer broke into a frightful, gasping laugh that sounded like the terrified chokes of a drowning man. The creature's sagging skin rippled like an overflowing sewer, and his drooping nose swung back and forth like a ghastly pendulum.

"Your Fortune Teller's suit won't protect you here," the Fate Sealer sneered at Damian's shimmering black clothes. "You've delivered the brat. Now, get lost! Or should I call my friends? It's been so long since we tortured one of your lot. Far too long..."

Will could see Damian's back tensing beneath his flowing, black cape. Then Damian stepped aside very slowly, but Will saw that his protector was reaching for something under his cape.

"A Fate Sealer's arrogance is his weakness," Will heard Damian whispering between them. "Entertain him. Play the fool, and he'll leave you alone. If not... don't worry. He'll be dead before he can touch you."

To play the fool was easy. Paralyzed with fear, Will's bloated body shivered and shook, while Will tried to explain all about Frederick Fingeldy, having no idea what to say, and hearing his medicated voice making everything he did say sound hopelessly moronic.

The Fate Sealer's robe of flesh shook in a thousand waves of mocking laughter, and just when Will couldn't stand the humiliation and fear anymore, he suddenly lost his balance and catapulted forward to fall flat on his face.

"Well done, well done... he's gone!" Will heard Deá

whispering over him.

Spitting snow, Will looked up and saw the Fate Sealer gliding away, laughing so hard his screeches frightened birds off every tree he passed.

But Will's embarrassment left no room for relief. "You tripped me," he hissed at Damian, as he lumbered to his feet, his swollen thighs almost tripping him again.

"And it worked," said Damian flatly. "Remember this lesson. From now on, you'll have to tackle Fate Sealers on your own. Without help... Without any help."

As he said this, Damian looked at Will sadly, as if he wanted to say so much more. That look reminded Will of Damian's face that night on the pond, when Damian had left to save Deá's life.

"You're not... you're not leaving?" asked Will, all of a sudden feeling terribly aware of how cold the Echo realm was.

"We can't stay," explained Damian. "It would look odd. Raise too many questions. Fortune Tellers don't go around escorting Castaways."

A frozen tear fell out of Deá's eye and disappeared in the glistening snow at her feet.

"Good luck... Fredrick Fingeldy," said Damian, glancing cautiously at Valerie. But the frail Echo girl was twirling her sapphire ring again, lost in her own thoughts, and Damian seemed to make up his mind to speak freely.

"So much has changed in the ten years since Deá and I were here... We didn't know the King was murdered... We didn't know about Fate Sealers roaming the land. But this doesn't change anything. The Orphanage is still the safest place for a Sound to hide."

"One Sound among hundreds, it makes sense," said Deá, all the glittering happiness now gone from her face.

"I know you hate it, but keep your disguise intact," said Damian. "Contact lenses, hair, slurry speech, everything. And don't draw attention to yourself."

"And the Fate Sealers?" asked Will, feeling that everything was suddenly going spectacularly wrong.

"It's up to you," said Damian. "Play the fool, and they'll think you're a fat nobody, someone to laugh at. Fate Sealer's are great at judging a book by its cover. And remember Peter, Emmy's friend. He'll help you find the fireplace."

Will nodded and looked away so Deá and Damian wouldn't see how scared he felt. Through the see-through trunk of a far-off tree, he saw the Fate Sealer slithering past a water fountain like a walking snake. Were Fate Sealers really as stupid as Damian said, Will wondered. And anyway, what difference would that make? You don't need to be a genius to freeze someone to death with an Ice Loom.

"Will you be all right?" asked Deá miserably.

"Of course, I will," Will lied to his childhood friends for the second time that morning.

The Ancient Headmaster

The Pet Selection Ceremony

The cool air was full of cheers and laughter, and the huge sun floated in the blue sky like a giant marble. Will watched Deá and Damian disappearing on their way out of the see-through garden. Then he took a deep breath and turned to face the waterfalls of ivy. No more Fate Sealers lurked there in the shadow between the icy bleachers, but suddenly an iridescent flying crystal ball zoomed out. It streaked past Valerie like some strange, glowing insect and came to a buzzing halt before Will's swollen face, its wings a streak of motion.

The bright blue words, *Follow Me!* lit up inside the crystal ball. They blinked on and off three times. Then the flying ball knocked Will on the head to make sure he was paying attention.

"Okay, I'll come," grunted Will, swatting the flying menace.

But another message lit up inside the ball. *Bring the girl!*

"Fine." Will grabbed Valerie's cold hand and started walking, to stop the crystal ball from giving him a concussion.

The flying messenger led them through the narrow, dark passage between the bleachers, then across a frozen lawn that crunched beneath their feet, to a gleaming ice-blue stage bordered with more iridescent winged crystal balls, which, thankfully, showed no intention of taking flight. Will could hear the crowd humming and whistling behind him, but when he tried to look back, the crystal ball smacked him on the head again and flashed its *Follow Me!* message in rapid succession.

Up ahead an old man in a shimmering ivory robe beckoned to Will and Valerie. His white, knee-length beard and hair fluttered in the frosty breeze like a wispy cloud. He wasn't quite see-through or solid, and Will couldn't decide if he was an Echo or a Sound, only that he was the oldest man he had ever seen.

Behind the ancient man, an assembly of Sounds and Echoes stood together, dressed in gleaming aquamarine robes that flowed from their shoulders like ocean waves. Nurse Flight was there, pretending she didn't know Will. The old Echo, Valerian, was several see-through faces to her left, his plastic hand gleaming in the sun as he waved hello to Valerie. But Will couldn't spot Drinkwater, and the crystal ball just wacked him again when he tried to look around.

"Come near! Come closer!" said the wrinkled old man on the gleaming stage. His words were magnified by a luminous horn that looked like a Fate Sealer's Ice Loom. "I and the staff of the Orphanage of Castaway Children welcome you. Come! Join us on the stage."

Up the Stairs! ordered the message inside the crystal ball, and Will tugged Valerie after him.

"The Echo Castaways welcome you," said the old man, sweeping his shimmering ivory sleeve to his left.

At last, the pesky ball flew away to take its place in the line of crystal balls edging the stage, and Will looked around at the cheering crowd.

Past the stage, a wide frozen lawn stretched to a pair of tall white bleachers that seemed carved from ice, like the doors inside the Orphanage. In the bleacher on the right, the seats were so packed that the spectators looked like a giant display of snowmen, all dressed in glistening Orphanage uniforms. But on the left, Will could see rows and rows of empty white seats, with only a few Echoes here and there, looking like a mirage from this distance, as if they weren't people at all just an illusion created by sunlight.

"The Sound Castaways welcome you," added the old man, sweeping his shimmering sleeve to the right.

Watching the two bleachers, Will realized that the races were separated, Sounds on the right, Echoes on the left. And there were at least ten times more Sounds than Echoes.

Rippling shadows suddenly glided over the bleachers, and a flock of giant white birds appeared in the deep blue sky. They were trailing an unraveling rainbow of shimmering ribbons: red, orange, yellow, green, blue, indigo and violet. From nowhere in particular the sound of wind chimes welcomed the birds, and soon another flock joined the first, this time with see-through wings and gauzy ribbons. Even the birds were divided into Sounds and Echoes.

"Whoever you are," whispered Valerie, tugging Will's

glistening sleeve. "Can you hear me, whoever you are? I want a bird like this. Can you hear me, whoever you are? I want a bird…"

"We shall come to that shortly," said the old man in the shimmering ivory robe.

He shifted his weight, and Will noticed that with his old, wrinkled hand, the old man was leaning on an ivory cane that was topped by a crystal ball. For a second Will thought he saw something moving inside the crystal ball. But whatever it was vanished before Will could be sure.

"I am Abednego," the old man spoke into the luminous horn that carried his sighing voice over to the bleachers. "Delmar Abednego, curator of the second largest library in the land and Headmaster of the Orphanage of Castaway Children… by Fortune's favor. Please tell us who you are, young woman."

The Headmaster stretched the horn to Valerie, who was still looking up at the birds, muttering, "Can you hear me, anyone? I want a bird…"

The crowd cheered, laughed and hooted, and Will saw what Damian meant about everyone at the Orphanage owning a pet. A wonderful menagerie of animals mingled with the glistening white spectators, spots of color in a pale, frozen world. There were dogs, cats, birds in cages, fishbowls glittering in the sun, and other smaller breeds, probably hamsters, rats, rabbits… though it was hard to be sure from that distance. Listening carefully, Will could hear the pet voices mingling with the cheers from the bleachers. And he was probably imagining it, but he thought he could hear Peter Patrick

Peterson's brindled mutt barking the loudest.

"By Fortune, that was spoken softly." The Headmaster bent his white beard over Valerie, who was now whispering her name. "Valerie Valerian," the ancient Echo repeated after her and added an introduction of his own. "Ward and niece of Victor Valerian, our very own Professor of Echo History. Who, as rumor has it, just rescued his niece from Shadowpain. An unsurpassed act of courage, by Fortune!"

The Headmaster swept his ivory sleeve to signal Valerian out from the assembly in aquamarine robes on the opposite side of the stage. The spectators in the bleachers broke out in loud cheers and waved their arms in the air. Valerian bowed to them and waved back with his gleaming plastic hand, and the cheers grew louder still. Only Valerie kept silent, watching the flying white birds, mesmerized.

Will held his breath, dreading speaking in the horn with his slurry voice. But already the Headmaster was turning to face him, his long white hair and beard fluttering in the breeze.

"And you?" said Abednego, bending the luminous horn to Will. "Will you tell us who you are?"

But suddenly the old man turned pensive, and for a moment he looked as if only just now he noticed how hideous Will looked.

"Hmm... Interesting..." The Headmaster nodded thoughtfully. Then he lowered the luminous horn and pressed his furrowed hand over its mouth, as if to keep his words from echoing far and wide. "Only seen it once before. Well..." The old Echo wrinkled his face in a smile. "Come, come... Cold Sleep got your tongue? Tell them who you are. In the Ice Loom, loud and clear." And the Headmaster raised the horn again.

"I'm..." Will stared into the gaping, luminous horn that Fate Sealers used to freeze people. What a strange place the Echo realm was where weapons were used for loudspeakers. Thoughts spun through Will's mind in a tornado of fears. The Headmaster guessed about the Cold Sleep. What if the Fate Sealers did too? What if they started asking questions? What if Fate Sealers searched him and found the Royal Shekel? From the corner of his eye Will saw a Fate Sealer gliding across the frozen lawn between the stage and bleachers, taunting the crowd.

"I'm Fredrick Fingeldy," Will said quickly, to get the introductions over with. But his moronic voice boomed much too loudly through the luminous horn.

The spectators burst out laughing and catcalling, and the large white birds overhead flew in faster circles, their rainbow ribbons streaking the blue sky.

Will looked down at his large gleaming shoes, his face burning with embarrassment. He never used to care what other people thought of him. But this was different. He wasn't just the smallest kid in class anymore. He was the weirdest kid in a dangerous world full of strangers and Fate Sealers.

"A crowd of strangers can make one feel terribly alone." Will heard the Headmaster's voice again and looked up. "For this reason," added Abednego, wrinkling his face to smile at Will and

162

Valerie, "it is our custom here at the Orphanage for new Castaways to choose a pet as a companion. Our dedicated Keeper of Pets and Keys, Rufus Warloch, will show you the pets awaiting adoption. Rufus... When you're ready."

A hush fell over the bleachers, but the chatter of pets grew loud and fearful. The Echoes and Sounds in aquamarine robes parted on the other side of the stage, and a hunched Echo pushed through them, limping and leaning on a long rusty rifle. He wore dark filthy clothes and muddy boots that hardly looked see-through with so many stains coating them. His shirt sleeves were folded over his elbows, and his forearms were covered in crystal ball tattoos that looked like watchful, evil eyeballs.

"Your Greatness," Rufus Warloch growled and bowed obsequiously to the Headmaster. The rusty spurs at his heels hissed like snakes. Then the Keeper of Pets and Keys chuckled wickedly and shifted his narrow gaze to Will and Valerie. "Follow me!" he barked.

But Valerie was rooted in place, her large blue eyes drinking in the sight of the giant white birds circling in the deep blue sky, their shimmering ribbons trailing behind them like the tails on kites.

"Ah, yes..." Abednego sighed into the luminous horn. "Valerie has already expressed a wish to adopt a *Diomedea Exulans*, more commonly known as a Wandering Albatross. Rarely do untamed pets wish to be adopted. But we shall see... Rufus, please be so good as to summon the flock."

A great cheer of surprise rose from the cloud of white

163

spectators. To his horror Will now spotted Fate Sealers inside the bleachers, gray blotches chasing frightened Echoes from seat to empty seat on the left, or causing a whole section of faces to disappear as the Sounds on the right ducked in terror.

"Which flock?" snarled the Keeper, his gruff voice loud enough for the horn to catch every word. "Echo or Sound, Illustrious Headmaster?"

Abednego shifted his weight tiredly, glancing up. "Both, if you please, Warloch."

"But which first, Great One?" insisted the Keeper, two gold teeth glittering though his evil simper.

Before the old Headmaster could answer, the glistening spectators rose to their feet in both bleachers, their voices unifying in a chant.

"TOSS A SHEKEL... TOSS A SHEKEL... TOSS A SHEKEL..."

A few Sounds shrieked in the bleachers on the right as a Fate Sealer raised his glowing Ice Loom and magnified his screech of the chant, sounding like a saw scrapping on bone.

Almost at once, Will guessed what was happening. It was the Memory of the Royal Shekel—reenacted. Will felt sick again, and before he could stop himself he was fingering the coin nervously in his pocket.

"By Fortune's Fate," declared Abednego, and the crowd fell silent, "I summon two who shall represent their kind."

The Headmaster walked heavily across the gleaming, ice-

164

blue stage and stopped where the crystal balls forming a luminous border fluttered their gauzy wings like strange, hovering insects.

The Echoes in the bleachers burst into applause as Abednego summoned Victor Valerian to represent the Echoes. Valerian jogged over cheerfully like a man half his age, beaming at Valerie, though she only had eyes for the birds in the sky.

Then the Sounds cheered their representative, retired Professor of Sound Science, and Will's heart slammed into his chest as a frail figure, dressed not in aquamarine blue but all in purple, crossed the stage tiredly, looking like a bruise. It was Drinkwater, and Will fingered the Royal Shekel guiltily in his pocket, feeling like a thief for the first time in his life.

Abednego turned his back to the icy bleachers, his white hair and beard fluttering like sea foam in the breeze. Then silence fell, even the voices of pets slowly fading.

"In the tradition of the Royal Shekel," announced Abednego in the luminous horn, "Make your selection!" And he tossed a glittering blue coin into the air.

"Words!" shouted Valerian, as the representative of the Echoes.

"King!" muttered Drinkwater, as the representative of the Sounds, his voice barely audible in the luminous horn Abednego was holding between the two men.

There was a moment of breathless silence. The coin twinkled as it lost momentum, hovered on the air for an instant, then fell, landing with a tiny clatter on the ice-blue stage. Abednego trapped

165

the coin in place with the base of his cane, and once again Will caught a flickering movement in the crystal ball top. Or was he imagining it?

"And the winners are… the Echoes!" declared Abednego.

The left side of the bleachers erupted in cheers, the right in raucous boos.

Still looking at Abednego's cane, Will saw the old Headmaster sinking on the icy blue steps as if all his energy had been spent. On the frozen snow below, Rufus Warloch put two grimy fingers to his mouth and whistled sharply. Then one by one the see-through albatrosses landed beside the Keeper, their shimmering ribbons folding under them like waves of color.

Warloch pulled dead fish from his filthy pockets and tossed them to the birds. Valerie rushed down the stage stairs, waving her thin, see-through arms excitedly. But she soon frightened the birds away in a chaos of see-through wings and ribbons, and the crowd in the bleachers hooted in disappointment.

Sniggering maliciously, the Keeper shoved Valerie aside with the butt of his rifle. Then he whistled again, more shrilly this time, and the flock of Sound albatrosses came to a landing, their shiny ribbons blending together like a melting rainbow. For a moment Valerie disappeared in a sea of white wings, and in the bleachers on the right waves of glistening arms cheered her on.

Watching Valerie from the stage, Will suddenly felt someone tugging at his sleeve. It was Drinkwater, a purple scarf now wrapped around his wrinkled throat and his glasses looking more taped than

166

ever.

"No! Don't look at me!" snapped Drinkwater, watching an albatross spread its giant wings and fly away from Valerie's outstretched arms. "Pretend we're strangers. Understand?"

Will nodded, his heart beating fast. "My parents," he whispered. "Did you explain? About why I left?"

"No!" snarled Drinkwater furiously. "Thanks to you, I had to rush to the Echo realm. Where's the coin, boy? I thought you had more sense than to steal it!"

"I'm sorry…" muttered Will, a jolt of biting disappointment falling over him like nightfall. No one told his parents anything. No one explained why he had to disappear.

"The coin," snarled Drinkwater, pinching Will's elbow.

Will flinched. "I'm sorry I had to take it," he muttered guiltily. "It's the only thing keeping me alive."

"It's the first thing that's going to get you killed. Stop looking at me!" Drinkwater elbowed Will's cheek gruffly, though Will had barely turned his head at all. "Look at the birds. Pretend we're talking about the Pet Selection. And keep your voice down! Didn't you hear anything I told you in the Sound realm? The false King needs only two things… the Royal Shekel… and your head! Are you so impatient to give him both at once? Now, where's the coin?"

Will dug his hands in his glistening pockets, watching Valerie nearing the last albatross left on the frosty ground.

"Well, boy? You'd better tell me."

"I'm going to destroy the coin!" said Will finally. "Why didn't you?"

"You what—?"

The rest of Drinkwater's words turned into a hiss, and he clawed at Will's wrists trying to pull Will's hands out of his pockets. Will flinched and crashed into someone. And suddenly the scent of cherry tobacco surrounded Will, as if his father was just behind him, smoking his old pipe.

"Dad...?" Will twisted back.

Victor Valerian was standing there, smiling serenely at Will. He looked thinner than in the Sound realm, as if he hadn't eaten in days. And an ugly cut now ran across his cheek, looking so see-through that at first Will had the impression that a piece of Valerian's face was missing.

"Valerian," snarled Drinkwater, "eavesdropping on our conversation? Or have you come to finish me off?"

"I apologize for intruding," said Valerian in his beautiful voice. He paused to puff on an icy pipe that glittered in the sunlight. "I only wished to thank Fredrick for his kindness to Valerie," he added, puffing sweet scented smoke.

Smiling kindly, the old Echo shook hands with Will, keeping his plastic hand in the pocket of his shimmering aquamarine robe.

"She's been through a lot lately, my little niece," said Valerian, unconsciously fingering the cut in his cheek.

"You rescued her... from Shadowpain?" asked Will. It seemed so incredible!

"I got lucky, by Fortune… Very lucky!" Suddenly Valerian's green eyes brightened like Waterweed near Echoes. "Wait a minute," he added, chuckling. "Is it really you? Is it possible?"

"Take your lucky, lying tongue somewhere else," snapped Drinkwater. He butted Valerian's elbow with his shoulder; so short was Will's old teacher beside the tall Echo.

Hardly noticing, Valerian kept smiling at Will, his eyes twinkling. "It is you, isn't it?" he whispered confidentially.

Will froze nervously, but Valerian chuckled. "After all the risks Damian and I took bringing you here…" Valerian shook his head and puffed on his gleaming pipe again. "Your secret is safe with me… Fredrick Fingeldy."

Perhaps it was the scent of cherry tobacco that reminded Will of his father and home and somehow made Will feel that he could trust Valerian. But Drinkwater grabbed Valerian's arm and tried to drag the Echo away, when suddenly a great cheer rose from the bleachers, and Valerian dashed off without any help, leaving Drinkwater spitting curses at thin air.

On the frozen grass before the stage Valerie was straddling the last albatross left on the ground as if it were a horse.

"No!" Valerian cried after her. "You mustn't, Valerie. You're not strong enough."

But already the frail Echo girl was riding the Sound bird, and soon they were soaring in the air together, the wind spiking Valerie's cropped hair into an imitation of Will's flaming picket fence hairdo. While on the ground, Valerian and the Keeper were jumping to-and-fro, trying to snatch the shimmering orange ribbons fluttering down from the bird's webbed feet, Valerian with a look of concern, Warloch with malice.

*   *   *

Once more on his feet and leaning on his crystal-ball-topped cane, Abednego spoke into the luminous horn, his voice sighing over the cheers and hoots of the glistening white crowd.

"Fredrick Fingeldy, your turn to select a pet has come."

To an explosion of cheers from the crowd, Will rushed forward, relieved to get away from Drinkwater. He would select a rabbit or a hamster, as Damian had suggested, and keep a low profile until his meeting with the Prince tomorrow. Easy! But a shriek at Will's back made him stop and turn.

The staff in shimmering aquamarine robes were jostling each other on the ice-blue stage, as if fighting to get a better look at something far away. Shrieks rose from the icy bleachers, and the chatter of pets grew fearful.

"The Wild One..." Nurse Flight chirped in a panic, glancing back at the Headmaster. "She's broken loose... The Wild One's heading this way!"

Rushing curiously to the edge of the stage, Will peered at the far garden.

Past the overlapping snowy trees and sapphire fountains, Will saw the far-off alabaster wall of the round fortress with a snowy forest curling at its feet like a giant snow heap. Something leapt away from the snow heap, an animal camouflaged so well in the wintry landscape that Will only spotted it because it wasn't see-through, like vanilla ice-cream set against pineapple sherbet. Soon the animal drew near enough for Will to recognize its shape. It was an arctic wolf, and in a moment of wonderful forgetfulness Will thought that he was seeing Deá the wolf running back to him, alive and well.

"Rufus will handle this!" declared Abednego in the luminous horn.

Jerked back to reality, Will saw the Keeper jumping off the ice-blue stage, the rusty spurs at his heels hissing like snakes. A wicked grin distorted Warloch's ugly face, as he raised his rifle to his shoulder and half ran half hobbled to intercept the wolf.

"NO!"

In a flash Will was off the stage too.

He dashed after the Keeper, kicking up snow, his fat legs feeling like tree trunks. See-through branches, fountains, topiaries flashed past Will, making him dizzy with seeing things through other things, as if he were somehow running in five icy gardens that existed one inside the other. And making things worse was the cold air that pierced Will's puffy cheeks like needles and froze his contact lenses until he could barely see for tears.

"Freddy, don't!" Valerie screamed, as she flew her albatross so low over Will that the shimmering orange ribbons trailing from her bird's legs kept flicking Will's face.

"Stay out of this," Warloch growled to Will's left. "Both of you. Or by Fortune, I'll make you pay!"

The Echo's grotesque limp slowed him down, but his malice lent him wings. Up ahead, the wolf cleared a clump of crystallized trees. It seemed to spot them through the sparkling splash of a distant fountain. Howling, it charged in the Keeper's direction, and the wolf's whole body became a blur of motion in the flurries of snow kicked up by its paws.

"You'll die for this!" Warloch hollered at the wild animal.

He threw himself on the frosty ground, taking aim with his rifle. And, the next moment, a shot echoed through the snowy trees, shattering the serenity of the snowy garden. But a second earlier, Will had thrown himself at the Keeper and knocked the Echo off balance.

Valerie screamed, and the beat of her bird's wings grew louder in the sky. Far off, the distant crowd booed and cheered. Will looked up breathlessly, blinking snow out of his eyes, hearing the rifle shot still echoing through the cold air.

It worked! The shot missed its target. The wolf was galloping still, drawing so near that Will could see the savage fury burning in the animal's dark-rimmed yellow eyes.

"You can't! You can't kill him!" Will yelled to the wolf, as he clambered to his feet, tottering stupidly on his bloated legs.

The Keeper cursed Will wildly from the frosty ground. The wolf stopped a few feet from them, its face wrinkled with a menacing growl, its front legs bent to spring forward.

"You can't kill him," Will yelled again, fighting to seem calm, though his heart pounded like a cannon. At least the painkiller

172

was working in his favor, turning his voice sluggish and unthreatening.

The wings of Valerie's albatross drew near again, beating an ominous cadence in the sky.

"If you kill him, they'll kill you," Will went on, as the wolf switched its savage gaze to him.

From the corner of his eye, Will saw the Keeper raising his rifle again. The Wolf jerked back, its growl turning into a snarl that bared its killer fangs. But suddenly someone was shouting behind them—

"STAY OUT OF THIS, WARLOCH!"

Will snapped his head back.

Through the iced topiary of a fairy riding a winged horse, Will saw Valerian dashing toward them, his aquamarine robe swelling over his knobby knees like a wave.

"Do you wish to adopt this wolf?" Valerian cried out to Will.

"Yes," Will shouted back. "Yes, I do!"

"Then tame it. Do, and it's yours."

Valerian stopped beside Warloch and helped the Keeper to his feet.

"You must give the boy this chance," said Valerian firmly, and he snatched the rifle before the Keeper could take aim at the wolf again.

Warloch grinned in a way that made Will shudder. "Tame the shrew?" the Keeper cackled, his twin gold teeth gleaming eerily. "I'll enjoy this."

"Be careful," yelled Valerie from her perch in the bright blue sky.

Will faced the wolf again. The animal no longer looked like Deá the wolf; fear was distorting the white muzzle. But in the dark-rimmed yellow eyes there was confusion.

Will took his chance.

"Don't be afraid," he said gently, "I'm a friend." Then Will crouched down cautiously.

The wolf arched its narrow back as if about to pounce and eyed Will, waiting for him to show the first sign of fear. The longer Will held the animal's gaze, the more his contact lenses stung. But instinctively Will knew that he must not blink. Even in the split second when his eyes would close the wolf would take its chance and attack him, because it was afraid of him.

"I'm a friend," Will repeated in his heavy voice. But he knew he would have to do more than talk to tame The Wild One.

Slowly Will straightened and started walking heel to toe toward the wolf. A hum of threatening growls rose ominously from the animal. Will shushed it soothingly and kept walking.

Slowly Will raised his right hand a little, his heart pounding a blast in his ears. Another step and then another, and soon the wolf had to look up to keep Will's gaze. The animal looked afraid and entranced at the same time, and it stopped growling. When the wolf started sniffing the air, Will was so close he could feel The Wild One's breath on his knuckles, warm and caressing, as if Will had slipped his frozen fingers into a glove. But he knew that this glove had teeth that could maul his hand in an instant.

Will waited, frozen, fighting the urge to flee.

The wolf sniffed Will gingerly. The animal looked starved and cold, the spine showing through its back as the ribs showed through its stomach. A rope was tied in a noose around the wolf's neck, and the noose was bloody from rubbing away the fur and skin.

"You're in pain…" Will realized, as drops of blood trickled from the noose on the snow between his feet. In a moment, Will's fear turned to compassion.

"I'll take care of you. I promise, I'll take care of you, I promise…" Will chanted soothingly, over and over; while slowly, ever so slowly, he raised his hands behind the wolf's right ear and untied the knot in the rope. Then Will blew cold air on the raw red neck, and the poor creature closed its dark-rimmed yellow eyes with relief.

When the wolf looked up at Will again, Will knew that the animal now trusted him. It didn't resist as Will tied the rope loosely around the wolf's thin stomach, nor even as Will lead The Wild One back toward the Keeper and Valerian

Overhead Valerie gasped in relief and flew off, the shadow of her mounted albatross gliding away over the glistening snow.

"I've tamed her," said Will, surprised to find Valerian aiming the rifle at him and the wolf.

"Just a precaution," said Valerian, lowering the weapon. "Though I had every confidence in your courage. We should head back," he added, glancing at the blue stage showing through the

175

glistening icy trees behind them.

Will saw a distant purple figure standing there, watching them with one hand shading its eyes. The mass of aquamarine robes was stirring restlessly on the stage like a storm at sea, and from the icy bleachers Will heard cries of disbelief.

So much for choosing a rabbit or a hamster, Will thought, remembering Damian's advice. He smiled down at his wolf and wondered what he should name her. Then he saw the fur bristle on the wolf's white back, and Will's eyes shot to Warloch.

The Keeper was eyeing him with bloodshot loathing, the tail end of an evil mutter still on his lips, "...see who blasts the last crystal ball, we'll see."

Wither Heart

The Crystal Ball Fireplace

Everyone at the glistening white Orphanage kept their distance from Will after seeing him tame The Wild One and rename her Wolfeá. Tame or not, however, the wolf was not allowed inside like other pets. But even without his wolf by his side, Will's slurry voice, puffy gray face and spiky red hair earned him the instant reputation of a weirdo. And, apparently, someone it was perfectly polite to stare at.

Only Peter Patrick Peterson, the strange boy with the bruised face, didn't stare at all. He just insisted on going everywhere Will went, like a slightly less stare-worthy sidekick. He showed Will around the crystal-ball-windowed corridors, the sparkling library with its towering shelves, and the Sound sitting rooms with their snowy furniture and warm fires that felt nothing like the caves of ice the Echoes dwelt in. Finally they stopped by their cozy dorm room with its tree-branch bunk beds and glistening snow-white canopies, where Will met his three roommates and their pets. Everyone kept staring; only Peter kept asking questions.

But Will decided not to answer any of them. Not yet. Not

until he could put Peter to some sort of test. Then it happened, in the glistening garden.

Charging out of nowhere, Drinkwater pinned Will against an ice sculpture.

"Let go of me—" Will writhed uselessly, his fat limbs weighing him down like an anchor.

"The coin! Tell me where it is!" snarled the old man. And he slammed a Crystillery to Will's forehead.

"Leave me alone— Aaahh!!!"

Through the fog of pain that slashed into Will's brain he heard angry barks. Something brown flashed before Will's bleary eyes and then—whoosh!—the pain was gone.

"Bring that dog back!" cried Drinkwater. And the last Will saw of Frankenstein that day was the old man running after Peter's silly-looking dog, as the brown mutt raced away with Drinkwater's Crystillery glittering in its mouth like a giant drool drop.

Still Will wasn't sure he could trust Peter. Not with the secret of the Royal Shekel, the coin that could make or break a king in this strange land. So Will asked to see the Sound kitchen, but kept shrugging at Peter's questions and answering stupidly, "Yeah, I've heard of shedding pounds. Are you saying I'm fat?" "Not shedding pounds. Beheading Sounds." Peter sighed.

Late that evening, when Will thought the day would never end, wind chimes tinkled through the cold Orphanage signaling lights-out. Curling between the snowy sheets of his warm bed, Will pretended to go to sleep and waited for his roommates to turn off their crystal ball lights and tuck away their pets for the night. Then he listened for the sound of soft snores, especially from Peter.

An hour passed before Will finally snuck out of bed and through the whooshing door of their dorm room. The door... thought Will nervously, looking over his shoulder as he crept down the cold corridor. If only the doors to Sound rooms didn't make such a racket as they whooshed a barrier between the cold air in the corridor and the warm air in the rooms... What if Peter heard Will slipping out? What if Fate Sealers did?

But Will saw no one as he slinked down the moonlit Orphanage corridor retracing the way down to the Sound Kitchen. No Fate Sealers lurked on the stairs or in the chilly corridor below. The sleepy Orphanage was strangely deserted, though Will had the strangest feeling that he was being watched by the crystal ball chandeliers, which looked like strings of eyeballs in the eerie moonlight slipping in through the crystal ball windows.

As Will finally passed the whooshing door of the Sound kitchen, he started running, though slowly because of his knocking fat thighs. The kitchen felt like a long tunnel, with an endless sink on one side and an endless counter on the other. Even the moonlight streaming through the barred crystal ball windows striped the flagstones with a ladder of light and shadow that went on and on, leading nowhere.

But suddenly dancing shadows appeared on the curving stone walls up ahead, and in a moment the giant fireplace stood before Will. It burned with a thousand flames. Every stone in its crystal mantelpiece shimmered like a small moon, as if the fireplace was built from giant pearls.

The almost unbearable heat made Will's skin tingle with relief. His hand closed on the coin in his pocket. He glanced back. No one was there. Will neared the shiny cauldron hissing steam in the fire like a sleeping dragon. The heat became scolding. Perfect for melting a coin.

Will took out the Royal Shekel.

Suddenly a terrifying voice hissed behind Will. "Ssstop—right there!"

Will froze.

"Pity, by dark Fortune," the intruder croaked. "If you ignored me, I could kill you right here... Or maybe I'll just say you ignored me when they ask me why I did it..."

Very slowly Will turned, hoping against hope that he wouldn't find what he knew was already there.

Ten feet or so away, just before the gleaming sink and counter curved out of sight, a Fate Sealer was standing in the moonlight, his Ice Loom glowing bright. Taller and thinner than any human, he looked like a deformed gray candle, trickles of skin hanging off him like melted wax. A black raven perched silently on his shoulder.

"Filthy brat! Step away from the fire," the creature croaked again. A terrible, bulging scar quivered on his sagging nose as he spoke, like a giant, slithering slug.

Fear strangled Will's voice, but his mind was racing. *What if the Fate Sealer searched him? What if he found the Royal Shekel? But the coin looked like an ordinary Echo coin. But what if the Fate Sealer tested the coin with a Crystillery?*

"NOW!" screeched the Fate Sealer, his long, sagging lips swinging from side to side like ghastly ropes.

Watching the Ice Loom growing brighter, Will braced himself for a hail of icy arrows. The Fate Sealer glared at him with enormous eyes that looked like pits of darkness. Inside each eye, a black whirlpool twisted faster and faster. But suddenly the Fate Sealer lowered his lustrous weapon and the spinning in his eyes froze.

"My lucky dark stars... The new boy, aren't you?" the creature croaked, his forehead rippling in a deformed frown. "Fredrick Finger-Me... You saved The Wild One?"

Will nodded tensely, ignoring the improvisation on his cover-name. His mind still hunted frantically for a way past the monster blocking the only exist.

"Step away from the fire, little Freddy." The Fate Sealer's lips swung from side to side as the creature took a few steps back himself, as if illustrating what he meant in case he was talking to an idiot.

Or maybe he can't stand the heat! Will realized with a rush of hope.

Suddenly Will's mind fixed on a plan. If he was right, the Fate Sealer couldn't come any closer. That was why real fire was banned everywhere in the Orphanage—fire was deadly to Echoes;

183

they needed cold to survive.

"I said, by blistering Fortune, step away from the fire!"

"No!" snarled Will, his hand already reaching high above his head to grab a poker someone had left on the shimmering crystal mantelpiece of the giant fireplace.

A second later, Will slipped the iron tip into the flames.

The folds of the Fate Sealer's skin bristled like a mountain of worms. "Little Freddy... putting up a fight," he croaked with relish. "How gallant... and deliciously stupid."

The fire cast Will's shadow on the flagstones before him, a long, stretched shadow, reminding Will of the long, stretched room he would have to run down to escape the Fate Sealer. Run and run and run, like in a nightmare. *Stay focused!* Will thought desperately and pulled the poker out of the flames.

The iron tip glowed red, letting off heat. Will brandished his makeshift weapon, his eyes still locked on the monster before him.

"I'm going to walk out of here," said Will, his voice heavy with medication and fear. "And you're going to let me pass."

The darkness writhed again in the Fate Sealer's eyes. "How ssstrange, by Fortune..." the creature hissed, flicking a passing fly with his long gray fingernails. "How very ssstrange, the Prince's Sound disappearing just as you arrived here... Freddy."

Will's heart banged in his chest like a caged beast, but Will forced his heavy feet resolutely forward.

The Fate Sealer flicked his long black tongue and scooped up the fly, which had splattered on the gleaming counter. "Where have you been all this time... Freddy?" he went on without pause. "You disappeared from your home ten years ago. I checked."

Will shuddered. Hiding from Peter in the bathroom that afternoon, he had snatched a few minutes to read Fredrick Fingeldy's story in the gravestone book. But Fredrick was killed, that's what Damian said, except that no one knew about it. So Will could pretend to be Fredrick, but how was he going to explain suddenly reappearing after ten years?

"The Fortune Teller... the one that brought me here..." Will improvised quickly, still marching forward, the tip of his poker glowing red before him, if already less brightly. "Yes, I remember... The Fortune Teller... he said I had a serious Brain Freeze or something..."

"Or *sssomething*," hissed the Fate Sealer. "Something colder perhaps?"

And, instantly, the creature flexed his sagging lips and blew into his glowing ice loom.

Will watched a hail of icy arrows shooting toward him, and he jerked the poker in startled shock. The arrows hissed against the throbbing red metal and dripped out of the air to make a puddle on the floor. But four icy arrows got past the glowing poker, and they pierced Will's swollen cheeks, his neck and his left hand, digging into him like frozen fingers. Will swung again, to stop a second volley. Even more arrows got through this time. One pierced his eyebrow, and the contact lens in his left eye turned into an icy veil that blinded him.

But with his right eye Will could still see—see that the tip of the poker had cooled back into lusterless metal. A fresh hail of arrows bounced off it unaffected and headed straight on for Will's chest, spreading numbness through him on impact. Will tried to retreat to the fire, but his body had become as frozen as the topiaries in the garden. He couldn't even blink.

And worse still, Will was starting to hear things, like the next volley of arrows singing at him. Except that the Fate Sealer seemed to hear the song too, and his drooping forehead rippled in a frown.

Somewhere out of sight someone was singing in a voice that was so off-key a dog could have howled better. Will was too terrified to laugh, but the Fate Sealer seemed unable to resist so stupid a sound. He chuckled, lowered his Ice Loom, and turned.

For a long moment Will stared at the Fate Sealer's sagging, quivering back, watching the creature watch the narrow moonlit kitchen. Then, at last, someone appeared there.

Peter Patrick Peterson, eyes closed and arms raised like a sleepwalker, rounded the curve in the kitchen walls. He was caroling at the top of his voice, and his puffy lower lip was wiggling to the rhythm like a hula-dancing banana.

"Jingle bells, jingle smells, jingle all the *wayyyyyy...*"

A second later, Peter's little dog darted out of nowhere and leapt at the Fate Sealer, making off with the creature's Ice Loom, the way Poudini had done with Drinkwater's Crystillery that afternoon. And the Fate Sealer swept after the fearless blur of fur in a cloud of drooping flesh, his black raven cackling in flight over his head.

"You followed me," said Will, thawing painfully as Peter pulled out the icy arrows stuck in Will's bloated face and hands. "Impossible to get away from, that's what you are. Ouch!"

"You're welcome." Peter grinned and finished pulling out the arrows stuck in Will's glistening sweater, which was rippling strangely as if trying to shake the arrows off. "Frozen cuts— You won't bleed to death, at least," Peter added happily.

"Marvelous."

With the contact lens in his left eye defogging, Will looked to see if Peter's dog or the Fate Sealer were returning, but both were gone.

"What about your dog?" asked Will, shaking the numbness out of his arms.

"Poudini?" Peter grinned. His bruised face looked worse than ever in the moonlight. "Fastest Sound in the Orphanage. Disappear into a pet passage, probably. Remember? Those tiny crystal ball doors I showed you this afternoon? —Can you walk?" Peter looked skeptically at Will shaking his legs.

"Think so."

Will limped after Peter down the moonlit, narrow kitchen, glancing back at the fireplace with regret. If only he could tell Peter everything, then Will could toss the Royal Shekel in the flames now and put an end to his biggest problem. He could even look for the chipped crystal-stone in the mantelpiece and test-open the secret room behind the fireplace, to be ready for meeting the Prince tomorrow.

But even if Will could trust Peter, how could he share his deadly secrets? How could he risk Peter's life just to make himself feel better? It was the same way Will felt about it when he didn't tell his best friend, Ben, anything back in the Sound realm. Deadly secrets were a lot like the flu virus; not something you should share with friends.

"What's wrong" asked Peter, twisting back.

Will hesitated. "Nothing," he said finally. "Let's get out of here."

"Let's see you then," said Peter, with his typical questioning grin.

To Will's amazement he realized that they had reached the entrance to the Sound kitchen. Somehow he had lost all track of time. Or was it one of Peter's magic tricks, to make the longest kitchen in the world feel like the shortest?

"How d'we get here so fast?" asked Will.

"Fast is a relative term. Are you ready?" Peter drummed his fingers on the door of the Sound kitchen, which seemed carved from gleaming ice. "It won't bite," he chuckled brightly, then passed through the swooshing air seal.

Will took a deep breath and followed, crossing through the tornado of air that wobbled his swollen cheeks, whipped his spiky hair and nearly sucked the contact lenses out of his eyes.

Peter grinned at him on the other side, his hair all tousled. "You'll get used to—"

"Yeah, you said." Will patted his spiky hair to make sure it hadn't blown off. "About a hundred times today."

"Right."

Chuckling, Peter led the way up the spiraling seashell staircase to the third floor, where the moon shone on the right through the crystal ball windows lining the cold stone corridor. And there, where before Will had seen no one, a group of Echo children now stood like human statues, silent, still, pale and see-through, staring up at the night sky with open eyes but blank, expressionless faces.

"Moon Worshipers," said Peter, without bothering to lower his voice as he brushed past them. "Totally hypnotized. Don't even realize we're here." And Peter waved his hand before a boy's face as proof.

"What's wrong with them?" Will was amazed to see that the Echo didn't even blink.

"Nothing that a good kick in the head wouldn't fix." Peter rolled his eyes, though his bruised one didn't seem to move much. "They think the moon's a crystal ball," Peter added, leading Will away. "Like Fortune's shining down on them or something. They go into a trance."

"Creepy," whispered Will.

"Yeah." Peter's nose wrinkled, as if he had picked up a terrible stench.

They hurried down the chilly, silent corridor. Through the crystal ball windows on the left Will saw Sounds sleeping in their

189

dorm rooms, their white canopies half drawn across their wooden beds like veils of snow hanging off bare trees. Far below the row of windows on the right, the silvery garden looked haunted with Fate Sealers that roamed the maze of frozen trees and sparkling fountains like ghosts.

"In here," said Peter, and Will caught sight of the little dog, Poudini, peeking at them through a sparkling crystal ball flap inserted at the bottom of the icy door Peter was opening. Happily, the Fate Sealer and his Ice Loom were nowhere to be seen.

WHOOOSSSSSHHHHH!

Will coughed off the effects of the Air Seal and dropped into a glistening armchair. The hearth before him was pleasantly warm, but the flames dancing inside it were just a hologram. The rest of the room was filled with scattered armchairs that looked like snow heaps from behind. No one sat in them now, no one stared or whispered. Even so, the unsettling sensation of being watched still haunted Will as he looked at the crystal balls edging the glittering hearth rug, crowding every painting hung on the stone walls, dangling over him in the unlit chandeliers—all looking like disembodied eyes in the firelight. Even the lustrous doorknob was a crystal ball. It was the same everywhere in the fortress, and Will felt as if he was forced to shake hands with Fortune before entering or leaving any room.

The little brown dog, Poudini, curled on the glittering hearth rug between Peter's glistening white shoes and went to sleep. Will yawned, absently fingering the shimmering arm of his snow heap arm chair. The fabrics in this strange world of the Echoes made him

190

feel as if he was indoors and out at the same time.

Peter's snow heap creaked. "So..." Peter sighed, and Will sighed back, guessing what would follow. "When are you going to tell me who you *really* are?"

Peter pulled a chicken bone out of Poudini's ear and dangled it like a pendulum before Will's eyes, as if trying to hypnotize him. He had performed such magic tricks all day, his way of proposing a trade: Your secrets for mine.

Will didn't fall for it. He had to wriggle out of this conversation and get Peter to go to sleep. Will yawned again and blinked, as if he couldn't keep his eyes open, which wasn't far from the truth.

"Sssssooooo..." Peter hissed, as if casting a spell.

"Told you." Will sighed. "About a million times. I'm Fredrick Fingeldy. Now, can we go to sleep?"

"Don't think so." Peter shook his head, and his puffy lower lip wobbled comically. "Took a peek... after dinner, when you went to the bathroom. Looked in your book... Weird cover—"

"You looked in the gravestone book?" Will sat up straight, forgetting how tired he was.

"I'm a curious person." Peter smiled sheepishly, and his black eye disappeared in a squint.

"Is that an apology?"

Peter shrugged. "Here— I tore the page out." He pulled a crumpled ball of paper out of his glistening white pocket. "Don't leave it lying around. No one's gonna think that dark baby is you.

191

Maybe if it was a picture of a baby elephant…"

Will snatched the Fingeldy page and tossed it in the fire in frustration, before remembering that the flickering flames were fake.

"I didn't tell anyone," said Peter, leaning back comfortably in his snow heap.

"How considerate!" Will bent to pick up the ball of paper. The hearth rug gleamed like ice under his glistening white shoes.

"Point is I could have," said Peter, "but I didn't. You can trust me, Fred… whoever you are."

Will fumed silently, watching the dancing holographic flames. The wounds from the Fate Sealer's arrows stung like wasp bites, and pain was creeping back into his bones as the painkiller he took with dinner was wearing off. At least Will's voice was sounding slightly less pathetic.

"Why do you want to help me?" he asked abruptly.

Peter scratched his head awkwardly then magically tied a knot in the chicken bone. "I promised Emmy," he muttered finally.

"Why?" insisted Will. "What's Emmy to you?"

"A friend— just a friend." Peter stared at the glowing hearth, looking embarrassed. "Don't make a big deal out of it, okay?"

Will stared at the flickering flames too, his eyes burning. The contact lenses felt like sandpaper in his eyes after the long, long day. He had to put a stop to this. Another day of badgering, and he would hurl Peter in the fire. And Will wasn't thinking of the one in front of them.

"I'm in trouble, Peter," said Will irritably. "Okay? So, the

192

last thing I need is you pestering me for information. Just drop—"

"What kind of trouble?"

Will rolled his eyes in exasperation. "The kind that gives you nightmares. Just trust me. I can't talk about it."

"Try," insisted Peter calmly.

"Honestly, Peter!" Will snapped furiously.

But a crystal ball lamp seemed to blink at Will inside a gleaming portrait hung above the fireplace, too quickly for Will to be sure, and yet that feeling of being watched made him lower his voice almost to a whisper.

"Someone's trying to kill me, Peter. And if I tell you about it, you'll be as good as dead too. So just drop it, okay?"

Incredibly, Peter started laughing. "You're kidding me, right? Everyone here had someone try to kill them. That's why we're here."

Will blinked stupidly. With all his troubles, he forgot to consider why everyone else was hiding at the Orphanage. "Someone's trying to kill you?" he asked.

"No, I just love living in this freezer. But you're different," added Peter thoughtfully. "You're not just hiding in here. You're hiding who you are. Your Echo must be real important... or you wouldn't have to look like this. I mean..." Peter suddenly reconsidered. "This *is* a disguise? You don't really—?"

"*Nooo!*" Will fumed. "Haven't you heard of Cold Sleep?" And still keeping his sluggish voice down, Will quickly recapped the unpleasant experience of being frozen until your bones seemed to crack.

"Brrrrr..." Peter shuddered.

"Times a million."

"But why?"

Will looked at Peter's bruised face and wished he could tell this strange boy everything, if only to shut Peter up. In a moment, Will turned his back to the crystal ball painting hanging over the fireplace.

"Ever heard of Crystilleries?" Will whispered, taking out his blue dome.

Peter gasped, his healthy eye widening so much from the shock that it looked ready to pop out of his head. "Illegal..." he blurted out finally, glancing nervously around the empty room. "Does it work?"

Will explained about the most recent and complex Memory and seeing everything from the perspective of the object you are reading, and Peter's awe-struck eye glinted in the firelight all the while.

"Almost as good as magic," said Peter finally, still not daring to reach for the blue dome.

"Wanna try?" asked Will, and Peter's face lit up like a Christmas tree.

They read the memories of Will's glistening sleeve, Poudini's brindled tail, the back of Peter's snow heap. And then Will turned serious again.

"You really want to know who I am?" he asked, still not

194

taking his Crystillery back as Peter looked up at him, head and puffy lip nodding eagerly. "You could make me tell you," said Will. "You've got my Crystillery. You could read my mind."

"Like Drinkwater tried to?" Peter shoved the Crystillery back at Will. "No, thanks! You're not that interesting. Okay, you are that interesting. But I'm not that desperate."

Will smiled and slipped the Crystillery back in his pocket. Then, very softly, Will whispered, "Peter... my Echo is the Prince."

Peter shot bolt upright, kicking Poudini awake. "You're—" The words got stuck in his throat.

"William Cleary." Will nodded. "Everyone calls me Will."

"Emmy's brother..." Peter stared at Will, good eye wide with amazement. "But... everyone says you're as good as... dead."

Will felt incredibly relieved to finally share his troubles with someone. *"This..."* Will whispered, taking out the Royal Shekel with his back still to the lustrous crystal ball painting, "is the only thing keeping me alive."

Peter's eyes exploded still wider, this time even his bruised one. "That's not—?"

"It is!" Will held out the see-through ice-blue coin, mesmerized as ever by the fact that the coin felt warm like hot sand but looked like running water that somehow didn't flow away.

"No, it can't be!" Peter flinched, his shock turning to horror. "Four months ago the King of Agám Kaffú died. You know about that? Okay, then you know what the Echoes think about it— Fortune killed him. But there's another rumor. Find the Royal Shekel, find

195

the thief who killed the King." Peter stiffened. "Are you the thief, Will?"

"No! Of course not!" Will frowned in horror.

"Then, how d'you get the coin?"

"Frankenstein," whispered Will.

"Who?"

"Drinkwater. I stole the Royal Shekel from him."

"Drinkwater…" repeated Peter breathlessly, twirling his tied chicken bone. "Then it was *him*— *He* killed the King. That's why he retired from teaching. He's been scheming to become King himself."

"But he didn't become King," said Will thoughtfully. "He took the Royal Shekel to the Sound realm—"

"To find you. To kill you. So the Prince would have to die without anyone suspecting anything. You know… the Law of Death."

"But he didn't kill me."

"Too many witnesses."

"Or maybe—" Will realized with a shudder "—maybe Drinkwater didn't think I'd survive the journey here…"

"The cunning creep!"

But Will shook his head uncertainly. "I dunno…" He twirled the Royal Shekel absently. "Frankenstein's the reason I went looking for the giant fireplace in the first place. But maybe… maybe we're overreacting. Maybe he's just… obnoxious. Anyway," Will added thoughtfully, "maybe I should just wait till tomorrow…"

"What's tomorrow?" asked Peter, a twinkle of curiosity in his good eye.

Still half lost in thought, Will blurted out, "I'm meeting my Echo—"

"The Prince...?" Looking awed, Peter fell silent, and for a while only Poudini's little snores and the crackling of the false fire made any sound in the empty room.

Then Peter asked, "Where's the meeting?"

"Behind the crystal ball fireplace, in the Sound kitchen. There's a secret room there."

A gleam of excitement brightened Peter's bruised face. "A secret room? For real?" But his expression soon darkened. "What did you mean before... about Drinkwater being the reason you went looking for the giant fireplace?"

"The Royal Shekel," said Will, blinking tiredly. The dance of the false flames was slowly putting him to sleep. "You saw what Drinkwater did this afternoon. I can't let him steal the coin."

"Well...?" Peter sat rigid, waiting to hear the rest.

"The crystal ball fireplace has the only real fire in the Orphanage, right? So, I went there to destroy the Royal Shekel."

Peter nearly tumbled off his snow heap from the shock. "Are you *insane*?"

"Sssssssshhhhh!" Will looked nervously up at the lustrous crystal ball painting. "It makes sense," he whispered and explained the logic to Peter, that the false King would keep hunting for the coin and not kill the Prince until he found it.

But Peter cut Will off. "It's like the biggest national heirloom around here, the Royal Shekel. You could sell it for a fortune. Or trade it for something— like your life! Or—" Suddenly a mischievous smile turned Peter's puffy lip into a wobbling second chin. "Fancy becoming King yourself?" he blurted out—and immediately asked Will to switch shoes with him.

"Switch shoes—? What for?"

Peter tapped the white heel of his glistening right shoe, and a secret compartment clicked open. "Perfect hiding place for a coin, don't you think?" He grinned. "I mean, if you're going to be King, you can't afford to lose the Royal Shekel, right?"

Peter started laughing and Will did too, because it was so late that it was actually early, and they were both so tired that anything seemed possible.

The Dining Hall

The Winter Break
Breakfast Feast

Will? Becoming King of the Echoes? No, no. With the light of day the next morning Will and Peter's imaginations shrank back to normal, especially at the sight of Will's reflection in the bathroom crystal ball mirror, which bore a close resemblance to a blue-eyed hippopotamus in a flaming wig—not exactly the face of a king. Then again, with his bruised, puffy face, Peter didn't look much like a King's close advisor either. The whole idea of Will becoming King of the Echoes just because he had the Royal Shekel seemed absolutely absurd.

As for Drinkwater, they had no idea if a Sound would even be allowed to rule over Echoes. And if the answer to this question was: *Never in a million twists of Fortune*, then Drinkwater had no motive to murder the true King or wish the Prince and Will any harm. At least no motive Will or Peter could think of.

"Better keep your distance from him anyway.... till we meet the Prince tonight," concluded Peter, as they meandered through the sunlit, sparkling garden on their way back from giving Wolfeá her breakfast.

To Will's relief, his pet had looked healthier even after just one day. The scabs around her neck were no longer bleeding, and her emaciated stomach bulged from wolfing down a bucketful of chicken wings.

"You're coming with me, then?" asked Will eagerly, no longer wishing to face his troubles alone.

But Peter was suddenly looking as still as a topiary.

"Shhhhh…" he hissed, his eyeballs sliding sideways meaningfully.

Through the fountain splashing on their left, two Fate Sealers were spilling out like sewage.

"Let's go—"

Peter dashed down a snowy path, his dog galloping beside him. Will ran after them, his swollen thighs knocking like wind chimes in a storm.

"Didn't follow us—" Will panted, catching up with Peter in a glittering, icy clearing.

"Not the idea," explained Peter, scanning the see-through garden for signs of more Fate Sealers. "Fate Sealers just frighten us around the garden. It's their morning exercise."

"Hilarious." Will pressed the stitch in his side and looked up to see what was making the shadow gliding on the snow between him and Peter.

It was Valerie Valerian, flying on her albatross, looking like

202

a fairy riding a swan in an upside down lake.

"Now, that's what I call morning exercise," said Peter admiringly.

Will nodded. "Anyway— then you're coming with me?"

"Tonight? Definitely!"

Peter grinned and magically pulled a dog treat from his nostril. He tossed it up at Valerie's bird, but the albatross wacked the snack back to earth with its wing, where it landed on a sundial floating in a sparkling pool. The shadow that was meant to tell time on the sundial was pointing at an ice sculpture of an elf eating. Presumably his breakfast, thought Will, as he watched Peter's dog leaping into the fountain after the snack and doing a bit of eating himself.

"Wither Heart," Peter kept talking. "You know, the Fate Sealer from last night… Did you see his scar? Makes you wonder what the guy who gave it to him looks like. Dead, probably. Anyway, don't get on his bad side. I mean, Wither Heart's already taken a shine to you. Last thing you want is a hug from him in a dark corridor, trust me."

"Other than the totally obvious, is there a special reason?" wondered Will, watching two beautiful see-through Echo girls strolling past. They stared so hard at him that they walked off the trail without noticing and got tangled in the low-hanging branches of an apple tree. Will chuckled. Looking like a blimp had its compensations.

"Chick magnet, you are." Peter smiled. "Wither Heart didn't

touch you last night, did he?" he added.

"Don't think so."

"You'd know if he did, trust me— Oh, brilliant!" Peter stopped suddenly and stood watching his dog drinking blue water from the mouth of a fairy fountain. "They're flavored, you know," he explained over Poudini's small explosions of lapping. "Each fountain's different. This one's *Strawberry Soda* flavor. See the dueling fawns behind it? That's how I tell. "

"Must be good," said Will, wondering how such a small dog could make so much noise.

"Delicious! Unless…" Peter squinted harder and pointed at another fountain splashing on the other side of the dueling fawns. "Oh yeah, I forgot. This could also be the *Blancmange* one. I always get these two confused."

"The what?"

"Blancmange. Echo delicacy… fish puke or something. Not that you'll find any *Hot Dog* fountains. Only foods Echoes love." Peter sighed. "Guess we should be grateful they eat some normal stuff sometimes."

"But it's got to be the right one," said Will, still watching Poudini lapping up gallons. "Your dog's Crazy about it."

"He's crazy about vomit," Peter reminded Will.

"Oh, yeah." Will grinned, remembering the little dog feasting on vomit at the hospital.

In light of Peter's uncertainty, they decided to save the taste test for another time and continued on their way back to the

Orphanage. Through the snowy labyrinth of see-through trees and fountains, they saw many Castaways walking their pets. The Sounds looked like walking snowmen in their glistening clothes, only their uncovered heads resembling children. The Echoes looked like icicle people in short-sleeved shirts.

Will felt as if he were seeing the garden through unfocused binoculars. But Peter seemed used to this glittering kaleidoscope of icicles, snow, and splashing blue water, with everything showing through everything else because everything was a little see-through. Well, everything except the snow.

"Over there," said Peter, as they crossed an icy bridge. Valerie's riding shadow glided on the sapphire river below them. "Not there. There." Peter pointed.

Behind a blur of white trees, Will saw the translucent white shapes of animals galloping, their manes and tales streaking behind them like shafts of light. "Unicorns…" he gasped.

"Horses, actually." Peter grinned. "Abednego's pets. He straps horns on their heads for effect."

"Does anyone ever get to ride them?" asked Will, wondering what that would feel like.

"When they're in the mood, definitely. It's like magi—" But Peter broke off, his face darkening. "Oh, joy!"

Will turned around, expecting to see more Fate Sealers. But instead he saw a boy dressed in the glistening white uniform of the Sounds waving at him. He was seated in a shiny black wheelchair, and all around him doves were pecking bread crumbs from the icy cobbles of the Orphanage courtyard.

With a happy bark, Poudini dashed at the birds, disappearing in a sea of fluttering white wings.

"I don't like dogs," said the boy sulkily, as Peter and Will reached him.

"That's all right," Peter shot back, "he doesn't like you either, Jeremy."

Jeremy shrugged haughtily, and a dark lizard leapt from the back of his wheelchair to the frosty courtyard, its bulbous eyes roving. "So, you're the Prince's Sound," he said matter-of-factly, looking up at Will.

Will blinked in shock, hearing Peter making a sort of choking sound beside him.

"Don't know what you're talking about," Will slurred in his medicated voice.

"Oh, you don't have to pretend with *me*," insisted Jeremy, smiling smugly and revealing a row of very long teeth. "Even if no one else around here can, *I* recognize the side effects of Cold Sleep. And your voice! You're obviously taking painkillers. Been there! Done that!"

"Done that...?" Will frowned thoughtfully. So that's who ended up in a wheelchair after his Cold Sleep, he realized, remembering the warnings from Damian and Nurse Bell who worried that the same thing might happen to Will.

"My Echo's Bram Fallon's grandson," Jeremy added resentfully, as if Will wasn't looking sufficiently impressed. "You know, *Bram Fallon*. The leader of the *Fate Sealers*. I'm an important Sound too." Jeremy sat up a little taller in his wheelchair. "You have nothing to worry about. I give you my word of honor—your secret's safe with me."

Will was still wondering how to react, when the lizard on the cobbles grew tired of Poudini sniffing it obsessively as if on the scent of treasure. With a quick flick of its tongue, the white reptile lashed Poudini on his nose, and the little dog burst out in a fit of angry barks.

"Last night..." said Jeremy, ignoring the commotion. "What you did to Wither Heart—"

"How do you know about that?" Peter cut in suspiciously, petting Poudini to calm him down.

Jeremy rolled his eyes, as if he had never heard anything so stupid. "Tell that *ordinary* Sound not to meddle with things he couldn't possibly understand," Jeremy said to Will, as if Peter was an insect of the lowest order. "And don't taunt Wither Heart again. True, the false King ordered the Fate Sealers to leave the Castaways here alone. But Fate Sealers have selective memories, if you know what I mean."

Jeremy winked knowingly and picked up his lizard, whose skin had turned pale and sickly.

"Natalia's a chameleon," he explained. "Black like my chair before— white like my hand now. Clever girl... blends with her surroundings. That's what you have to do. And don't trust just *anyone*—" Jeremy flicked his eyes to Peter "—if you know what I

207

mean."

Peter didn't stick around to be insulted again. He led Will away, Poudini galloping ahead of them into the fortress to the sound of Valerie's albatross beating its giant wings behind them, coming to a landing.

"He knows who I am," muttered Will, glancing over his shoulder at Jeremy waving goodbye.

"Don't worry," said Peter. "Jeremy won't say anything. Not because of his *word of honor*. Because no one talks to him. It's like he's cursed, *if you know what I mean.*" Peter mimicked Jeremy's pompous manner perfectly.

*   *   *

The hum of many voices echoed all around them as Will and Peter entered the Orphanage, and a wonderful aroma of food beckoned them forward.

"Winter break starts today. There's a feast," explained Peter, licking his puffy purple lower lip in expectation of wonderful treats.

They joined the Sounds streaming into the dining hall, their pets squealing in their arms or barking at their feet; while on their left a few solitary Echoes strolled leisurely in through the Echo entrance. Valerie slipped quietly behind them, her large blue eyes downcast, but her cheeks glowing and her zigzag hair looking wild from her flight over the garden.

There was no Air Seal to vacuum Will's lungs out of his chest. And even though this meant it was nearly as cold indoors as outside, he didn't mind it, not when his glistening white clothes grew warmer around him the longer he wore them, trapping his body heat over time.

The dining hall was magnificent. Light from at least ten crystal ball chandeliers gleamed off the curving icy walls of the great white hall. Ice sculptures of fairies fluttered between the pearly lights, their frozen wings actually moving, and their crystal lips blowing iridescent bubbles that rained down on the hall like many, many more crystal balls. As in the garden, fountains splashed here too, though not in straight lines but in arches of blue water that shot across the ceiling from fountain to fountain, creating a liquid sky. Will had seen it all yesterday, but the Orphanage dining hall was just as enchanting on second sight.

The three curving tables stretching before Will still amazed him by looking longer than any tables he had ever seen. And, like his uniform and so many other things in this strange Echo world, the tables glistened in perfect imitation of ice in sunlight. By the middle table, no one sat. But on the right, Sounds were jostling in a thick throng of white, cold breath spilling from their mouths, enveloping their faces in mist. While on the left, Echoes lounged so comfortably spread apart that they had to shout to have a conversation.

"And we're stuffed like sardines," said Peter resentfully.

"Rotten sardines," someone sneered behind them.

Will turned, hearing Peter muttering a curse under his breath.

A beefy Echo was towering over them, flanked by two friends, one with a crystal ball tattooed on his see-through forehead, the other with slanted, asymmetrical black eyes. They might have been sixteen years old by the look of them, but all three boys wore the petulant expressions of toddlers about to throw a tantrum.

"You still *stink*, Tongue Twister," the one in the middle spat at Peter, his smooth black hair gleaming like a puddle of petrol, his pimpled face looking like a—

"Dartboard... how's it going?" Peter smiled crookedly; while Poudini growled at the see-through Doberman snarling behind the Echo's tree-trunk legs.

The boy's thick lips curled in a sneer. "Time for another art lesson, by filthy Fortune. Black and blue's wearing off— I can make out your ugly face again, Tongue Twister."

The Echo's see-through friends grunted their appreciation of the joke, their pets, a green and brown snake, dangling from their necks like hissing scarves.

Will stepped closer to Peter, realizing who had decorated his friend's face with bruises. The bully cracked his knuckles and lunged. But a gray mass of sagging flesh caught his fist in midair.

"AAARRRRRRRRR—"

The overgrown boy writhed in agony, broke free and fled, his friends already leading him. Sounds shrieked out of sight, buffeting Will and Peter's backs as the two boys looked up, and up and up, until they faced an eerily familiar scar that twisted in a sagging, swinging smirk straight over Will's face.

"Well, well..." Wither Heart's long black tongue flicked out of his drooping mouth like an eel. From his sagging shoulder, the Fate Sealer's pet raven stared at Will with beady little eyes. "Hello again... *Freddy*. And that little pest—" The Fate Sealer's eyes squinted down at Poudini like collapsing caves. "Took me half the night to find my Ice Loom. Just wait till I get my—"

"No, no, *no!*" a frail voice, like talking wind, snapped irritably behind them, as the little dog shot away from the Fate Sealer's claws. "Out of the way! Not the time, not the place, Fate Sealer! Everyone— to your seats." And leaning tiredly on his crystal-ball-topped cane, the ancient Headmaster, Abednego, shuffled into the glittering hall, aquamarine-robed staff members streaming in behind him like a shimmering river.

"Come on—" whispered Peter, and Will rushed after his friend to the Sound table, diving into the throng of white backs and misty faces.

"Watch it!" someone snarled, as Peter squeezed between two boys and made room for Will, who took up the space of two more people with his swollen thighs.

The next instant the center of the icy Sound table flipped open from one end to the other like an incredibly long revolving door. Glittering, covered trays rose up with a clatter and with them appeared sparkling porcelain plates and goblets, silver utensils and napkins that looked like giant snowflakes. And still the rain of bubbles continued to fall from the Ice fairies flying between the crystal ball chandeliers and the liquid blue ceiling overhead.

In a whirl of voices and arms, the silvery lids were flung aside and a frenzy of eating began. Will glanced back at the beefy boy staring daggers at them from the Echo table, where glittering

211

trays had emerged also. The Echo's strange-looking friends were beside him still, too busy sneering to eat. But further down the half-empty table, the Fate Sealers were tearing into raw meat, their hollow mouths collapsing in ghastly chews that sent pale, see-through blood dribbling down their sagging, swinging chins.

"Who was that?" Will asked Peter, turning away from the Fate Sealers with revolution.

"Dartboard? Poof—" Peter puffed an iridescent bubble out of his face. "A toad trapped in a human. Like in the fairytales, only backwards." Peter piled mashed potatoes on his sparkling white plate and sausages on Poudini's. "His real name's B.S.... Bog Slippery. Dumbest Echo name on the planet. Other two morons are close seconds. Rain and Water Drops. They're brothers."

"Rain Drops and Water Drops?" Will spluttered into his icy goblet. "Thought Echoes were named after their Sounds."

"Yeah, but their parents give them Echo nicknames. Didn't think you could top Peter Patrick Peterson... till I got here. Save the bone for my magic trick," Peter added, watching Will biting into a drumstick.

"By all the flying crystal balls," grumbled a boy at Will's elbow. "Alexander the Great— you're sitting on him!"

Will slid off the long tail of a white mouse. "Sorry, Brainy." He smiled sheepishly at the spectacled boy he recognized as his least favorite roommate.

"Yeah, well... next time, by Fortune, look before you land!"

"Is Brainy having an attack of Echo-speech again?" asked a

dark-skinned boy sitting opposite. A long black curl hid his left eye. Will smiled. He liked Michael Silver. He was a good roommate. Funny and respectful of other people's privacy.

"Yes, by Fortune," grinned the boy next to Michael, who was the last of Will's roommates, Evan something... Will couldn't remember his last name, nor which of the frogs peeking out of his puffy hair was supposed to be Galileo and which Galilei.

"Can't you turn that mouse into a pumpkin?" Michael suggested to Peter.

"Poudini wouldn't like chasing a pumpkin." Peter grinned.

"Ha! Ha!" Brainy scowled and tossed a carrot at the parrot squawking on Michael's shoulder.

They ate on, jibes making their way across the table as frequently as bits of food. Will ducked to avoid a flying sausage, and Poudini burst a passing bubble in his face. Without thinking, Will licked the splatter off his lips.

"Chocolate..." He realized in surprise and swallowed another bubble whole, to see if it would taste as good.

"Not chocolate?" guessed Michael, when Will scrunched his puffy face and quickly wiped his tongue on a snowflake napkin.

"Sawdust and...radish?"

"Oh! Yes, Radish Cereal." Peter nodded sagely. "Got to watch out for those Echo Breakfast Bubbles— Nasty!"

"How exactly?" Will dodged another iridescent bubble. "They all look the same."

"Next time let a pet taste it for you," suggested Evan, holding

213

his frogs up to burst a bubble floating near his face. "No Sound's stupid enough to like Echo Bubbles, not even frogs."

"No Sound except Poudini," Peter grumbled to himself.

"The dog with no taste buds," Brainy gloated. "Fortune help us…"

All up and down the table Sounds were staring at Will between bites. He felt as if everyone was talking about him. But the spectacled boy beside him was staring worse than anyone, especially at Will's red hair. Even the mouse perched on Brainy's shoulder was twitching its nose like someone picking up a bad scent.

"Problem?" Will turned to him.

"Natural color is it?" asked the boy.

"Errr…"

"Drink! Drink!—" Peter came to Will's rescue, shoving a goblet of grape juice at him. "Radish Cereal can kill you."

Will took the opportunity to swallow a painkiller secretly. Sounding slow and stupid seemed like a good idea if his least favorite roommate was about to repeat yesterday's performance and turn into a human quizzing machine.

"Interesting article in today's *Crystal Monitor*," said Brainy, pulling out a rolled newspaper from his glistening back pocket. A bubble burst on his forehead, splattering his glasses. He hardly blinked. "Fascinating, By Fortune!"

"Yeah…?" Will slurred his heavy voice to sound bored. "I prefer fiction, actually."

Brainy looked far from discouraged. Without warning, he

slapped his palm with the newspaper as if he had made a momentous decision. Then he climbed on the gleaming white bench, unfurled his newspaper with one hand and swatted bubbles out of his way with the other. His white mouse settled on his glistening shoulder, flicking its long tail like a baton at an orchestra.

"What now?" Will muttered to Peter. "Why can't he just stare at me like everyone else?"

"Going to bore us to death, Brainy?" asked Michael, his multicolored parrot still squawking loudly on his glistening white shoulder.

Brainy ignored him, stretched his sweater collar, cleared his throat and started reading at the top of his voice. He had to reread the title several times, but soon the glittering hall filled with whispers repeating his intriguing words: "The Prince's Sound Disappears... The Prince's Sound disappears? Disappears... disappears..." Until silence fell except for the splash of the liquid ceiling and the chatter of pets.

His heart pounding Will spotted his sister, Emmy, further down the Sound table. Fear flashed in her melancholy brown eyes, as Brainy shook the folds out of his newspaper and, looking nervous but pleased with himself, began reading the article in the voice of a herald.

"On Monday, December 10th, the Sound of our Royal Prince, William Cleary III, disappeared from his home in the Sound realm. It is not yet known whether Fate Sealers or Fortune Tellers were involved. However, reports have confirmed that the Royal Sound

215

was brought into the Echo realm, specifically into Agám Kaffú. Where he might be hidden remains a mystery, though sources close to the Palace have hinted that the boy is as well concealed as an icicle in winter. Could this perfect camouflage be a clue? Might this not mean that this single Sound is lost among many of his kind—" Brainy paused for effect *"—at the Orphanage of Castaway Children?"*

Suddenly, as if every eye in the great hall was being drawn by a magnet, the Echoes, the Sounds and the Fate Sealers, all turned as one to stare at Will. Even pets seemed to watch him through the rain of iridescent bubbles. And at the far end of the Echo table, Will saw the darkness inside Wither Heart's eyes swirling in a storm. For the first time since waking in the Echo realm, Will breathed a sigh of relief for every uncomfortable, hideous, dim-witted part of his disguise.

Then, suddenly, the heavy silence was cut by a challenging voice.

"Sit down, Brainy— Before you make a complete fool of yourself!"

It was Emmy.

His heart pounding, Will watched his sister climbing on the gleaming bench, a white cat leaping on the cluttered table before her. She didn't glance at him, but Will could see what Emmy was thinking. It was like looking at his own reflection... the way he used to look about a million years ago. Emmy was about to say things she didn't really mean, just as she had warned him at the hospital. The

216

water fountains shooting blue water across the ceiling suddenly sounded incredibly loud in the quiet hall. Will could see hands wrapped around muzzles and beaks, silencing pets everywhere.

"Maybe it slipped your minds," Emmy's voice rose harshly, "but William Cleary is my twin— *Identical* twin. His Echo's still alive, but mine isn't. Right? We all know that! Princess Emmy was murdered. Why? Because the Fate Sealer made a mistake."

Will shot a quick glance at Wither Heart. Inside the creature's eyes the darkness gurgled like boiling black water.

"My Echo died because she looked just like her twin," Emmy continued, her voice even harsher. "The Fate Sealer couldn't tell them apart. So he killed the wrong kid. Get that? When they were two years old, Princess Emmy and Prince William looked exactly the same. So honestly—" Emmy rolled her eyes "—it doesn't take a genius, like Brainy thinks he is, to figure out that if my Echo looked like her brother... so do I!"

And suddenly, so fast that Will didn't see it coming, his sister's melancholy eyes were locked on him. A sickening sensation twisted in his stomach. This wasn't the family reunion she wanted; he could see it as clearly as if her eyes were screaming an apology at him. Will tried to send his sister a subliminal message of his own, to tell her she was doing the right thing. But he doubted she could read anything in his deformed face.

And still, all those eyes were staring at Will.

Emmy spoke again, but her voice was different, heavy with ridicule. "I'd like to know—" She glanced around at the hall.

217

"Which one of you *exactly*— thinks that this—" She pointed at Will "—this... *freak*... has anything to do... with *me*?"

Will didn't need a mirror to make the comparison everyone around him was making. Emmy looked so beautiful with her blond hair streaming down her glistening sweater. He looked like an overgrown rat with chili peppers sprouting out of his head.

It didn't take long for giggles to begin rippling through the hall, then swell into open laughter that snapped the tension.

Michael shot a carrot at Brainy's head, narrowly missing his mouse. "Dumbest idea you ever had," he shouted happily, his parrot squawking in outrage to see good food go to waste.

Evan, with his frogs bobbing by his ears, glanced at Will sympathetically and tried not to laugh, which made him look constipated. Brainy folded his newspaper wordlessly and sat down again.

"It was just a thought," he said resentfully. And glancing at Will, Brainy added a little sheepishly, "Not that I was trying to get you in trouble or anything. But the truth's the truth— No point hiding from it."

"No point talking like an idiot, either," snapped Peter sourly, blowing his frosty breath into the shape of a magician's hat that whacked Brainy on the head before disintegrating.

And yet, the damage had been done. Will could see it when he glanced at Wither Heart again. The Fate Sealer was watching him closely through the rain of iridescent bubbles. A moment after, the creature whispered to two of his kind, and they rose obediently and glided toward the icy Sound door, positioning themselves on either side of it like ghostly pillars.

And, with a shudder of fear, Will realized that they were waiting there for him.

*   *   *

At the back of the shimmering dining hall stood a fourth, horizontal table, which faced the other three from a stage that looked like an iceberg. The ancient Headmaster, Abednego, sat at the center of the icy table in a high-backed icy chair, his long white beard and hair covering him like sea foam. Echo Orphanage staff members talked and laughed to his left, Sounds to his right, their aquamarine robes dripping from their shoulders like small lagoons. But there were no animals at the table, and Will concluded that staff members didn't adopt pets.

"Hold your unicorns! Settle down!" the Headmaster ordered for the fourth time, his wispy voice magnified by a luminous Ice Loom.

Grudgingly Castaways stopped talking, though their pets kept up a happy chatter. Without commenting on the passing moments, the Headmaster requested that all dirty plates, utensils, goblets, and lids be placed in the silvery food trays. A minute or so later, the centers of the glacial tables flipped once more, and the messy stacks disappeared with a muffled clutter. And at the same time exactly, the fairies circling against the liquid ceiling stopped blowing their iridescent bubbles.

"Your two week Winter Break begins today," said

219

Abednego, his voice tinged with resentment as he went on to issue a general warning over the bursts of excited cheers. Castaways must not mistake his beloved library for a playground, not under any circumstance. "By all the crystal balls! Not your garden variety stomping ground for frolicking fools," the Headmaster concluded.

Then he sighed and lowered his luminous horn as if he had second thoughts about what came next. But after a moment Abednego raised the glowing horn again and announced, "Let the performances begin."

"What performances?" Will glanced at Peter.

"Oh, you'll love this," Peter promised, grinning over Poudini's floppy ears, which seemed to be dripping something brown; probably gravy left over from the feast, thought Will.

Across from Will, Evan stuck his frogs back in his thick bouncy hair. "They're a holiday tradition, the performances," he said gravely, as if this explained everything.

Michael leaned across the table, his colorful parrot still squawking on his shoulder. "The staff pretend they have talent," he explained confidentially. "We choose our favorite."

"Right." Will nodded. It didn't sound too bad. Anything to get people to start staring in another direction.

And indeed, on the left side of the glistening iceberg, a frizzy, white-haired Echo was already piping a tune on a smoking pipe, and the smoke was curling into crystal balls that wacked him on the head then exploded. Next to him, a whiskered Echo placed a fishbowl on his head and, ever so carefully, started pirouetting like a ballerina with a sore back.

On the Sound side of the iceberg, Nurse Flight was juggling seven crystal goblets with white mice peeking out of them. While behind her, a fat Sound was taking his cue from the great fountains in the corners of the hall and tossing blue water between two jugs, thoroughly soaking himself in the process. More and more performers joined them, bumping into each other on the narrow stage, and the great hall filled with laughter.

"Over a million books in the Orphanage library, and I have read them all, by Fortune's grace!" Abednego announced in the luminous Ice Loom, joining the host of performers without leaving his icy seat. "Ask me any question. My knowledge is vast, so Fortune will attest."

"With Fortune's permission, what's the oldest book, sir?" cried Brainy, too tempted by an open call for questions to remember his recent humiliation.

"Crystal my ears, what's that?" Abednego scanned the sparkling hall for the speaker, and Brainy waved his mouse in the air, shouting his question again.

"Ah, yes. Oldest book, not scroll…?" Abednego considered, his voice, as ever, sounding like a sigh even in the luminous horn. "That would be the dome-shaped book. The oldest book in the Echo realm, by Fortune."

Brainy jostled in his seat next to Will like someone with corn popping inside him. "Sir. Please, sir! By Fortune's favor, what does the book look like?" Brainy nearly deafened Will from shouting so loudly.

"By the Lake of Eternal Ice, humble it is!" said the Headmaster faintly. "Ever so humble for its kind! Embossed leather binding of a red deeper than the color of wine. A sapphire blue spine. And a gilded title in an ancient language few Echoes know."

"What's it about?" shouted a girl from the Echo side of the hall. A white bird circled over her jet black hair like a halo.

Cups suddenly crashed on the stage as Nurse Flight's juggling act went terribly wrong, propelling mice into the air. One splashed into the liquid ceiling and disappeared. Another landed in Abednego's white beard.

"I guess you could say it is a road map," said the Headmaster, his gnarled old hand leaving the cane he was leaning on, even while sitting. Will watched the ancient man fishing out the startled mouse, and then something else caught his eye.

"Did you see that?" Will breathed at Peter.

Peter was too busy laughing. "See what?"

"There it is again. Look— The crystal ball on Abednego's cane."

"What about it?"

"There's... an *eye* inside it."

"Oh, that. Yeah, I know." Peter shrugged and glanced around to see why people were suddenly cheering, and Poudini barked happily in his lap.

But Will sat frozen; the old sensation of being watched came back to him. He thought he imagined seeing eyes in the chandeliers last night. But maybe he didn't. He glanced at the crystal ball chandeliers of the dining hall, then at the crystal ball windows and the crystal ball pedestals of the fountains. Even the glistening shoes of the flying Ice Fairies looked like pearly orbs. But if there were eyes inside any of these crystal balls, Will couldn't spot them.

"By Fortune! I believe Valerian has joined us," Abednego's whispering voice boomed from the Ice Loom, before Will could ask Peter more about it.

The icy hall was suddenly wild with cheers, laughter, hoots. Faces lit up with smiles and wide-eyed wonder, all staring at the gleaming entrance. Will glanced back but saw no one there, except the two Fate Sealers who stood like sentinels by the Sound doorway, watching him with swirling eyes.

And yet an aquamarine bag was floating away from the icy Echo door, like a puddle carried on wings it didn't have. The bag made for the Sound table and was soon bouncing off people's heads, and any Castaway who tried to snatch it was quickly distracted by his pet turning into a wingless, screeching, flying fur ball.

"What the—?" Peter gasped.

A memory flashed through Will's mind. "Some Echoes can turn invisible," he said breathlessly.

And, as if in answer, Valerian's beautiful voice spoke out of thin air, rising above the laughter and cacophony of voices filling the dining hall.

"Yes, it's me. Victor Valerian. Your Echo History Professor. Quiet down and I'll explain."

Once again, hands closed on muzzles and beaks, and moderate silence fell through the shimmering white hall.

"Thank you," said Valerian's beautiful voice, with the hint of a smile. "Yes, I'm invisible. But how—? I'll explain. As you know, all Echoes are made of gas. A cloud of gas, if you will... trapped inside a bubble of ice that keeps it from evaporating. Without this gas, we die... the way a Sound dies when all his blood flows away. And wonder of wonders, this cloud of gas is entirely—invisible.

"But a healthy Echo produces an enzyme in his blood. An enzyme that gives this gas a paler shade of milk in white Echoes, or the palest shade of chocolate in black Echoes. And so, the body of an Echo gains its color... though we are still somewhat see-through.

"A sick Echo will produce less of this enzyme. He might even become almost invisible. But I... I have the *rare* ability to stop making this enzyme altogether. Whenever I wish. To cleanse my blood—until I disappear."

The aquamarine bag was still bouncing from head to Sound head. Brainy cringed when his turn came. Will felt his spiky hair tingling. Then suddenly the smell of cherry tobacco enveloped him with memories of home, and Valerian's disembodied voice whispered in his ear, "Pay close attention to my gift!" before the bag bounced on, to everyone's happy cheers.

"Brilliant!" cried Peter. "Better than magic!"

"Can't you shut Prattle up?" complained Brainy, as Michael's parrot found a way to resume its incessant squawking even through a clamped beak.

"A parrot called Prattle... and you think he likes to shut up?" Michael raised a single skeptical eyebrow.

Peter's face suddenly darkened. "A bit late, isn't he?"

A second later, a flash of purple darted past them.

"Drinkwater...?" Will frowned at his old teacher's receding back.

A little ahead of Drinkwater's limping, hurrying figure, Valerian was materializing, dressed in the fluid robe he had pulled from his aquamarine bag. Cries of disgust and laughter followed him as the Echo jogged lightly up the iceberg stage, screwing his gleaming plastic hand in place. Drinkwater followed him, keeping his distance. All other performers were back in their icy seats, not wishing to compete with so spectacular an act.

"I'm thrilled to be here," declared Valerian, his beautiful voice still needing no Ice Loom to be heard, despite the happy cheers greeting him from every direction. "This is the first Christmas break my niece and I will spend here, at the Orphanage."

Valerian gestured at the glistening Echo table, and Will saw Valerie seated somewhere on the edge of the Echoes, entirely alone, looking all the more frail and see-through because of it.

"Crash and Splash!" Brainy shook his head in horror. "An Echo girl adopting a Sound bird. What next? Sounds and Echoes falling in love?"

"You don't just talk like them, do you?" Michael stared hard at Brainy with the eye that wasn't covered by his long, dangling curl.

All at once, Will realized why Valerie was sitting alone. Her choice of pet was even worse than his. He only chose a wild animal that could kill people. Valerie was an Echo who adopted a Sound. Apparently not a popular thing to do.

Seeing how frightened and miserable the frail girl looked, Will wished he could cross the glittering hall and talk to her. But he was in enough trouble already. The two Fate Sealers, who stood guard by the icy Sound doorway of the great hall, were watching him still, the darkness in their eyes swirling like hypnotic, bottomless wells. If he was going to make it to tonight's meeting with the Prince, Will knew he would have to find a way past them.

"I want this Christmas to be special," Valerian continued on the stage, beaming down at his admiring audience, his voice alluring. "And so I propose—a contest. A gift to the Castaway who will do something *extraordinary* by Christmas day. I will place my gift on top of the giant Christmas tree. Look outside..." Valerian gestured at the crystal ball windows with his plastic hand. "Warloch is dragging the tree into place as we speak. On Christmas... just eight days from now... one hero among you will win... *this*—"

With a flourish of his Echo hand Valerian was suddenly swinging a large gold medallion that glittered on a long gold chain. The staff members shot to their feet behind him, their aquamarine robes rippling like waves. Drinkwater swept across the stage, pushing his taped glasses up as if not believing his eyes. Only Abednego seemed too weary to react.

"It's just a coin," Brainy snapped irritably, knocking into Will as he tried to get a better look. "Isn't it, isn't it?"

226

"Stuff a crystal ball in it, and maybe we'll find out," said Michael dryly.

"Beautiful, don't you agree?" said Valerian in his beguiling voice, raising the medallion beyond Drinkwater's reach. "And as valuable as it looks. But not merely for its beauty. Echo History records an ancient invention—"

"No, Valerian! You mustn't!" Drinkwater roared suddenly, leaping desperately at the medallion dangling just over his balding head.

"A safeguard of past treasures," Valerian went on calmly, smiling at his audience as if Drinkwater wasn't there at all, jostling desperately beside him.

"No!"

"A coin... that isn't money—"

"Stop! Before it's too late!" insisted Drinkwater.

"A coin that is, in fact... a KEY."

Drinkwater froze as if turned to stone. The glittering hall fell silent with anticipation. Only a few pets still barked or squawked here and there, Michael's parrot among them.

Valerian smiled serenely, still keeping his medallion out of Drinkwater's reach.

"This is a Coin Key," he explained in his enchanting voice. "Embossed on both sides is the image of the beautiful Queen Illyria, the Queen who disappeared in the Lake of Eternal Ice so many years ago. A reflection of this image is said to be engraved into the base of a golden chest known as Illyria's Treasure. Should the two images

227

ever touch, the chest will unlock. If only..." the old Echo laughed softly. "If only the chest wasn't lost..."

As a hum of whispers swallowed the last of Valerian's chuckles, Drinkwater snapped back to life with all his former fury. Will watched his old teacher's lips moving spitefully, doubtless hurling curses at Valerian. Why was Drinkwater so upset, Will wondered. Could Coin Keys have something to do with—?

And then it hit Will!

What if the Royal Shekel wasn't just a coin? What if it was actually—a key? To a treasure... a gate... a door to a secret place...?

By the glitter of excitement in Peter's unbruised eye, Will saw that his friend was thinking the same thing, wondering if this was why Drinkwater was so desperate to get the Royal Shekel back.

"What?" demanded Brainy suspiciously, craning his neck to stare at Will and Peter.

But the feast had ended. Glistening Sounds rose from the icy table, furry heads pushing between their elbows, wings fluttering over their excited faces. And Will and Peter dashed away also, Poudini barking before them.

"Wither Heart's spies... by the door... waiting for me," whispered Will, trying to duck so his red spikes would disappear in the streaming, glistening crowd.

"I saw." Peter nodded tensely. The shadow of a flying Ice Fairy fluttered over his face. "Have to let us pass, though. Too many witness."

Will hoped Peter was right.

228

But as they slipped through the icy Sound door unharmed, Will realized something worse.

The Fate Sealers had never intended to trap him. They wanted him alive and free, going anywhere he wanted, meeting anyone he pleased—for the two Fate Sealers crept behind him all that day like ghostly shadows, never letting him out of their hollow sight, never fading out of his; not when he and Peter tried to lose them in a maze in the glittering, see-through garden, or among the stalagmites of books in the sparkling white library, or down the curving, narrow corridors of the chilly fortress, with Poudini disappearing into pet passages and reappearing two floors above.

Though, every hour, one of the Fate Sealers would leave for a short time, and Will guessed that Wither Heart insisted on regular reports.

Cold Fire Mushrooms

The Prince

Will opened half an eye for what felt like the hundredth time and looked out the crystal ball window overlooking his snowy bunk bed. One Fate Sealer was finally gliding away down the dark corridor beyond. But the other loathsome, sagging creature was still there, watching Will with an eerie green gleam swirling in his hollow eyes.

Past the Fate Sealer Will could see the crystal ball windows of the corridor. The blue sky of the morning was black now with dark, brewing storm clouds. Lightning flashed, and Will blinked his eye shut and continued faking sleep.

"Well?" Peter whispered from the top bunk. The combined snores of Will and Peter's roommates and pets nearly drowned Peter's voice.

Will snored the agreed upon sign for *One freak's still there*.

"Almost midnight." Peter sighed. "Better do your thing… before the other one gets back. I'll leave Poudini here. He's sleeping."

A knot twisted in Will's stomach. They had planned it in

advance, just in case the Fate Sealers didn't give up: Will would play the fool to create a diversion, and Peter would go and meet the Prince alone. Will braced himself for a chilling, probably agonizing, experience. He had to do it, he thought, wishing desperately that he didn't. But staying warm under the covers wouldn't return his life back to normal... wouldn't bring him and Emmy home... to their parents... who were probably looking for him desperately, as well as Emmy, through the hole in the middle of the pond.

Will took a deep breath and opened his eyes again—and a purple figure streaked past his window.

A second later, the Fate Sealer swept after the purple figure, his Ice Loom suddenly blazing like a giant lantern.

"He's following Drinkwater," gasped Will, leaping out of bed.

"Drinkwater? Ouch—"

Rubbing his head, Peter grumbled about the low ceiling over his top bunk. But Will was already slipping through the vacuuming swoosh of the Air Seal insulating the heat of their dorm room. He passed into the cold dark corridor, and Peter popped behind him in a moment.

"You'll get used—"

"Don't say it!" Will coughed, pressing his spiked hair back into his skull.

They crept through the sleeping Orphanage, seeing nothing of the garden past the rain-streaked crystal ball windows, nor anyone in the narrow, chilly corridors when lightning bleached the night.

Down the spiraling staircase they slipped, barely daring to breathe, watching wide-eyed for the wicked glow of an Ice Loom on the stone walls curving before them.

"Look," gasped Will, on the first floor landing.

Outside the dining hall, the strings of crystal balls in the unlit chandelier had been rearranged to spell the words: *Merry Christmas*.

"Someone trying to win Valerian's medallion, probably," whispered Peter. "Come on."

But Will stood frozen. His eyes were bleary from wearing his contact lenses all day, but he didn't think he was imagining it. Inside a few of the dark orbs—Will saw eyes. Watching him.

"Come on." Peter tugged Will down the spiraling staircase.

"They're spying on us?" whispered Will, staring at the glowing crystal ball handrails.

"Who?"

"The crystal balls."

"Can't be." Peter darted nervous glances right and left. "Seeing things— You must be."

"No, I'm not," insisted Will, though he saw no more eyes here. "You said it yourself, there's an eye inside Abednego's—"

"Yeah... just for show."

"For show?"

"Like the horns on his horses. Stop making me nervous— Oh, finally... we're here—"

Peter's sigh of relief was sucked away by the whirl of the Air Seal guarding the enormous icy door of the Sound kitchen. Will

235

fought back his coughs. And then came the long march between the endless gleaming sink and counter, with flashes of lightning casting fearsome shadows at their feet, making Will see all sorts of things, like Fate Sealers coming out of the walls or Drinkwater dangling from the ceiling, until Will started to think that perhaps he had imagined the eyes upstairs. And then, at long last, the warm glow of the great fireplace dispelled all his fears.

Tonight no cauldron was hissing on a hook. Even the thousand flames were small and tame.

"You know what to do?" whispered Peter.

Will nodded.

The mantelpiece was five feet tall. Its crystal ball stones sparkled as if someone was in the habit of polishing the soot off daily. Teetering on tiptoes, Will slid his palm along the curving, shimmering stones, until his fingers scraped against a chipped edge.

"This one," he breathed, the blood throbbing in his veins as he pushed the stone up, then down, then up again—exactly as Damian had told him the secret passage was to be opened.

Nothing happened.

"Try again," whispered Peter.

But, suddenly, Peter snatched Will's glistening white sleeve, his eyes bulging with terror.

Right beside them, a man was appearing out of thin air. Only it wasn't a man at all, just the outline of a human being formed by spots of light, like a connect-the-dots drawing without any of the dots connected. The strange being walked to the edge of the

236

gleaming hearth, raised the collection of fireflies that formed its forefinger, then motioned for Will and Peter to follow him—before he slipped behind the hearth and disappeared.

Will blinked, now totally convinced that his contact lenses were making him see things; except that Peter was mumbling, "Trick of the light, must be," which proved that he had seen the thing too.

Will and Peter shrugged at each other in amazement, then followed the vanished apparition.

Soon they could see that something *must* have been there— for the reason the secret passage had not opened for them before was that someone had opened it already. They slipped into the black crack between the back of the fireplace and the stone wall. The connect-the-dots man was gone. But a secret room opened before them.

It was a dark place, without windows, musty and cold like a cell in a dungeon. A broken crystal ball glowed by the mildewed back wall. And in its halo, surrounded by shadows like yolk trapped in a rotten egg, stood a handsome blond boy. He looked like a Sound of about fifteen, and he was holding a man by his throat. Thick cobwebs dangled from the low ceiling, casting an evil shadow over them both. Will stared, amazed. The man was dressed in a purple robe. It was Drinkwater, no doubt about it. Though how he had eluded the Fate Sealer and arrived here first, Will had no idea.

"Don't lie to me—" the blond boy snarled at Drinkwater. "You sold me to the false King."

"*I?*" Drinkwater choked on the word. "Sold… *you*—?"

"What a bargain," the boy cut Drinkwater off fiercely. "A Safe Passage Ring. For the life of your *son*!"

Drinkwater's son... Will could hardly believe it. He never imagined his old teacher could be so normal as to be someone's father. Peter was probably as surprised, for Will felt his friend's warm hand on his wrist, pulling him deeper into the dark edge of the cell.

"But the dagger..." Drinkwater pleaded.

Will saw that his old teacher was holding the gold knife he had used to hide the Royal Shekel in the Memory Box, back in the cellar of Will's crumbling home.

"A Crystillery can't lie," insisted Drinkwater. "I saw it happen! I saw you fall! This knife slashed your throat. You must believe me," he pleaded, his pale lips twisting to the horror of his words. "Auralius, listen to me! I saw you die—"

"Do I look dead?" sneered Auralius, rage flashing in his blue eyes. Or was it the lamplight shining through them? For the boy's head seemed see-through in places, though not all the time. As if he was a Sound, but wasn't.

Will wished he and Peter could slip away. This was a private meeting. He felt embarrassed to keep eavesdropping. He crept even further back until he bumped into the wall. It felt cold, damp and slimy.

And then, Will nearly screamed.

Something sticky had smeared over his face. And things were crawling inside it. Will wiped his cheeks frantically, feeling Peter

238

thrashing beside him, clearly fighting off the same revolting touch. They were making too much noise. But in the pool of light Drinkwater and his son continued staring at each other, hearing nothing.

And then Will saw it, tiny shadows starting to crawl over the stony faces of Auralius and Drinkwater. Overhead, spiders emerged in the cobwebbed ceiling, hundreds of them, crawling toward the illuminated wall of the cell. Will blinked in disbelief, for the mildew back there was suddenly spilling out of the cracks between the stones. And worse still, the clammy moisture behind Will's back began stirring too. The walls of the cell were filling with ants.

"My pets," hissed Auralius, not taking his eyes off his father. "Ants and spiders. I flick the light on, and slowly they come out... to keep me company. The only company I have left, thanks to you."

In a flash, the boy snatched the golden dagger from his father's hand and pressed the blade to the purple scarf encircling Drinkwater's throat.

"I should kill you..." snarled Auralius. "I should kill you here and now—"

"Auralius... don't," breathed Drinkwater, as from the depths of a grave. "You mustn't! Not for my sake... for yours."

"What was that—?" Auralius hissed suddenly, twisting his head back, though his knife remained pressed to his father's throat.

Will saw it too.

Something was stirring in the air beside Drinkwater and his son.

239

At first Will thought that a spider was swinging itself on invisible cobwebs. But then he realized that a small shimmering pouch was hovering there like a silver bird without wings. "Shhhh," a warning hissed from the pouch, as if it could speak. And then the raspy voices of Fate Sealers crept into the cell through the secret passage still open at Will and Peter's backs. The voices were far-off, still somewhere down the Sound kitchen, but they were drawing near.

"A tiny bag... I'm sure of it," one of the Fate Sealers was croaking. "Flying— A flying bag!"

"Kidnapped Drinkwater and Vomit Face, did it?" answered a voice that sent shudders down Will's spine.

"I swear it, Wither Heart. By blood and guts, I do! That foul Fingeldy was sleeping when I left him. I had to follow Drinkwater. He was up to something, I could tell. And now this flying bag! I feel it in my rotten flesh! By dark Fortune and bloodshed, something dastardly is going on."

"Sleeping?" hissed Wither Heart's voice.

"What—?"

"Fingeldy, you imbecile."

"Yes, I swear it, Wither Heart. Fast asleep, by all the evil omens!"

"Eyes closed? Snoring? Shut up, you moron!"

There was a shrill scream of pain that in the croaky voice of a Fate Sealer sounded like firecrackers exploding amid howling wolves.

In the musty cell, Drinkwater slipped free of his son's grip and darted for the exit. He moved so fast that Will had barely enough time to freeze against the slimy wall for fear of being detected. He felt Peter stiffening also as the darkness stirred beside them, sweeping a sticky web over their faces.

As Will wiped his eyes, he heard Auralius snarling, "Coward!" Then Drinkwater's shadow disappeared through the hidden passage as it rumbled shut.

*   *   *

The hovering silver pouch stopped over a black bag, which Drinkwater had dropped on escaping. Still hidden in darkness, Will watched in amazement as the bag suddenly opened by itself, and a short-sleeved Orphanage uniform drifted out of it. The glistening white clothes unfolded in mid-air, then moved about in a funny way until they dressed someone who wasn't there.

And then it happened. The invisible person began to appear, first like a misty presence with the silver pouch hanging around its neck; then like the outline of a boy; and finally like someone Will knew better than anyone else in the world.

Will was face-to-face with his Echo at last.

Mesmerized, Will stared at this see-through version of himself, a scrawny boy who looked like a scarecrow with strawy hair and melancholy brown eyes. But, at the same time, Will remembered bitterly that he now looked like an overgrown pickle in trousers.

Auralius stared just as much as Will until the Echo finished materializing. Then Auralius bent on one knee and bowed his golden head, looking like a homeless orphan dressed in rags that were as soiled and wrinkled as his cell was damp and creepy.

"Your Majesty," said Auralius, as calmly as if he was used to speaking with monarchs.

The Prince motioned for the blond boy to rise, but his manner was dumbfounded. "But you're dead, Auralius…" he gasped.

"Alive!" snarled Auralius resentfully, his fist tightening around the golden dagger. "As Fortune is my witness, my father lied to you, Your Majesty."

"Lied…?" The Prince shook his head in wonder. "I never met a more honest man." Then the Prince drew his thin shoulders back, as if seeking to regain his regal composure. "Please forgive my intrusion, Auralius," he added. "I had no idea a Mongrel was hiding in this—" the Prince frowned at the sagging cobwebs still teeming with spiders overhead "—this… room. But I've come a long way, at great risk… to meet someone. There's nowhere else safe."

Turning his back to Auralius, the Prince faced the darkness and asked. "Are you there?"

Will's breath caught in his throat.

Silently Will stepped out of the shadows. He could see his gray cheeks swelling under his eyes like deformed mushrooms, but he couldn't stop himself smiling. At long last, he was going to meet his Echo.

A short exchange of introductions followed. To begin with Peter rushed into the light also and, staring at the Prince, blurted out his amazement at how un-blimp-like Will really was in his normal

242

state. The Prince, who had better manners, congratulated his Sound on his disguise. Then Peter seemed to remember himself, and he bowed gallantly to the Prince, offered his full tongue twister name, and blew his frosty breath into the shape of a magician's hat. The Prince laughed and with equal gallantry, if less ostentation, asked to be called *William* instead of *Your Majesty*. Only Auralius kept apart, brooding, perhaps wondering how long the two trespassing Sounds had been hiding in his cell, and what they may have witnessed.

"What's that?" asked Peter suddenly.

Will tore his fascinated gaze from his Echo and saw Peter bending to pick up a square of paper from the mildewed flagstones.

"Must have fallen from the bag Drinkwater left me," said the Prince, holding his hand out imperiously.

But Peter failed to take the regal hint. Shaking off a few ants and a spider, he unfolded the note and read it aloud. "*Someone you thought was dead is waiting to see you.*"

"Was that note meant for Drinkwater?" wondered Will, trying to sound more normal, more like his Echo, though his voice still came out slurred and foolish.

Will glanced at Auralius to see what he thought. But the blond boy was still silent, staring daggers at them, the mildewed wall flickering through his blue eyes like an image someone was turning on and off.

The Prince frowned thoughtfully, wiping his see-through cheek from the trickling, cobwebbed ceiling. "Turn the note over," he commanded Peter, who was already doing it anyway.

243

Astonishingly, the back of the crisp sheet of paper was a three-dimensional map.

It took Will a moment to realize that it must be a map of the Orphanage of Castaway Children, with its icy walls and double-windowed corridors. He guessed that the glistening white crystal balls he saw down one side of every corridor marked the Sound rooms, and the silvery crystal balls on the other side signified Echo rooms. All these crystal balls lay on the map the way ink dots are supposed to, with a beautiful shimmering blue script curled inside each, specifying which room was which.

But there was a third set of crystal balls, red ones, and these were doing things normal drawings never do. These emblems on the map were actually moving, flickering like flames—*inside* some of the walls. And one of the crystal balls was even leaving round red footprints on the parchment as it bounced like a ball straight through the drawing of a giant fireplace into a dark square room labeled: *The Ant Chamber*.

"It's a map of the Orphanage," snarled Auralius, trying to snatch the note from Peter.

But Peter darted back, shoving the paper into his glistening pocket.

"A map with everything!" Auralius glared at Peter. "Secret rooms. Secret passages. How to get in here. Give it to me."

Peter didn't budge.

For an instant, Will saw the lamplight and cobwebs flickering through Auralius' furious eyes and even his entire head, as if the blond boy were an Echo, not a Sound.

"Yes, a map." The Prince nodded gravely at Auralius, who looked as if he was deciding whether to break Peter's knuckles to get at the note, or get the note first and then break Peter's nose for good measure.

"Looks like someone left the note for your father," the Prince kept addressing Auralius, as if he saw nothing of the brewing fight, or didn't care if he did. "Someone who wanted Drinkwater to come here," added the Prince. "Late at night... to surprise you. Maybe that person guessed how much you hate your father. Why is that, Auralius? What did Drinkwater do?"

Auralius laughed coldly. The shadow of a spider crawling in the cobwebs above fell on his handsome face like a moving bruise.

"You mean, what did my father do other than have a child with an Echo?" demanded Auralius. "Nothing much. One day he decided that his half-breed of a son didn't deserve to live anymore, that's all. Or maybe he wanted to put me out of my misery. Hand over one more filthy-blooded Mongrel to the false King— no big deal!

"Don't look so surprised, Your Majesty," Auralius added bitterly, his blue eyes turning lucent again. "My father had his reason. My life in exchange for a Safe Passage Ring... So he could run back to his precious Sound realm."

"Who told you that?" snapped the Prince, amazed and furious.

Auralius shrugged. "I figured it out... Your Majesty."

"Then you figured it wrong—" The anger drained from the Prince's melancholy eyes, and he looked at Auralius with pity. "*I* gave your father the ring. *I* asked my uncle... the *false* King, for a favor. He wanted to keep me happy, make me think we could be friends—" the Price chuckled bitterly "—so he granted my wish."

Auralius stared, his face horror-struck. "*You* gave my father the ring?" he asked, shaking his beautiful head.

The Prince just nodded, then he turned away slowly to lock his eyes on Will. "I had my reason for wanting Drinkwater to return to the Sound realm," he said meaningfully—and, at once, Will knew that his Echo was alluding to the Royal Shekel.

With a thrill of excitement, Will quickly changed the subject. He wasn't ready to admit that the coin was here with him.

"Can we sit?" said Will to his Echo. "I'm still getting over my Cold Sleep."

Will sat beside his cold Echo on the only piece of furniture in the damp cell, an old wooden bed standing beside the cracked crystal ball lamp. The snowflake sheets on the bed were filthy, and the blanket looked like a puddle of slush. Water could be heard trickling behind the headboard, and the lucent ants still streaming in through the mildewed cracks in the stone wall glistened as if they were wet.

The Prince spoke first.

"Thank you for coming to the Echo realm." He smiled at Will.

"It's really thanks to Deá and Damian." Will smiled back. "They're my—"

"I know who they are."

"Oh..." Will felt glad he wouldn't have to explain about his dead pets. "Drinkwater also convinced me," Will added, deciding to mention his old teacher in light of everything that happened in this cell.

"I know," said the Prince. "I asked him to."

"You did?"

The Prince brushed away a see-through spider that fell on the glistening sleeve of his Orphanage uniform. "The Law of Death," he said, his voice suddenly as heavy as Will's. "Drinkwater told you about it."

It wasn't a question! Will wondered what else Drinkwater had mentioned to the Prince. Did he warn the Prince that Will stole the Royal Shekel? That he couldn't be trusted? As if thinking the same thing, Peter knocked his foot against the secret compartment in Will's glistening white shoe, where the Royal Shekel lay hidden. Will glanced up at his friend. Without saying a word, Peter's blue-green eyes, even his bruised one, were telling Will not to say a word.

"The King..." the Prince went on, wiping his strawy hair back as if to push away a sad thought. "The *true* King... my father... His whole life was dedicated to abolishing the Law of Death. But the Fate Sealers and the Fortune Tellers resisted him at every turn...

"Then one night, four months ago, my father came to my room. It was very late. He looked troubled. Worse than ever before. He paced and paced. Finally he told me he found a solution to the problem. He found a way to free the Echoes from the Law of Death.

He wouldn't tell me how, only that he was going to look for a passage to a place called Olám Shoné, because the answer was there. He never came back."

Moisture kept trickling from the cobwebbed ceiling as if the room was weeping. Will wiped a drop from his forehead.

"He was murdered," said Will, watching his Echo sadly; it felt like telling yourself that your Dad was killed.

"Worse than murdered," said the Prince, anger flashing in his melancholy eyes, turning them even more see-through. "Someone trapped him inside the Lake of Eternal Ice."

"To defame his name!" said Peter angrily. His fingers toyed restlessly with his tied chicken bone, which he must have pulled out magically from his ear or his nostril.

The Prince nodded, and to Will, who knew nothing of this, the Prince explained that the Lake of Eternal Ice was no ordinary lake. Not only was it eternally frozen, which in itself was unique in Agám Kaffú, but beneath the icy surface thousands of precious stones were trapped, as if the lake was a giant jewel box. Will tried to imagine this fantastic place. He wanted to ask how the stones got there, and what kept people from stealing them. But the Prince was talking again.

"The Echoes believe the stones belong to Fortune... That She keeps the lake frozen forever to protect Her treasure. To steal even one stone is the highest crime possible in our Land. It's a crime against Fortune Herself. Most Echoes believe that a thief, and even his family, will suffer greatly. And when a King steals a stone from the lake… the whole Land will suffer."

"And the Echoes think that your father went to the lake to steal?" Will began to see what Peter meant by someone scheming to defame the true King's name.

"Yes."

"And your uncle took the throne…"

"And will remain King—" the Prince frowned, his eyes disappearing from his face for a moment "—until I can clear my father's name."

"Even if you turn thirteen?" asked Will, bewildered. He still remembered Drinkwater telling him he could help his Echo take the throne two and half weeks from now. On their thirteenth birthday.

"The bloodline is tainted," said the Prince.

"But then, why did he say…?" Will shook his head. "Drinkwater," he explained. "He made it sound like I could help you. Like all this—" Will dug his swollen fingers in his jutting hair "—All this *nightmare* could be over."

In his dark corner Auralius chuckled bitterly. "By all the flying crystal balls… My father… telling a lie…?"

"You're wrong, Auralius." The Prince's angry voice echoed through the dank, dark cell. "Talk to Drinkwater. Check your facts. You can always go back to hating your father, if you feel justified. But be crystally sure that you are, Auralius. Be sure!"

With his heavy head in his hands, Will stared at a column of ants making their way across the moldy, wet cobbles. But a cold tap on his shoulder made him glance up at his Echo again. From this angle, the shadow of the cobwebs made the Prince look wrinkled and weary, nothing like a twelve-year-old boy. But the Prince didn't break down in self-pity, thought Will.

Will sat up. "Sorry," he said.

"No, I'm sorry," said the Prince. "I know you didn't ask for any of this, Will. But I had to involve you. If I can just take the throne, I'd make sure nothing like this ever happens again. To you... or any other Sound," the Prince added, looking up at Peter.

"But you can't take the throne, can you?" said Will bitterly.

"I can! I will! After I clear my father's name."

"But how will you do that?" asked Peter, his eyes twinkling with curiosity, even his bruised one.

"It will be dangerous," admitted the Prince. "But it can be done."

"But...?" Will could read the hesitation in his Echo's face.

"But both an Echo and his Sound are needed. I can't do it without you, Will."

*   *   *

The Prince opened the shimmering silver pouch dangling from his neck and withdrew a folded parchment. Will caught sight of a black vial and a glowing ball that remained behind in the silver pouch. Both looked so beautiful that Will almost asked what they were, but he didn't want to be a busybody like his roommate, Brainy.

The Prince unfolded the crinkled parchment and handed it to Will, and with a regal gesture he invited Peter and Auralius to draw

250

nearer. But Auralius lingered in his dark corner, brooding. And Peter had already bent down, unable to contain his incorrigible curiosity.

Then, silently, Will and Peter read the letter, though Will took longer with his bleary, tired eyes.

To My Dear Son,

I have told you tales of a land where Echoes and Sounds live in harmony. This land is real. I have found the proof.

- *Map points to Lake of Eternal Ice as the Passage Well.*
- *Both an Echo and his Sound are needed to pass (?)*
- *Cold Fire Mushrooms grow in the field outside the city.*

That you are reading this letter, my dear son, proves that I failed to cross into Olám Shoné, despite my map. Learn from this that both an Echo and his Sound must enter together.

Your Loving Father,

The King

"Looks more like a *list* than a *letter*," said Peter suspiciously, as Will looked up from the faded parchment. "Handwriting's darker… here… and here." Peter tapped the top and bottom segments of the letter. "Like someone added those bits later…."

"You have the mind of a magician, Peter." The Prince smiled. "But this isn't a trick. That's my father's handwriting. And I saw in a Crystillery that the letter was written in his private chamber. By someone dressed in his robe. It had to be my father. No one else was ever allowed in there. And my father had the only key… The ink is faded in places because the letter probably got wet," added the Prince. "You can see how stiff the parchment is. Besides, my father mentions a map. I think I know which map he means. He used to keep a road map on his library desk. But it disappeared the night he died."

"How did you get this letter? My father?" asked Auralius from his dark corner, cutting off Peter's objection about the ink not bleeding on the page the way it should have, if the parchment really had gotten wet.

The Prince didn't seem to hear Peter. His melancholy brown eyes narrowed. And, seeing as the Prince's face was really a reflection of Will's, it wasn't hard for Will to guess that his Echo was getting annoyed. Though only his eyes showed it.

"Not your father," the Prince said sharply to Auralius. "Valerian gave me this letter. He found it in the library with my father's private papers."

Turning to Will and Peter again, the Prince explained.

252

"Valerian was Chief Royal Advisor when my father was King. He lost everything when my father was dishonored. Paid for his loyalty with all his lands, his home, everything he owned—and his left hand. My uncle, the false King, cut off Valerian's left hand himself. A mark of shame, he called it. Then he sent Fate Sealers after Valerian's only living family... his dead brother's wife and daughter."

For a moment, Will imagined the terror Valerie Valerian had felt that day, fleeing from the Fate Sealers only to be caught and dragged into Shadowpain. He wondered what happened to her mother....

"Drinkwater couldn't tell you about this letter," said the Prince to Will. "Drinkwater couldn't risk a Fate Sealer stopping you on your journey to the Orphanage... and reading your mind with a Crystillery. Don't be angry with Drinkwater. He only did what I asked. He always does."

The Prince smiled to himself and added, "Drinkwater was my royal tutor... until two years ago, when he came to teach at the Orphanage, because he thought Auralius will be happier here, mixing with Sounds and Echoes."

In his dark corner Auralius chuckled bitterly. But the Prince ignored him and went on with his explanation. Overhead the spiders stopped scurrying in their cobwebs, as if even they were listening.

"I can't clear my father's name without you, Will" said the Prince. "This letter proves it. My father tried to find the passage to Olám Shoné without *his* Sound..."

"Without my Dad," said Will.

The Prince nodded. "That's why my father failed. There's no other way. I have to ask you to come with me."

"But why do you want to go to this… Olám place?" asked Will.

"Because of the Cold Fire Mushrooms." The Prince tapped the parchment. "I'm sure that's what my father was after. These mushrooms glow, as if they are on fire. But it's the only fire that won't kill an Echo. And it's a perfect form of energy.

"Right now," explained the Prince, "all Echo energy comes from the Hydro-electric plant controlled by the Fortune Tellers at Mapál Anák. Without it, there would be no sky, no moon, no sun, no rain, no weather at all. Echoes have to create all these things, because we live underground. And there's also electricity used for lighting people's homes, plowing fields, healing the sick. For all this, we're dependent on the Fortune Tellers."

"And the Fortune Tellers want to keep it that way?" muttered Peter, twirling his tied chicken bone, making it appear and disappear.

"Yes."

"And when your father wanted to abolish the Law of Death, the Fortune Tellers stopped him?" guessed Will.

"By threatening to shut down the power plant," said the Prince, wiping his cheek from the drizzling, cobwebbed ceiling.

"So the King had to find another form of energy. But…" Will frowned thoughtfully, and felt his swollen forehead puffing over his eyebrows. "Why can't you use your father's letter to clear his name?"

"I wish it was that simple..." The Prince wiped another drop. "All Echoes know of Olám Shoné, but they don't believe it really exists. It's a legend, a bedtime story. If I revealed that my father went looking for a fairytale, everyone would think he was out of his mind. Insanity can run in the family... I could be insane too... They'd never let me take the throne."

Will glanced down at the King's letter again.

"And both an Echo and his Sound are needed to get through the passage to Olám Shoné?" he asked.

"Yes. But there's more," said the Prince. "I've spent the last three nights crisscrossing the Lake of Eternal Ice, searching. I couldn't find the passage. I think both an Echo and his Sound are needed to make the passage appear in the first place."

"Let me get this straight," Peter cut in, accidentally propelling his tied chicken bone into the spider webs, where it remained stuck. "You want the two of you to go to the lake and start searching together? And this with the false King desperate to kill you both? And with Fate Sealers everywhere? Worse ones out there than in here?"

Auralius chuckled dryly, leaning against the shadowy wall where the dark mildew had stopped stirring, as if the ants had gone back to sleep.

"You're as mad as your father was..." he muttered, forgetting to treat the Prince like a prince.

The Prince's eyes flashed. "Do you believe my father was

killed by the Spirits of the Lake?" he demanded

"I know it!" snarled Auralius.

Will and Peter exchanged baffled smiles.

"It's not a joke," said the Prince gravely. "Echoes really believe in them, the Spirits. So many stories... repeated over and over— no one bothers to ask for proof anymore."

"Fine, by Fortune!" Auralius slammed the hilt of his dagger into the wall. "Go to the Lake of Eternal Ice if you think I'm wrong."

The Prince seemed to notice the golden knife for the first time, and he rose stiffly from the filthy bed.

"Is this the dagger that killed—" The Prince paused and corrected himself. "—The dagger we *thought* killed you, Auralius? It would be interesting to see its Memory in a Crystillery.... The forged Memory, I mean... the one in which you die."

Auralius darted forward, an unmistakable flash of curiosity turning his eyes slightly see-through. The shadows of the still spiders lay like flies on Auralius' cheeks as the blond boy stopped before the Prince, towering a little over him.

"Of course, you'll need your father to teach you how to use a Crystillery," added the Prince.

"Or someone else," Auralius shot back.

"And you'll need one of these—"

The Prince withdrew a blue dome from one of his glistening white pockets. Auralius gasped. His hand shot forward greedily. But the Prince held the Crystillery back.

"Only if you take Will and me to the Lake of Eternal Ice...

tonight," said the Prince. "And bring us back safely. Then you can have this Crystillery."

"But the Fate Sealers." Peter drew closer.

"I know a safe way!" Auralius shoved Peter back, suddenly looking as eager as the Prince to reach the Lake of Eternal Ice.

"And you'd trust him—?" Peter glared at Auralius. "With your life? And Will's?"

"Tell you what…" said the Prince. "You stay here, Peter. Keep this safe—" The Prince handed his Crystillery to Peter. "If we're not back by morning, go to Drinkwater for help."

"And how do I know I can trust *him*?" Auralius glared at Peter. "I'm a Mongrel. He could have Fate Sealers waiting for me when I get back—"

"And you could tell them all about the Prince's Sound. And his best friend!" Peter shot back.

The Prince stepped between them. "You're wasting time. Do we have a deal?"

Auralius' breath quickened. "One more thing—"

Without warning he snatched the note with the map of the Orphanage from Peter's glistening pocket.

"Hey—"

"It's a map to *my* room!"

Auralius rushed off, disappearing in the darkness edging his cell.

"Secret passages—" Peter yelled to Will, and they darted forward.

But already the strange prisoner of this cell had opened a secret window only he knew about. The giant fireplace flickered on the other side, and through the dark silhouette of Auralius' head— which had suddenly turned as see-through as an Echo's—Will saw the map catching fire.

"Now we can go," said Auralius, closing the window again.

Returning to his old wooden bed, Auralius dragged it sideways. A horizontal crack appeared in the mildewed wall. Auralius pressed his dirty fingers to it, and instantly one giant stone began to slide forward, ants spilling over its top, cobwebs dangling in the dark opening growing behind it.

"Told you— I know a safe way," Auralius snarled at Peter.

Then the beautiful blond boy pulled on a pair of worn leather shoes, tucked the dagger in his frayed pants and wrapped himself in a tattered cape, which Will had mistaken for a filthy blanket on the bed.

"Follow me…" Auralius said to Will and the Prince, already wriggling into the secret passage.

"First sign of sunrise," Peter called after them, "and I'm getting help!"

The Prince Finds His Father

The Lake of Eternal Ice

Advancing on hands and knees, Will followed the rustle of Auralius' motions in the pitch darkness. The cold ceiling of the secret passage pressed on his back like a cold, giant hand. The rumble of distant thunders mingled with the thudding of his heart. Up ahead a greenish glow shone eerily, and when Will passed through it he saw that it was Waterweed, and he shoved some in his pocket. On they crawled like moles, until suddenly lightning flashed through a crack in the tunnel roof.

A skeletal, sagging hand reached through it.

"A branch— just a branch—" Will heard the Prince gasping at his back, before they crawled forward once more.

And then, at long last, the tunnel widened, and they climbed out into a chilly night.

They were in an icy dark forest rich with the scent of a fading storm. The giant moon was lost behind a filthy brew of inky clouds. A frosty wind stirred the dark branches all around them, showering them with shattered ice and wilted leaves. Silently, they followed Auralius' silhouette, seeing no Fate Sealers; though they ducked low each time a distant lightning bleached the night, threatening to bring back the rain.

After a while, a dim sparkle covered the land beyond the forest.

"The Spirits of the Lake, do you believe the trees will keep you safe from them?" the Prince asked Auralius.

The Mongrel nodded, though darting wild glances at the somber sky.

"Good." The Prince nodded too. "Hide in that rotting tree… over there— in case of Fate Sealers. And wait for us."

The Prince promised to return before sunrise, then he guided Will past the last of the trees into the open, where the wind blasted unimpeded, and the muted radiance of frozen ice spread far and wide.

"The Lake of Eternal Ice," said the Prince, as they began shuffling their feet over the slippery surface.

"It's huge," sighed Will, hugging himself against the bitter cold. Even the Prince was shivering in his short-sleeved Orphanage uniform, as he pointed left.

"Let's head there first. We'll walk back and forth, crisscrossing, the way I did before."

"There's something I want to ask you," said Will as they set off, hunched against the wind, their white clothes too lost in darkness to glisten. "My parents, when I left… I didn't leave them a note or anything. They won't know what happened to me."

"Don't worry," said the Prince. "I can send a message with

Flit... Drinkwater's carrier pigeon." Will remembered the white dove that lived inside a Sound. "I'll ask for a message back," added the Prince. "Make sure your parents are all right. Get down—"

Lightning flashed in the distance. They lay flat on their stomachs for fear of being seen by Fate Sealers lurking on the distant shore. The wind whipped over their heads; thunder rumbled far off. Soon lightning flashed again, closer now, and the lake was suddenly lit up.

Will gasped.

Only inches from his face, trapped under the veil of ice, was a scattered treasure of precious stones. Red rubies, blue sapphires, yellow diamonds—hundreds of them, all shaped like stars. The sight was more beautiful, more enchanting, than Will could ever have imagined. And, at once, he knew where the stones had come from.

"They're Crystillery stones," said Will, mesmerized, as they rose and walked on in a darkness that felt heavier still.

"Yes, from thousands of Crystilleries," said the Prince. "Shattered. Two hundred years ago."

"Shattered? Why?" A blast of wind hurled Will's sluggish words back into his mouth.

"Punishment—when the people revolted against the Law of Death. It began with the man who invented the Crystillery," explained the Prince. "Fluid Conway. A Sound with an Echo's nickname. He wasn't just a scientist. He was a businessman too. He convinced Echoes and Sounds to invest in his factory, so he could make thousands of Crystilleries. He knew that Crystilleries keep

263

happy memories alive," added the Prince, raising his voice to be heard over the shrieking wind. "And happy people fight back when Fortune Tellers come to kill them."

"So what happened? What happened with the Law of Death?"

"The King stopped the revolution. With his army of Fate Sealers and Fortune Tellers. Then he rounded up all the Crystilleries. And shattered them all over this lake."

The wind flicked Will's hair into his eyes, making them water as if he was crying. But it was too dark for the Prince to notice.

"So, how come the stones are *under* the ice?" Will shouted over the wind. There was no risk of Fate Sealers hearing him on the shore. Nothing could be heard for more than a few inches in such weather.

"Fluid Conway," the Prince shouted back. "The inventor of the Crystillery. The King was going to execute him. But Conway melted the lake— And disappeared into it. That's the legend, anyway. No one saw Conway do it. No one knows how it happened. But the next morning the lake looked like this. And it hasn't changed again, not for two hundred years."

Lightning flashed, quite close this time. As Will threw himself on his stomach, he nearly screamed. A face—a man's face— was staring back at him through the thick layer of ice, eyes wide and terrified.

"Thieves. Men who tried to steal the stones," said the Prince, rising stiffly. "Fortune Tellers throw them into the holes they melt. The Echoes think Fortune does it. They're left here, the thieves… as a warning to others."

"Then your father—?" Will realized.

"Yes— he's here, too. The greatest warning of all."

They walked on in silence, crisscrossing the frozen lake seven times before something suddenly loomed before them in the darkness: a glossy sphere, a giant crystal ball.

"My father's grave," said the Prince, his voice bitter. "And a cursed crystal ball to mark the spot."

The Prince threw himself on the lake and pressed his face to the ice. Above him the ball of smoky glass hovered like a strange cloud trapped inside a sphere.

Will bent beside his Echo, pulling out the Waterweed he collected in Auralius' tunnel. In the green, eerie glow, he felt the blood freezing in his veins. His father's face, eyes glassy and bloodshot, was looking back at him through the frozen lake, as through a window leading to the realm of the dead. A dark scarf encircled the frozen man's neck, monogrammed with the golden letter M. And only as Will realized that the *M* must stand for *Monarch* did his shock begin to fade, and he remembered that his father was still alive, back in the Sound realm.

Then silently, Will stepped back to give his Echo time to grieve alone.

*   *   *

It felt like hours later when the wind blasted their backs as

265

they turned and headed across the lake for the twenty-third time. The Prince had kept silent, his thoughts no doubt still with his disgraced father, but presently he spoke again.

"Thank you for taking the Royal Shekel from Drinkwater. He sent Flit with a message… to warn me."

They had been silent so long that for a moment Will thought the wind was playing tricks on him.

"What?" Will asked, wondering what to say if the Prince asks him about the coin.

"Valerian was desperate," continued the Prince, the wind sweeping his voice away. "His niece was in the hands of devils. We'll never know what would have happened… if he found the Royal Shekel on Drinkwater. Maybe Valerian would have rescued Valerie without giving up the Royal Shekel. But maybe not. It was good fortune that you took the coin in time."

"Drinkwater wasn't this understanding," said Will, his jaw so stiff from the cold he could barely speak.

"He can be gruff, I know." The Prince tucked his shirt in his pants, against the whipping wind. "But he'll do anything for the people he loves. My Father trusted Drinkwater more than all his advisors. That's why he left the Royal Shekel with him before he went to the lake."

So that was how Drinkwater got the coin, Will realized. How wrong Peter and he had been!

For a moment, the wind thrashed too loudly for speaking. Then the Prince added, "I want you to keep the Royal Shekel. Maybe give it to Peter… I know it's risky, but there's no one I can trust at the palace. Deá and Damian are in danger all ready."

"Danger?" repeated Will, as they rose from the ice after another lightning. "You mean… because they used to be Fortune Tellers?"

"They're wanted for High Treason— For turning their backs on Fortune. They're here tonight… waiting for me by the Orphanage gate."

"Here…?" Will's heart leapt faintly in his frozen chest.

On they walked, Will thinking of his childhood friends, wishing he could see them again. Turn succeeded turn, and still nothing but darkness and wind stretched before them. His feet frozen like blocks of ice, Will began to doubt that the passage would ever appear. But even if it did, and they went through it and returned with the Cold Fire Mushrooms—what then? Was the false King likely to surrender the throne without a fight?

"Not without a fight," agreed the Prince, when Will asked him. "But we'll clear my father's name by proving why he really went to the lake— to find the Mushrooms. Then Fortis Fortuna… he's the Leader of the Fortune Tellers… He'll place me on the throne. He has the power to do that."

"And the King will just… surrender?"

"*False* King," said the Prince bitterly, as they turned again and the wind gusted in their faces. "He'll have no choice. Without the backing of the Fortune Tellers, the false King will have to rely on the Fate Sealers to keep him in power. But the Fate Sealers sell their services to the *highest* bidder. And no one has more ice-gold than Fortis Fortuna."

"Then... couldn't this Fortis person become King?" Will wiped his stinging eyes on his sleeve.

The Prince chuckled bitterly. "He doesn't want to— Already, as the Leader of the Fortune Tellers... he has more power than any king ever had."

"And you're sssure the Fortune Tellers will help yyyou... us?" Will was starting to shiver.

Perhaps the cold was getting to the Prince as well, for he took a moment to answer. "In exchange for Fortis Fortuna's services— Deá and Damian will surrender and stand trial," he said finally.

Will stopped still. "They'll dddo wwwhat?"

"They won't be killed, Will," said the Prince quickly, urging Will to keep walking. "Fortune Tellers are never executed. Fortis Fortuna will never set such a dangerous precedent."

"But this is crrrazy," Will shot back, his insides stiffening as if the icy wind had finally succeeded in freezing him. He started walking again but his stiff legs felt like massive icicles that he could barely control.

"This is totally crrrazy," Will shouted again. "No wwway this Fortis Fffortuna will be happy to see Cold Fffire Mushrooms. Not when they'll ppput him out of bbbusiness. Remember? That's what it's all abbbout! Giving the Echoes another source of energy, so they wwwon't have to bbbow down to the Fortune Tellers anymore!"

"Yes… But I'll pretend I know nothing about what makes the mushrooms special," said the Prince earnestly. "Nothing about what the mushrooms can do. Fortis Fortuna thinks that I'm young… Stupid. A King he could control."

Will wanted to argue, to plead, to scream how unfair it all was! How Deá and Damian had *already* sacrificed ten years of their lives living inside animals! And shouldn't have to sacrifice anymore! But, at that moment, something strange happened.

A sphere of white light appeared beneath their feet, as if Will and the Prince had stepped on an invisible light switch.

Brighter and brighter grew the light under the ice, gems twinkling inside it like shooting stars. Deeper and deeper the light sunk, until the white glow illuminated a crystal blue round door that lay flat on the bottom of the lake. There beneath layers and layers of ice it lay, a door with two circles glittering at its center. The first was a mirror the size of someone's head. The second, glittering inside the first, seemed fashioned from a diamond the size of a small coin.

"The Passage…" gasped Will, collapsing on the ice, shock and illation draining all his strength at once.

"But it's not supposed to have a door," snarled the Prince, sinking to his knees also, his fists clenched. "Passage Wells never have doors…"

Will felt warmer by the light, as if sitting by a fire. "We could open it… just need to get rid of the ice somehow."

"Oh, I can melt the ice!" The Prince pulled a copper crossbow from his bulging pocket and slammed it down on the

269

shimmering lake. It was the same type of weapon Valerian had used to kill the Fate Sealer back in the Sound realm. As it had then, the arrow was melting the ice it was touching.

"The lock," said the Prince bitterly, pointing at the silver cavity inside the round mirror. "The door's locked."

"It's the same size..." muttered Will. And his heart pounding, he snapped the heel of his shoe open and pulled out the Royal Shekel. "Maybe it's a Coin Key..."

But the Prince shook his head at the ice-blue coin and its spiraling waves of strange letters. A Coin Key is unique," he said. "The one and only to fit the mirror image inside its matching lock. This lock is different. It's *blank*... It's blank, and I've never seen anything like it. I don't know how to open this door. But nice hiding place," added the Prince with a half-smile, as Will slipped the Royal Shekel back inside its secret compartment.

Slowly the Prince rose, pocketed his wet crossbow, taking care not to touch the arrow, and retreated one step—and, instantly, both the door and the glowing white light disappeared as if they had never been there at all.

Will and the Prince memorized the spot by its distance from the shore and hurried away, in case they had been spotted by Fate Sealers while the light had shone at their feet. The wind felt even more biting than before, the night darker than a grave. But suddenly a ray of hope flashed across Will's mind.

"Your father's letter," he said, seeing the faint presence of the silver pouch at the Prince's throat, where the parchment lay hidden. "Your father mentioned a map..."

The Prince shuffled silently on, too tired or too disappointed to speak.

"Maybe the map can show us how to unlock the door," Will insisted.

The Prince shook his head, or perhaps the wind was shaking it for him; Will couldn't be sure in the darkness. "Disappeared..." the Prince said dryly. "Remember? I haven't seen the map since my father died."

"But maybe there's another copy..."

"Yes... maybe..." the Prince answered after a moment. "My father divided his library in two, about fifteen years ago. He sent half his books to the Orphanage, just in case anything ever happened to the palace library."

"Then I'll sssearch the Orphanage lllibrary for another cccopy of the mmmap," shivered Will, the warmth the passage had spread through him now all gone.

"I'll search the palace library," agreed the Prince, and Will could hear renewed hope in his Echo's voice. "But you have to watch out for the eyes—"

"Eyes?"

"Abednego's Eyes. They're scattered through the Orphanage... hidden inside—"

"Crrrystal bbballs," said Will, "I've sssseen them—"And he started shivering uncontrollably, feeling too tired and too cold to fight his aching muscles anymore. "But they cccan't really sssee, can they?"

"They're surveillance cameras. That's how Abednego keeps watch on the Orphanage. But hardly anyone knows what the eyes can really do."

"Peter doesn't…" muttered Will.

"You'll have to be careful. The library especially is full of eyes. Abednego guards his books jealously. The eyes will blink open when they sense motion. If Abednego puts them on high alert, you'll start seeing them everywhere. You'll need a Blinker to shut them again."

"A wwwhat?" The wind now blasted into Will's right ear as he and the Prince veered toward the black mass of the shore.

"It's a gadget for putting the eyes to sleep. It confuses their motion detectors. I'll send you one by Carrier, my private one— Not a pigeon, a bat. You'll need this," added the Prince, pulling out a faintly glowing glass marble from his silver pouch. It was the beautiful ball Will had seen earlier.

"Take it—" The Prince handed the cold marble to Will. "It's my Pitch Beacon. A human ear can't hear its signal, but my bat can… from miles away. He'll find you. I'll send him with the Blinker as soon as I get back to the palace. Be careful until then."

"Thanks," said Will, trying to imagine what Peter would look like when he heard about Abednego's eyes.

Will was slipping the marble into the heel of his shoe, when the wind seemed to shriek suddenly.

"We did it!" The Prince glanced back at the frozen lake. "We found the passage. I can't believe it—"

"Did you hear that?" Will straightened nervously.

And in the next instant, the windswept night was torn by the unmistakable screeches of Fate Sealers.

*   *   *

"A mongrel! Grab him!"

On the shore, three Ice Looms had turned lustrous, and tall, sagging Fate Sealers were moving in the pearly haze. At first Will saw two, then a third. He glanced at the Prince, not sure what to do, and saw that his Echo was tossing his Orphanage uniform on the ice and turning invisible, as if someone was erasing the Prince out of a painting.

"Can't fight them with one Incendiary," the Prince whispered and shoved his small crossbow into Will's hand. "Just in case. But keep it in your pocket. If they spot you, tell the Fate Sealers something stupid. Buy time. I'll be back with Deá and Damian in ten minutes."

All that remained of the Prince now was the dim silver pouch dangling from his neck.

"Will you be—?"

"Yes, go!" whispered Will.

A Fate Sealer was rushing to the frozen shoreline, his glowing Ice Loom held high, lighting the darkness.

"Told you!" the creature screeched triumphantly. "Someone's there. *There!*"

And before Will could decide what to do, the Fate Sealer was

273

sweeping across the ice toward him like a speeding car. A second later, a sagging hand clamped on Will's shoulder.

"AAAAAARRRRRRRRRR!"

A scream erupted from Will's throat like searing lava. The touch, the mere touch of a Fate Sealer was agony. Acid and swords swirled together. The world zoomed and shook as the pain tore into Will's shoulder, and he felt himself dragged across the ice back to the shore.

Through bleary eyes, Will saw Auralius by the forest's edge, twisting in the grip of the other two Fate Sealers. The beautiful blond boy's face was contorted in agony. He was screaming his soul out. And pale blood was oozing everywhere through his torn shirt.

"Two little boys... alone in the forest at nigh..." screeched the Fate Sealer at Will's side, his voice shrieking like the wind. "How careless. Lost...? Or looking for something?"

Will felt himself dragged fiercely forward, legs flailing, feet kicking, every muscle spasming through his body as if he was being electrocuted. He knew if he didn't answer, the torture wouldn't stop. But his brain had melted. He couldn't think.

"AAAAAARRRRRRRRRR!"

An iceberg must have pierced Will's stomach. Vomit shot up his throat. "I... I'm an idiot," he spluttered, frantically trying to think. "An idiot... not just a pretty face."

All at once, the pain vanished.

Will collapsed on the frozen shore, coughing and drooling. Sagging lips swung before him to the sound of gasping laughter.

274

Will flinched to avoid their searing touch, and through the swinging, see-through lips he spotted a Fate Sealer preparing to slash Auralius' throat with the golden dagger.

"Leave him alone!" Will snarled, and rolled to his left, wrenching the copper crossbow from his pocket.

All three Fate Sealers squealed with amusement. But the one beside Will acted as well as laughed. Already his clammy, skeletal fingers were shredding Will's throat with their touch. Will's own hands felt like swords thrust into his chest, and every movement cut him like a knife. Any moment now Will would pass out from the pain. "I... I'm an idiot," he choked. But the joke had worn thin, and the Fate Sealer breathed his foul breath into Will's face, until Will felt his stomach lurching.

Suddenly, the pain vanished once more.

For a moment white spirals and shrieks were all that Will could see or hear. And then he realized that his hand had collapsed on the trigger of his crossbow, and the weapon had fired. The Fate Sealer was dying.

Will tugged the copper arrow free of the melting Fate Sealer curling over him into clouds of putrid stench. Quickly, Will rearmed his crossbow and, kicking a backwards escape, fired again, this time intentionally; while the cold sagging fingers of a second Fate Sealer were already folding over his Incendiary, pulling the weapon away.

This time, the copper arrow went through the Fate Sealer's palm. The creature's scream shattered ice off nearby trees, and the wind blew the shards at Will's face. Like an unraveling scarf the

Fate Sealer slipped out of existence at lightning speed, his sagging hand dissolving one moment, his hollow eyes the next, until all that remained for a flickering instant were his flailing feet, and then they too were gone, leaving behind the rotting stench of an incinerated Echo.

"You'll pay for this—" screeched the last Fate Sealer, dropping Auralius free.

Will looked around for the Incendiary arrow. This time it had lodged in a distant tree. Will started running, but cold numbness weighed him down, and pain... so much pain still flowed through his body like lava. He looked down and saw that his pants were coated in icy arrows... Ice Loom arrows. And another hail of arrows was flying through the air toward him.

Suddenly another shriek shook the night.

Will ducked instinctively, and the icy arrows zoomed over his head. He twisted back to see who was screaming, and there was Auralius, standing tall. Will could see him through the see-through body of the last Fate Sealer, as the creature sunk to the ground, writhing as he died, his glowing Ice Loom still spitting icy hail.

"Filthy monster," snarled Auralius, pulling his dagger free of the creature's cold heart.

"He didn't melt..." Will staggered to his feet, watching see-through white blood trickling from the golden blade.

"This isn't Heat Metal," said Auralius. He wiped the knife clean on the folds of gray flesh spread at his feet. "Too bad," he added, tucking the dagger back in his belt.

276

The wind whistled through the dark frozen branches of the forest behind the shore, as if the dead Fate Sealers had turned into ghosts and were hovering there. And suddenly, in the glow of the fallen Ice Looms, Will saw black specks begin to buzz like evil flies. More and more of them pulsed out of the night, until the shape of something too tall to be a man was towering at Auralius' back.

"Watch out—" screamed Will, rubbing his eyes in disbelief.

The next instant, a Fate Sealer had emerged entirely, one unlike any Will had seen before, for he was black from head to toe, and so misshapen that the skin of his cheeks reached down to his feet. And like a giant jellyfish, he folded over Auralius, swallowing him whole.

Almost blind with horror, Will twisted back and dashed for the arrow lodged in the tree.

But the arrow was gone.

Then a flash of purple streaked past Will.

"Not my son!" cried Drinkwater, bursting out of the icy forest to hurl himself at the billowing, black Fate Sealer.

Auralius fell limply on the frozen ground, unconscious or dead, Will couldn't tell. And, screaming with agony, the old man reached for his son, or maybe it was the golden dagger he was trying to get. But already the terrible monster fell over Drinkwater like a dark cloud.

"AAAAAARRRRRRRRRR!"

Drinkwater's scream of agony writhed on the wind, before the old man's eyes rolled back in their sockets, and he fell unconscious by his son's side.

Then, for a moment, an Ice Loom glinted between the sagging folds of the Fate Sealer's hand as he looked down at Drinkwater. But, in a moment, the creature seemed to change his mind, and he reached for the golden dagger instead.

"Nooooooooo!"

Will dashed forward, terror blinding him as he watched the Fate Sealer raise the dagger, then let it fall. The gold blade glinted in the eerie light of the fallen Ice Looms of the dead Fate Sealers. It rose into the air, then plunged into Drinkwater's chest— into the air again, then into Drinkwater's neck— into the air, then into the old man's stomach—

Then, suddenly, two arrows shot out of the forest, one white, one black.

The knife froze in midair, dripping dark blood. An instant later, it fell on the icy shore. And over it rose a howl like a raging tornado. The gruesome black Fate Sealer started melting into billowing dark smoke that poisoned the night with fumes so putrid, so foul, that Will's insides twisted in revolution. He vomited and choked, unable to catch his breath, the black ribbons of foul mist curling around his throat like fingers trying to squeeze the life out of him.

*   *   *

Peter was slapping Will's face.

"Stop, stop, STOP!" Will shouted, flinching back.

"Wake up, wake up, WAKE UP!" Peter shouted back.

"I'm awake— Stop hitting me—"

"Oh, sorry… You were in a trance or something. Shaking all over."

And then Will noticed Deá and Damian.

They were leaning over Drinkwater's motionless body, trickling a thin stream of crystallized water into his wounds from two glowing Ice Looms. The Prince was with them, wrapped in Damian's black cape, scowling and looking nearly invisible. Auralius was leaning on his shoulder, his face entirely see-through.

"This will slow the bleeding," said Damian, rising. "We must get him back to the Orphanage immediately."

Auralius insisted on carrying his father himself and led the procession, with Deá and Damian lighting the way with the glowing Ice Looms.

"What was that… thing?" muttered Peter at Will's side, as they followed the Echoes. He had taken the Incendiary from Will, after finding the copper arrow where the black Fate Sealer had died. Like Deá and Damian, Peter held the weapon armed and ready.

"A Fate Sealer… I think," said Will, his voice sounding normal, his bones telling him he was long overdue for his dose of painkiller.

"His name was Black Heart," said the Prince. "The only Fate Sealer who can turn invisible… as far as I know. He was my uncle's right hand man. He wouldn't be snooping outside the Orphanage, unless he suspected I was here. I'd better get back to the palace," added the Prince, nodding at Damian. "Yes, I'll be careful."

They reached the opening to Auralius' tunnel. Above them, branches shook ominously in the wind, raining down shards of ice.

"I'll be back on Christmas Eve," said the Prince, turning to Will. "We'll celebrate our birthdays together."

"Good luck looking for the map," said Will, trying to smile, though it hurt.

"You too." The Prince smiled back. And leaving Damian's cape behind, he disappeared.

But not right away, not if you looked closely.

For the first time Will took in what he saw: The faint sprinkling of light hovering on the air as the Prince slipped invisibly away. *The firefly dots by the great fireplace— the dark specks from the black Fate Sealer— and now the flecks of light from the Prince—*

"Look!" Will caught Peter's sleeve, to stop him slipping into the tunnel.

"What?" Peter squinted at the darkness past the light of the Ice Looms. "You mean those buzzing things over there? Flies or something?"

"Not flies, Peter," whispered Will. "Traces of an invisible Echo. That's the Prince."

"The Prince…?"

By the shock spreading over Peter's face, Will could see that his friend understood what this meant: Earlier that evening, outside the giant fireplace, they weren't seeing things, they weren't dreaming. An invisible Echo had shown them the way into Auralius' secret room. But who could it have been?

280

The Library

The Library

Will would never forget how Auralius looked when they got back to his dark, mildew-coated cell. Tufts of his blond hair were missing where the Fate Sealer pulled it by the roots. His torn shirt was soaked in pale blood, paler than a Sound's. And Auralius' beautiful features were full of grief and guilt. "He saved my life," he whispered, as he rested his unconscious father on the dirty bed beneath the ceiling of cobwebs. "I hated him... and he saved me."

Deá and Damian stayed to help, but Will and Peter rushed away to get back to their snowy beds before dawn. Even as Brainy was sticking his head through his glistening white canopy and muttering, "What's going on?" Will was already drifting into sleep, though still thinking about Auralius in his prison, his Mongrel eyes flashing on and off from solid to see-through, as if something inside him was trying to put out the light of his life.

It felt like minutes later, but the giant Echo sun was already high in the cloudy sky outside the corridor crystal ball window when Will woke up at last, to the sound of someone practicing asking questions before the dorm room mirror.

"By all the crystal balls! Awake at last!" declared Brainy triumphantly, spinning to face Will. His mouse, Alexander the Great, was knocked off Brainy's shoulder and landed head first in a shoe.

Will rubbed his sore eyes, then remembered his contact lenses and stopped, sitting up groggily. "What time is it?" he asked, his heavy voice as slow as a snail.

"Time to feed Poudini," Will heard Peter's voice, and looked up to find his friend's head dangling upside down from the fluffy top bunk, which was creaking and stretching oddly, as if someone was using it for a trampoline.

"Hold on! You've got some serious explaining to do," Brainy shouted after them, as Will and Peter jumped out of bed and slipped into the chilly corridor with Poudini in the lead. And for the first time, Will hardly coughed from the Air Seal, not after experiencing the blasting wind of the Lake of Eternal Ice.

It was Peter who first spotted the two sagging creatures waiting for them where the stone walls curved, their hollow eyes widening greedily. Will's heart froze in terror, memories of dying Fate Sealers swirling through his mind. *Did they know? Were they here for revenge?*

"Let's start with this morning," Brainy rushed after them, his glasses still askew from the Air Seal. "Where were you, by Fortune? And why—?"

"In the bathroom!" Peter rounded on Brainy fiercely. "Freddy had diarrhea. Next time, we'll save you the evidence. Now, go pester someone else, Brainy." And Peter blew a magician's hat in

Brainy's face.

The Fate Sealers should have been amused; it was their kind of humor. But they seemed petrified this morning, cast out of melted stone, unmoving like a tiger that freezes for a moment before it springs on its prey.

"In here—" whispered Peter nervously.

Will followed his friend into a balmy blue bathroom, where boys were whispering by the gleaming crystal ball sinks about dead Fate Sealers and a fight on the shore of the Lake of Eternal Ice. The walls behind them were overlaid with thin blue waterfalls, and overhead crystal ball chandeliers spread soft illumination.

"Thirteen dead— Fate Sealers, by Fortune!" shouted a thin Echo, from the Echo side of the bathroom.

"Professor Drinkwater's disappeared. And Professor Valerian," a Sound hollered back.

"Dead too… maybe," said a short Sound to his shorter friend.

"Who—? That Fingeldy weirdo?" Will heard another pair of boys ahead of him. "He knows something? You sure?"

"Ssshhhh… behind you."

"Let's get out of here," Will whispered to Peter, finishing spiking his flaming hair in the gleaming crystal ball mirror.

They slipped back into the chilly corridor. The Fate Sealers were there, leaning against two crystal ball windows, watching Will and Peter with hollow, spinning eyes. Suddenly they swept forward like moving lumps of cooled lava. But still, they did not pounce.

"If they wanted to get us, they would have by now,"

whispered Peter.

Will nodded, trying to ignore the glistening white Castaways retreating as he passed. More than ever, everyone was staring at Will wide-eyed and startled, hardly noticing Poudini skipping ahead of Will and Peter, sniffing for food.

"Never missed breakfast before." Peter pointed at his over-active pet. "Better feed that dog before we start searching for the King's—" But Peter broke off, suddenly staring up.

Will saw them too, the twin cold eyes watching them from the double O's in the crystal ball sign spelling Girl's WashrOOm.

"You sure— they're not just for show?" Peter whispered, and Will nodded.

Will had explained it all already, when he and Peter exchanged stories as they crawled back to the Orphanage in Auralius' dark tunnel. Peter learned about Abednego's Eyes, the door in the lake, and the King's map that might hold the secret to unlocking the passage. Will learned about Drinkwater. How the old man arrived in his son's room for the second time that night and saw the open tunnel. When Peter told him where Auralius had gone, Drinkwater rushed into the tunnel and Peter followed him. And so they arrived in the midst of the fight on the shore of the Lake of Eternal Ice, just in time to save Auralius from the dark Fate Sealer the Prince had called—

"Black Heart?" a girl was whispering beside Will. He listened tensely for more, but the conversation was sucked away by an Air Seal, as the group of Sounds spotted him and fled back into their dorm room, their ponytails whirling.

"They all know about last night..." Will whispered incredulously. "They know I had something to do—"

But Peter wasn't listening. "No, no, no, no..." He shook his head, staring down the crowded, bright corridor.

And there, parting the glistening white Castaways, Will expected to find more Fate Sealers closing in on him from the front. Instead he spotted a shimmering purple hat hovering beneath the crystal ball chandeliers like a flying saucer. And very soon the Castaways staring at Will with suspicion were suddenly snickering and giggling, as a strange man swept through the crowd like a shiny ship.

"Ah— There you are! My valiant friends!" he called to Will and Peter. And with a few gallant strides the strange man was before them, blocking the way forward with his bronzed arms akimbo and his thigh-high gleaming boots spread apart like a human archway.

If they were standing on the deck of a ship, Will would have sworn that the strange Sound was a pirate. After all, his shimmering black shirt and crimson pants ballooned like sails in a storm, and a sword, a dagger, and a pistol glittered wickedly from his silver belt. But the man had the face of a fairy prince: golden ringlets, startling blue eyes, and a thin mustache that curled into heart-shapes in the corners. Will had never seen anyone so beautiful... or so absurdly out of date, by about three hundred years.

"Cyrano de Bergerac," the swashbuckling Sound introduced himself in a theatrical voice, bowing graciously. He swept his voluminous hat off, and Poudini leapt after the peacock feather wafting over the shimmering brim.

"Errr… Fredrick Fingeldy," Will stammered back, to chuckles all around.

"Ah! A name to rival your hair, by Fortune! Neither common, hardly pretty." Cyrano patted Will's spikes gingerly as if petting a porcupine. "To each his own and so forth…"

"Not really a good time, Cyrano." Peter tried to pull Will away, though curious Castaways were closing in on them, making escape impossible; except a retreat to where the Fate Sealers where leaning against a crystal ball window, watching the proceedings with interest but still not pulling out their Ice Looms to attack.

"Surely five minutes will cost you little," Cyrano retorted magnificently, like an actor performing on a stage. "Think of the rewards! Think of the glory!" And he flourished his shimmering purple hat once more, withdrawing a lustrous crystal ball with a flaming eye burning inside it.

"Whoa…" Will jerked back.

"It's just a camera." Peter rolled his eyes in exasperation. "No… I didn't mean like Abednego's—"

"*Just* a… *camera?*" Cyrano twirled his heart-shaped mustache in outrage. "By all the flying crystal balls! Why, you might as well call a snowflake a puddle. No, no, no!" He cast his twinkling eyes on Will. "This is a Snap-A-Fortune. A reader of destinies. One click *here* and *now*—" the flames inside the eye of the camera flickered hypnotically "—and you will see yourself *anywhere* but here, and *anytime* but now. This is your chance to receive a message from Fortune. A riddle from your future. Five minutes of your time is all I ask in exchange for unraveling the mysteries of your fate."

"Sounds fascinating," said Peter impatiently.

A group of girls nodded fervently behind him as if they had never heard of sarcasm. Will was startled to spot Emmy among them, holding her white cat. Her face turned serious as their eyes met. Then she looked away, nodding inanely with the rest, as if everything that was about to happen here was nothing but a silly joke.

"Thing is—" Peter frowned up at Cyrano "—we can't think of any compliments today. So, we wouldn't really be able to tell you how *wonderful* you are. And you wouldn't want to tell our fortunes for free, would you?"

"Three minutes then…" Cyrano negotiated. "Use big words. Tell me I'm gorgeous, nonpareil, Fortune's Favorite…

"A god?" suggested a pretty Echo girl, her see-through cheeks glowing in what Will guessed was an Echo blush.

"Well…" Cyrano glanced around approvingly. "Where is this paragon of Fortunerific good taste? Ah… yes, my beauty. You and I shall meet again… But first—" he swiveled to face Will once more "—you are an enigma. I must read your Fortune! I must! At least once!"

And suddenly the flaming eye inside the camera blinked, making a clicking noise just like an old-fashioned camera, and a white square popped out at the top of the crystal ball.

289

"Hey…" Peter tried to snatch it. But Will pulled Peter back. If he understood correctly, if Cyrano could somehow tell his future… well, that could prove useful.

"Good news?" Will smiled politely as Cyrano snapped up the Fortune Photo.

But the heart-shaped mustache had already wilted on the strange man's face, and his blue eyes were wide with amazement.

"Indeed— a fateful omen!" Cyrano shook his beautiful head somberly, spreading flecks of dandruff… or was it frost? "Never before have I seen the likes of it. I am speechless!"

"You're never speechless!" It was Peter's turn to look amazed.

"What is it?" stammered Will, his insides somersaulting. Castaways all around were suddenly holding their breath. Even their pets fell quiet. Brainy appeared at Cyrano's elbow looking as if only his glasses were keeping his bulging eyes in their sockets. Emmy stopped nodding, and in her brown eyes Will saw fear.

"It's… *nothing*—" Cyrano's sapphire eyes narrowed ominously "—and, therefore… *everything*!" And with a single flourish, Cyrano laid the Fortune Photo in Will's swollen hand.

Will saw at once that *nothing* was indeed all there was to see, for there he was, a fat kid, slightly on the gray side of the spectrum, except on his head that looked like a bonfire—but *nothing* Will didn't already know, and *nothing* to do with revealing his future.

"You are here…" sighed Cyrano, tapping the photograph meaningfully. "Here, by Fortune— in this corridor! Here… and, therefore, *nowhere*. You *are*, so to speak… but you *aren't*."

Will could feel Peter tensing beside him. "You're supposed to be somewhere else— Like in a mansion… that would mean you'll be rich one day."

"Or in a crypt." Cyrano's golden eyebrows met in a frown. "At least then death would have been your future. But this… this means you have *no* future."

Shaking his head again, his golden ringlets raining frosty flecks, the strange man trudged off. The peacock feather dangled limply in his shimmering purple hat, and his glittering sword swung forlornly by his sparkling crimson hip.

With a shiver Will caught sight of the two Fate Sealers staring at him, their hollow eyes looking darker than ever. Though even now, they came no closer.

"Everyone has a future," Will heard Peter trying to sound reassuring. Behind him Emmy was nodding again, her eyes wide with worry.

"Not someone who doesn't exist." Brainy elbowed his way forward. "By Fortune, I *still* think—"

"Not necessarily!" someone cut Brainy off. And to Will's relief he saw Michael Silver emerging from the glistening crowd, his multicolored parrot squawking on his shoulder. "Thinking doesn't happen to you that much, Brainy," Michael added, straight-faced. "Most of the time your mouth gets in the way. Talking Echo rubbish."

"I resent that!"

"Excellent." Michael nodded, his long black curl swinging before his left eye. "Let's talk about it."

The diversion worked perfectly. Will and Peter snuck away down the spiraling stone staircase, Poudini skipping before them, sniffing the luminous crystal ball handrails for traces of food.

"Let's try to lose the Fate Sealers," said Will, already running.

He veered between glistening white Castaways, who jerked back nervously on seeing who was coming up behind them.

Peter looked worried about something else. "You shouldn't have done it," he panted, running beside Will, dodging the Castaways jumping out of his way. "You never know what Cyrano's going to say. He's not a Sound. He's an Echo—living in a Sound. For ages. He's supposed to be really ugly or something... like a midget... with scales and a frog face— That's why he lives in a gorgeous Sound."

Dogs skipped out of Will's path, but a raven got tangled in his spikes, and started pecking and pulling.

"Not worms!" Peter yelled and swatted the bird away.

"But an Echo can't live in a Sound forever," said Will, straightening and starting to run again.

He took two stairs at a time, ignoring the see-through faces grinning at him from the Echo side of the stairs, waiting to see the fat Sound stumble and fall head over heels.

"That's why Cyrano looked frozen today." Peter dashed beside Will, Poudini skipping to his left, barking happily. "That wasn't dandruff on his shoulders... Frost!" Peter nodded meaningfully and nearly missed a step. "Every few days Cyrano leaves his body in a freezer. Goes back to being an Echo. No one knows exactly where he disappears to. But there's a rumor about a troll living in the forest. —Finally..."

Peter sighed with relief, as the second floor landing appeared past the curving walls of the spiraling staircase. "Almost at the library."

Slowing down, Will glanced back to see if his Fate Sealer shadows were still out of sight. "Oh, not again," he grumbled.

"Good grief, he's persistent," said Peter

And soon Brainy was yelling down to them, panting for breath.

"Not so fast! Last night... you were trying to do something Fortunerific. That's it, isn't it? You were trying to win Valerian's medallion! Admit it— AAAAAARRRRRRRRRRR!"

Brainy screamed as a wave of drooping gray flesh billowed past him, knocking his mouse off his glistening shoulder. And then the two Fate Sealers were behind Will again, following him as he and Peter gave up running and split up on the second floor landing. Peter stayed behind to blow distracting hats in Brainy's face, while Will slipped away in the direction of the library, over the flagstones that looked like an ice rink today with an Echo girl painted in gold from head to toe ice-skating there like a statue come to life.

"See!" Brainy yelled after Will. "You're not the only one trying to win Valerian's Medallion."

But Will stepped under an arch of books carved from ice, and Brainy's voice was drowned by the crystal ball fountain splashing on the library's doorstep. The two Fate Sealers slipped after Will like evil shadows, and the pale, almost invisible eye swimming inside the fountain blinked open to watch them pass.

*　　*　　*

The library was a majestic place, so white and so bright that crystal ball sunglasses were provided at the entrance by an Ice Fairy that flew down to meet each visitor, though she was only a statue. Will accepted a pair from her frozen moving hand, then watched the luster of the gleaming white walls dim to a bearable shimmer as he put his sunglasses on.

Overhead the lofty ceiling drifted like a cloud. And all around, circular bookcases rose like stalagmites of frozen blue ice. Castaways circled around the towering round shelves on moving, glass ladders, everyone wearing crystal ball sunglasses. The sight of all those crystal balls with all those living eyes behind them sent a shudder down Will's spine.

He glanced back. His evil shadows were still there, wearing especially large sunglasses now and flicking their black tongues out of their sagging gray mouths, as if hunting for his scent.

Will hurried on, along the weave of crystal balls edging the snow-white carpet. Everywhere he looked he saw books. Hundreds. Thousands. And his heart sunk as he wondered how many days, weeks, months it would take him and Peter to search for the King's map, which might not even be here.

294

And worse, Will suddenly realized. How stupid of him! He never asked the Prince what the map looked like. Maybe he was walking past it this very second without even knowing it. Will sighed inwardly, remembering what Abednego said about the library during the Winter Break Breakfast Feast.

Over a million books.

And suddenly the flaming hairs on the back of Will's neck stood on end.

Brainy had asked about the oldest book, and Abednego answered: *I guess you could say it is—*

"A ROAD MAP!" In his excitement, Will had shouted.

An eye blinked open in a crystal ball floor lamp to Will's right. A few feet behind it, the Fate Sealers stiffened and took off their sunglasses, the darkness in their hollow eyes spinning like whirlpools. Glistening Castaways frowned down on Will from their glittering glass ladders, and an Echo librarian snapped her see-through finger at an enormous, icy plaque declaring in gilded letters that *Silence Is Crystal.*

Will sunk into one of hundreds of glistening white armchairs scattered through the sparkling hall and tried to make himself invisible; though he knew that his hair must stand out like a lighthouse in a storm. He had to remember! Abednego had described the ancient road map. Yes... the words were coming back to him...

A dome-shaped book, with a cover of red leather. Or was it blue? The spine was a different color. Maybe that was blue? And there were gold letters on the front.

The three colors fluttered through Will's mind like fireflies.

Red.

Blue.

Gold.

And then, all at once, Will realized what they meant.

"I'm back!"

A magician's hat floated into Will's face, Peter grinning behind it, wearing crystal ball sunglasses. His glistening white sweater bulged in the middle as if Peter had put on twenty pounds in the last ten minutes. And Poudini was jumping between Peter's legs, as if consciously trying to trip him.

"Have something to tell you," whispered Will urgently. But suddenly he noticed an eye watching them from a crystal ball bookend.

"Not here—" Peter glanced at two girls glistening in snow-heap armchairs, watching them curiously.

Will and Peter found an ideal spot behind a corner bookcase. No one could see them from nearby ladders or armchairs, not even the sharp-eyed librarian. And no crystal balls of any kind were overlooking them. It was even dim enough in the shadow of the icy pillar to take off their sunglasses. But the two Fate Sealers were still there, loitering by a splashing blue fountain, chuckling to see Peter deflate his new stomach by pulling out sandwiches and drinks from under his sweater.

"Will they hear us?" Will whispered warily, biting into his hamburger.

"Nah." Peter tossed Poudini a hotdog. "They're actually a little deaf, Fate Sealers."

"Good." Will took another bite. "I just realized something about Abednego." Crumbs flew out of Will's mouth from talking in whispers, as he reminded Peter of the Headmaster's oldest book: the ancient road map. "The book's dome-shaped," Will concluded. "And it has three colors: Red, blue and yellow. Just like—"

"Crystillery stones!" Peter gasped, spitting bits of bun as well.

"A ruby, a sapphire and a yellow diamond." Will nodded then glanced back to check on the Fate Sealers. One of them was flicking his black tongue indolently. The other was yawning. Neither showed signs of overhearing an interesting conversation. "Could they be faking it?" Will wondered.

"Too stupid for that." Peter tossed Poudini another hotdog. "Except Wither Heart. He's seriously dangerous. Anyway… so Abednego's map looks like a Crystillery, so what?"

"A Sound called Fluid Conway invented the Crystillery," whispered Will, and he repeated the Prince's tale of last night. When he reached the part where Fluid Conway's Crystilleries were shattered, Will added, "That was two hundred years ago. The King was going to execute Fluid Conway. So Fluid Conway just disappeared. In the Lake of Eternal Ice."

"You think he found the passage?" Peter swallowed hard.

"Maybe… and figured out how to unlock the door."

Peter frowned thoughtfully and tossed Poudini his third

297

hotdog. It fell on the carpet, and for a moment a dark, greasy stain remained behind as Poudini chewed up the evidence. But then the smudge simply disappeared, as if wiped by an invisible eraser, and once again the carpet looked as white as freshly fallen snow.

"Auralius needs something like that," said Peter, distracted for a moment. "I've never seen clothes that filthy."

"No wonder, considering…" The memory of Auralius' cell, its damp darkness and crawling insects, made Will shudder. "To be trapped in there all the time." He shook his head.

"Like being buried alive," said Peter.

"Yeah…"

They tossed the rest of their food to Poudini and watched the carpet clean itself again.

"Our clothes do the same thing," Will realized, absently wiping his knee. "No marks from Auralius' tunnel."

"You need another painkiller." Peter handed Will an icy bottle. "You're starting to sound normal. Go on, it's blueberry soda… should be."

"Should be?" Will studied the cool blue water suspiciously. But he was beginning to feel pain everywhere, so he turned his back to the Fate Sealers and swallowed the pill he pulled out of his pocket.

"From the crystal ball fountain outside the library." Peter took a swig from a second bottle. "Only one fountain there. Keeps me from getting confused. Of course, sometimes the Echoes change the flavors around. Last month— Thanksgiving… Turkey Frappe.

Don't ask." Peter rolled his eyes. His bruised one was almost looking normal again.

Will leaned back against the translucent aquamarine bookcase, thinking. "Abednego's ancient map is shaped like a Crystillery, right? The book's dome shaped. Fluid Conway invented the Crystillery. And he disappeared in the Lake of Eternal Ice. What if there's a connection? What if Fluid Conway sent back a map?"

"Like to friends he left behind?" Peter's lips parted in amazement, the lower one finally looking like a lip again. "Are you saying—?"

"How many of them can there be?" Will's gray cheeks ballooned under his eyes in a grin.

"You think… they're the same? The ancient road map Abednego was talking about—"

"Is the map the King was talking about!" Will nodded eagerly, feeling his spiky hair tingling with excitement. "It's the map to Olám Shoné, Peter. Has to be. And it's here somewhere."

*   *   *

The august white library had seven floors, and seven shallow stone wells at the entrance displayed a three-dimensional map of each floor. Will and Peter bent their heads over the rippling surfaces, examining the miniature replicas of icy pillars with silvery names drifting over them.

"Sixth floor's our best bet for finding a map," concluded Peter, grinning like a pirate on the scent of treasure. And he led the way up a glistening glass staircase, Poudini skipping happily in the lead.

Soon they alighted into a pillared space that looked just as gleaming and white as the one they had left below. Here and there Castaways in their glistening uniforms and crystal ball sunglasses looked up from their books as Will and Peter passed. Their startled expressions darted from Will to his evil shadows, who were gliding on behind him, silent and ominous, not letting him out of their hollow sight.

"What are we going to do about them?" Will muttered in frustration, as Peter led the way across a floating walkway that seemed made of frozen snow. Below Castaways on the fifth floor were weaving between the icy blue bookcases like walking snowmen.

Peter's eyebrows flicked up mischievously. "Magic, what else?" he said, grinning.

With one swift motion, Peter pulled a tied chicken bone out of each of Will's ears and tossed one over the rail of icicles to his right, the other to his left.

"What was that—?" shrieked the Fate Sealers.

In a blur of flapping skin, the ghastly creatures swept forward.

"You'll never ffffind them," stammered Peter, his grin suddenly reduced to quivering lips. Poudini, on the other hand, growled fiercely, bounced a lot and nearly tripped Peter.

"Oh, yes we will!" The first Fate Sealer took up the challenge, already gathering his sagging stomach and climbing the

300

glittering rail of icicles so he could jump below.

But the second Fate Sealer stopped still, inches from Will, his legs rippling like a swamp over Will's feet. And Will flinched back, a stab of searing pain penetrating even through his glistening white shoes.

"Himmmm!" The Fate Sealer hissed, his features swinging over Will.

For the first time Will saw something solid floating in the creature's hollow eyes: A black oval-shaped pupil thrashing about like a deep-sea monster getting ready for the kill.

"Only himmmm!" the hiss went on. "Nothing but himmmm! Let him out of our sight again— and Wither Heart will have two more Fate Sealer heads to mount over his fireplace."

A second later, Will realized that he could breathe again.

The hypnotic pupils were drawing back. The Fate Sealers were retreating, turning into his shadows again, waiting to follow him everywhere he went.

"If only *we* could turn invisible…" Will muttered, letting Peter pull him away.

"At least we know they can't." Peter picked Poudini up, to stop him barking like a crazy dog. "The Prince said only Black Heart could."

Will spotted a sinister eye in the chandelier above them, circling around in its sphere to keep them in sight.

"How far's the palace from here?" Will whispered, thinking about the Pitch Beacon the Prince had given him, which even now was emitting its silent signal in the secret compartment of his shoe.

"Just a few hours, I think." Peter gulped nervously, following the movement of the eye above them.

"Hope we get the Blinker soon."

"Yeah."

Peter gestured at a silver ring glittering halfway up the icy blue column to their right. "*Cartography*," he read the words etched on it. "We're here."

Silently, they began their search.

The Fate Sealers smeared themselves into glistening, snowy armchairs, yawning a lot, though not daring to close their hollow eyes. Poudini fell asleep on the snow-white carpet, which lapped over the little dog's front paws as if trying to clean them away. Craning his neck beside Peter to scan the books within eyesight, Will contemplated what he should do when they found the King's map. Between the Fate Sealers and Abednego's eyes, there was little chance Will could sneak anything unseen out of the brightly lit library....

His neck was getting sore. One hour elapsed. Every book was a disappointment.

"Let's try with the ladder," suggested Peter, sighing.

They took turns gliding with the glistening glass ladder around the higher shelves, until two more hours elapsed, the highlight of which came when Will mistook a globe-shaped book for a dome-shaped one, but quickly realized his mistake.

"Have to look somewhere else," Peter muttered, as he

climbed down for the last time, his crystal ball sunglasses sliding off his nose.

The Fate Sealers swept behind them as they headed down the spiraling glass staircase again.

"Invisible Fate Sealers," said Peter suddenly, Poudini snoring in his arms.

"What—?" Will looked down nervously at the glittering hall spread below them.

"Black Heart... The Prince didn't actually know for sure, did he? About him being the only invisible Fate Sealer. Remember what he said?"

And suddenly Will did remember, with chilling clarity. *"As far as I know,"* he repeated the Prince's tentative words.

"Exactly."

"Echoes are never totally invisible, though," said Will, when they alighted on the first floor.

They followed the weave of crystal balls in the snow-white carpet, all the way to the glittering Map Wells at the entrance.

"Dots of light—" Peter nodded thoughtfully "—like the Prince last night."

"And outside the secret passage to Auralius' room."

Peter leaned over a stone well to study its rippling content. "Who do you think that was?"

"Valerian can turn invisible..." Will scanned the crystal ball lanterns illuminating the stone wells, but he could see no spying eyes inside them.

"Yeah... But if Valerian was planning to sneak around, he wouldn't let everybody know he could, would he? Besides, he always smells like his pipe... even when he isn't smoking. Okay—" Peter dipped his finger in the wet map "—second floor."

"Anyway," Peter added, as they climbed the glistening glass staircase again, the Fate Sealers creeping behind them, "Brainy says he saw Abednego turning invisible after the Winter Break Breakfast feast. Then again— Brainy sees conspiracy theories everywhere."

"Yeah," Will muttered softly, "like thinking I'm the Prince's Sound."

They expanded their search into the gleaming section labeled *Echo Geography*. Here they discovered that Agám Kaffú wasn't the only Echo land. Each book title disclosed more locations on the earth with Echo lands underground: Shélleg under Greenland, Kárr under Iceland, and more lands with terribly long names under Norway, Sweden, Finland and Siberia. Finally Antarctic Echoes spoke of a land called Daróm Kaffú under the South Pole. The hours crawled slowly by, but nowhere did they find Olám Shoné mentioned, and the smooth-edged, shiny covers of the books all seemed too new to hold an ancient road map.

"Perhaps under *Echo History*," suggested Peter wearily, Poudini yawning by his glistening shoe.

But at that moment the sound of wind chimes filled the sparkling hall, announcing the closing of the library. Will and Peter returned their crystal ball sunglasses to the flying Ice Fairy and joined the many Castaways streaming past the blueberry-flavored

304

fountain into the stone corridor, where the snowy garden could be seen glittering in the sunset outside the crystal ball windows. The giant Christmas tree rose high over the garden, not yet decorated, though Valerian must have kept his word about placing his medallion on the top, for something was twinkling there like a star.

And very soon Will and Peter were climbing down the spiraling, seashell stairway to dinner, the two Fate Sealers keeping close behind them.

*   *   *

The strings of lustrous crystal balls in the chandelier outside the dining hall still spelled the holiday greeting: *Merry Christmas*. Beneath their glow, a great icy poster now hung between the Sound and Echo entrances, carved with delicate golden words that seemed to promise wonderful things, though a Fate Sealer was blocking the view, spray-painting ugly black letters over the golden ones.

"Oh, no…" sighed Peter, as he and Will left the spiraling staircase.

Castaways broke into angry chatter all around. Poudini sprinted off down the stone corridor, disappearing in a sea of legs and paws.

"What's going on?" wondered Will, accidentally stepping on the tail of an Echo cat, which hissed at him and darted off.

"I don't believe it! They've just gone and cancelled the Veiled Village Trip." Peter's face was turning red. "It's supposed to be amazing. Leave the Orphanage— go see the Christmas Fair— the *famous* Christmas Fair at the Veiled Village."

"Not tomorrow, we won't," said someone dryly.

Will turned and found Michael Silver staring at him intently, his left eye half hidden as always by his long black curl.

"Last night…" Michael added softly, spotting the two Fate Sealers lurking behind Will, looking like two hideous rocks jutting from the river of Castaways. "…Strange things happened… when you were in the bathroom, Freddy. How's your stomach, by the way?"

"Better…" said Will guardedly. He caught sight of Evan and Brainy rushing in from the snowy garden with so many other glistening Sounds and Echoes, as twilight fell past the crystal ball windows.

"Treacherous things, toilets." Michael's dark face looked somber. "Let me know if you ever need help… flushing." And he signaled for his colorful parrot to land on his glistening shoulder and sauntered off.

Evan stopped beside Peter, who was still staring at the gleaming, icy poster, heartbroken.

"Don't worry—" Evan shook one of his frogs in Peter's face "—only the first day's cancelled."

"For now, by Fortune's Fate!" Brainy pushed between them. "And Alexander was really looking forward to it!" he added sourly, adjusting a tiny top hat on his mouse's head.

"Didn't know you could speak mouse, Brainy," said Evan, sounding genuinely surprised.

"Speak mouse…?" Brainy stared at Evan, dumbfounded.

306

"Oh, forget it."

"Was that mouse wearing a tuxedo?" asked Will, relieved to see Brainy stomping off.

"Brainy's brilliant idea for winning Valerian's medallion." Evan grinned.

Up ahead, the Fate Sealer finished defacing the beautiful icy poster with ugly black graffiti, and someone started clapping in appreciation. Will looked past the glistening Castaways streaming with him and Peter toward the glittering doorways of the sparkling dining hall. And there, leaning against the crystal ball windows, was Rufus Warloch, the Keeper of Pets and Keys. He was still applauding with a pair of leather gauntlets, which must have had metallic palms, for his claps resounded eerily through the chilly stone corridor, despite the chatter of voices all around.

"Gives me the creeps," muttered Peter.

Indeed, there was something deeply malicious in Warloch's furrowed, grimy face. A cross between a hyena and rat. Will thought of Wolfeá and how this Echo, whose job it was to care for unadopted pets, had starved and tortured her. And anger bubbled in Will's chest.

But only for an instant.

For, in the next, cold fear washed over him.

"*Someone...* left the Orphanage last night," Will heard a familiar, chilling voice, and realized that Wither Heart had joined Warloch.

The Fate Sealer spoke too loudly for a private conversation,

307

clearly wishing to be overheard by everyone. Castaways fell quiet, their hands silencing their pets. The light of the crystal ball chandeliers seemed to grow brighter, and in one or two Will spotted a pale eye blinking open.

"A murderer!" concurred Warloch, ceasing his clapping to lean on his long rifle. "How many Fate Sealers killed?"

"Four." Wither Heart punched the air to his left to frighten a passing Echo girl, who screamed and fled. The raven perched on Wither Heart's sagging shoulder cackled wickedly and flew after her. "Four dead Fate Sealers. And Valerian… if he's dead too."

"What about Drinkwater? Vanished and dead can mean the same thing." Warloch snorted, his two gold teeth glinting wickedly through his lucent purple lips. "You think the demented fool cracked finally? Went on a killing spree?"

"And got himself killed in the bargain?" Wither Heart chuckled; it sounded like someone gasping for air. "A tempting version of events. But one old man… killing four Fate Sealers? I hardly think so. And with Valerian disappearing at the same time…."

"Strange…" The Keeper nodded thoughtfully.

"Very! Which leads me back to my original conclusion. Ssssomeone left the Orphanage last night."

And suddenly Wither Heart was scanning the sea of frightened faces staring at him, until he found what he was seeking and locked his hollow eyes on Will.

"Four Fate Sealers— murdered!" he rasped, his mouth

twisting in hate. "The first three... oh, well." Wither Heart waved his sagging hand dismissively. "It happens. But Black Heart! BLACK HEART! I'll find who murdered... *my brother*. And I'll kill him. So slowly that time will lose all meaning. It could take a year for my brother's murderer to die, or ten, or twenty... Maybe I'll turn him into a Fate Sealer before I finish him off."

"Something to look forward to." The Keeper's evil laugh rippled through the hushed corridor.

An avalanche of fear shuddered down Will's spine. Beside him, Peter's face was ashen.

"Black Heart was Wither Heart's brother," Peter choked out.

Luckily, Sounds all around started buffeting Will and Peter into the dining hall, as everyone tried to escape into the safety of the sparkling hall.

"What if it runs in the family, turning invisible?" whispered Will. "What if Wither Heart can do it too?"

Will's heart felt like a caged beast pounding against his chest. He could feel his skin tingling as if something evil was creeping over him. He twisted back in a panic. But Wither Heart was still out in the stone corridor, not in the least invisible, watching Will over the jostling stream of glistening Castaways; as were the other two Fate Sealers, Will's constant, evil shadows. In a moment the two creatures slipped into the hall and positioned themselves by the icy Sound door, beneath the arch of blue water splashing from fountain to fountain across the liquid ceiling.

If Wither Heart knows who I am, Will thought desperately. If he knows what happened…

But a shrill shriek tore the thought from Will's mind.

At the center of the glittering, curved hall, Valerie Valerian was climbing on the empty, middle table. Dark circles still engulfed her blue eyes as if trying to drown them out. She looked as pale and see-through as the fairies fluttering their icy wings above her, blowing Flavor Bubbles. But Valerie's wild, cropped hair was more like a fawn's than a fairy's.

"Fortune will punish you!" Valerie shrieked, as three large Echo boys climbed up on the glistening table after her, a see-through Doberman growling at their heels.

"Bog!" Peter snarled at Will's side, swiping a bubble out of his face.

"And the Drops Duo. Come on!" Will shot forward, forgetting his own troubles.

Within seconds they were bounding on the glistening table, ramming one Drops brother each, ignoring the evil hissing from the snakes curled around the Echoes' necks. The Doberman shot after Poudini, and from the corner of his eye Will saw the dogs disappearing under the Sound table, where Castaways were climbing on the gleaming benches, slapping Flavor Bubbles away to better see what was happening.

"Fortune will punish you!" Valerie shrieked again, frozen teardrops rolling down her see-through cheeks.

"Leave her alone!" Will snarled, trying to shelter Valerie behind him. Until he realized that her frail arm was trapped.

310

"The ring! I want your ring!" Bog Slippery twisted Valerie's wrist.

For one short moment, the Drops brothers burst out laughing, before Peter rammed the one with the tattooed forehead, and this time the huge boy lost his balance and tumbled off the bench, taking his brother with him like two oversized dominos.

"Your ring!" Bog tugged Valerie so hard her small, see-through shoes came off the table.

She screamed even louder, a bubble bursting before her face.

Then, suddenly, she was a wild animal. Her hand clawed at Bog's bulging eyes, over and over, as if she wanted to shred his skin, tear out his eyeballs, gouge her way into his brain.

"Tried to blind me— Tried to blind me—" hollered the Echo, flinching back.

His beefy fingers dabbed at the white liquid trickling from his eyelid. The Drops brothers peeled themselves off the gleaming floor, cracking their knuckles.

"Fortune's fire—get her!" Bog snarled the sign for them to attack.

And then, suddenly, a fierce cry cut the air in the gleaming hall, not another scream from Valerie, but a reedy voice twittering, "Out of my way! Out of my way! By all the flying crystal balls— GET OUT OF MY WAY!"

Like an enraged canary Nurse Flight fluttered up on the table, her red hair flickering like flames, her thin arms already shoving Bog and his friends back to the floor.

311

"Attacking Professor Valerian's ward?" she twittered. "Are you out of your minds? Hospital Duty! All three of you! Tomorrow morning! Seven sharp! Now, get out of my sight!"

Comically, the overgrown Echoes obeyed the little woman. Still glaring and sneering at Will, Valerie and Peter, Bog ran his fat finger across his see-through throat. Then he whistled to his Doberman and walked away with the Drops brothers, whose pets were once again hissing around their necks like a punctured tire.

"My poor little thing..." Nurse Flight hugged Valerie, though still eyeing Will and Peter sharply. "These two were trying to help, I assume?" she asked. But Valerie was absorbed in twirling her beautiful sapphire ring inches before her see-through face, as if she didn't quite believe it was still there, and Nurse Flight seemed to make up her own mind on the subject.

"Well done, boys!" She smiled. Then, leaning very close to Will, she added, "I don't believe rumors as a rule. But do you know anything... about Victor... Professor Valerian, I mean? He's gone— No note, no message. Vanished, by Fortune! Drinkwater too. Do you know anything? Anything at all? No..." Nurse Flight looked crestfallen at Will and Peter's blank expressions. "Well, never mind, my dears."

The little woman turned to Valerie again and coaxed her off the table, muttering soothingly, though shaking her spiky red head sadly.

Will looked at Peter in wonder.

"Valerian's disappeared..." he said thoughtfully. Poudini

312

was back by his leg, exploding Flavor Bubbles with his nose. "Do you think he was with us... last night... invisible? Maybe something happened to him?"

"Then he'd turn visible again, wouldn't he... if he died or something. Savage," Peter added, watching Valerie go. "Nearly took his eye out."

"Bog? He had it coming, didn't he?" said Will.

"Yeah." Peter massaged his ramming shoulder. "All three idiots did! But remind me never to get on her bad side. Especially if it runs in the family..."

"What?"

"Turning invisible."

Valerie Valerian

The Mapless Road Map

The first thing Will noticed the next day was that someone had looked through his things in the night and stolen the gravestone book. His roommates were still sleeping, and he and Peter quickly searched everywhere, especially around Brainy, whose mouse was sleeping in an icy cage on Brainy's pillow, still dressed in a tuxedo. But the book was definitely gone.

"Good morning," Will shot a sarcastic greeting at the Fate Sealers waiting for him in the chilly crystal-ball-windowed corridor. He wondered if one of them was the thief.

"And a foul morning to you too, Vomit Face," one of them croaked, as the Fate Sealers fell into step behind Will, flicking their shriveled black tongues at Poudini, which only made the little dog growl at them more.

"At least they're talking to us today," mumbled Peter sarcastically, magicking a snack out of his nostril to comfort his little dog.

"Lucky us." And after a while something else occurred to Will. "At least you tore out the Fingeldy page!"

They stepped out into the glittering snowy garden, where the sunrise was painting the snow pink. Here and there glistening Castaways were walking their pets between the see-through trees and icy topiaries, their voices lost in the splash of the blue fountains. Valerie was flying her albatross in the cotton candy sky like a fairy riding a white kite, and even from this distance Will could see her sparkling sapphire ring.

On the far side of the wintry garden, Abednego's horses were galloping free, their fake horns looking like real unicorn horns. And by the giant Christmas tree with Valerian's medallion glittering at its top, Rufus Warloch was opening boxes of Christmas ornaments, his rifle slung over his shoulder, the rusty spurs on his heels hissing each time he kicked a lid off.

"Hey there, Filth," he growled, the moment he caught sight of Will. "Keep your wolf tied up, you hear? One more scratch on my fence, and I'll have her shot."

"You stay away from her," snarled Will, but his moronic voice made it sound as if he was snoring.

"Maybe I will... and maybe I won't." The Keeper cackled to himself and returned to beheading the Christmas boxes, his gold teeth twinkling like two demon's eyes in his mouth.

"He's evil, that one," hissed Peter, rushing away with Will.

They found Wolfeá wagging her tail under her tree, leaping up to greet them.

"Here—" Will spread a napkinful of chicken wings before his wolf, and Poudini quickly stole one for himself.

"We should stay with her," Will said bitterly, loosening the knotted rope around his pet's stomach, which didn't seem so hollow anymore.

"Can't... Have to look for the King's map, remember?" Peter walked over to the tree, to double the knot there, just in case.

Will shook his head, wishing he could set Wolfeá free. The sparkling white garden with its splashing blue fountains spread before his wolf, and the frosty forest sprawled at her back. But both were out-of-bounds. Wolfeá was a prisoner, and there was nothing Will could do about it.

"We'll think of something," promised Peter, as they left to have their own breakfast.

But Peter was soon distracted by events in the dining hall, where two Echoes were contending for Valerian's medallion in a most amazing way; though Valerian himself was not there to see them surfing the arches of blue water crisscrossing the ceiling, splashing people below as their surfboards cut through the waves, appearing and disappearing behind the flying Ice Fairies and the rain of Flavor Bubbles. Brainy was wringing his mouse like a wet towel when Will pulled Peter away, to head for the library and another boring day of searching. Even the two Fate Sealers dripped a little as they swept behind Will and Peter.

"The sooner we find the King's map, the sooner we can get back to Wolfeá," said Will at the entrance to the library. He bent to drink from the blueberry-flavored fountain and swallowed a painkiller. The eye inside the fountain blinked open to watch him.

"Right," agreed Peter. He pushed a pair of crystal ball sunglasses up his nose, trying to wipe the smile off his face, but already something wonderful was distracting Peter again.

And not just him, Will realized, for Cyrano de Bergerac was standing by the rippling Map Wells, his preposterous hat pushed far back as if he was trying to get a better look at something. Even his fortune-telling camera was rolling by his shiny boots, as if he had dropped it in amazement.

Stranger still, everywhere in the gleaming, snow-white hall crystal balls were full of eyes today: in the chandeliers, the bookends, the lanterns over the Map Wells; in the snowy carpet, the lamps, the knobs that turned the glass ladders around. Crystal balls everywhere, and all watching a single bookcase that rose to the cloud-high ceiling like a glistening pillar of blue ice—without a single book to be seen on it anywhere.

"Emmy..." gasped Will.

A girl was perched on top of the bare pillar, swinging on the floating silver section plaque: *Invisibility*. She was laughing and waving to the frantic librarians in fluid aquamarine robes, who were clambering up the empty bookshelves to get at her, all cackling furiously.

"Get down!"

"Wicked Castaway!"

"Not Valerian's medallion, you won't!"

"Not for this, by Fortune's fury! Never!"

And over and over again, they shouted, "Where are the

320

books? Where are the books? WHERE ARE ALL THE BOOKS?"

"Right under your noses," Peter chuckled, and Will noticed a seating area that he could have sworn hadn't been there yesterday. He would have remembered armchairs made entirely from books, and no ordinary books either, but Invisibility Books, with covers that looked like flowing water and pages that rippled.

"Hi Lee… Hi Jenny…" Peter blew a magician's hat at the two pretty, oriental girls sitting there, petting three white cats and grinning.

"But… Abednego's eyes," Will wondered, as he and Peter turned down a carpeted aisle, a weave of crystal balls stretching before them like Fortune's footprints, some blinking open.

"The library's closed at night," said Peter, still grinning. Poudini skipped between his legs with a tied chicken bone in his mouth. "The eyes were probably turned off."

"They never are… not in the corridors, not on the stairs," Will remembered. "Not even in the middle of the night."

"Yeah, but the library actually gets locked up."

"You think Emmy hid somewhere before closing time?" Will's skin tingled at this new idea for searching the library safely, until he remembered his evil shadows.

"Stayed overnight. With Lee and Jenny, has to be." Peter nodded. "That explains why they weren't at dinner yesterday. Hold on—" Suddenly Peter tore his crystal ball sunglasses off. "Of course! That's it! Almost as brilliant as magic!"

Will thought he saw what Peter was talking about. Just in

321

front of them, on an icy shelf was a book titled: *War of the Roses.* Except that someone had doodled over the title, changing it to *War of the Noses.* "Cute." Will smiled. "Not that amazing, though."

"Not that—" Peter's blue-green eyes sparkled like Valerie's ring in the sun. "I mean, if you had a special book... like an incredibly old map."

Peter twisted back to check on the Fate Sealers. But they were too far to hear, not to mention busy untangling their swinging lips after a monstrous yawn.

"Would you leave that book on a bottom shelf?" continued Peter. "Not unless you're stupid. So, no. You'd hide it, right? Somewhere safe. Somewhere high. Somewhere people didn't get to that much."

"Yeah, so?" Will was beginning to feel embarrassed for not getting it... whatever *it* was.

"The knobs! You can't make the ladders move without the knobs. If someone hid something up there—"

"We could see it!" Will caught on at last, and his hand slipped into his pocket, feeling for the cold, smooth surface of his Crystillery.

"Almost as brilliant as magic," repeated Peter, and now Will could share in the joke.

Trying to look stupid and lost, for the benefit of the Fate Sealers, Will and Peter meandered through the gleaming white library, dawdling here and there by an ice-blue bookcase, until they reached the *Echo History Section* and pretended to settle in out of sheer exhaustion.

"And if you don't find anything here," whispered Peter, as Will began climbing the sparkling glass ladder, "we'll go back to *Cartography*. Maybe we missed something yesterday."

From the height of the topmost rung, Poudini and Peter looked like toys to Will, and the two Fate Sealers like grotesque candles stuck in the middle of a frosted white cake.

Will's nose was swollen enough to keep his crystal ball sunglasses from slipping off, even as he bent his head awkwardly not to bump into the ceiling, which up close looked like a misty river. The eyes in nearby crystal ball chandeliers ignored Will completely, as they kept gazing over the gleaming white hall in Emmy's direction.

Will fished his Crystillery out of his pocket, keeping his hands concealed in the glistening sleeves of his white sweater. Then he kicked the crystal ball knob that turned his glass ladder around until he was sure it didn't conceal an eye. Finally, he bent over the ball and swirled his Crystillery awake.

Almost at once, a Memory came to life inside the blue dome.

An old, wrinkled hand floated up to the top of the Crystillery, until it seemed to be peeking out of the little dome resting in Will's palm. It wasn't exactly the hand of a Sound, but it wasn't see-through either. It seemed more like the hand of a mummy.

And there was something else. The ancient hand was clutching a jeweled green case. Except that it wasn't a case at all, but a book, a book with a jeweled cover. Will could tell because the hand in the Crystillery gently lifted the emerald cover to one side until the jewels peeked out of the dome in Will's hand for a moment. And then Will watched the hand flipping through the pages of the book.

It was then that a frail, windy voice rose out of the Crystillery. "You don't belong here, my beauty," it muttered lovingly. "The *Restricted Section* is the place for a book like you."

Will recognized the voice and the hand at once.

His heart pounding, Will shoved the Crystillery back in his glistening white pocket and climbed down from that dizzying height to the brilliance below. The Fate Sealers yawned lazily to see him back so soon and carrying no chosen book besides.

Peter was also skeptical. "Found something already?" he asked, before Will's foot touched the snowy carpet.

"You could say that." Will grinned and his puffy cheeks swelled like parachutes. "Where's the *Restricted Section* of the library, Peter?"

"The what?"

"I heard Abednego in the Crystillery," said Will. "He said something about a *Restricted Section*."

"*Restricted Section*! *Restricted Section*? Mmmm..." Peter rolled the words around in his mouth as if he could taste them. "*Restricted Section*..." He smacked his lips and smiled. "There's a door," he suddenly whispered. "Always figured it led up to Abednego's tower. But maybe...."

They set off for the glittering, spiraling staircase, trying to waste time on looking stupid and lost so the Fate Sealers won't suspect anything. But Will and Peter were just too excited. Soon they climbed the glass steps to the seventh floor, where they walked to the back of the gleaming white hall. Poudini cantered behind them, growling at the Fate Sealers, who kept smacking their swinging lips, as if they were less bored now… or perhaps they were hungry… Will found it hard to read emotions in faces that looked like mole hills, with the mole still flinging mud.

"Almost there," whispered Peter.

And, indeed, an icy tree suddenly appeared before them, sunk into the back wall of the gleaming library as if someone had incased it in glass. It was a bare tree, branches with no leaves. And instead of fruit the icy tree bore two crystal balls that hung side by side like pearly apples.

It took Will a moment to realize that the shape of a door was carved into the center of the icy tree. And the crystal balls, which stuck out of the wall, were actually doorknobs, with the word *Private* carved into them for all time, as if the writer had refused to put his faith in a mere plaque.

"Now what?" said Will, as he and Peter turned their backs to the door and smiled innocently at the Fate Sealers.

"Lean back, pretend you're tired," said Peter.

He yawned at the Fate Sealers, while his hands groped behind his back, testing both doorknobs.

Suddenly Will saw a shadow crawling over Peter's face. "Peter!"

They looked up.

A strange sort of spider was descending toward them on a web of silk, its legs as see-through as glass, its belly as round and lustrous as a crystal ball. An eye blinked open inside it.

"Not another one…" groaned Will, wishing the Prince's bat would arrive already with the Blinker for putting Abednego's eyes to sleep.

But Peter was already pulling out a white glistening handkerchief from his pocket.

"Going to blow your nose at it?" asked Will skeptically.

Peter just smiled. In a moment, the handkerchief ballooned in his hand like a tiny parachute and then it started rising, by sheer magic. It drifted over the spider and, in a flash, collapsed all around it, covering Abednego's spying eye completely.

"How did you…?" Will gasped.

"A magician never reveals his tricks," said Peter, as he went back to testing the doorknobs behind his back while yawning at the Fate Sealers.

"Locked," said Peter finally. "Definitely locked."

"No keyholes, either," said Will, after glancing back at the doorknobs while pretending to scratch his back.

Will was secretly reaching for his Crystillery to see how the door was last opened, when Peter grabbed his swollen wrist and whispered.

"Someone's coming."

*   *   *

Will and Peter ducked behind the nearest stalagmite of books, and Will tripped over Poudini. His crystal ball sunglasses flew into a shimmering fountain with an icy sundial floating at its center, encircled with books in place of numbers to tell time, which apparently was *Alice in Echoland* at the moment, whatever that meant.

The Fate Sealers were so amused they clapped their sagging hands in ovation until their fingers become knotted.

"They're enjoying this," muttered Will resentfully. "And attracting attention." He sighed, as an eye blinked open in a distant chandelier and swiveled to see what the Fate Sealers found so amusing.

The noise, which warned Peter that someone was coming, grew louder. It was an annoying squeak, or squeaks really. And it was definitely heading their way.

"A collection cart," said Peter, after peeking behind the glacial bookcase. "Librarian. Putting books back. This could take ages."

He sunk on the snowy carpet, which was cleaning itself where Poudini drooled happily over a tied chicken bone.

Will fished out his sunglasses and shoved them back over his swollen nose. "How do you tie a knot in a chicken bone, anyway?" he asked Peter.

"A magician never reveals—"

"Yeah, yeah," said Will, and he reached blindly over his head for something to read in the meantime.

Peter looked down at the book. "*Earthworms through the Ages*... Excellent choice."

Will was shoving the book back in place, when a sharp voice startled him.

"By all the crumbling crystal balls, is that dog eating?"

The suspicious question came from an Echo in a short-sleeved, flowing robe, who rippled toward Will and Peter like a miniature waterfall. Sticking out of the billowing robe were scrawny arms and legs that moved about really fast, like dancing chopsticks. But funniest of all was the woman's face, which looked like a water balloon with a pointy nose and hair pulled in a tight bun at the back of the head.

"Another librarian?" Peter groaned. "They're multiplying."

"—Because I will not stand for pets eating in the library!" snapped the librarian, and she went on and on for about five minutes, lecturing on the horrors of mixing food with parchment.

Peter magicked the tied chicken bone out of existence, and Will and Peter were finally let off after Will pulled out another random book and explained that *Irresistible Tales to Worm Your Heart* was exactly what they were looking for.

They descended one floor and Will quickly dumped the book, whose worm-illustrated cover was actually writhing under his fingers. The Fate Sealers were close behind, but the creatures were sweeping across the white carpet in zigzags, as if trying to stave off boredom... Or maybe they were dancing. And one of them was even waving hello.

"What's gotten into them?" asked Will

"Jeremy Fallon," muttered Peter sullenly.

Facing front again, Will spotted the dark-haired boy in his shiny black wheelchair. Jeremy had taken his crystal ball sunglasses off, and he was waving hello indolently like a queen or a famous movie star. Behind him, an especially thick bookcase rose up to the shimmering white ceiling. The books on it were all wrinkled and gray, and something about them was disturbingly familiar.

"Always there," said Peter, as Poudini started growling both forwards and back. "Reading about them. Thinking about them. Talking to himself about them. Obsessed— that's what he is."

Will looked up at the silver section plaque glittering like a giant halo high over Jeremy's head.

"*Fate Sealers.*" Will read the plaque with bitter understanding. "Jeremy's Echo is the grandson of a famous Fate Sealer, right?" Will remembered what the boy in the wheelchair told him when they first met. "Look what happened to him because of it. Wouldn't you be obsessed? Let's go talk to him," added Will, glancing back at the waltzing, waving Fate Sealers. "Maybe Jeremy can tell us what to do about my shadows."

"Terrific." Peter sighed.

Jeremy looked even more sickly today. His black hair was oily, and his face looked waxy. He smiled with his big teeth and kept waving, which explained why the Fate Sealers were waving back. Though Will wondered if Jeremy's waves were intended for him or the creatures behind him.

Poudini rushed over to the wheelchair, and the white lizard jumped off Jeremy's lap right beside the little dog.

"Keep that dog away from Natalia," Jeremy shouted at Peter, losing his smile.

"Keep that lizard away from Poudini," Peter shouted back.

"Natalia wouldn't come near that mutt with a ten-foot pole."

"It's not the pole I'm worried about!"

"What's that supposed to mean?"

But another librarian rushed over in her billowing aquamarine robe and put an end to the argument.

"Silence is crystal!" she snapped at Peter and Jeremy, then stormed off, her long white hair flying after her like a cape.

Will didn't want to tower over Jeremy in his wheelchair, so he sunk into a bean bag that looked like a cloud. Peter landed on the other half, with Poudini munching his tied chicken bone in his lap. Then Will tried to break the tension by being polite.

"Do you have time to talk, Jeremy?" he asked.

"I'll make time... for *you*." Jeremy picked up his lizard and stroked her pointy back. "If you know what I mean. You and I... we're special."

"Aha..." Peter grumbled quietly.

Will smiled tensely, beginning to think that talking to someone who knew his true identity may not be the wisest thing in the world, especially with two Fate Sealers listening in. And... Will realized, two spying eyes blinking open in the crystal ball chandelier overhead.

"Wither Heart's spies?" asked Jeremy after a moment. He glanced over Will's shoulder at the Fate Sealers, who were standing close by, holding their sagging palms up to their drooping ears to hear better.

"Hey, Evil Deed... Evil Dude." Jeremy waved to the Fate Sealers like old friends. Then leaning closer to Will, he congratulated himself on being the only Castaway able to tell Fate Sealers apart.

"Don't worry," Jeremy added with a toothy smile, "they're harmless. Won't do anything to you... not without Wither Heart's permission. Perfectly harmless."

"Fate Sealers? Harmless?" Peter choked, but Jeremy ignored him.

"But what if they get Wither Heart's permission?" asked Will nervously.

"Even Wither Heart has to get the false King's permission before he can execute a Castaway. But—" Jeremy glanced up at the lustrous chandelier, where an eye was blinking, and he lowered his voice. "If Wither Heart finds proof that you killed his brother—*that* will be bad. Very bad. No, no, don't tell me..." Jeremy shook a pompous finger at Will. "I'd like to make it to my sixteenth birthday."

Will chuckled politely. Peter rolled his eyes.

"Anyway..." Jeremy pushed his long greasy bangs out of his dark eyes. "Wither Heart isn't convinced you did it. Not yet. We chatted about you this morning, as a matter-of-fact. Nothing

331

compromising. Just a friendly get-together. Wither Heart thinks I'm the only Castaway worth talking to in this cursed Orphanage."

"Lucky you," said Peter, looking at Jeremy as if he were a strange specimen in a museum.

"That's why Evil Deed and Evil Dude are following you," said Jeremy to Will, as if Peter wasn't there. "Just following. Nothing worse, if you know what I mean."

"But I need to get away from them," Will whispered back.

"I see." Jeremy frowned and put on his crystal ball sunglasses again. "On important Sound business, are you? I understand. Well... let me see. Yes, I know... I'll tell you a bit about the Fate Sealers. First of all, do you know how a Fate Sealer is created? I say *created*, not *born*."

Delicately, Jeremy petted his chameleon, enjoying the suspenseful silence that followed. Even Peter looked too intrigued to interrupt.

"It starts with a kidnapping," Jeremy began, relishing every word. "Before he can reach his intended parents, an Echo baby is snatched. Poof! And he's gone." Jeremy blew on his fingertips as if casting a spell.

"And where does that poor, unfortunate baby go? Into Shadowpain. To begin his training. Twenty years of torture... Horrors you couldn't possibly imagine. The body is stretched on torture racks, until the Fate Sealer becomes distorted— taller, flatter, longer than any human being. His skin starts to sag and rot and turn gray. His hair falls out. His fingernails drop off, and talons grow in their place. His teeth decay... they fall out too. His eyes sink into his skull. His vocal chords change forever from years of screaming."

With his long, worm-like fingers, Jeremy kept stroking his lizard's head, where her chameleon eyes were roving in their sockets like Abednego's spying crystal balls.

"Like the body of a Fate Sealer," Jeremy went on darkly, "the mind also becomes deformed. A Fate Sealer isn't taught how to think, do math, speak eloquently... He learns to scheme. To lie. To cheat. To do whatever it takes to put someone else on the torture rack instead of him.

"We should pity them," concluded Jeremy, sliding his gaze sideways over the rim of his crystal ball sunglasses, until Will took up the hint and looked behind him.

Evil Deed and Evil Dude were leaning sleepily against a glacial pillar of books. Their large crystal ball sunglasses had slipped off their drooping noses, and Will could see that the Fate Sealers' eyes were closed. Although just then one of them opened a single drooping eyelid to see why Jeremy had stopped his gruesome tale.

"Fate Sealers are victims of circumstance," Jeremy went on, and the eyelid sealed again. "None of them asked to become monsters." Then to Will, Jeremy whispered, "I'll keep talking— you sneak off—" Before Jeremy raised his voice again and plunged deeper into tales of suffering, horror and doom.

A moment or so after, only the eye in the crystal ball chandelier watched Will and Peter creeping quietly away with Poudini at their heels; for the Fate Sealers had sunk sleepily on the snowy carpet, mesmerized by the story of their own tragedy.

*   *   *

Will and Peter hid behind a glittering, icy bookcase, with Poudini still doing battle with his tied chicken bone. Castaways and librarians were all heading down to lunch. When the last of their footsteps faded from the library's spiraling glass staircase, Will and Peter slipped out and climbed to the seventh floor.

Soon they were standing by the Ice Tree that was a door. No eyes had blinked open at their approach. Peter's handkerchief still hung from the silk string, wrapped around the mechanical spider, blinding that eye completely. Best of all, there was no sign of Evil Dude and Evil Deed.

Peter tried the crystal ball doorknobs again, but they were still locked. So Will pulled out his Crystillery, to try and see how the door was last opened. But Peter was suddenly in the way.

"Another magic trick?" asked Will, watching Peter bending to kiss... No! To lick the doorknobs.

"Sssssssshhh..." Peter stopped licking and stared at the crystal balls. "No eyes," he said finally.

"You had to lick them to find out?"

"Wouldn't you open your eyes if someone was licking your face?" Peter grinned.

"Good point." Will smiled back.

Then Will began to swirl his Crystillery, rocking the ruby, sapphire and diamond on the frothy waves inside the blue dome. "Let's do it," he said, when the stones crashed and sparked like fire.

"Let's find out how this door was opened in the past."

The Memory began just like the one Will saw earlier. There was the hologram of that ancient mummy hand again, half peeking out of the Crystillery like a real, living hand.

"Spooky," said Peter.

"Abednego," said Will.

Now a second hand appeared, looking just as old and wrinkled. And the two hands started caressing two crystal ball doorknobs. Caressing them at the same time. But not in the same way. Each hand was forming a different pattern. And then suddenly, there was a click inside the Crystillery, and the old hands pushed open an icy door that looked like a tree encased in glass.

"Did you get all that?" Peter glanced nervously up at the crystal ball chandelier.

"Think so. See any eyes?"

Peter shook his head. "Looks like the spider's the only guard dog."

"Wish we had the Blinker already," muttered Will.

Will slipped the Crystillery back in his glistening white pocket and placed his swollen hands over the doorknobs. He closed his eyes in concentration, took a deep breath and began repeating what he saw in the Crystillery.

Right hand two circles to the left. Then one half to the right.

At the same time, left hand half a circle to the right. Then three to the left.

It didn't work the first time, nor the second. But after the third try, there was a soft click. Will exhaled in amazement and pushed the crystal ball doorknobs just like Abednego's hands had in the Crystillery. And the Ice Tree Door parted in the middle, opening on the landing of another glittering, glass staircase that spiraled up and out of sight.

"You're a genius," whispered Peter in awe, taking Poudini in his arms and following Will across the threshold.

They climbed as softly as possible, looking up at the ceiling of icicles that seemed to be drawing nearer with each step they took; until Will was sure the glass stairs would run into the ceiling and end abruptly. But then the wrought-ice banister curved one last time, and a circular, gleaming white gallery opened before them, offering them a place to alight—on a round lustrous rug, the exact color and shape of a crystal ball.

The next moment, something terrible happened.

The entire rug blinked open under Will and Peter's feet, as if they had woken it up. For the entire rug was an eye.

In a flash, Peter dropped Poudini and threw himself over the pupil emerging at the center of the eye. But the ice-colored pupil fought back.

The little dog started barking insanely, running in circles around the eye rug. Peter's body jostled violently as he held on tight. His feet flailed. His head wagged like an out of control jack-in-the-box. His crystal ball sunglasses smashed against a wall.

Other eyes appeared in the crystal ball chandelier overhead, but they were all still closed, trying to blink open but failing.

"Keep it covered," shouted Will, realizing that all the eyes were somehow interconnected.

"Not exactly wanting to—" snarled Peter, his back quivering like a small earthquake.

Will darted his glance around the gleaming curved walls. No more eyes! But the room was a kind of museum, and museums were usually guarded by silent alarms.

Icy pedestals surrounded Will, each displaying a giant jewel worth a fortune, no doubt. And suddenly Will realized that the jewels were actually books with covers of gem-encrusted gold, of pearl-decked silver, of ruby and amethyst… and the one he had seen Abednego taking down in the Crystillery with a cover of jade edged with emeralds.

"We have to— get out— of here," Peter grunted from the rug, his hair thrashing madly.

But Will's heart was suddenly racing with excitement. A small chest caught his eye, hidden in the shadow of the only crystal ball window in the room.

Wood! The chest was made of wood! Not faux-ice like everything else at the Orphanage. Not jewels like everything else in this room. It was plain, very old, and very Sound-like. *Fluid Conway was a Sound… Could his road map really be in there?*

"What— are— you— doing—?" Peter groaned. "Get— out! I'm right behind— Argh!" Peter's head slammed into the rug.

"Hold on— Maybe the map's here—" shouted Will, bending over the old wooden chest. But the chest had a rusty keyhole. "Oh, no!" Will muttered. "I think it's locked."

"Hurry!"

Will tore his Crystillery out. He had to find out where the key was hidden.

"Come on—" Peter shouted, Poudini still running frantic circles around him and barking madly.

Will jammed the Crystillery over the keyhole. His hand slipped. The Crystillery flew up, pushing the lid up as it went. The chest was not locked after all.

"*Yes!*" Will cheered in amazement.

But as if the hinges of the chest were wired to an alarm, soft shrieks suddenly echoed through the room. And they kept getting louder by the second.

Will flinched back from the chest. The pupil froze under Peter for a second. Then it went mad and started spinning Peter's body like a merry-go-round.

"What did you do?" screamed Peter, trying to hold on to the eyelashes.

"I don't know," Will shouted back. "Stop barking, Poudini."

It was impossible to hear. Will thought the shrieks were coming from the box. But now, he thought they were coming from the crystal ball window.

Will looked out, and there was a see-through bat, zooming in and shrieking. It dove for Will's shoe, where the Prince's Pitch Beacon was emitting its silent signal. And, without stopping to think, Will collapsed his hand over the crystal ball eye dangling like a locket from the bat's shimmering neck.

Silence fell so abruptly that Will heard the last snap of something locking inside that tiny crystal ball the bat had brought with it.

"It's the blinker…" Will muttered in disbelief.

The bat perched tamely on Will's shoe and waited until Will removed the blinker from its chain and tied the Pitch Beacon on it instead. Then the beautiful, silvery creature shrieked softly one last time, as if saying goodbye, and took flight, disappearing into the blue, blue sky beyond the glistening crystal ball window.

"And about time too!" Peter sat up, Poudini licking his face.

Only the faint trace of a closed eyelid showed in the lustrous rug that was a giant eye.

Will looked up at the chandelier, still not believing it. The eyes had all gone to sleep—like the small eye he was clutching in his palm. He looked around, still expecting to see something staring back at him from the glittering books or the gleaming white walls.

"Helllllooo?" Peter pulled Will's crystal ball sunglasses off. "Thought you blinked yourself to sleep too." He grinned. "You said something about a map…?"

"The map!"

In a flash Will and Peter bent over the wooden chest and lifted the lid.

The soft light of the room slipped through the widening opening. First they could see an ancient leather book with a rounded top like the shape of a dome. Then they recognized the color of the cover, sapphire blue and worn around the edges. They saw the ruby red spine and, finally, the strange title spelled in letters that glittered like gold.

Speechless, Will and Peter simply stared at each other—until the magic of the moment was suddenly shattered by the sound of someone shuffling his tired feet up the spiraling glass staircase outside the room, tapping as he went, as if he was leaning heavily on a cane.

*   *   *

It was only later, breathing normally again as Will lay stretched beside Wolfeá, that he realized the magnitude of this discovery.

The road map to Olám Shoné was now tucked under his glistening white sweater, pressing on his thumping heart. He still wasn't sure that taking the book was the right decision. But at least he had paused to close the lid of the chest before joining Peter in a frantic escape out the crystal ball window onto a soft snow heap; then down the winding trail of a shimmering white garden until two ice-carved doors, which a moment before had looked like wings on a flying horse topiary, suddenly flew apart, revealing a dark passage that led into a freezing tunnel and, after a while, into a cage of branches with no visible exist, as if no one before them had ever fought his way out of that tangle.

Wolfeá was licking the scratches left in Will's face. Valerie was flying her albatross above him. She was fearless, clinging tight as the giant white bird dove and thrust, playing with the air currents.

340

Maybe she'll win her uncle's medallion, thought will, if Valerian ever shows up again.

Peter had been gone for some time, to fetch food before lunch ended, and at long last Will spotted his friend behind a see-through cluster of trees, tossing something to Poudini, probably a tied chicken bone.

"They saw me," Peter grumbled, dropping on the soft snow beside Will. Peter's face was just as scratched from the cage of branches, which in the end had released them into the tangled, frozen forest behind Wolfeá's tree.

Will didn't need to ask what Peter meant. He could see his Evil Shadows slithering behind a nearby fountain like two upright snakes.

"Didn't try to kill me, at least." Peter shrugged. "More afraid of Wither Heart than annoyed with us, I guess. Here—" Peter pulled two stuffed napkins from under his glistening white sweater.

Will and Peter shared their food with their pets and watched the Fate Sealers watching them, until it seemed safe to turn around and lie on their stomachs, pretending to talk, while Will pulled out the road map. Even in the joint shadow of their heads, the gold letters on the front of the book glittered like jewels.

"Ready?" whispered Will. And, ever so carefully, he opened the book to the sound of the ruby spine crackling like fire.

"But…" Peter shook his head, bewildered. "Where's the map?"

They were staring down at an actual book, with parchments

for pages. Will flipped through them one by one, only to find yet more pages all lined from top to bottom with beautiful, strange letters scrawled in shimmering silver ink.

"An ancient language few Echoes know..." Will suddenly remembered Abednego's words from the Winter Break Breakfast Feast. And then his fingers froze, as his eyes locked on the drawing of an ice-blue coin near the bottom of page five.

"You think—?"

Will sat up and snapped open the secret compartment in his glistening shoe.

He shook out the Royal Shekel with his back to the Fate Sealers. The ice-blue coin and the drawing were a perfect match, and more than that—the unfamiliar letters flowing like water on the coin's surface looked just like the letters crowding every parchment in the book.

An ancient language few Echoes know.

There had to be a link between the Royal Shekel and the map, and Will pulled out his Crystillery, hoping to learn more. But Crystillery Reading was still an art he had to master, and seeing the most recent, complex Memory told him and Peter what they already knew—that they had stolen the book.

"What now?" Peter sat up glumly.

But they couldn't think of anything.

"It's still probably a road map," said Will a little later, as they walked back to the Orphanage, past strolling Castaways who hadn't a care in the world.

Far off, Valerie was flying over the garden pond where boats of glass were twinkling in the sun. And by the now fully decorated Christmas tree Warloch was spraying water, which froze around the colorful ornaments, making them sparkle like lights.

"So it's a map… How is that helpful, if we can't read it?" grumbled Peter, watching Poudini drinking from a fountain that smelled so bad, instead of a fairy, two icy skunks were perched at its center. "No taste buds," Peter added dejectedly, to gasping laughter from their Fate Sealer shadows.

"Didn't think fountains had smells." Will wrinkled his nose.

"Only Poudini's favorites." Peter rolled his eyes. "It's not intentional… some just go bad. That's why the warning skunks."

"I have another idea," said Will, getting back to talking about the map. "We know the passage is in the Lake of Eternal Ice. That leaves one option. We can try Memory Crossing."

"Memory what—?" Peter lured Poudini away with a tied chicken bone.

"—Crossing. It's what happens when a Crystillery reads two Memories at the same time," said Will. "Like the lake and the road map together. That could tell us how to unlock the passage. *If* we could get to the lake without being followed, that is," Will added skeptically.

"If crystal balls had wings," said Peter, "to quote your favorite roommate".

"There's Auralius' tunnel…" Will suggested, wincing inwardly at the prospect of running into Fate Sealers in the middle of the night again.

"Tempting." Peter cringed.

"We could ask Jeremy Fallon to help," it occurred to Will.

Peter cringed even more. "Don't think I'd survive making him that happy. But there's another way. And I'm pretty sure it will work."

"Pretty sure?" Will didn't exactly feel overwhelmed with confidence.

Like a Fairy Riding a Kite

The Coin Key

The plan was simple. The first day of the Veiled Village Trip was cancelled... but the second *wasn't*. Will and Peter would go with everyone else to the famous Christmas Fair and disappear in the crowd. The Lake of Eternal Ice was just behind the village wall. Before Will's evil shadows realized where he had gone, Will and Peter would slip away to test the road map and the lake together under a Crystillery.

But, as with all simple plans, complications soon ruined everything.

"But how did Brainy guess?" huffed Peter, as Will and he dashed down a windowless Orphanage corridor.

Three crystal balls flew ahead of them for a few seconds, spelling the message: *Veiled Village Fair, This Way* ↓.

"I knew it..." answered Will, clutching the strap of the shimmering black bag slung across his shoulder. "Should have stuck the map under my sweater."

"And risk losing it? No Way! We'll lose Brainy. Follow me."

Peter plunged into an indoor forest of Christmas trees that

seemed to have been delivered to the Orphanage of Castaway Children that morning, since crystal ball shipping labels still hovered over each tree.

"Eighty seven, eighty nine..." someone was counting the trees from the ceiling. "Crystal madness! Slow down!" she called after Will and Peter, and Will caught sight of a staff member riding an Ice Fairy and holding what looked like a packing list a mile long.

"Wait! Your bag! That's Fortune Teller fabric." Brainy's voice could be heard through the trees, calling after them. "I'm absolutely sure! Wait up, Freddy!"

"Crystal madness! Slow down!"

"The brainless wonder's back," sighed Will.

"Not for long," promised Peter.

They burst through the last of the trees into the second half of the windowless corridor leading in and out of the Orphanage. And here a jumble of voices met their ears, for the narrow passage was jam-packed with Castaways waiting to leave for the Veiled Village Fair. On the right the Sounds crowded together; on the left Echoes strolled in open space. Will followed Peter through the crowd of glistening white Sounds, and, for once, he didn't care that everyone flinched at the sight of him. But just when Will thought Brainy was reduced to a bad memory, he felt someone clutching his shimmering bag from behind.

"Let go!" Will twisted back.

"Crash and splash! What's in your bag?" Brainy huffed so much his cold breath fogged up his glasses.

348

"For the last time… GET OFF—" Will snarled.

But suddenly Will noticed two creatures rippling out of the forest of delivered Christmas trees, walking in Brainy's footsteps.

"Evil Deed and Evil Dude," grumbled Peter.

"Thanks a lot, Brainy." Will snatched his bag free.

Brainy took his pet out of his pocket, too determined to be distracted by anything. "If you don't tell me, I'll send Alexander the Great on a mission." He waved his mouse in Will's face. The little rodent was still looking sharp, dressed in a tuxedo.

"You dare," snarled Will, though in his medicated voice the threat sounded more like a yawn.

"What's in your bag?" repeated Brainy.

"A change of diapers?" a sneering voice called out from the Echo side of the corridor.

"Why? You need some?" Peter shouted back.

Will looked over. It was Bog Slippery, his face looking more pimpled than ever. As usual, the Drops brothers were sneering beside the overgrown Echo, their pet snakes hanging round their necks like hissing ties. Over their heads Will noticed five staff members riding Ice Fairies to decorate the crystal ball chandeliers with shimmering Christmas ribbons. One red ribbon fluttered down and stuck over Slippery's Doberman like an eye patch, and the dog shook his head stupidly and walked blindly into the wall.

"A diaper, yeah… to wipe your dirty face, Tongue Twister." Slippery was too busy sneering at Peter to notice his pet.

"At least my dirt comes off, Dartboard," answered Peter,

before he turned his back on the Echoes to stop this stupid conversation.

"You're meeting Fortune Tellers in the village, that's it, isn't it?" Brainy kept poking Will's bag, hardly noticing the cold mist hats Peter started blowing in his face.

Suddenly, loud squawks drowned out Brainy's voice, though his lips kept moving. A colorful parrot appeared over his head, and then Michael Silver rammed him out of the way

"Hey—"

"Abednego— Looking for you—" Michael panted urgently at Will.

"Looking for you—" echoed Evan, who popped up behind Michael, pointing backwards with his two frogs.

"Cooking for you—? What—?" Brainy darted angry looks overhead. "For Fortune's sake, someone shut that parrot up! Can't hear a word I'm saying!"

"Lucky you." Michael tossed his bird a thank-you carrot.

Will exchanged a nervous glance with Peter.

He could see the Headmaster pushing past the Fate Sealers. The old man waved his cane in a rage to chase the loud parrot away. His face was so see-through today that the wrinkles in his cheeks looked like rippling water and his eyes like ice cubes.

"Impudent boy," the Headmaster hissed as he stopped beside Will, his voice as faint as a sigh. Though it was clearly audible in the silence that fell all around.

In Abednego's almost see-through forehead a vein appeared,

350

pulsing as if about to explode. Poudini sniffed feverishly at the ancient man's shimmering ivory robe, but the Headmaster seemed to see no one but Will.

"Impudent," he hissed again in Will's face, "and stupid. I will not be provoked twice. Remember that! Never— never attempt your impudence again! Never!"

His heart pounding violently, Will nodded, too startled to think of anything to say. He tried to read in Abednego's almost invisible features how much the Headmaster knew... About Will and Peter's visit to his forbidden tower of treasured books... About who stole the ancient road map... About the Blinker that put Abednego's eyes to sleep...

Suddenly something glinted at Will under the Headmaster's wispy, water-like beard. Not an eye for once, but something smooth and blue and crystal clear.

A Crystillery!

"Oh, yes— You're not seeing things," said Abednego, his faint voice suddenly lighter, as if the sigh in his throat had turned into a yawn. "It is what you think it is. And I, as even you might guess, am an *expert* reader. Expert! Doorknobs present no challenge at all... not to mention old wooden chests."

"Reading doorknobs...?" Will could hear Brainy muttering in confusion somewhere behind his back.

But beside Will, Peter stiffened with understanding and kicked Poudini away from Abednego's shimmering hem, though the old man still had eyes for Will alone.

"You may have this back," continued the Headmaster enigmatically. "It isn't yours to lose, after all. Oh yes… I know who gave it to you. And I know why. Don't think you could ever keep anything from *me*."

And stretching his withered hand, the Headmaster dropped a small eye in Will's palm.

The Blinker! The Prince's Blinker!

Will's heart seemed to crash into his stomach. He hadn't even realized that he had lost the Prince's gift! He glanced at Peter, who looked just as startled. *But why are you giving it back to me?* Will almost asked Abednego, but he didn't want to push his luck.

"Remember my warning," sighed the Headmaster—before he swept away, his long see-through hair and beard fluttering behind him like rain, his cane tapping on the flagstones with an eye blinking inside its crystal ball top.

The ancient Echo brushed past the Fate Sealers, who kept watching Will hollowly, their lips swinging a little as if they were laughing quietly to themselves. All around, a murmur of voices filled the chilly corridor. And overhead three staff members flew down with their Ice Fairies, trailing Christmas ribbons in their wake as they urged the line of Castaways to move along down the corridor.

"What, in Fortune's Name, was all that about?" Brainy exploded, his mouse now perched on his shoulder, top hat all aquiver.

Michael whistled for Prattle, and his parrot returned, squawking happily.

Brainy simply raised his voice. "And what's that thing... that... that eye? It's no good hiding it, I saw it!"

"It's not polite to pry," Evan objected timidly.

A funny thing to say, thought Will, with the entire corridor staring and listening in. While on the Echo side of the passage, Rain and Water Drops joined Bog Slippery in cracking their knuckles and blowing inane kisses at Will and Peter.

"A smooching dartboard... that's all we need," Peter grumbled.

"Move along down there," a decorator called from her flying fairy. Putting a luminous crystal ball to her see-through lips, she whistled over Brainy, startling the top hat off his mouse. "Around the curve! There you go. Move on every one. The Village Fair awaits you."

Castaways started flowing forward finally, and soon Will spotted two giant, open doors at the end of the curving stone corridor. Castaways around Will forgot all about him as they gaped at the perfect blue sky shining beyond. On both the Echo and Sound sides of the corridor pet birds fluttered their wings impatiently. Dogs barked, Poudini the loudest. And Prattle flew away, squawking over the sea of heads.

"Echoes to the left! Sounds to the right!" shouted a frizzy white-haired Echo.

He hovered by the icy doors, directing the glistening white crowd and, at the same time, somehow managing to pipe a tune on his smoking pipe. Just as he had done during the Winter Break

Breakfast Feast, Will remembered.

"Catch! Five Echo Shekels each. Don't spend it all at once." The Echo tossed large raindrops at the Castaways streaming out of the Orphanage, which were actually purses sewn from Echo fabric. "There it comes... Good catch! One more... Oh, crash and splash! Hamster overboard! Never mind, he'll live, my young Sound, he'll live. Now let's keep moving. Echoes to the left! Sounds to the right!"

"And what were you impudent about, Freddy?" Brainy was still at it, his face scrunched, as if the mass of questions cramming his mouth was giving him a toothache.

"Give it a rest, Brainy," huffed Peter, magically pulling a key from behind Brainy's ear. "Or I'll lock your mouth up."

"Yeah, right... when Fortune flies. Lock my mouth up— Hey!"

"Mouse overboard!" The frizzy Echo cringed at his latest mis-throw. "Pick him up, my young Sound. Go on. Is that a tuxedo?"

The girl walking before Will held up the watery purse she just caught. The beautiful fabric twinkled in the light streaming in through the doors up ahead. Soon the girl pulled out a coin from the purse, and the coin looked like a circle of ice with water trapped inside it.

For a split second Will thought the girl was holding up the Royal Shekel, and his heart missed a beat. But then Will remembered the incredible truth: The greatest heirloom in this strange land was nothing but an ordinary coin, like a million other

Echo Shekels—unless you tested it with a Crystillery and read its Memories.

"See you later, Diaper Boy," Will heard someone sneering on his left.

He turned and spotted Bog Slippery stepping out into the sunshine, smirking smugly and running his finger across his see-through throat in a silent threat.

"And don't forget..." the Echo riding the Ice Fairy cried down to them, "haggling is the spice of Fortune to the village vendors. —Oh, I do apologize," he added, accidentally tossing a watery purse into Will's nose. "At least we're not playing darts." The Echo chuckled at his own joke and blew a quick tune out of his pipe. "Never mind, keep moving everyone. Echoes to the left! Sounds to the right!"

Will and Peter stepped out into the sunshine too.

The giant Echo sun welcomed them like a huge hot air balloon blazing in the deep blue sky, with Valerie flying her albatross against it, her ring twinkling like a star. A river of Castaways glistened down the snow-covered hill of the Orphanage, all white in their uniforms, pets skipping between their legs or flying over their heads. Far below Cyrano de Bergerac's hat was bobbing like a shimmering purple boat, the peacock feather wafting like a flag. Here and there a few Fate Sealers jutted out of the white stream like blobs of filth. And, far below, a crystallized, wild forest spread far and wide.

Soon Will started to believe that Peter was right. With so

355

many Castaways all dressed the same, how hard would it be for him and Peter to get lost in the crowd? Already the glistening procession was fanning out as it slipped beneath the shadows of the wild, icy trees, where the road grew wider.

But suddenly Poudini started barking fiercely. At Will's side Peter muttered, "Oh, no..." and quickly drew a crystal ball on the air. And then Will felt something searing into his arm, as his Fate Sealer shadows took up brand new positions, one on either side of him and Peter, their sagging flesh swinging as they moved.

Arrrgh! Another burning caress brushed across Will's arm. He could see Peter flinching too.

"So sssorry," screeched the Fate Sealers together, sandwiching Will and Peter even more.

Castaways all around them cringed as far back as the thick crowd would allow.

"Your fan club?" Michael Silver passed them, his parrot squawking in the air above him. "Impressive— Fate Sealers with taste. Never thought I'd see it."

But the Fate Sealers weren't going to be teased from their purpose. "We're not going anywhere," the one beside Will promised, his sagging mouth grazing Will's ear vindictively. "Eh?" The creature straightened suddenly, twisting back. "By rotting Fortune, what was that?"

"The bag? What's in the bag?" a muffled whisper reached them. And there was Brainy, passing them swiftly with his mouse walking in the lead.

The Fate Sealers stiffened to attention.

"You'd forget your own funeral—"

"You'd forget your own deathday—"

The creatures hurled recriminations at each other. And then, in a flash, the shimmering black bag was torn from Will's grasp, and shivering with pain he saw the road map floating out into the light on a wave of gray flesh.

"A book?" screeched Peter's Fate Sealer, his hollow mouth twisting in a sagging sneer.

"A book?" screeched Will's Fate Sealer, gasping out a hollow laugh.

"Just something to read. Heard the Christmas Fair can be boring," muttered Will, trying to sound foolish, which wasn't hard.

Bitterly, Will watched Brainy staring at them from a safe distance, his spectacled eyes all lit up with curiosity. The next second, Brainy tripped over his mouse and tumbled off the trail.

"Way to go Alexander the Tiny." Peter grinned.

The Fate Sealers tossed the book and the bag back at Will, snorting in amusement. No one spoke again, though Poudini kept on growling. The narrow road meandered through the frozen forest as if it would go on forever. Valerie flickered into view past the glittering, icy branches cutting across the sky. The sea of glistening Castaways streamed on and on, and Will wondered how he and Peter could ever have imagined that getting lost in the crowd would be easy.

At long last the road curved one more time, and suddenly the icy forest branches parted like a thousand fingers. Will saw a cluster of tall, sparkling buildings rising against the sapphire blue sky, with a giant waterfall gushing at their feet. Only, in a moment, Will realized that it wasn't a waterfall at all, but a wall of water built around the city, with crystal balls floating on the wall like shimmering lights. Or maybe they were security cameras, thought Will, like the one embedded in the crystal ball knocker hung on Will's home in the Sound realm.

In the middle of this strange, gushing wall stood a wide open gate. Like a huge mouth, the opening swallowed the road and everyone streaming toward the beautiful city. As Will passed through the icy gate he stared at the crystal ball knocker gleaming at its center, and once again Will thought of the crystal ball knocker on the front door of his home, though this one was a hundred times bigger.

"Well, well… looks like we're here," croaked the Fate Sealer at Will's side, pulling out his glowing Ice Loom.

*   *   *

Christmas ribbons decked every crystal ball knocker on every sparkling door as far as the eye could see. Through the snowy streets of the Veiled Village, Echoes and Sounds rushed to and fro, their shimmering clothes looking like pouring rain or ice or waves. Before them multi-colored parcels fluttered like strange birds carried on small see-through wings, and every once in a while two parcels would collide and rain down gifts. There were great crystal ball vats on every corner, where eggnog was sold to Sounds and fishnog to Echoes. And between the crystal ball streetlamps Ice Fairies were flying, singing Christmas carols, their frozen lips actually moving. It was a perfect place for disappearing in a crowd, but the Fate Sealers, their Ice Looms glowing bright, stuck ever closer to Will and Peter.

Crystal ball jugglers jumped out of the creatures' way. Christmas ribbons that fluttered in the air like butterflies flew off at the sight of the Fate Sealers. Flying parcels kept whooshing before their eyes in a frantic attempt to avoid them, until Peter snatched Poudini up for fear of losing his little dog to a particularly vengeful box. One more snowy street lined with twinkling Christmas trees, and then, all at once, the crowd grew so thick that no one could keep his distance from them anymore, though people were flinching at the painful touch of the Fate Sealers.

"Wow!" Will and Peter gasped together, and even the Fate Sealers froze for a moment as an icy temple came into view, an enormous crystal ball shining behind its glistening columns as if someone had caged the moon.

And soon Will, Peter and their Fate Sealer guards were swept into the bustle below the temple's stairs.

Here blue-green stalls covered the sky like drifting lagoons, and vendors everywhere were shouting and shaking crystal balls of every size and purpose. Crystal ball amulets and crystal ball socks, pastries, flying carpets; crystal ball flyswatters, balloons and even just plain crystal balls, though some had eyes inside them. Glistening Castaways pulled out their raindrop-purses, laughing and stuffing their mouths with crystal ball candy, and Will glanced sadly at Peter, guessing what his friend was thinking: *Why couldn't they be like everyone else, with nothing better to do than have fun?*

But then, out of nowhere, something yanked Will, and he toppled backwards into a display of crystal ball baskets.

"Sound menace!" A fat vendor rolled after his scattering baskets, looking like an enormous crystal ball basket himself. Behind him, a boy kicked a basket at Will's face, sneering down at him.

"Told you we'd meet again, Diaper Boy!" Bog Slippery smoothed his oiled black hair, swinging something shimmering and black on his fat, see-through finger.

"My bag!"

Will scrambled to his feet, kicking up snow. Peter darted to his friend's side with Poudini barking in his arms. But Slippery and his ever-present friends, the Drops brothers, were fleeing already, tossing Will's bag between them as if playing catch. They shoved shimmering shoppers out of their way and scattered flying parcels in every direction, with Slippery's Doberman snarling at their heels.

"Let's go!" hissed Will, as he darted forward—and smashed into a sagging gray arm that fell on him from the sky.

"AAAAAAARRRRRRRRRRRRR!"

Twisting in agony from the Fate Sealer's grip, Will heard a terrible screech. "NOT AFRAID OF *USSSSSSS!* HOW DARRRRRRE HE!"

And when Will could see again, a shadow was hiding the sun. A Fate Sealer was sweeping across the blue sky in a giant leap that knocked an Ice Fairy off her lamppost and scattered crystal balls far and wide. And still unable to move, Will realized that one Fate Sealer had stayed with him and Peter, while the other was swooping down from above, villagers scrambling out of his path as he dropped like a parachute of sagging gray flesh on the jostling mass of Bog Slippery and his friends.

"You wanted to play?" the Fate Sealer screeched at them, muffled cries of agony bursting under him in a flurry of snow. "Get up, you sniveling cowards. Up!" And, waving his sagging hand like a flag, the Fate Sealer turned and beckoned to his partner to shove Will and Peter over.

Poudini twisted out of Peter's arms and leapt at Slippery's Doberman in a fury of growls. The brown snake tightened around Rain Drop's neck until his asymmetrical eyes started to bulge, and the green snake bit Water Drops on the crystal ball tattooed on his forehead.

"Play!" screeched the Fate Sealer, slapping Will and Peter forward with one hand, and using the other to ward off any villager foolish enough to try and intervene.

"Stop it!" A desperate scream reached them from the sky. And Valerie appeared, plunging toward them on the back of her albatross, her hair looking wilder than ever.

"Play!" screeched the other Fate Sealer, heaving Bog slippery to his feet and tossing Will's shimmering black bag between the boys, before swatting Valerie and her albatross away.

Slippery moved first in the shadow of the startled bird, but Peter snatched a shimmering black strap, and for a second the bag didn't seem to move at all. Until the Drops brothers joined in, kicking Will as his fingers slipped into the bag, closing in on the road map, which toppled out into the light. And then the shimmering bag was forgotten and a tug-of-war began for the book. And in the confusion of arms and legs, shouts and barks, Will imagined he could hear the spine of the book crackling—until someone commanded them all to stop!

It was only one word, but the voice was deep and beautiful, and everyone seemed to recognize it immediately. Will looked up in astonishment, smelling cherry tobacco suddenly, as if his father was right there.

It was Victor Valerian, smoking his icy pipe as if he had never disappeared from the Orphanage at all. His plastic hand gleamed in the sun, his aquamarine robe shimmered, and his sharp green gaze fixed on Peter's hands snatching up the ancient road map.

"This is no way to win my medallion, boys," said Valerian, looking into every face, and it sounded as if he were saying, *I dare you to move.* Then he laughed and looked around at the sellers and buyers, who had stopped all their wheeling and dealing.

"With such splendors everywhere, we waste our time watching children brawling...."

Chuckling, Valerian swept his arms over the colorful, glittering street, nodding at nearby vendors who were quick to take up the hint and present their wares for all to see.

As villagers all around muttered and shrugged and resumed their holiday shopping, Will watched Valerian blowing scented smoke in the Fate Sealer's sagging faces and whispering softly. And whatever the old Echo said, after a moment, incredibly... the two creatures simply slithered away.

They kept on slithering, like two monstrous serpents parting the sea of shimmering shoppers. And Will kept watching them, expecting at any moment to see the Fate Sealers turning back. He could hear Valerian ordering Bog, Water and Rain to go and enjoy the fair. And from the corner of his eye, Will saw Peter flinching back, hugging the road map tightly, just in case.

But there was no need anymore. The Echo boys turned and left, looking too stunned or perhaps too frightened to make another attempt to snatch the map. And even as the Fate Sealers kept fading out of sight, Will wondered if Valerian could call them back if someone didn't do as he asked.

"May I?" asked Valerian, in his silky voice.

Will turned, scented smoke curling before him. The old Echo's plastic hand was reaching for the road map.

"Don't trust him!" Valerie shouted from the sky, before she kicked with her heels and soared away with her bird.

Valerian watched his niece for a moment, sadness washing over his face. Then he stretched his plastic hand to the ancient book again.

"No, don't," Will muttered to Peter, who was hugging the road map even tighter.

"I can't... I'm sorry, Professor," mumbled Peter, shuffling his feet.

Just for an instant Will saw Valerian's green eyes darting sideways, as if the old Echo really was going to summon the Fate Sealers back. But then Valerian slipped his plastic hand back in his rippling sea robe and puffed thoughtfully on his pipe.

"You're making a mistake," he said very slowly, looking more at Will than Peter. But Valerian was nodding with resignation. "I'm staying at the *Moon Hotel*," he added, "until tomorrow afternoon. Have been for a few days now. Waiting for a new Castaway to arrive. If you need my help... need anything at all, ask for me there. Oh, yes..." Valerian turned back when it seemed that he was already leaving. "Take care of this map, boys. Keep it safe. Books in this language are very rare. Very rare indeed."

Then Valerian walked away and disappeared in the glittering swirl of the bustling fair.

An Ice Fairy flew down to Will and Peter and waved her glistening hand before their stunned faces. "Doing a garden gnome impersonation?"

Will blinked first and shook Peter. "Come on!"

With Poudini barking before them, they dashed away down sparkling snowy streets and festive icy alleys. Flying parcels fluttered out of their way. Shimmering shoppers shouted after them to watch where they were going!

"Lake's this way!" said Will, pointing at a shimmering street sign.

They turned down another frozen alley, where stilt walkers were decking the snowy rooftops with strings of crystal ball

364

ornaments. Then down an avenue with a giant twinkling Christmas tree at its end, and suddenly Will and Peter found themselves in a beautiful street with the waterfall wall cascading on their left in a gleaming curve.

"What did Valerian say to them?" Will panted, darting his glance forwards and back in search of his Fate Sealer shadows. "Still gone."

"They didn't even argue," Peter wheezed, out of breath too. He leaned on a crystal ball lamppost and swatted the air over his head, where three flying Christmas ribbons were whizzing in circles. "Too afraid of Wither Heart to leave us for one second— Then suddenly they just up and go... Get off!" Peter gave the flying ribbons another good swat.

"Something's weird." Will nodded in agreement. Then squinting up at the shimmering waterfall wall, he said thoughtfully, "Lake's on the other side, I think."

"So how do we get past the wall. Swim?"

"Or look for a gate."

"Fine. Be boring." Peter grinned.

"Jeremy Fallon might know, about Valerian and the Fate Sealers," suggested Will, as they set off up the street.

The frosty storefronts on their right twinkled with Christmas lights and ribbons. Some flew out into the street, and Poudini chased them round and round.

"Jeremy Fallon?" Peter puffed away a Christmas ribbon that settled on his upper lip like a festive mustache. "Really looking forward to that. There's something else strange—" Peter looked down at the road map he was still hugging. "Doesn't exactly look like a map, does it? So how did Valerian know? He called it a map!"

"Maybe he saw it in Abednego's tower. Maybe he knew all about it. He said it was rare. But then—?"

"Why didn't he confiscate it?"

"Yeah." Will frowned.

"And why didn't Abednego, either?" said Peter. "He made sure we knew he knew... You know, about what we did... So why leave the map with us? Oh, honestly—" Peter rolled his eyes, as Poudini swallowed a flying light and his nose started to smoke.

"Is he okay?" Will tried not to laugh.

"Perfect." Peter shoved his dog's nose in a snow heap. "Who needs taste buds anyway?"

"So why did Abednego return the Blinker?" Will got back on topic, toying with the Prince's gadget in his pocket.

"Exactly what I'm wondering. Oh, there it is—"

Peter released Poudini and pointed up the street. A few steps more and Will could see it too. A hole came into view in the middle of the waterfall wall not so far from them.

They rushed over and discovered a dark, winding tunnel. As soon as they stepped inside, flying crystal balls appeared all around them, and the luminous spheres glowed like lanterns before Will and Peter, with two Ice Fairies flying in the lead, pointing the way they should go.

"There," said Peter excitedly, as daylight appeared at the end of the tunnel.

Already Will could spot the Lake of Eternal Ice shimmering through bare tree branches outside the tunnel. The fairies waved them farewell, and the lustrous crystal balls zoomed around Poudini's head before flying back into the dark tunnel. Will and Peter peeked outside in search of Fate Sealers. And, when they saw no one, they dashed into the chilly air and didn't stop until they reached the great sheet of ice stretching far into the distance.

"Wow…." Peter gasped in awe.

Even Will couldn't tear his eyes away from the sight that looked so different by daylight. Beneath the frozen surface of the Lake of Eternal Ice, the treasure chest of starry stones twinkled in a dazzling display of red, blue and yellow.

"Rubies… Diamonds… Sapphires…" Peter's blue-green eyes twinkled like the gems in the ice. "We could be rich, Will!"

"Or dead—" Will pointed to their left.

A terrified, frozen face was staring at them through the ice.

"That's not—" Peter choked.

"That's what they do to thieves." Will nodded. "They're all over the lake, Peter. Like a graveyard… but you can see the corpses. Look over there…" Will pointed at a dark crystal ball that hovered over the frozen lake in the distance. "That's where the true King's buried."

Peter gulped and looked around nervously. "We'd better hurry."

"Before my shadows find us," Will agreed, taking out his

Crystillery.

"Will it really work... this Memory Crossing thing?" Peter handed Will the road map, as they bent down to the ice.

"Only one way to find out."

Placing the book on the frozen lake, Will rocked his Crystillery until the starry stones sparked like fire and disappeared in a whirlpool of blue waves. Then the noise of the marketplace rose up from the Crystillery, and the road map appeared half inside the dome, half sticking out. Hands tugged at the ancient volume and the parchment pages fluttered like fragile wings—until one was torn in half.

"Dartboard!" Peter flipped through the real road map until he found a page torn in the middle, half of it gone. "Come on—" He shot to his feet, kicking up snow.

Poudini burst into barks beside Peter.

"No!" Will fought the urge to rise too. "The lake— We haven't tested it yet."

Quickly Will turned to the previous page in the road map, with the drawing of an ice-blue coin near the bottom. The ancient book still lay flat on the frozen lake, the Crystillery not yet touching the parchment. Even so, something strange started to happen right away.

The drawing of the coin floated up out of the page, turning three dimensional and sparkling as if it were real. The rest of the drawing came to life beside it, framing this perfect replica of an Echo Shekel with a round mirror inserted in a crystal blue round door.

"The door in the lake—" Will gasped.

"Put the Royal Shekel on it! No, Poudini—" Peter stopped his dog from clawing at the hovering hologram.

Holding his breath, Will set the ice-blue coin on top of its hovering mirror image—and the Royal Shekel remained suspended there over the road map, as if it were resting on something real.

But still, nothing more happened.

"Crystillery— Try it—" Peter's voice was choked with excitement.

Will nodded. They kept coming back to the Crystillery. It seemed to lie at the heart of the mystery of the lake.

This time, no sooner did the starry stones sparkle inside the blue dome then both floating Royal Shekels—the real one and the hologram—began to turn by themselves. First came a quarter turn, then another and two more until the drawing brought to life inside the road map altered for the last time. The crystal blue door hovering there opened by itself to reveal a grassy trail cutting through an icy cave.

"It's giving us instructions." Peter blinked in awe. "The Royal Shekel is a... *Coin Key*."

"*Yes!*" A surge of excitement rippled through Will's mind. "And I know what the lock is— Has to be! It's a Crystillery lock. That's why it's blank. No carvings— No mirror image of anything. The key doesn't have to be a perfect fit... not the way Coin Keys are supposed to. It just has to be the coin with the right *Memory*. Peter you know what this means?" Will laughed in amazement. "We've figured out how to unlock the door in the lake. We can go to Olám Shoné on Christmas Eve... when the Prince comes back. That's only five days—"

All of a sudden Will realized that the glimmer of the lake had dimmed all around him. He was standing in a fluttering shadow. He even knew that the shadow had covered him a while ago, bringing with it the sound of something beating the air above him—but he had been too distracted to notice.

"What the—?" Peter seemed to finally notice Poudini wagging his tail like a propeller and barking at the sky.

"Hi, there," a distant voice called to them.

"Valerie—" Looking straight up, Will found Valerie Valerian waving hello at him over the neck of her flying albatross.

"How long have you been there—" snapped Peter, slamming the road map shut.

"We didn't hear you," added Will, hiding his Crystillery quickly.

"I know you didn't, silly." Valerie laughed. "I'm practicing."

"What?" asked Will.

"Spying?" muttered Peter under his breath.

"No!" Valerie frowned, as if she somehow heard Peter. "Silent flying. Goodbye, Freddy. But not you." Valerie glared down at Peter. "Spying, my crystal foot!"

And suddenly she kicked her see-through heels into her bird, and the two of them fluttered away like a cloud.

"No way she could hear me without a spying tool," snarled Peter.

"There is such a thing?"

"Well, there must be. Mustn't there?" Peter shrugged.

Evil Deed

A Different World

Late that night, Jeremy Fallon gave Will and Peter a warning.

"Don't trust everything you *think* you see, if you know what I mean? Valerian couldn't make the Fate Sealers just give up on following you. Must be a trick. Maybe Wither Heart is following you now—*Invisible*."

Peter wanted to know if Jeremy was making this up as he went along. But it hardly mattered that the morbid boy in the wheelchair was only fifty percent sure. Will and Peter had one more thing to worry about.

And then there was Valerie. And Peter had some fanciful ideas when it came to her.

"What if the Fate Sealers don't need to follow us anymore..." he suggested, sitting with Will by the fake sitting room fire, talking things over late into the night. "It's simple, if you see past the magic. The Fate Sealers don't need to follow us... because Valerie *is*."

"Is what—?" asked Will, turning tiredly away from the holographic flames.

"Following us."

"You think Valerie's working for the Fate Sealers?" Will sighed, but suddenly he froze. "D'you see that—?" He stared out the crystal ball corridor window.

Peter twisted in his snow heap armchair. "What?"

"Gone now," muttered Will. "Two Fate Sealers. Stared at me... then walked away. Like they were looking for me... but changed their minds."

"What d'I tell you?" said Peter, folding his arms decisively. "Valerie's taken over for them. They brainwashed her, that's it. In Shadowpain... She was a prisoner. And they brainwashed her. Not impossible, is it?"

"No..." Will had to admit. "No, it isn't."

"I know you like her," Peter added, grinning. "Sorry about that."

"Like her?" Will felt himself turning red. "She's ten, Peter."

By the next morning, Will and Peter decided that, until the Prince arrived four days from now, they would have to be extra careful. This meant avoiding Valerie and watching for signs of an invisible Echo, just in case Jeremy was right about Wither Heart. And finally Bog Slippery and the Splash Brothers were added to the danger list, when they stared daggers at Will and Peter through the crystal ball bathroom mirrors and mimicked cutting their own throats in a silent threat.

And so it was that while the whole Orphanage came alive with Christmas cheer, fluttering red and green lights and hovering

376

crystal balls decked with holly— And while flying Ice Fairies rained down sugarplum Flavor Bubbles, and glistening Castaways rushed about sampling every splashing fountain, for suddenly the blue water everywhere was amazingly delicious— while all this was going on, Will and Peter had no time for fun at all.

It occurred to them, talking over breakfast by Wolfeá's tree (and as far away from Brainy's snooping ears as possible) that learning how to open the door in the lake was only the beginning. Now they would have to figure out how to find the Cold Fire Mushrooms. After all, this was the reason for going to Olám Shoné in the first place, to clear the true King's name so the Prince could take the throne.

But what if the mushrooms grew thousands of miles away from the door in the lake? How could Will and Peter find them? Once more they looked down at the road map wondering what the words in shimmering silver ink were saying. *Words in an ancient language few Echoes know*, as Abednego described it at the Winter Break Breakfast Feast. Determined to figure it out, Will and Peter left Wolfeá with a fresh bucket of water and a pile of chicken bones and headed for the glacial library in search of a dictionary.

"We don't even know what language we're looking for," complained Peter, as he descended the glass ladder of the Ancient Languages section in the great orphanage library. He had climbed up and down the precariously tall ladder at least eight times, and every time he lugged down a heavier dictionary than the one before.

"Not Ancient Greek," decided Will, after quickly comparing

the book with the road map.

Peter swatted away a Christmas light that was buzzing around Poudini's head, driving the little dog insane. Then Peter climbed the sparkling ladder again, the misty ceiling floating high above him like a cloud.

"They're watching us," Will muttered to himself.

He was seeing eyes in every crystal ball around him, even the flying ones, which hovered past every once in a while, wearing wigs of Christmas holly. Will pulled out the Prince's Blinker and clicked it shut. But it came as no surprise when nothing happened. Will had first realized that something was wrong the night before, when he couldn't blink the painting to sleep over the sitting room fireplace. Will's finger was already blistered from testing the Blinker so many times since.

"Any luck?" asked Peter, climbing down with another heavy book.

"Nope. At least now we know why Abednego gave it back to me..." Will shoved the sabotaged blinker back in his glistening white pocket.

"Forget the eyes," said Peter. "You heard him— Abednego doesn't really care what we do, as long as we stay away from his tower. Not this one either?" Peter added glumly, as Will shook his head at the dictionary.

Up the glistening ladder, and ten dictionaries later Peter was getting breathless and Will took over and brought down ten more books. But none of them matched the strange letters scribbled in the ancient road map. And there were still at least a hundred dictionaries on the shelves above, hours of boring comparisons to go through— when suddenly Will froze, staring at Peter.

"Did you feel that?"

Something cold had brushed against Will's cheek, as if an Echo had passed between him and Peter. Except that no one was there. And yet Poudini started growling.

"No dots of light," whispered Peter.

Will cast around for the faint outline of an invisible Fate Sealer or a girl, though with so many Christmas lights buzzing everywhere like fireflies it was hard to tell.

"No, look... It's all right." Peter heaved a sigh of relief as two Ice Fairies flew overhead, raining down Flavor Bubbles. "Their wings— They push down cold air."

"Maybe," said Will, but he still felt nervous.

Peter climbed the glistening glass ladder again, while Poudini gave up growling in favor of bursting sugarplum bubbles.

Will took his crystal ball sunglasses off and scanned the brilliant white hall all around him. He could see no glistening Castaways anywhere; everyone was outside competing for Valerian's medallion, having fun in the sun. No Fate Sealers, either. No librarians in watery robes. Still, the library felt crowded with eyes watching him and Peter. And here and there a Christmas tree twinkled as if an invisible Echo was crouching inside it.

"This is it— hope so..."

Peter returned, carrying a dictionary twice the size of all the others and blowing a magician's hat in self-congratulation. And soon they were sure of it: *Hebrew* was the ancient language few Echoes knew! There was no doubt. The strange letters in the dictionary looked exactly like the strange letters in the ancient road map.

"We did it." Peter grinned.

"Yack—" said Will, scrunching his face. "Sorry. Swallowed a painkiller without water. Meant to say 'yay'. You know... 'Yay! We did it.' "

Sitting on the snow-white carpet behind a twinkling Christmas tree, which seemed free of invisible Echoes (for Poudini didn't growl near it), Will and Peter opened the enormous dictionary.

A lustrous crystal ball bookmark rested between page one and two. It blinked its eye open, stared at Will then at Peter before going back to sleep.

"What d'you think?" whispered Peter. "A deadly book alarm?"

"Too late, if it is." Will shrugged.

But the bookmark didn't turn violent, so Will turned the page.

A word leapt off the second paragraph and disappeared in the self-cleaning carpet of the library.

"What next? A juggling act?" grumbled Will.

But, thereafter, the pages of the dictionary, yellow and faded with age, behaved quite normally.

Each page contained words written in English, with the Hebrew version written beside them. Will and Peter took turns pointing out an interesting word here and there, like Fate Sealer or Mongrel, until suddenly they were both pointing at the same word.

"So that's what *Crystillery* looks like in Hebrew," Will realized. And he suggested that they search for the same word inside the road map. But they might as well have tried to pick out a single raindrop in a storm!

"They're all kind of the same." Will sighed, when the sea of shimmering silver words started swimming on the parchment before his eyes.

"But totally different." Peter nodded, pushing his slipping crystal ball sunglasses back up. "And lethal. I'm about to die of boredom."

"Then, what can we—?"

But at that moment a sweet voice found its way into their secret corner, and Will and Peter snapped their heads up suspiciously.

"Thought I heard voices..." said Valerie Valerian, her see-through face peeking at them past the twinkling Christmas tree.

She was wearing no crystal ball sunglasses, and her blue eyes looked like tiny swimming pools in her pale face.

"I was looking for you—" she added shyly, smiling at Will.

"Told you!" grumbled Peter, slamming the road map on a buzzing Christmas light. "Working for them!"

"—To give this back to you," Valerie went on, sidling past the tree to pet Poudini. The little dog had cleared a whole patch of needles on the tree from wagging so much. "Your name's on the inside cover, Freddy," explained Valerie. "It is yours, isn't it?"

Valerie raised the book she was carrying—a book that looked like a slab of marble stolen from a graveyard.

And, suddenly, all three of them were gaping in amazement.

"Where did you get *that*?" they asked together. But Valerie was staring at the road map, while Will and Peter were staring at the gravestone book.

"On my pillow. Someone left it," Valerie answered first. And stretching her see-through hand timidly to the road map, she added in wonder, "Is that really the King's—?"

"On your pillow?" Peter shot to his feet. "Special delivery from the tooth fairy?"

"You've seen this book before?" Will rose also, holding the road map out to Valerie.

"Of course, she did!" hissed Peter. "On the lake—"

"—In the palace." Valerie nodded, her cropped hair juddering. "My uncle was Chief Royal Advisor. Is it really…?" And as if to convince herself that her eyes weren't playing tricks on her, she moved a see-through finger beneath the gilded title, mumbling softly, "*Mapá*."

"Did you just read this?" Will shoved his crystal ball sunglasses up on his head, staring at Valerie in awe.

"It's in Hebrew," said Valerie shyly, "the ancient language of the Echoes. It means: Map."

"You can read Hebrew?" Peter frowned skeptically.

Will fumbled to open the King's map.

"No— It's upside down." Valerie turned the road map around in Will's arms. "You read Hebrew from right to left. *Ma— pá—*" She moved her see-though finger beneath the title again.

"And this?" Will flicked to the title page and the three silver words scrawled at its center.

"Meéver Le-Olám Shoné." Valerie moved her delicate finger beneath each shimmering word as she translated, "*Beyond a Different World*. Olám Shoné means a Different World. It's like a fairytale place. But it's real. Well... *I* think it's real, anyway."

"And this?" Will had already turned another of the road map's parchments, his heart beating wildly in his chest.

But suddenly Valerie shook her head.

"I can't really read Hebrew, Freddy," she said shyly. "I just remember the title, that's all—"

"I knew it!" Peter crowed.

"Crash and splash! I never said I could read it!" Valerie stiffened, and her pale face glowed with an Echo blush. "You don't believe me about this book, either— Do you?" She shoved the gravestone book at Peter. "You think I'm lying. Just because my uncle's a liar— about rescuing me— about Shadowpain... You think I'm like him? I'm not."

Valerie twirled her sapphire ring miserably and started walking away with Poudini skipping merrily after her.

"No, wait—" Will grabbed Valerie's thin, see-through arm. It felt as cold as ice. "We don't think you're lying."

"I do," Peter grumbled, but Will cut him off.

"We don't think your uncle's lying either."

This seemed to make matters worse. Valerie shook Will's hand off.

"I don't know anything else in the map, Freddy," she said coldly. "Just translate it. It shouldn't be too hard. Is that a Hebrew dictionary?"

Valerie looked down at the thick volume left forgotten on the snowy carpet, which was trying to clean the dictionary out of existence.

"It certainly is," said Peter. And in a moment, he returned the favor for the gravestone book and shoved the dictionary into Valerie's frail arms. "Let's see you then..." he said dryly, "if it's so easy."

Wordlessly Valerie walked away, taking the dictionary with her. But before Will could finish congratulating Peter on scaring her off, they saw Valerie sinking into a snowy armchair. She pulled out a sheet of paper and a pen from the glistening side pocket of the chair. Then she started copying the Hebrew letters cascading in flaps down the fore-edge of the old dictionary.

"Come on," said Will to Peter.

All the lights flew off the Christmas tree and followed Will and Peter as they walked over to Valerie. But Poudini launched himself into the twinkling swirl and scattered the lot.

"Is that the Hebrew alphabet?" asked Will, as Valerie finished copying the ancient looking letters.

Valerie nodded. "So, give me the King's map," she

demanded.

Will handed over the road map and watched as Valerie started to translate the shimmering title of page one. She referenced her column of letters again and again, to remind herself which letter came before which in alphabetical order. Peter opened the gravestone book to pass the time, making it very clear that he expected nothing good to come of Valerie. But Will watched the frail Echo breathlessly.

"Mushrooms!" Will gasped, when Valerie finished.

Peter closed the gravestone book, looking amazed.

"Told you—" Valerie said to Peter, staring at the gravestone book. "Property of Fredrick Fingeldy. Says so inside. I wasn't lying."

"You sure…?" Peter gasped at Will, looking as if he hadn't even heard Valerie.

Valerie, on the other hand, seemed to think that Peter was talking to her, and she sighed and started twirling her beautiful ring again, as if it brought her comfort.

Will tapped the Hebrew word and double-checked its English translation. "This definitely means: *Mushrooms*, Peter. We were looking at the dictionary the wrong way. Had to start on the right… not the left. Valerie, you're amazing!" Will smiled so widely he could see his gray cheeks ballooning under his eyes like bullfrogs.

Valerie laughed softly, shyly, her see-through cheeks glowing again and her eyes glittering like her sapphire ring.

"I've translated other things written about him… Fluid

Conway, I mean," she said shyly. "He wrote this book." Valerie placed her see-through hand delicately on the road map. "I've learned everything about him. Conway invented the Crystillery. But the King wanted to execute him *and* the woman he loved. It's all *so* romantic... She was a queen..." Valerie sighed. "The beautiful Queen Illyria."

"Queen Illyria?" Peter's blue-green eyes narrowed thoughtfully.

And, all at once, two flying crystal balls fluttered closer, eyes blinking open between their Christmas holly wigs.

"As in *Illyria's Treasure?*" Peter added, lowering his voice.

"You mean... the Winter Break Breakfast Feast," Will remembered. "Valerian's medallion..." And, seeing more crystal balls flying low, Will pressed his blistered finger to the Blinker in his pocket. But, of course, nothing happened.

"The medallion..." Valerie nodded, oblivious of the hovering eyes. "Yes, it's the Coin Key for Illyria's Treasure. Chest is lost, though," she added, petting Poudini, who was trying to sniff a buzzing light out of her see-through shoe. "My uncle wasn't lying about that—"

"No! Not about that!" Peter suddenly looked suspicious again. "Only about rescuing you from Shadowpain. That's what you said before..."

"Yes, he did lie about that." Valerie's large blue eyes filled with hurt. "But you still don't believe me, do you?"

"Not especially, no," said Peter. "Want to explain what

386

exactly did happen in Shadowpain? I mean, if your uncle didn't rescue you, how did you get out? The Fate Sealers just let you go?"

"Oh, you're just horrible, you know that? Peter Twister Person... whatever your name is."

Valerie burst into frozen tears, which rolled down her cheeks and disappeared in the self-cleaning carpet. In a moment, she rushed away, twirling her large ring once more. And the eavesdropping crystal balls raced after her, their sprigs of holly fluttering behind them like scarves.

"Peter Twister Person...?" grumbled Peter.

"Did you have to do that?" Will sighed, gathering their things to go after Valerie.

Peter pushed his crystal ball sunglasses defiantly up his nose. "You heard what she said— if Valerian didn't rescue her, what is she doing out of Shadowpain? I'm telling you, she's working for the Fate Sealers. And now she knows we have the road map! And she knows we're translating it!"

"So what now?" asked Will.

"Let's just take the dictionary to Wolfeá and translate there. *Alone*. All right?"

"All right," said Will. "At least I'll get to spend some time with Wolfeá. She hates being tied up like that. But she's looking better, isn't she? Fur all grown around her collar. And you can't see her ribs anymore."

"Yeah, that's great. But there's another thing... about Valerie, I mean," said Peter, when they were heading down the

387

glistening glass staircase, on their way out of the library. "Don't you think it's just a bit odd how friendly she's getting suddenly? Popping up everywhere... Looking for you. Here—"

Crystal ball candy-canes dangled from the banister and grew back as Peter picked one for each of them, Poudini included.

"Ever since Valerie got to the Orphanage, she was always by herself," Peter went on. "Flying her albatross—alone. Twirling her ring, mumbling—to herself... unless she was busy trying to blind Dartboard. And suddenly she shows up with the gravestone book— after someone stole it! And look— It does say *Property of Fredrick Fingeldy* inside. And we're supposed to believe she didn't write it in herself? How lame can you get...? *'Someone left it on my pillow'.* Honestly!"

Will was sure Peter was rolling his eyes behind his crystal ball sunglasses. "Yeah, it is lame," he admitted, finishing off his candy cane and wishing he had taken another for the road. It tasted like nothing he had ever had before, kind of fizzy and amazingly sweet. "That's why I believe her," added Will. "If Valerie was lying, she'd come up with something better, wouldn't she?"

Peter grumbled a response, but they had reached a giant crystal ball by the library entrance, and an eye blinked open inside it, beneath the silver letters *Checkout Desk.* Behind the crystal ball, a see-through librarian was stamping the spines of books with crystal ball stamps of many different colors. As she fluttered her thin, see-through arms, her aquamarine robe rippled like a miniature waterfall.

"We'd like to check this book out, please," said Will, laying the Hebrew dictionary on the crowded desk and smiling politely.

"Oh no— Don't smile!" The librarian scrutinized Will over the rim of her crystal ball sunglasses. "With a face like that, a smile is not the way to go. Oh, Fortune help me!" She suddenly clapped her ink-stained fingers to her mouth. "Said that aloud, didn't I? Books, books, books! All day long surrounded by books. Tell them anything… never take offense. But people— Good Fortune! Always have to watch what you say to *them*." And the jittery librarian sighed, which seemed like the only apology Will was going to get.

"We want to *check— this— book— out—*" said Peter very slowly, as if the librarian was hard of hearing.

"Yes!" The Echo pursed her see-through lips at him. "Heard you the first time. And…" She flipped the dictionary over to its side, scattering her rainbow of crystal ball stamps across the desk. "Aha! As I thought, by Fortune!" the librarian said with satisfaction. "Not a book you're allowed to take anywhere! Which is as it should be," she added to herself, "and should be more often.

"*Red— crystal— ball—*" It was now her turn to talk to Peter as if he were an idiot. "See this stamp on the back, mmmm? Seeing it now, are we? Not to be allowed out of the library! I'll keep it here, thank you very much!"

It took fifteen minutes of patient promises, not to mention bountiful compliments, to regain possession of the dictionary with the strict vow to use it only in the library, and only in the *Ancient Languages Section*, and only with Poudini keeping at least two feet away.

389

*　　*　　*

Late that afternoon, their necks sore and stomachs growling from missing lunch, Will and Peter finished translating *Page 1*. Now they knew about the Cold Fire Mushroom Field, which grew in the shadow of a giant Crystillery, surrounded by clouds of purple smoke and the fresh smell of apples.

"Apples? You sure we translated this bit right?" wondered Peter.

Will just nodded.

And yet they still had to discover how far the field was from the door in the lake. And the way to get there. The answers might lie hidden in the remaining pages of the road map, eleven in all, or ten and half to be exact, thanks to Bog Slippery and the Splash Brothers. But if each page took half a day to translate, Will and Peter would never finish before the Prince arrived on Christmas Eve, just four nights and three days away.

They thought of splitting the work between them but found they each took twice as long without the other's help. Working around-the-clock was out of the question because the library closed in the evening. And they couldn't checkout the dictionary, though they did try to sneak the enormous book out tucked under Peter's glistening sweater. But they discovered that the red crystal ball stamp on the book's spine was a silent alarm that summoned two Ice Fairies, who blocked the exit with their frozen wings.

"We need someone to help us," concluded Will a little later.

They were sitting with Wolfeá, eating roast beef sandwiches

and watching the giant Echo sun setting behind the curved alabaster wall of the gleaming Orphanage. A shadow kept fluttering on the snow between them: Valerie flying her albatross in the dark purple sky just above them.

"Help translating? Well, not her," said Peter, spitting crumbs. "And not Brainy, obviously. Michael's all right, but...."

Will nodded. They both knew it, though they didn't say it aloud. They weren't just translating a book. They were plotting to replace the false King with his nephew, the Prince. And the false King had agents at the Orphanage. The Fate Sealers were everywhere, their footsteps muffled, their motions silent. Will and Peter couldn't drag their roommates into this. Even Brainy didn't deserve that. But there was someone else whose life was already in danger.

"Auralius," said Will, petting Wolfeá's head in his lap. "The false King is hunting down Mongrels, right? Auralius is stuck hiding in the creepy Ant Chamber. Like a prisoner. But if he helps us get the mushrooms, the Prince will stop the killing. Mongrels will be safe again."

Peter shook his head doubtfully. "Don't know if we can trust Auralius."

"The Prince trusts him," insisted Will. "Besides, this could be Auralius' only chance to be free again."

"Yeah, maybe... But, anyway, it's too risky. Catch—" Peter tossed Poudini the last bite from his sandwich. "Takes ten minutes to cross the Sound kitchen," explained Peter. "And it's full of shadows at night. What if someone follows us? At least before we could see them. Now… who knows?" Peter glanced angrily up at Valerie circling above them, Christmas lights buzzing around her.

"Isn't there a shortcut in the kitchen, though?" asked Will. "I mean… the night you saved me from Wither Heart… we crossed the kitchen in a couple of minutes, didn't we?"

"Yeah." Peter grinned. "And, no it wasn't magic. You just have to know which flagstones to stand on at the same time. But it only works one way. From the fireplace back to the door… You know, so cooked food can be delivered quickly."

"Too bad."

"Yeah…"

"But maybe there's another way," said Will after a moment.

And he closed his eyes and cast his thoughts back to the night the Prince had met them in Auralius' cell.

It wasn't until long past midnight that they got to test Will's idea.

Lying in their beds, pretending to sleep, Will and Peter listened to Brainy tiring himself out with fake snores until he finally fell asleep for real, with his tuxedoed mouse sleeping in the icy cage by his head. Then Will tucked the road map under his sweater, and Peter left Poudini sleeping on his pillow.

They slipped out through the Air Seal guarding their dorm room into the chilly corridor, seeing no one, and pretty soon they turned into the balmy boy's bathroom. The waterfall walls rustled faintly like whispering voices, but there was no one here either. And even in the crystal ball chandelier, which cast a faded glow for nocturnal visitors, no eyes blinked open.

"You sure you remember it right?" whispered Peter.

"Think so…"

Will led the way past the eyeless crystal ball sinks and mirrors, going over the memory in his mind.

The note with the map of the Orphanage… before Auralius burned it… It had crystal ball signposts drawn on it. White for Sound rooms, silver for Echoes, and red for secret passages…. One flaming crystal ball in particular bounced across the parchment… showing the secret tunnel into the Ant Chamber… where Auralius was hiding.

"It starts here," Will whispered, as the shower stalls came into view, their water curtains rippling. "The fifth shower stall. There—"

But suddenly Will froze.

"What was that—?"

Something was stirring in the dark corner behind the last stall. Then a shrill voice rose above the rustle of water echoing through the empty blue chamber.

"A tryst? Lovers meeting in the sssilver sssilence of the night?"

A sagging arm slithered into the light, gruesome red fingernails curving from it like waterfalls of blood.

"Oh, no… Hydra Agonia," whispered Peter, and Will could feel his friend shuddering. "Only female Fate Sealer at the

Orphanage. Comes out at night. To spy on—?"

"Come boyfriend and girlfriend... Hold hands for me... Kisssss for me!"

The Fate Sealer slithered free of the shadows. Her skin was tucked fashionably around her waist with a string of pearls, as if she were a decomposing princess come back from the dead. "Hug for me! Ssssnuggle for me!" she screeched. "I'm a sssssucker for a good love sssstory."

But suddenly Hydra Agonia's sagging mouth started writhing.

"BOYS! Ssssmelly, troublemaking BOYS! Come to pop your pimplessss?"

And instantly the romantic Fate Sealer flew at Will and Peter, her skin flapping like a thousand insect wings.

"Not good—" Peter drew a crystal ball on the air and tried to blow another with his cold breath; though only his usual magician's hat came out, looking a little flat around the edges.

Play the fool, Will could suddenly hear Damian's voice in his mind.

"Eh... actually, we're here to do laundry," Will improvised quickly, slurring his medicated voice to sound like a complete moron.

Hydra Agonia slowed down and gasped a hollow laugh, waving her bloody fingernails. "Laundry? In the shhhhower?"

"Saaavvves tiiiiime," Will bleated like a sheep, smirking stupidly.

Then he shoved Peter into the fifth shower stall and pulled the water-curtain closed behind them.

"Start looking," Will whispered, to the sound of the Fate Sealer coughing a hollow laugh behind the rippling curtain.

"Looking for what?" stammered Peter.

"Secret opening. It's here somewhere."

"Can't hear the water running," screeched Hydra Agonia, her voice drawing dangerously near.

"Coming up."

Peter twisted the crystal ball faucet, and the rain cloud hovering over the stall erupted in a freezing shower.

"The road map—" grumbled Will, trying to keep the front of his sweater dry. He slapped Peter's hand off the crystal ball faucet, then he pushed the faucet up, then down, then up again—just as if he were opening the secret door behind the great fireplace.

"Please, please work," muttered Will.

The next moment, the waterfall wall to Will and Peter's right slid silently apart like a stage curtain.

"Need detergent?" Hydra Agonia screeched again. "Fabric softener? Bleach?"

"Doing fine," gurgled Peter, sticking his dripping head through the shower curtain.

"Don't forget to rub those stains off— Or is that your face?"

Will could hear Peter laughing stupidly, before he stuck his head back through the curtain.

"She's leaving," Peter spluttered under the stream of ice-cold water. "Had to be an Echo shower stall… I'm fffreeezzzing."

"Let's go."

A moment later, the cascading wall shuddered shut behind them, as Will and Peter slipped down the secret passage. Wet and shivering, they groped their way through the darkness until their fingers grew numb from the cold. But still only clammy walls stretched on at their sides into the silent gloom. Until, at long last, they bumped into a barrier.

Will raised his frozen hand and knocked.

There was a rumble, and light appeared in front of them through a widening crack. For a moment Will was blinded. When he could see again Auralius was flying at him, his golden dagger glinting in his fist.

"It's us!" Peter shouted.

"You!" snarled Auralius.

The Mongrel's eyes were see-through with rage. And his face was dotted with the shadows of the spiders crawling in the cobwebbed ceiling over him.

"Anyone follow you?" asked Auralius warily.

Will shook his head, and slowly Auralius withdrew the point of his knife from Will's throat.

"Who is it Auralius, dear?" a sweet voice rose from the cold cell.

"You'd better come in," muttered Auralius.

Will and Peter entered the musty ant chamber. Tonight, the broken crystal ball light glowing on the dirty floor illuminated two other people beside Auralius. A beautiful Echo sat on a snow heap by the narrow bed, oblivious of the ants crawling on her waterfall apron. And a man lay in the bed, covered with a snowy sheet that kept cleaning itself from the dirty drops trickling through the cobwebbed ceiling.

"Drinkwater…?" stammered Will, barely recognizing the pale, sleeping man who looked like a corpse. "Is he dead?"

Auralius shook his head and dropped by the woman's snow heap. "He saved me. And now he's dying for it."

"He isn't dying," said the beautiful Echo, kissing Auralius on the cheek. "I won't let him. And now…" She rose and smiled kindly at Will and Peter. "Who are our guests?"

"I'm… Fredrick Fingeldy," said Will, shivering badly in his wet clothes.

"Peter Pppatrick Peterson," said Peter, shivering even more.

"Well, how wonderful to have friends come over. But you look chilled to the bone. We'll soon fix that."

The beautiful Echo lifted the top off the snow heap she had been sitting on. She pulled out one blanket and then another, both of which looked like icicles sewn together in rows upon rows.

"They're warmer than they look," she promised, handing one to Will and one to Peter. "Wrap yourselves in them. That's right… all around. In no time you'll be as toasty as a crystal ball toast. I'm Auralius' mother, by the way," she added, smiling brightly. "Well… you didn't think Auralius was born a Mongrel by accident, did you? Sound for a father, Echo for a mother. Just call me Professor

397

Flower."

"Had you for Sound Physiology last year, Professor Flower," said Peter, "before you—"

"Oh, yes… the Fortunate days! Before Mongrels were hunted. I did love teaching… All the fun we had taking skeletons apart and putting them back together again like jigsaw puzzles. Well… now I work in the kitchen to be near my boy. Head Chef for the Echoes. Isn't that right Auralius?"

The blond boy grunted a response without looking up from his father's pale face.

"So…" Professor Flower beamed at Will, who was already beginning to feel strangely dry beneath the blanket of icicles. "Fredrick Fingeldy is it? Well… just between the four of us, Auralius already told me all about you."

"He did what?" snapped Peter, staring furiously at the boy kneeling by the bed.

"You're the magician, aren't you?" Professor Flower smiled at Peter. "I do remember you now. Well no wonder you can't trust anyone… How can you, if you're always expecting some magical mischief? All splash and nonsense in my case, of course."

Professor Flower turned to Will. "So what was I saying…? Oh, yes. Not easy being the Prince's Sound, I'm sure. So when the Cold Sleep symptoms wear off, as they're sure to eventually— just come and hide with Auralius. We'll keep you safe."

Will smiled awkwardly, not to seem ungrateful, though he hoped things would never come to such a gloomy end.

"So… all dry then?" said Professor Flower, pulling off the two blankets from Will and Peter. The icicles looked fatter now, and some of them where dripping.

Peter pinched his dry clothes in disbelief. "How…?"

"Absorbed every drop, didn't they?" Professor Flower tossed the blankets back in the snow heap and replaced the lid. "Did wonders for my Nicholas, they did."

"Who's Nicholas?" Will glanced at Peter, who gestured at Drinkwater's still body.

"And never scolded my Echo hands," continued Professor Flower. "Amazing invention! Thank you Fluid Conway, Fortune rest your soul. Well, if you'll forgive me now. It's time for Nicholas' medicine. Auralius, entertain our guests."

Professor Flower gave her son a soft kick, before pulling out a vial of medicine from her watery apron and bending over her husband.

Auralius stood up resentfully, his dagger still glinting in his fist.

"How did you know—? About the shower stall?" he asked, glaring at Will and Peter.

"The map," said Will. "On the note—"

"Which I burned?"

"Yeah," said Peter, really proud of Will at the moment.

"You have a good memory," said Auralius politely. But he sounded as if he wished he could get inside Will's head and slice the memory out with his dagger. "So what was so important you had to come here?" added the Mongrel suspiciously.

Will took out the road map, the translation of *Page 1*, and Valerie's column of the Hebrew alphabet. Then he told Auralius everything he and Peter discovered about the mushrooms, the King's road map, and the secret to opening the door in the lake with the—

"Royal Shekel—" gasped Professor Flower. Her beautiful face turned see-through from shock as Will pulled out the coin from the secret compartment in his glistening white shoe.

"All Shekels look the same," said Auralius skeptically.

"Not to a *Crystillery* lock, they don't," said Will.

Peter grabbed Will's arm, as if he was worried Will was saying too much.

"You know how to use a Crystillery....?" Auralius' eyes turned invisible for a moment.

Will shook his head. But Peter jumped in before Will could explain anymore.

"We're only telling you all this 'cause we need your help. But if you say anything— To anyone—"

"Say anything? Who to— my pets— or my walls?" Auralius gestured with his hands around the miserable, dank cell he called his home.

"—Need our help...?" Professor Flower laid a calming hand on her son's shoulder. "You mean... with translating the road map?"

"The Prince is coming back in three days," said Will urgently.

"On Christmas Eve... I see." Professor Flower nodded. "And

you want to finish the translation before that. Then it's settled."

She clapped her see-through hands soundlessly.

"I'll bring the dictionary here every night," Professor Flower decided. "And return it to the library before dawn. I have a key to the library, all staff members do. We'll start immediately. Just leave the road map with Auralius tonight. Tomorrow you'll find both the dictionary and the road map waiting for you in the *Hold Section*... on the second floor of the library. I'll leave the books under your name, Mr. Peterson, shall I...? Excellent," Professor Flower added without waiting for a reply. "I'll be off then."

Without another word, Professor Flower dashed away into the passage Will and Peter had come by.

"No— wait!" said Auralius, when Will and Peter turned to follow her.

"What?" asked Peter suspiciously.

"I'll help you... if you help me," answered the Mongrel. He pulled out a blue dome from the filthy rags hanging on his thin body and added, "The Prince left his Crystillery here. I tried to use it... But I don't know how to see what my father saw. If he saw it.... I need to know the truth."

His hand shaking a little, Auralius stretched his golden dagger to Will.

"A Crystillery can't lie," explained Auralius. "If my father really saw this knife killing me, I need to know. I need to know he was telling the truth— That he didn't abandon me and my Mom. You can read a Crystillery. Show me the Memory."

Auralius looked like a boy trapped in hell asking for just a little ray of hope. Will was almost tempted to invent some lie that would make Auralius feel better. But he knew that a lie couldn't change facts. And, worse—a lie could later be found out, and end up doing more harm than good. Will shook his head and told Auralius the truth.

"I know how to activate a Crystillery. But I can only see the last complex Memory."

"The last complex Memory..." repeated Auralius, as if the words were acid in his mouth. "I already saw *that*." And he turned away, to face the narrow bed where his father lay dying.

Will said nothing as he slipped into the secret passage after Peter. He didn't have to ask. He guessed what memory Auralius had seen: His father hurling himself at a black Fate Sealer to save his son; and the golden dagger—Auralius' own knife—rising and falling in the evil creature's sagging hand, slashing Drinkwater's chest, his neck, his stomach....

*　　*　　*

The next day, freezing rain started falling after breakfast. The blue fountains froze in mid-splash and the topiaries turned to glass. The flying crystal balls came out to float like bubbles of light beneath the crystal sky. And the Christmas Fireflies, all coated in ice, twinkled like rubies and emeralds as they buzzed around the garden.

"Feels like being inside a snow globe," said Will, as he and Peter rushed to Wolfeá's tree with a warm blanket.

They looked like walking snowmen; even their heads were covered with glistening hats.

"Okay... this is getting creepy!" Peter scrunched his face at the tenth Echo they saw trying to win Valerian's medallion by standing in the rain so long she was turning into an ice sculpture.

"Orphanage of Castaway popsicles." Will grinned.

And then, just above Wolfeá's twinkling, Christmas-ribboned tree, they saw an albatross shattering the freezing rain with its flapping wings.

"Again!" Peter snarled in outrage, pulling out a pair of sticks he seemed to carry everywhere since last night. "Her! *Again!*" And rubbing the sticks together, Peter glared up at Valerie as if he wished he could knock the see-through girl off her bird.

"Maybe she's trying to be an umbrella," suggested Will.

"What—?"

"Over Wolfeá. She's kept her dry. Look—"

Will reached his shivering wolf. Above her no rain was falling, because the giant flying bird was sheltering the spot.

"You're welcome." Will laughed, as he wrapped Wolfeá in the plush glistening blanket and received a thank-you lick across his nose.

"Or maybe Valerie guessed you would come here," said Peter, still rubbing his sticks.

"What are you trying to do?" asked Will. "Make a wand?"

"A magician never reveals his tricks," said Peter, before he shoved his sticks back in his pocket.

Will shrugged and wrapped Wolfeá tighter. She wasn't shivering anymore.

"Look—" said Peter, suddenly brightening. "Not there— There—"

Suddenly Will saw them too.

Past an orchard of crystallized apple trees, Abednego's unicorns were galloping free, their pale see-through bodies looking like glass. While Wolfeá was a prisoner, thought Will bitterly. And all because of—

"Warloch!" Peter's face changed again, this time darkening with anger.

"Where?"

But already Will had spotted the Keeper watching them. The seedy-looking Echo was leaning on an icy fence not far from Wolfeá's tree, with his rifle half raised and his gold teeth glittering eerily. Three boys leaned on the fence beside him, all Echoes who seemed too large for their Castaway uniforms.

"Dartboard— and the Drops Duo— How totally marvelous," muttered Peter, as the three Echoes started blowing mock kisses his way.

"Check the knot on the tree," said Will, making sure Wolfeá was still safely tethered around her stomach. "Warloch's just itching to see her escape."

"You're right, Freddy," Valerie yelled down from the sky, somehow hearing what Will had said. "Warloch hates Wild pets."

"Is this idiot day or something?" grumbled Peter.

Will kept his eyes on Warloch's rifle, shielding Wolfeá with his body.

"Keep your wolf tied," Valerie shouted again.

"Thank you, Captain Obvious," Peter shouted back.

"We can't leave," said Will. "He'll kill her."

"Don't think so." Peter shook his head, and icicles rained down from his hat. "Warloch could have shot Wolfeá anytime. It's not about that."

"Not about that?" asked Valerie skeptically, as if she was part of the conversation.

"Will you stop spying on us?" Peter shouted up at her.

"No need to shout," said Valerie, sounding hurt.

"Clearly— Listen," Peter added, whispering into Will's ear. "Scaring you— That's what this is about. Just look at him... Warloch's loving it. The longer you stick around, the worse you'll make it. We have to go. Now! Before Warloch really starts to enjoy himself!"

Peter tugged Will back toward the white Orphanage, which curved majestically around the frozen garden like a giant ring. Valerie and her albatross followed them up in the sky like a far-off umbrella. And on the ground, Poudini barked greetings up at the flying girl, as he skipped ahead of Will and Peter.

"Everywhere— She's everywhere—" Peter grumbled.

Will cast a farewell glance at Wolfeá. His white wolf looked like a lonely snow heap under her blanket.

"In the bathroom— *Boy's* bathroom," Peter kept venting. "In

the dining hall— *Sound* side! *Inside* our dorm room— I know I'm
going to have nightmares about that one! Took over for them."

Peter gestured meaningfully as two Fate Sealers glided past,
stopped for a moment as they seemed to recognize Will, then glided
on, uninterested.

"Only logical explanation!" said Peter. "She's spying on us,
so they don't have to. Next time Valerie *accidentally* bumps into us,
I'm *accidentally* dumping a Christmas tree on her head!"

And very soon Peter did just that, by the library fountain,
leaving two Ice Fairies to untangle Valerie from a mess of buzzing
lights and branches, while he and Will fled up the nearest glass
staircase.

They stopped by the *Hold Section* and found the two books
Professor Flower had left for them, camouflaged in crystal ball
wrapping-paper. Up two more sparkling flights, and then a glittering
section plaque seemed to wink at Will and Peter.

"Brilliant!" Peter grinned.

"No one's ever going to look for us here!" Will agreed.

And so they settled beneath the silvery, hovering section
plaque: *Sewers.*

Only a single lazy eye watched them, half closed, from a
chandelier. The flying crystal balls were all outside, basking in the
rain that came down like needles. And the only specs of light
hovering around the library buzzed like ordinary Christmas Fireflies,
hardly the telltale signs of an invisible Echo.

"Way to go, Auralius!" Peter beamed as Will opened the
406

road map. "Two pages! *Two* pages translated in *one* night. I knew it was a good idea... getting him to help."

"*You* knew?" Will raised a skeptical eyebrow, and his entire puffy forehead swelled like a mushroom.

"What—?" said Peter innocently.

"Nothing."

They pushed their crystal ball sunglasses up on their heads to see better, then bent over the pages of translation.

But Will's heart was only half in it. The other half was worrying about his pet... out there in the freezing rain storm with Warloch plotting to kill her. And yet the more Will read Auralius' translation, the more his fears for Wolfeá disappeared.

"*Wolf Packs...*" Will tapped the words scribbled in Auralius' messy handwriting. "Wild wolves... I can't believe it."

It turned out that the Cold Fire Mushroom Field was guarded by a family of wolves, both Echoes and Sounds. No intruder had ever slipped past the wild animals. No thief had escaped their sharp fangs. But the road map explained how to tame the wolves.

"Wolfeá... she could go live with them," said Will, his heart almost floating out of his chest like a flying crystal ball. "She'll be... *free*. Peter, did you see this?"

But Peter had lost his smile. He shook his head, and Will thought his friend was trying to shake off the pair of flying Christmas bows that settled on his ears to decorate him. But Peter tapped the second page of translations.

"A bridge that plays tricks on you..." he muttered. "Don't

like the sound of that!"

Will leaned over. Christmas lights twinkled happily between him and the page.

There was only one way to reach the mushroom field— across a metal bridge. And the bridge hung over a raging river. The floor of the bridge was made of ice that never melted. But beneath the ice knives lay in wait.

"In wait... for what?" Will swallowed hard.

"Keep reading," said Peter.

At the lightest pressure the blades beneath the ice would start to spin. Not in one direction, but in a mad, confusing chaos of rotating blades. And good luck to anyone trying to cross! Unless...

"*Unless a Primary Safety Measure is used to render the bridge passable,*" Peter read the last line of Auralius' translation.

"What Primary Safety Measure?" asked Will, puffing at a buzzing Christmas firefly, which tried to fly up his nostril.

"We'd better find out."

Breathless with anticipation, they set to translating *Page 4* of the strange road map.

And here they discovered the answer to the question they had worried about most. How far was the field from the door in the lake? Only as far as a grassy slope that began in an icy cave and ended at the bridge. But beware of the silver handle halfway down the path! For if anyone pulled that handle—the bridge would break free from the cliff. And anyone crossing at the time would fall into the raging river and the freezing depths of a circular waterfall so vast it was named Whirlpool Chasm.

"Who would be stupid enough to pull the handle, anyway?" Peter tried to laugh it off.

"So why is it there?" wondered Will.

They turned to the next page, still seeking clues to how the bridge might be crossed safely.

And here, the page bearing the drawing of the Royal Shekel revealed the secrets they had already discovered for themselves on the Lake of Eternal Ice. Even so they translated every word, hoping that somehow, somewhere one of the strange looking Hebrew words would reveal a secret they didn't know. And then it happened, near the bottom of the page, where the Primary Safety Measure was mentioned once more, along with another most interesting clue.

"*The Crystillery Lock is one sided,*" Will read the last line they had translated, "*applying only to strangers coming into our world.*"

And suddenly an idea flashed through Will's mind.

Will sat bolt upright, too excited to care that an eye was blinking open to watch him from a crystal ball bookend on a nearby shelf.

"Peter," he whispered, "we're reading the road map backwards."

"What—?" Peter slapped a Christmas ribbon off his nose, straight into Poudini's waiting paws. "Backwards?"

"Backwards! As in... the wrong way. The road map... it's giving us directions *out* of Olám Shoné—not *into* it. But we'll be coming *in*, so we have to read the book backwards. We come by the door—that's *Page 5*." Will tapped the road map. "Then we go down the path. We avoid the dangerous handle, not to collapse the bridge—*Page 4*." The parchment crackled as Will flipped back a page. "Then we cross the bridge—*Page 3*." He kept going backwards page by page. "We get past the wolves, doing everything it says here, on *Page 2*. And in the end... in the end, Peter, we get the mushrooms! *Page 1*." Will slapped his hand down one last time.

"But then... Valerie!" Peter's blue-green eyes flashed with rage. "It's her fault. She said we were reading the road map backwards. '*It's upside down'*," he mimicked her voice ludicrously. "If she hadn't stuck her see-through nose in, we'd be fine! She set us up!"

Will shrugged, Christmas lights buzzing around him like flies around ice-cream. "Maybe... Doesn't—"

"No maybe about it! Get off—" Peter set Poudini on the lights, which fled in a fiery trail. "She did it! She wanted to trick us— Why are you smiling?"

"All these other pages..." Will rifled through the road map. "Who cares...? We don't have to translate them. Peter, we've figured out the important bit. We know how to get the mushrooms."

"But the Safety Measure—"

"They're all Safety Measures." Will couldn't stop grinning, though half his vision was blurred by the gray hills of his cheeks. "That's how Olám Shoné is protected. The Crystillery Lock is a Safety Measure. The door in the lake appears only when an Echo and his Sound are together— Another Safety Measure."

"But the Bridge of Knives," insisted Peter. "We can't get to the mushrooms without figuring out how to cross it."

"The answer's probably on the next page."

"You mean this one?" asked Peter, and he turned to the page Bog Slippery and the Splash Brothers had ripped in half.

Flying Crystal Balls

The Lost Safety Measure

That night the moon looked bigger than ever, floating like a giant crystal ball in the black sky. Its eerie light flooded the chilly corridors of the Orphanage, and Moon Worshipers gathered in a trance to watch Fortune gazing down on them.

"Beyond creepy," muttered Will, as he and Peter slipped past the still, see-through figures. For a moment, Will thought one of the Echoes had turned to watch them, but it was only a flying crystal ball with an eye blinking open inside it.

Peter swatted another flying spy. "Maybe we shouldn't go."

But they had to see Auralius. They had to tell him about that evening's terrible events.

It began after dinner. The freezing rain of the morning had coated the forest behind Wolfeá's tree in drooping ice. By nightfall, all the trees resembled Fate Sealers shivering in the chill evening wind, which blew so fiercely it chased Valerie and her albatross out of the sky. Twice Will and Peter had heard someone howling through the frozen trees, and they stayed with Wolfeá, afraid to leave her alone. Poudini leapt into Peter's arms when a third howl shivered on the wind—and then, suddenly, a hunched figure burst through the shadows before them.

It was a man with scaly black skin, which glistened eerily in the moonlight. Dressed only in a pair of torn pants, he gazed here and there at the crystallized forest as if looking for something. With his hunched back and hanging arms he resembled an ape.

"The troll," gasped Peter, grabbing Poudini's muzzle to stop him growling. "Cyrano de Bergerac... but in Echo form."

"Who's there?" The deformed man twisted back, his bulging eyes gleaming. "Castaways—? No!" he shrieked. "Mustn't see me!" And, covering his face in shame, he fled.

"Look! Eight toes." Peter pointed at the hideous footprints left in the frozen snow. "Can't believe we got to see him— Really cool!"

"Really horrible, you mean..." Will searched the shadows where poor Cyrano had disappeared.

"Yeah. Totally. Let's see if we can spot him again."

Another howl pierced the night as Will and Peter tied Wolfeá's rope around her neck and let her lead them into the sinister forest of Fate Sealer trees. They followed the many-toed tracks left in the snow, and every shadow startled them, though not enough to make them turn back.

"The howling, think it's him?" whispered Will.

"Hope so..." Peter's voice shuddered.

Overhead, the frozen trees shook in the wind as if laughing.

"Can't really blame him for living in a Sound." Will

416

shuddered.

"Yeah, he looks worse than a Fate Sealer. There—"

Peter stopped still, pointing at a waterfall of sagging icicles. On the other side, a man was standing in the shaft of a moonbeam. But it wasn't Cyrano.

The man heard the frozen snow crunching under Will and Peter's feet, and he looked up. On his see-through arms crystal ball tattoos shimmered like evil eyes.

"Warloch..." hissed Will, his insides turning cold.

Wolfeá snarled at the end of her rope, tugging Will forward.

"Well... well..." The Keeper greeted Will and Peter with an evil leer. He looked like a vampire with his sharp gold teeth glinting in the moonlight. "Come to watch the fun?"

He laughed and leaned over a crystal ball tub brimming with filthy water. With gauntlets covering his hands, the evil Echo submerged a sponge or a tiny pillow—except that whatever it was started thrashing and splashing as if it was drowning. Or perhaps it was only an illusion, thought Will, for in a moment all motion stopped.

"What are you doing?" shouted Peter, Poudini barking madly in his arms.

"Want to see?"

The Keeper laughed again and fished out the sodden bundle.

Will blinked in horror. This was no pillow. The bundle had eyes, and paws, and a tail.

"You drowned it!" cried Peter.

417

"One less." The Keeper flashed his evil smile at Wolfeá

"One less wild pet?" snarled Will.

"Not just wild... a *Mongrel*." The Keeper dropped the lifeless wolf cub. "And its *filthy* Echo." he added with an evil laugh.

In horror, Will saw another drowned pet lying in the snow. But this animal was as see-through as water.

"That's not—" Will's voice choked in his throat.

"The Mongrel's Echo?" Warloch smirked wickedly. "Oh, yes it is, by Dark Destiny! So what do you think of my performance?" added the Keeper, turning sideways to talk to the trees.

Only they weren't trees, Will realized. They were Echoes, which the moonlight turned as pale as ice. And Will was seeing the frozen trees through their bodies.

"Your wolf's next, Diaper-Boy," one of them snickered.

"Dartboard." Will recognized the unmistakable, pimpled face of Bog Slippery.

"Inspiring stuff, Mr. Warloch." The beefy Echo grinned. Between his muscular legs, his Doberman growled fiercely at Wolfeá.

"Splashingly brilliant," the Drops brothers chimed in at Slippery's sides. "Deserves a medallion." Around their necks, their pet snakes hissed eerily.

Will's insides twisted with revulsion. He let Wolfeá jerk him forward. "You twisted... Sick—"

"Look!" Peter yanked Will back.

But already Will had frozen stiff, watching the crumpled

Parchment Bog Slippery was pulling out of his glistening pocket.

"*Page 6*," hissed Will. "The missing half."

Slippery laughed, and his pimples rippled in his lucent cheeks. "Yours?"

"Hand it over!" shouted Will.

"Come and get it."

"No!" Peter yanked Will back again—as Bog Slippery ripped a corner off the parchment.

"Don't like waiting." Slippery ripped another corner off, to the hoots of his friends.

"He'll just tear it all up!" Peter hissed in Will's ear. "Let's get out of here. Now!"

As Will tried to decide what to do, another corner of parchment was snatched away by the wind. But this time a spear of pain shot up Will's back as if his arm had been torn off as well. He heard Peter screaming in agony and Poudini howling. Wolfeá's rope twisted in his fist like a writhing snake. And then a quivering gray mass bent over Will, and he recognized the hideous scar slithering like a slug up Wither Heart's nose.

"Past your bedtime, little brats," the Fate Sealer croaked, and his swinging lips slapped Will's cheeks. "Want to make your nightmares come true? No...?" The darkness swirled in Wither Heart's eyes, as in the eyes of the raven perched on his sagging shoulder. "Then I suggest that you... GET LOST!"

The Fate Sealer's scorching touch had barely faded from Will's face, when Bog Slippery and his friends were already gone, scrambling over the icy forest floor in a mad dash back to the gleaming Orphanage, the Doberman whimpering at their heels.

"Poudini—" Peter gasped in horror.

The little dog had fainted in Peter's arms. By Will's leg, Wolfeá was panting and shivering.

"Waiting for an encore, Vomit Face?" Wither Heart's sagging mouth loomed over Will, covering the moon.

Will shook his head frantically and dragged Peter and Wolfeá away. Behind them he heard Warloch laughing and clapping the metallic palms of his gauntlets in a cruel ovation.

*   *   *

Three hours later Will and Peter were still silent and gloomy over what they had seen in the forest. At least, Hydra Agonia did not lurk in the boy's bathroom as they slipped inside. Past the rustling blue walls, and soon they had slipped into the fifth Echo shower stall, from where they made their way down the secret tunnel to the Ant Chamber.

Before long they were sitting on the mildewed floor of Auralius' prison. The faint light of the broken crystal ball lamp cast shadows around them as they explained about Bog Slippery and the missing half of *Page 6*. All the while, the ceiling of cobwebs rained dirty drops on them, and their glistening uniforms did battle with the stains.

"It's too early to start worrying about *Page 6*," was Auralius' conclusion.

He shrugged, and a spider fell off his filthy shirt. For some reason, the Mongrel didn't wear self-cleaning Echo clothes.

"Too early to worry?" asked Will, scowling. "The Prince will be here on Christmas Eve."

"Christmas Eve...?" repeated Auralius indifferently.

"Ya, you know," said Peter. "What Winter Break's all about. And why there's silly holiday decorations everywhere."

"Not everywhere," said Auralius bitterly. "Everything gets ruined here. It's the leaky ceiling... Even my clothes gave up trying to clean me."

"It's in two days, Christmas Eve," said Will, really feeling sorry for Auralius, and he made a mental note to bring some Christmas candy canes next time. "If we can't figure out the Primary Safety Measure by then, we won't be able to cross the Bridge of Knives. No bridge— no mushrooms —no point going to Olám Shoné at all!"

"Agreed." Auralius nodded his beautiful blond head. "But you're forgetting something. We still have the second half of *Page 6*. Maybe the Primary Safety Measure's on that. Haven't had time to translate tonight, though..."

Auralius glanced gloomily at the narrow bed where his father lay motionless. Drinkwater was looking so pale that he seemed to disappear into the blanket of icicles Professor Flower was tossing over him.

"Frosty Fortune, but it's cold here tonight," she muttered anxiously.

This seemed to remind Peter of something. He pulled out the

two sticks he carried everywhere lately, rubbed them together, and suddenly the sticks burst into flames.

"Fake fire." Peter beamed, already shaking his head at Professor Flower. "A magician never reveals his tricks," he added proudly. "It's perfectly safe. Here— take it."

With her hands protected from the heat by her watery apron, Professor Flower carried the tiny fire to the bed. She rested it on Drinkwater's covered chest and sat on her snow heap beside her husband, her beautiful face lit up by the fake flames.

"The missing half of *Page 6*," said Will, wanting to get back on topic. "What if the Primary Safety Measure is on it? Warloch saw us with Slippery— Maybe Wither Heart did too, I'm not sure. If they get involved, we'll never get the page back."

"I'm sure the magician will figure something out." Auralius jerked his head at Peter.

Peter finished magicking another fake fire and set it on the floor between the three of them. For the first time the Mongrel smiled, and his blue eyes glittered with amusement.

"You like it?" said Peter, astonished. "That's great. Didn't think you liked anything... no offense."

"Don't get excited. I'm still not sure about you."

"Feeling's mutual." Peter grinned, because Auralius hadn't stopped smiling. "Well, anyway," added Peter. "There's something else we came to talk to you about. Something serious."

"Okay..."

"Mongrels have Echoes, right? Just like Sounds do?"

422

"Yeah…" Auralius nodded. In the firelight he looked even more beautiful than usual.

"*You* had an Echo," said Peter meaningfully. "Someone who looked just like you… only more see-through?"

"Almost entirely see-through," said Professor Flower from her snow heap. "You're talking in the past tense, Peter," she added thoughtfully, spider shadows crawling on her pretty face. "You think Auralius' Echo is dead?"

"Yes," said Peter, glancing at Will. "We both do."

"Oh, my Fortune." Professor Flower blinked in amazement. "Are you thinking what I think you're thinking? This luckless knife…" She pointed at the golden dagger Auralius was balancing absently in his hand. "Almost killed my Nicholas. And you think it killed Auralius' Echo too, don't you? You think the Memory in the Crystillery wasn't of Auralius dying at all. But if it's true…" Professor Flower blinked back tears of joy. "If it's true, Auralius dear… then your father never lied to us. He did see someone murdering you! He did see your throat cut! He did see you die! Only it wasn't *you*!"

"Not me…" said Auralius in amazement.

Suddenly a rain of dirty drops fell from the ceiling and put out the little fire on the mildewed flagstones. But Auralius didn't seem to notice.

"Murdered…?" he muttered to himself. "My Echo? With this knife—?"

He flinched and dropped the weapon with a clang.

423

"A sick magic trick," said Peter, starting another small fire. "An illusion to make your Dad *think* you were dead."

"Why would anyone do that?" asked Auralius in horror. And, for a moment, his whole head was see-through in the rekindled firelight.

"That's what we can't figure out," said Will.

Peter nodded in agreement.

"But the answer is simple," said Professor Flower darkly. "Why didn't I see it before....? The true King loved my Nicholas like a brother. Such close friends— I knew one day we would pay for it. Too many ambitious men were jealous. And they knew, they all knew how much Nicholas blamed himself for the fate of his son. The Mongrel..." She smiled gently at Auralius. "Your father would have given his life to make you all Sound or all Echo... Doesn't matter which, just so you wouldn't have to suffer for being too see-through, or not see-through enough. It was our fault. We fell in love, an Echo and a Sound... but you had to pay the price. You... our innocent boy.

"Your father couldn't stand it," she went on, three frozen tears dropping at her see-through feet. "He wanted to change the world for you, Auralius. He and the King dreamed about freeing the Echoes from the Fortune Tellers and the Fate Sealers. But such dreams are dangerous— They make enemies. Someone in the palace, one of the lords maybe... must have decided to get rid of *Drinkwater the Troublemaker*. Not by murdering him... no, that would look suspicious. But if Drinkwater's son was murdered... and if Drinkwater blamed himself. Then he would go insane, maybe even kill himself. Certainly go away somewhere he would never be any trouble again—"

"Who? Who did it?" hissed Auralius, and his eyes vanished from his face in rage.

Behind the Mongrel ants crawled out of the cracks in the mildewed wall as if drawing near to listen.

Professor Flower shrugged bitterly. "Pellucid… Watercress… Azurian… The false King, even. Or Valerian."

"Valerian?" Peter darted a meaningful glance at Will.

"—Any one of them…" Professor Flower wiped away a spider that fell on her see-through forehead. "All of them… Someone else…. The King's best friend is never short of enemies."

"Valerie Valerian's working for the Fate Sealers," said Peter, flicking his magic fire nervously. "Maybe she—"

"—Is just a girl," Will cut in.

Auralius grabbed Peter's wrist to stop him filling the cell with writhing shadows. "But why murder my Echo?" he asked. "Why not just murder me?"

"Less risky," said Professor Flower. "You were hidden here. But your Echo… Echoes of Mongrels are so see-through, so fragile… they live in a vault of ice. Orphanage of the Damned, it's sometimes called. They never come out. And no one would ever realize if one of them disappeared. I should have thought of it myself," she added, shaking her head. "I should have thought of your Echo. It all makes sense now."

They fell silent, the tragic tale casting a chill over them. Peter's hands rested limply in his lap. And yet suddenly his little fire flickered again, as if someone were playing with it. Or as if wind was blowing in from an open window, though there were no windows in Auralius' prison.

"Quick!" hissed Auralius, shooting to his feet.

Will and Peter jumped up after him.

"Stay here," ordered Professor Flower, darting to the front of the Ant Chamber.

A gap of light appeared there, and a rumbling noise filled the cell.

"The passage behind the fireplace," whispered Will. "Someone's opening it."

He stomped out the flames flickering on the floor, while Peter put out the second fake fire burning on Drinkwater's chest.

The soft light of the broken crystal ball lamp didn't reach the corner Auralius shoved them into, where cobwebs smeared on Will's cheeks and things began to crawl on his hands. Will could feel Peter fidgeting beside him, as silently they listened to Professor Flower greeting the silhouette of the man who appeared at the entrance to the cell.

"By all the crystal balls..." Professor Flower gasped. "Valerian..."

"Good Evening, Cully," said Valerian, his voice as enchanting as ever.

Cherry-scented smoke drifted into the cell and into Will's

426

corner, reminding him of home.

"Don't worry, I wasn't followed," said Valerian soothingly. "No one can follow an invisible man. I would have stayed invisible, if I didn't fear it would give you a start. My opening the passage suddenly was probably just as bad, though. I am sorry for frightening you."

"You're not dead?" said Professor Flower. She stepped closer to the silhouette, as if she was trying to block the way into the room. "The Orphanage is full of—"

"Rumors... Yes. I've heard." Valerian chuckled. "Nothing so dramatic as death. I just spent a few days at the Veiled Village, that's all. A new Castaway was set to arrive."

"And did he?" asked Professor Flower warily. "Arrive?"

"As a matter-of-fact, no. And so I'm back. No one knows yet. I wanted to see you first. I brought you something... For Drinkwater."

"Drinkwater?" Professor Flower laughed nervously. "Why would my good-for-nothing husband be here? Abandoned me and my son, that's what he did! I haven't spoken to him since."

"I think you have," said Valerian gently. "Don't look so startled, Cully. I'm not a mind reader. Just common sense, that's all. A fight on the shore of the Lake of Eternal Ice... Fate Sealers dying... and Drinkwater disappearing—all at the same time. He must be wounded, I told myself. And where else would he hide but here? The Ant Chamber is the only secret room in the kitchens... and you are always in the kitchens nowadays, Cully, aren't you? So

427

take this medicine with my best wishes. Goodnight."

Bowing slightly, the silhouette slipped back into the shadows in a cloud of scented smoke. Soon footsteps echoed softly away. Professor Flower retreated into the dim cell, holding a blue glass vial in her hand. Behind her, the back of the great fireplace rumbled shut.

Auralius shot back into the light of the crystal ball lamp, with Will and Peter close behind him, wiping ants off their glistening clothes.

"Valerian knows about this room?" said the Mongrel.

"Hmmm...?" Professor Flower looked thoughtful. "This room? Yes... yes, he would. The Orphanage was built when he was Chief Royal Advisor. He must have seen the plans. But I don't think he knows you're here, dear." She twirled the vial of medicine absently and added, "I just remembered something. Your knife, Auralius... You said your father gave it to you?"

"He said the knife murdered me..."

"Yes." Professor Flower nodded sadly. "But when we still lived in the palace... ages ago it seems now... I saw someone else using this knife."

"Someone else?" asked Will.

"He was peeling an apple in the garden... using a gold knife."

"This knife? You're sure?" asked Peter. And he magicked a rope from under his glistening sweater and lassoed the golden dagger from the floor where Auralius had dropped it before. All in less than two seconds.

"Maybe..." Professor Flower's cheeks glowed with excitement. "The blade, the secret is in the blade. When that man saw me, he dried off the apple juice quickly. But not before I saw *them*. Wet the blade, Peter. Over there— the ceiling is dripping... Now let me see. Yes..."

They could all see it happening. Beautiful etchings of crystal balls magically appeared all along the smooth, gold surface of the blade, as if an invisible artist was etching them at this very moment.

"I've never seen another knife like it," said Professor Flower. She stretched her see-through fingers to the gold crystal balls, which were disappearing already as the water dripped off the knife.

"Who did you see using this knife, Professor Flower?" asked Will.

"Didn't I say...?" She looked up. "Why, it was Valerian. Victor Valerian."

"Valerian?" said Peter. "Then how did the knife end up with Drinkwater?"

"And how, in Fortune's fate, did it end up murdering my Echo?" added Auralius bitterly.

*   *   *

Hydra Agonia was still nowhere in sight when Will and Peter slipped out of the fifth Echo shower stall a little later. They saw no signs of an invisible Echo in the balmy boy's bathroom, though a cluster of Christmas Fireflies gave them a start for a moment. Pretending to wipe their faces on crystal ball towels, they hurried past the eyes that popped open in the crystal ball sinks and mirrors.

The rustle of the blue waterfall walls sounded louder somehow. So they raised their voices, but only a little.

"I don't think he killed Auralius' Echo," whispered Will. "Valerian, I mean."

"Valerian's knife did." Peter wiped cobwebs off his hair. "That's all we know."

"When we met the Prince..." said Will thoughtfully, "... the invisible Echo behind the fireplace... think it was him... Valerian?"

"I didn't smell his pipe. You always smell cherry tobacco around Valerian, even if he's not smoking."

"Maybe he showered."

"Maybe..."

"Coin keys," said Will, "that's another one down to Valerian. Before the Winter Break Breakfast Feast, I didn't even know they existed."

"Me either," agreed Peter. "Here— give me yours," he added, shunting their towels down a crystal ball laundry chute.

"And Valerian helped Damian get me here," said Will, before he peeked out at the moonlit corridor. "Moon worshipers all gone," he reported back. "One Ice Fairy... but looks like she's sleeping."

"Valerian helped us in the Village too," said Peter, as he followed Will out of the bathroom. "Coincidence—?"

Suddenly Will slapped Peter's shoulder. "Shhhh... Over there—"

Not far from them, a crystal ball was hovering between the

twinkling branches of a Christmas tree. It moved here and there, to get a better look at something behind the tree. And as Will and Peter craned their necks, they managed to see what the ball was spying on. There were two figures standing there, whispering.

The moonlight had bleached them, making the sagging gray shape of the Fate Sealer look more like a rippling pile of dirty sheets. Only the hideous scar across the creature's sagging nose still looked unchanged, as did the raven perched on his shoulder. The Castaway he was talking to seemed ever so small by comparison. Will could clearly see her glistening Echo uniform, but her face was hidden in the shadow of the sleeping Ice Fairy hovering over the corridor. And yet the girl's short, spikey hair was unmistakable.

"Valerie..." Will spotted the blue glitter of Valerie's ring.

"I knew it!"

Peter's breath caught in his throat as Wither Heart reached under his sagging arm and pulled out a white sheet of paper. At the same time Valerie slipped her sapphire ring off her finger. In a moment an exchange was made, the ring for the paper. Then Wither Heart croaked a hollow laugh and floated away down the spiraling staircase, with the spying crystal ball zooming after him.

"Payment— for a job well done," hissed Peter.

They ducked into the boy's bathroom, as Valerie turned nervously to search the moonlit corridor for more flying spies.

"That wasn't a payment for anything." Will shook his head, amazed, still trying to make sense of what just happened. "A trade— has to be. She gave her ring for that piece of paper. Maybe it was a

431

letter… No, I know— If she's really following us, she knows about *Page 6*—"

"She's definitely following us. Ugh!" Peter bent his head upside down and shook out one of Auralius' leftover spiders. "But that wasn't *Page 6*. Too white— Parchments in the road map are kind of yellow. Instructions probably, that's what it was… off with our heads. She's working for them— Totally brainwashed. Just handed her ring over… after she almost blinded Dartboard over it."

There was no sign of Valerie the next morning, not at breakfast, where a Sound thought he could win Valerian's medallion by turning all the food blue. Nor by the garden pond, where a crowd stood watching as an Echo shot a paintball rocket at the giant sun and turned it purple for a few seconds. Neither was Valerie in the library, where the *Flight Section* books had grown wings and were whizzing around, whacking Castaways on the head, with a librarian chasing after them, yelling frantically, "No— no— That's not what I meant— Dust off! Not take off!"

"And no Fate Sealers, either," remarked Peter, as he and Will stopped by the *Hold Section* to pick up the dictionary and road map, which Professor Flower had once again camouflaged in crystal ball wrapping-paper. "And no Fate Sealers can only mean one thing," Peter added. "Valerie's still around. Probably invisible!"

"We don't even know if she can turn invisible," said Will. Nevertheless, he looked around for spots of light between the flying books and Christmas Fireflies buzzing through the sparkling hall. "Besides, the Prince is coming *tomorrow*," added Will. "We've got

432

other things to worry about."

A few spying eyes blinked open in a glittering chandelier as Will and Peter sunk into snow heap armchairs beneath the floating silver section plaque: *Sewers*. A flock of crystal balls circled over them like vultures. But if Abednego had wanted to stop them, he certainly could have done so by now. And deciding to ignore the eyes, Will and Peter set to work with Poudini chewing a tied chicken bone beside them, while the snowy carpet tried to clean the little dog out of existence.

"*Primary Safety Measure!*" Will read the first line of Auralius' translation of the portion of *Page 6* they still had. But Will's medicated voice got stuck in his throat. He stared down at the Mongrel's messy handwriting, stared and couldn't bring himself to read on—for beneath the title Auralius had written: *Information Lost!*

"Then, forget it! We can't cross the Bridge of Knives!" Peter slapped away a flying book in frustration.

The book landed in a small fountain where the sundial was pointing, in the obscure time-telling fashion of all the library book-clocks, at half past The Ugly Echo Duckling.

Unable to speak for disappointment, Will and Peter read Auralius' translation in silence.

Page 6 (Top Half Missing)
Primary Safety Measure:
Information Lost!!!

???

Index of Perils:

Another flying book knocked Will and Peter out of their shock by scattering a swarm of Firefly Lights in their faces.

"Get off!" Peter swatted the lights with the rope he pulled from under his glistening sweater.

"Auralius translated *Page 7* too," said Will, not even smiling to see Peter accidentally catapulting his crystal ball sunglasses into a passing Christmas ribbon. "It talks about Whirlpool Chasm," added Will. "That's the first item in the Index of Perils."

"You think the rest of the road map's about this other stuff?" Peter shoved his sunglasses back up his nose, which had turned a throbbing shade of red. "Five more pages—" he flipped through the road map "—for five disasters? Invisible Plants... probably eat us alive. Giant Echo Spiders... Don't wanna know—"

"They're probably all Safety Measures." Will sighed, hardly noticing an eye blinking open in a glass ladder by his elbow. "Maybe the Primary Safety Measure deactivates all of them. Not that we'll find out if the bridge shreds us first."

"Or collapses under us." Peter sighed too. "If we're lucky."

"Lucky? Falling into Whirlpool Chasm, the waterfall from

434

hell?" Will's expression darkened. "Dartboard—" He fumed. "There has to be a way! We have to get the first half of *Page 6* back!"

"As what, confetti? The second Bog sees us he'll start shredding faster than the Bridge of Knives. Let's translate more." Peter slapped the dictionary open, scaring off a flying book as an added bonus. "We have to find another clue. Have to."

Again they set to work, with Peter flicking his rope at Christmas Fireflies or Butterfly Ribbons when they flew too near, and Poudini seeing them off with a barking ovation.

Page 8 described the strange invisible plants that grew inside the raging river. Not man-eaters after all, to Peter's relief, the plants were just ordinary plants, though they were as strong as ropes. And anyone who fell in the river could grab them and hold on for dear life."

"But how are we supposed to grab something we can't see?" said Peter.

"*Note: see Primary Safety Measure,*" Will read their last translation bitterly.

Page 9 proved equally disappointing with its description of a shore of steaming rocks that would surely melt an Echo but could save the life of a Sound; only to leave the Sound stranded there forever—unless the Primary Safety Measure was employed.

"See *Page 6* for details," read Peter.

Soon after, wind chimes announced the closing of the library. Hours had passed, and Will and Peter were still no nearer to finding an answer. But the Prince was coming tomorrow.

"Okay, okay we're going," said Peter to an Ice Fairy, which signaled for them to pack up their things. "No choice—" he added. "It's Dartboard or nothing. Even if we have to grovel."

"He'd love that," said Will.

They headed for the *Hold Section*, Firefly Lights twinkling all around them, making it impossible to tell if an invisible Echo was following them through the sparkling white hall.

"Too bad *we* can't turn invisible," said Peter.

"Yeah, too bad…"

They couldn't risk going to dinner. Bog Slippery might destroy the parchment at the mere sight of them. They needed to come up with a plan.

"We could drop a Christmas tree on him," suggested Peter, as they left the library. "It worked on Valerie."

"They don't make Christmas trees big enough," said Will.

"Then how about setting Wolfeá on him?"

"Tempting…" Will smiled wryly—but suddenly he grabbed Peter's arm.

Out in the corridor two figures were standing, just as they had stood together in the night.

"Again!" hissed Peter, as Valerie shook her head at Wither Heart. She looked so lost in conversation that she didn't notice the flying crystal balls and glistening Castaways stopping in their tracks to gape at her. "Out in the open. Not even trying to fake it," grumbled Peter. But suddenly he noticed Will's expression. "You okay?"

436

Will nodded slowly, a smile puffing his swollen gray cheeks until he could barely see past them. But he saw all he needed to see... Wither Heart's hideous scar wriggling on the Fate Sealer's face.

"I have an idea," whispered Will. "Dartboard— There's a way!"

*   *   *

"It's insane," Peter hissed at Will.

Peter's blue-green eyes blazed in the setting sun, which shone through the crystal ball windows, painting the corridor and everyone in it like a brush dipped in blood.

"It's worse than insane," insisted Peter. "Suicidal, that's what it is. You can't do it! I won't let you do it!"

"It's the only way." Will slapped a red Firefly Light off his nose. "We have to get that page back. Have to!"

"Not like this, we don't!"

"You said it yourself, confetti!" insisted Will. "That's what we'll get if we go to Dartboard. But if Wither Heart goes.... It'll work, you'll see. It worked for Valerie. She traded her ring—"

"No!" Peter shook his head desperately. "Don't you get it? She's working for them—"

But Will was already walking away down the crowded corridor.

The setting sun blinded Will with its spears of red light. He raised his voice and called out to the Fate Sealer. "Mr. Wither Heart... Mr. Wither Heart... Do you have a minute?"

437

Even the Firefly Lights froze in the reddish atmosphere. Castaways and flying crystal balls, Ice Fairies and two staff members in waterfall robes, all swiveled to watch Will. He stopped beside Valerie, ignoring her horrified expression, and forced himself to keep talking while Wither Heart's swinging lips lost momentum and set in an evil sneer.

"There's a piece of pppaper—" Will stammered, too frightened to care how stupid his medicated voice made him sound. "—Yeah, paper…"

The darkness in Wither Heart's eyes started rippling, as if something evil was trying to swim out of them. His pet raven cackled once on his shoulder, peering at Will with its small beady eyes.

"Parchment, really," Will continued. "Dartboard… I mean, Slippery… He's got it, the parchment. Bog Slippery. He's a Castaway. Echo Castaway. I want to… —NO! WAIT!"

Will froze as Wither Heart's dripping fingers zoomed towards him in a gray smear of speed.

A split second later, all light, all air, even the floor seemed to disappear under Will's feet. He writhed, feeling as if someone had thrust a burning sword through his mouth and was twisting it just to see how much torture he could stand. And then far, far away, Will heard a girl screaming. The world came back, painted crimson by the sunset. Castaways and crystal balls were all staring at Will as if no time had elapsed at all, though to him it seemed that at least an hour had gone by.

Will wiped the wetness from his cheeks; he must have been crying. Someone was keeping him from falling. "Let's go!" that person whispered, and Will realized that Peter was trying to pull him away.

Will shook his friend off and cleared his throat again.

"Mr. Wither Heart… Let's trade. I have a Crystillery."

"A Crysssssstillery?" Wither Heart's croak slithered through the silent, stunned corridor.

"—Not with me," gasped Will. "Not here! I'm not as stupid as I look."

"You look pretty stupid, Vomit Face."

Wither Heart pulled out an Ice Loom and set it glowing with a single shake of his sagging wrist.

"You? A Crystillery?" he croaked, his whole face twisting with loathing. "How did you get it? Tell me. —NOW!"

Already a whirlpool of needles was spinning inside the glowing horn, inches from Will's face.

"A Fortune Teller—" Will stammered the first thing that popped into his head. "—Yes… Pickpocketed a Fortune Teller, that's what I did… In the Veiled Village."

A gasp of laughter choked its way out of Wither Heart's sagging throat. "Idiots! One and all! Fortune Tellers… Fortune Sellers, more like it. But *you*—" In the darkness of the creature's hollow eyes an oval-shaped pupil surfaced, green flames flickering inside it. "By Darkest Destiny, there is something wrong about you… Who are you, Frederick Finger-Me? What are you doing

439

here? Why risk dying for a piece of paper?"

Wither Heart's voice had sunk into a hiss, like a snake talking. The sibilance slithered up Will's spine. He shuddered. But in his mind, he could hear Damian saying, *Play the fool... play the fool... PLAY THE FOOL!*

"Abednego—" Will spluttered. "He'll kill me if he finds out. It's his— The paper's his. From his private—"

"WHAT?!"

The fearful croak shook the crystal ball windows. Castaways shrieked in fear.

"More afraid of Abednego than ME...?" The burning green pupils spun madly in the Fate Sealer's hollow eyes. "ME! Congratulations, idiot of the century! You are more stupid than you look. An undisputed champion. Want my help, Vomit Face? Want *my* help? Very well...."

And suddenly Wither Heart swept away in a tornado of gray flesh that scattered Castaways, crystal balls and Firefly Lights like leaves in a storm all down the corridor.

In a flash, Valerie turned on Will.

"Are you insane?"

She flew at Will with her fists. And her face was so see-through that Will could see the panic-stricken corridor straight through her cheeks, as if he were looking through a window.

"Never!" screamed Valerie. "Never bargain with a Fate Sealer! Don't you know that? What, in Fortune's name, possessed you, Freddy?"

440

"Me?" Will flinched back from her sharp nails. "What possessed *me*?"

"Yeah, you," Peter jumped in, warding Valerie off with his rope.

"*She's* the one hanging out with Wither Heart," screamed Will.

"You don't understand!" Valerie got around Peter and punched Will in the nose. "Wither Heart sold me letters. From my mother. She's trapped—" Valerie's voice cracked in a sob "—in Shadowpain. Oh, nobody believes me, nobody..."

And, suddenly, Valerie was gone. Vanished completely! Only her see-through uniform fluttered down the corridor between the gaping crowd of Castaways, Sounds on the right, Echoes on the left.

"Told you she could!" Peter's eyes lit up like bonfires—then went up in smoke.

"The Crysssssstillery," hissed Wither Heart, rippling toward them, Castaways shrieking out of his way, his pet raven cackling in flight over his head.

"The pppaper," stammered Will, knocking back against a crystal ball window.

And then Will saw it, the yellow parchment trapped between the Fate Sealer's long, black fingernails. But something was wrong! The parchment was wet, soaking wet, dripping inky drops like blood from a wound. Every drop—a word lost forever!

Pain stabbing up his arm, Will shoved his Crystillery in

Whiter Heart's sagging gray hand and snatched the parchment. He dashed away, Peter beside him, Poudini in the lead. Up the stairs they ran. Will tried to dry the parchment on his glistening sweater, but the rows of foreign letters trickled like black rain between his fingers, and the sweater cleaned them off.

"Stop! Stop! There's no point!" Will finally fell against the crystal ball handrail, where eyes blinked open to watch him.

"I don't believe it! Another Safety Measure!" Peter slammed his fist into the stone wall in frustration, as Poudini licked the last two drops of ink from Will's glistening white shoe.

Abednego's Watching

A Chilling Christmas Eve

The next morning the sparkling garden still looked carved from ice beneath the pale blue sky and the giant orange sun. Will's heart felt just as frozen. Even the Christmas decorations twinkling and fluttering around the festive corridors failed to cheer him up. Castaways everywhere wore bright red Santa hats with crystal ball pompons, and everyone raved about the feast planned for that evening. But Will and Peter doubted they would get to see Christmas Eve at the Orphanage of Castaway Children. Instead they would huddle in Auralius' creepy cell, waiting for the Prince. And after all their hard work, they had nothing but bad news to share.

"The last three pages… Maybe they'll tell us something about the Primary Safety Measure," said Peter, as they walked through the glistening trees to breakfast with Wolfeá.

"Don't think so," said Will glumly. "Maybe the Prince… *If* he finds another copy of the road map. That's our only hope."

They skirted a sparkling crystal ball fountain, its blue water still frozen mid-splash. Behind it, the garden's giant Christmas tree glittered with ice, crystal ball ornaments and Firefly Lights.

445

"You can see it, Valerian's medallion." Peter pointed at the glittering treetop. "Would be amazing if we end up winning it. You know, for going to Olám Shoné. What if we find Queen Illyria's treasure? We'd have the key!"

"Amazing? Yeah, it would be," muttered Will. "About as amazing as us getting across the Bridge of Knives in one piece. At least they're not following us," he added, spotting two Fate Sealers glaring at him through the frozen topiary of a fawn.

Peter lost his smile. "Why should they? They've got the spikey menace working for them."

And as if Peter had summoned Valerie Valerian, there she was, dismounting her giant white albatross under Wolfeá's twinkling tree. All morning she had followed Will and Peter through the merry Orphanage, and every time they had turned to confront her—about Wither Heart and the ring she traded for the letter crushed between her see-through fingers—the frail Echo girl burst into frozen tears and fled. Will was hardly in the mood to start all that again.

"Three Christmas trees!" Peter rolled his eyes as Poudini dashed to greet Valerie with his usual delight. "Three! Dropping on her in one hour! You'd think she'd get the hint."

"Really can't stop to chat—" Will swept past Valerie and her bird and crouched in the snow by his wolf.

For some strange reason Wolfeá was still lying down. She didn't even raise her beautiful white head to lick a wet hello across Will's nose.

"Don't bother." Valerie glared at Peter, who started leaning on Wolfeá's tree. "It has roots."

"Something's wrong." Will stared up at them. "Wolfeá... she can't get any air. Her tongue... it's totally swollen."

"Let me see." Valerie dropped beside Will, Christmas Fireflies buzzing around her wild hair, which was sprinkled with pine needles. "Yes, by Fortune." She blinked her wide blue eyes in amazement. "Has to be! I know what's wrong."

"You know?" asked Will suspiciously.

"Did you do something to her?" asked Peter, grabbing Poudini just in case. "And don't start crying again!"

"Me? No!" Valerie's pretty, pale face glowed with emotion. "The water... your wolf's water—"

"What about it?" snapped Peter.

But Will was already dipping his hand in Wolfeá's cold bucket and drinking.

"Salt—" he spluttered, spraying them.

"Salt?" Peter glared at Valerie. "You put salt in there?"

"You know what?" Valerie glared back at Peter. "You're pretty dumb for a magician, Peter Twister Person. Maybe you should blow a hat and whack yourself on the head."

"Maybe you should stop calling me Peter Twister Person—"

"Who? Who did this?" shouted Will.

"Not me!" Valerie blinked back frozen tears. "Warloch! He tried the same thing with Pegasus... He tried to dehydrate my albatross." She kissed her giant bird on the forehead then climbed on its back. "What sort of Keeper of Pets doesn't know an albatross drinks seawater?" she added bitterly. "Merry Christmas, Freddy. But not you, Twister."

In a moment, the bird took flight, scattering Christmas Fireflies with its giant white wings.

"She's turning invisible," said Peter, watching the frail Echo rider disappearing. "What d'you think? Believe her about Warloch?"

"Yes," said Will, sounding dangerously calm.

He scanned the sparkling icy forest for the evil Keeper. But he wasn't there.

"Me too," admitted Peter grudgingly. "I'll get fresh water," he added and walked away, still hugging his little brindled dog.

Will dropped his head on Wolfeá's, feeling as if his life was spinning from bad to worse. For a moment he imagined that he was back in the Sound realm, looking down at his dead pets... He couldn't let Wolfeá die too!

"I'll get you away from here," he promised.

And the memory of the lost Safety Measure stabbed him like a knife.

*   *   *

Watching Wolfeá drinking half a bucket of fresh water, Will determined to get her away from the garden before nightfall, when Rufus Warloch seemed to practice his worst deeds. If the Prince found another copy of the road map, she could go to Olám Shoné with them. If not...? Peter suggested sneaking Wolfeá into Auralius' room in a Christmas crate. But, in the meantime, there were two more pages to translate in the road map, without hope, just to be sure they had left no page unturned in their search for the Primary Safety Measure.

They waited for Wolfeá to fall asleep before they left. The albatross with its invisible rider followed them back to the alabaster fortress. It wasn't hard to spot the dots of light following them inside, not with the Christmas Fireflies still buzzing in the air where Valerie's head should be. She must have taken off her clothes to be completely invisible, but the letter she was clutching in her absent fist still floated everywhere she went. By the library entrance Will swallowed a painkiller, drinking from the crystal ball fountain that tasted like eggnog for the holiday. And Peter blew a magician's hat at the girl who wasn't there, his cold breath outlining her invisible features for a few seconds.

"Hello... *again*," he said to Valerie, starting to lean on a Christmas tree.

Will watched the piece of paper floating in the air in front of Peter. "It's your mother's letter, Valerie, isn't it?" he spoke to thin air. "How did Wither Heart get it? Is your mother a prisoner... in Shadowpain? Is that how they got you to follow us for them?"

Passing Castaways rolled their eyes to see Will talking to himself.

"Having a nice chat?"

A girl giggled at Will, and he found himself staring at his sister, before she walked away with her two pretty friends, pretending not to know him, her white cat hissing a warning at Will not to follow.

"She's gone!" Peter tugged Will's glistening sleeve. "Valerie. Look! Left a trail of frozen tears. Let's get out of here before she comes back."

Before long they were hiding in the *Sewers Section*, behind a row of snow heap armchairs, the dictionary and road map already open in their glistening laps. Eyes watched them from the chandeliers, bookends and flying crystal balls. But no dots of light appeared around them, except for a few buzzing Firefly Lights. Peter magicked the usual tied chicken bone for Poudini, and the snowy carpet took up its losing battle with dog drool.

"Great," said Peter sarcastically, when they finished reading Auralius' translation of *Page 10*. "So now we know. The Chilling Mist kills all Sounds. And the Heat Rocks kill all Echoes. Brilliant! We all get to die!"

"Not Auralius," Will realized, "if he's coming with us…. A Mongrel's half Echo, half Sound. Chilling Mist won't freeze him. Heat Rocks won't melt him."

"Well, that's all right, then." Peter pulled his customary rope from under his sweater and started twirling it in frustration.

"Come on, two more pages," said Will with a sigh, opening the dictionary.

They had become experts at translating by now and worked fast, ignoring the watchful eyes in nearby crystal balls. But the description of the Giant Echo Spiders on *Page 11*, far from offering any hope, promised another excruciating death.

"*Larger than cows, quicker than rabbits*," Will read their last

450

translation glumly.

"*With Pinchers for mouths,*" said Peter, still twirling his rope, which seemed to get magically longer by the second. "A Magician never…" he added.

"I know, I know." Will shook his head at the rope.

"Too bad we can't set a cow-spider on Bog Slippery," muttered Peter.

"Or Warloch."

Will flipped to the last page in the road map, his heart beating fast with the knowledge that this was their last chance!

But more bad news met their eyes with every word translated, for here was a description of a towering cliff that offered no foothold for climbing, except the occasional cave in which the giant spiders dwelled. This was the final Safety Measure guarding Olám Shoné. There was no escape after falling off the Bridge of Knives. Only different ways of dying.

"Brilliant!" Peter sat up, his rope dangling off his mummified hand. "So, we get on the bridge, and it shreds us. But if we're lucky, it just collapses… and we get to drown in Whirlpool Chasm. No, wait, I forgot the invisible plants. We grab them and make it to the shore. Of course, the Prince melts the moment he steps on the Heat Rocks, and we freeze to death in the Chilling Mist, but Auralius survives. Until he gets to the Cliff of Doom. Then he can sit down, relax and wait for the spiders to come eat him. Absolutely brilliant! I'm definitely looking forward to this."

Will took off his crystal ball sunglasses and gently rubbed his

451

sore, sore eyes, wishing he could take the contact lenses out. "Nothing more about the Primary Safety Measure!" he said glumly. "The whole road map translated for nothing. If the Prince can't find another copy... I dunno know. We'll just have to figure out how to cross the bridge when we get there."

"*If* we get there," muttered Peter, turning very pale suddenly as he pointed over Will's shoulder.

Will turned and gasped.

Where the icy bookcase curved out of sight, flecks of light were hovering together, so tall they couldn't be Valerie's invisible outline.

"Wither Heart?" breathed Peter.

The next instant, the dots vanished.

*   *   *

That afternoon a storm blew in without warning. Wind and rain battered the icy garden, chasing the giant orange sun behind a swamp of dark clouds. All the Castaways ran indoors holding their Santa hats for dear life. Only Will and Peter rushed outside to sneak Wolfeá back into the Orphanage, hidden in a Christmas crate they found abandoned behind the garden's giant Christmas tree.

"That's all we need," cried Peter over the shrieking wind, stuffing his dog under his sweater.

"Can't believe Echoes make this weather on purpose," Will shouted back.

But Peter wasn't talking about the storm. "Over there—" he pointed.

Through the layers of see-through, icy trees, Will caught sight of Jeremy Fallon wheeling himself at top speed down the snowy garden path, his elbows flapping like bizarre wings.

"Going for Valerian's medallion?" Peter shouted at him.

"Have— to talk— to you—" Jeremy shouted back, flapping his wheelchair around a Fairy Fountain. And suddenly one of the wheels hit a rut, and the gangly boy almost fell out of his chair. His chameleon catapulted off his shoulder and landed on the fairy's head.

"You shouldn't be out here—" Will reached Jeremy in time to stop the shiny black chair from toppling.

"Wither Heart—" panted Jeremy, rain battering his sallow face. "Looking for you— He knows—"

"What's going on?" Peter shouted again, stopping to rescue the lizard.

"Shut up, Peterson!" Jeremy clawed at Will's hand. "He knows— Wither Heart knows who you are! Thinks you killed his brother— Black Heart— Wants revenge—"

"Revenge?" Peter reached them, Poudini's wet face peeking out of his collar. "Wither Heart? What's going—?"

"Shut— up—! The tower—" Jeremy clawed at Will again. "—He's in Abednego's tower— Coming for you— He'll kill you! Hide! Go!"

"What about you?" Will looked frantically through the battering rain. "He'll know you warned—"

"Just go!"

Icicles shattered on the frozen ground like raining arrows as Will dashed away with Peter, deep into the glistening, windswept garden. Explosions of cracking ice burst over them, cold blasts whipped their faces, raindrops stabbed their eyes.

"We have to get Wolfeá?" yelled Will, jumping over a sparkling sundial at the last minute.

An icy branch slashed down, inches from Peter's arm. "Where to?"

"Abednego's tower— remember?" Memories of escaping that museum of treasure-books flashed through Will's mind: The trail winding through a shimmering white garden... The icy doors that looked like wings on a flying horse topiary... The dark passage, the freezing tunnel and the cage of branches in the end. "The passage— It ended in the forest— Remember?" Will shouted at the top of his voice.

"You cra—zy—?" The wind chopped Peter's words. "Wither— Heart— There!"

"Not— Anymore! Look— Over there."

Gray smears were billowing far on their right, as if the rain clouds had plunged from the sky. And one of them was storming in the lead, a raven perched on his sagging shoulder.

"It's him!" shouted Will.

"Watch out!"

A hail of icy leaves shattered over them. Peter tugged Will past the swaying swords of an army of glittering white branches— and suddenly an avenue of towering trees swallowed them in its

454

glacial tunnel. The wind was shut out. The rain became a quiet mist. And Abednego's unicorns trotted over to nuzzle them, their fake horns glittering like diamonds.

"Brilliant!" cried Peter, grabbing the shimmering mane of the horse neighing an invitation at him. "They want us to— Let's ride!" Suddenly, as if by magic, Peter was flying up onto the animal's translucent back, Poudini barking over his glistening collar. "Behind you— Just touch it—" Peter beamed at Will.

Will's frozen fingers barely grazed the radiant white horse nuzzling his shoulder, when his feet were swept in the air and he mounted the beautiful, see-though animal without a clue how he did it.

"Go!" shouted Peter, streaking away as on a shaft of light that looked like a unicorn.

The last thing Will saw before his own unicorn shot forward was a smear of Fate Sealers breaking through the shield of frozen trees behind him. But already everything was turning into flowing glass, and Will was flying forward.

A rainbow shimmered in the fluttering mane of Will's horse. His heart felt light for the first time in days. It was like riding an ice sculpture, so cold that Will's legs didn't feel like they were there at all. The rushing air froze his cheeks numb. His contact lenses flew out of his eyes. He couldn't remember ever being this cold—or free. As if the frosty wind was shrinking him back to normal, back to the Will he used to be before his disguise, before the Cold Sleep, before his life was torn apart.

Will wanted to ride like this forever. But suddenly there was Wolfeá up ahead, huddled under her windswept tree, and Will grabbed the shimmering mane of his horse and pulled, until the animal slowed down and bucked him into a snow heap.

"Behind us!" shouted Peter, dismounting gracefully.

Will twisted back and saw the gray cloud of Fate Sealers still billowing after them. Abednego's unicorns streaked away at the hideous monsters, buying Will and Peter a second or two, enough time to untie Wolfeá and plunge into the shuddering glacial forest. But the thick trees slowed them down, and the ice was slippery under their feet.

"We'll never make it—" shouted Will, barely seeing for the wind whipping frozen leaves in his face.

"There—" Peter pointed at a thick nest of glistening thorns. "The opening to the passage. Hurry!"

"Behind us—" Will twisted back, as the shrieks of Fate Sealers joined the howling wind.

A river of Ice Looms was glowing on the forest's edge, shaped in a half-circle like a giant scythe.

"They're cutting down the trees!" shouted Peter, as the forest started to shake.

"We'll never make it—"

"Watch out!"

Will flung his head back. The tree above him had shaken off all its ice, and the rain was coming down like knives.

Suddenly a frosty hand tore Will off his feet, whipping

456

Wolfeá after him. The deadly downpour crashed harmlessly beside them. And a black, see-through Echo towered over them, his bare torso scaly, his frog-face dripping.

"Cyrano!" shouted Peter. Poudini barked under his chin.

"In there!" growled the hideous Echo. He ripped an icy bush by the roots and tossed it to the wind. A hole was torn in the frozen ground, dark and deep. "In there!" Cyrano growled again.

Trees fell like dominoes behind them. The eerie light of a hundred Ice Looms blazed through the storm.

"Thank you!" shouted Peter, and he jumped into the hole with Poudini.

"Keep my secret!" snarled Cyrano, as Will glanced at their hideous rescuer one last time.

"I swear!"

Will lowered Wolfeá and jumped in after her, ice and frozen dirt already raining down on him as Cyrano sealed the hole again.

And then there was only darkness and a terrible cold. They were buried alive, the earth shaking over them with fallen trees, the shrieks of Fate Sealers piercing near and far as the hunt aboveground continued.

"Is he okay?" whispered Will, hearing Poudini whimpering.

"Just afraid. Wolfeá?"

"She's fine." Will groped for the wolf's warm fur, feeling better for hearing Peter's voice in the darkness. *If only they had a small light… Maybe Peter could start a fire—*

And, suddenly, a green glow appeared down the pitch black

tunnel. Someone or something was heading their way.

*   *   *

The green light grew brighter, glowing in the hand of a shadowy figure that was crawling on hands and knees toward them through the cramped, murky tunnel.

"It's Waterweed," whispered Peter.

"Glowing bright," Will whispered back. "It's an Echo."

Will held his breath. It was too late to crawl backwards into the darkness. The glow was only a few feet away. And then the figure looked up and saw them.

"Merry Christmas," said a voice Will knew as well as his own.

For a moment Will felt as if he was looking in a greenish mirror, seeing a see-through reflection of himself, the way he used to look before the disguise: thin features and melancholy eyes. Except that his reflection was a little see-through.

Peter sighed with relief. "It's your Echo, Will."

"You came to meet me?" said the Prince, as he reached them. His hair dripped green rain between them. "What's going on? I could hear the thumping all the way back at the lake... You're wet... Didn't you come by Auralius' room?"

"Is this his tunnel?" wondered Peter, calming Poudini with a tied chicken bone.

"Wither Heart," explained Will, his teeth starting to chatter. The tunnel was so cold. "He knows who I am. They're looking for me... Fate Sealers everywhere. Cutting down trees."

"So that's why this storm's so wild… and why it started so suddenly." The Prince wiped his dripping hair. "Echoes create their own weather. The Fate Sealers must have taken control of the Weather Loom. Created the storm to make you run for cover."

"I can never go back to the Orphanage," said Will, the thunder of falling trees shaking dust over his head. "My wolf can't either."

The Prince noticed Wolfeá for the first time, as he shared the glowing Waterweed between them. "Beautiful," he said, petting the white wolf as if she were a tame dog. "I can't return to the palace either," he added, watching Peter magicking a fake fire between his hands. "I forgot… Magician by fame. How?"

"A magician never reveals—"

But Will kept talking to his Echo. "Why not? Why can't you go back to the palace?"

The firelight danced in the Prince's eyes. "I have so much to tell you. The door in the lake, I know how to open it."

"So do we," Peter boasted, the fire flickering on his knee.

"Yep." Will smiled back at his Echo, already feeling warmer by the flames.

"Then you brought the Royal Shekel?" asked the Prince.

Will tapped the heel of his shoe. "Still here. A Coin Key… for a Crystillery Lock."

"You *did* figure it out!" The Prince beamed, and Will nodded so much he bumped his head on the roof of the tunnel.

"We found your father's road map." Peter grinned. "Did you

459

find another copy?"

"No. But—"

The shrieks of the Fate Sealers drew suddenly near. Frozen dirt rained through the green glow, and thunderous booms shook the ground overhead. They waited for the earthquake of falling trees to pass.

"Let's get out of here," breathed Peter, when the tunnel stopped shaking.

"Too early," said the Prince cryptically, blinking dirt out of his eyes. And he went on with his story. "Four nights ago I couldn't sleep. I was just lying in bed, thinking. Then I saw a square of light opening in the floor. Just like that! Sliding open like a window."

"Magic?" asked Peter.

"A secret compartment. I found a leather journal inside. When I took it out, the floor sealed again."

"Magic." Peter seemed convinced.

"No. The journal was my father's. He explained everything inside. Every four months he'd reset the trap door, so it wouldn't open as long as he was alive. But if anything ever happened to him..."

"Which it did..." Will coughed in the settling dust. "Four months ago."

"So the secret compartment opened." Peter nodded. "I bet it still felt like magic, didn't it? You sure about staying here?" he added, as the earth thudded in the distance to the fading shrieks of Fate Sealers.

"For a bit," insisted the Prince. "My father wrote about three things. Two, you already know about: the Cold Fire Mushrooms, and how to open the door in the lake. The third thing was about the crystal ball knocker. On your door, Will."

"What door? You mean, on my house?" Will pointed a baffled finger at his own chest. He loved the pearly knocker that hung on the front door of his crumbling home, back in the Sound realm; loved the way it glowed brighter as its motion detector was activated, and especially how the secret camera inside the knocker projected a hologram into Will's crystal ball clock. "My Dad never knew how the knocker got there… or my clock," Will added. "They just appeared after Emmy disappeared."

"My father." The Prince nodded. "He did it himself… installed the knocker on your door in the middle of the night. And he left the crystal ball clock on the porch. It's more than a security camera, Will."

"Magic?" Peter ventured again, petting Poudini and Wolfeá to keep them calm.

"No." The Prince shook his head, amused. "There's a Safe Passage Ring inside the crystal ball. Whoever wears the ring can jump into the pond behind the house… and end up here. Well, not here… here." The Prince gestured at the tunnel. "In a secret garden under the palace. A special hiding place for the royal Sounds, in case they'll ever need it."

"But what's the point if they don't know about it?" Will frowned, remembering his mother diving into the frozen pond every

461

day for ten years, searching for Emmy. And all this time, she could have put on the Safe Passage Ring and crossed into the Echo realm...

"Remember the message I promised to send your parents?" asked the Prince, his melancholy eyes twinkling a little. "I did. I told them about the ring."

"You mean...?" Will's heart leapt into his mouth, kidnapping his voice.

"Your parents arrived at the palace two days ago. They can't wait to see you—and Emmy."

Will felt as if a Fourth of July fireworks show was exploding inside him, flooding him with light and color and warmth—and, most of all, hope. "My parents... here..." he stammered in disbelief.

"That's great, Will." Peter clapped Will's shoulder, raising a small cloud of green dust. "Really great," he added, but his voice broke strangely in the end.

"You'll see your family too," promised the Prince. "When I'm King, I'll abolish the Law of Death. No Sound will be in danger because of an Echo again. And the Castaways will be free to go home, those that want to. A Brain Freeze can erase their memories to keep the Echo realm a secret. With proper medication it won't even hurt."

"Like Emmy..." said Peter, half lost in a dream of what might be.

Again the forest shook but far away, and the shrieks of the Fate Sealers faded.

The Prince glanced at his watch. It was an icy sundial with smoke pointing out the time. "Fifteen more minutes," he muttered to himself.

"To what?" asked Will, wondering what other wonderful news the Prince had in store for them.

"Deá and Damian," said the Prince sadly.

"Deá and Damian...?" repeated Will. And in a flash all his happiness vanished like a coin plunging down a dark well. "They're bringing the Leader of the Fortune Tellers," Will added stiffly, remembering what the Prince had told him on the Lake of Eternal Ice. His childhood pets would now make the ultimate sacrifice to save the Prince and his Sound. They will give up their freedom.

"Yes... They're bringing Fortis Fortuna," said the Prince, looking frozen in Peter's fake firelight.

"What's all this about?" asked Peter suspiciously.

"A deal," said Will. "Deá and Damian are going to rot in a dungeon, so we can clear the King's name."

Peter blinked in amazement. "That's insane."

"No, it's a trade," said the Prince softly. "We need the Leader of the Fortune Tellers to witness us going to Olám Shoné. He agreed for a price."

"Deá and Damian," repeated Will bitterly.

"The only two Fortune Tellers who turned their backs on Fortune," said the Prince. "Or that's how the Fortune Tellers see it. But I'll find them," he added. "No one's going to rot anywhere."

"It's all for nothing anyway," said Peter, flicking his fake fire impatiently. And angrily he told the Prince about the lost Primary Safety Measure.

The Prince chuckled dryly, shaking his head. "Ironic. The one page... half a page... that's missing. And it's the one we need. Not that it matters." The Prince withdrew a glittering black vial from the shimmering silver pouch dangling from his neck and added, "Last night, my uncle tried to poison me. This healing potion saved my life. But he'll keep trying, because tomorrow I turn thirteen... old enough to take the throne from him. It's too dangerous for me to stay anywhere in Agám Kaffú. You too, Will... with Wither Heart on your trail. We have to go to Olám Shoné. We can take our time figuring out the Primary Safety Measure after we get through the door in the lake."

"I'm coming too," said Peter, his fingers fidgeting with the rope bulging under his sweater.

"So am I," said a determined voice deep within the tunnel. And Auralius emerged in the green glow of the Waterweed just past Wolfeá's sleeping head.

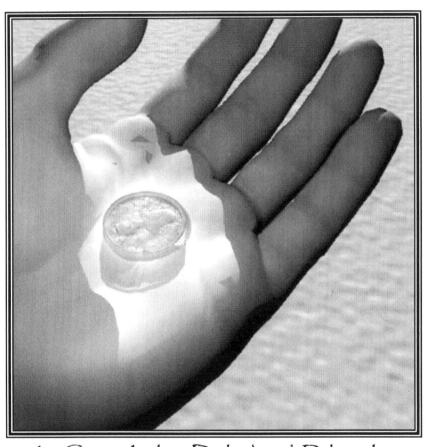

A Coin Like Polished Blue Ice

Beyond the Door
In the Lake

Will crawled after his Echo down the long dark tunnel with Wolfeá between them and Peter, Poudini and Auralius behind. The fake fire and Waterweed cast more shadows than light between them, and far away they could hear the earthquake of falling trees still rumbling like distant thunder. After a while a chill wind reached them. The flames flickered and died. Then the tunnel walls widened, and they left the Waterweed behind and crawled outside.

"Storm over the Orphanage." The Prince pointed at the somber sky behind them.

"Hopefully the Fate Sealers still think I'm there," said Will.

"Won't help you with the Spirits of the Lake," muttered Auralius, clutching his golden dagger nervously.

"Just keep to the shadows," said the Prince. "Follow me."

Will saw the Lake of Eternal Ice gleaming through his Echo's body as the Prince led the way into the moonlit, windswept forest. Before long the precious rubies, sapphires and diamonds came into view, twinkling like fallen stars inside the ice. Far in the distance Will saw a crystal ball of smoky glass hovering over the lake to mark the spot where the Prince's father was frozen forever.

"No sign of Deá and Damian," said Peter, peeking behind the last of the trees with Poudini in his arms.

"Or Fortis Fortuna," said the Prince.

"Or the Spirits," muttered Auralius.

But a ripple of motion caught Will's eye. "There—" He gasped.

Out of the frozen forest on their left, three Fate Sealers emerged like dark phantoms, a moonbeam slashing the scarred face of the tallest one.

"Wither Heart…" Will blinked in horror.

"I knew it," hissed Peter. "She told them. Valerie! Invisible. In the forest. Saw Cyrano helping us."

As if picking up the scent of humans on the chill night wind, the Fate Sealers swept forward, their Ice Looms glowing bright. A cackling raven flew over the head of the tallest one.

Suddenly a black ball shot past the bird and the swinging ears of the Fate Sealers. The creatures shrieked as another and another ball shot out of the sky, as if the storm clouds were suddenly raining down rocks. Already two of the Fate Sealers dropped their Ice Looms in startled anger, when Wither Heart shot his sagging arm up like a flapping sail and shone the last Ice Loom up at the brooding sky. And there, leaving the cover of the trees to circle over the Fate Sealers, was a white albatross with a small, see-through girl riding it fearlessly.

"Told you!" hissed Peter.

"No— She's protecting us," Will realized.

"Victor Valerian's niece...?" the Prince gasped in wonder.

"GET HER!" shrieked Wither Heart, as the see-through girl reached inside the dark sack tied to her stomach and hurled another stone at his scar.

Then the albatross flew off, low to the ground but just out of reach of the Fate Sealers. Wither Heart's black raven disappeared in the night, but its cackles carried far and wide, as all three Fate Sealers swept after the white albatross in a blur of speed, ducking each time Valerie hurled another rock in their billowing faces.

"They'll come back," said Auralius.

"We can't wait for Fortis Fortuna," agreed the Prince. "I know Damian promised," he added, glancing at Will. "Fortis Fortuna will be here. He'll see us coming back."

"*If* we get back," muttered Peter.

"We'll get back," said the Prince. "With the Fire Mushrooms. Ready?"

They nodded in agreement. Then, hunched like moving boulders, they crept across the frozen lake.

And now more than twinkling gems met their eyes beneath the ice. Faces—men, women, even one boy—stared back at them through that cold, frosty window, stared with sightless, terrifying faces that seemed perfectly preserved, as if the thieves of old were waiting to rise and wreak vengeance on their jailors.

As the four of them neared the smoky crystal ball that marked the King's icy grave, the Prince and Will kept close, searching for the passage that would only appear for an Echo and his Sound. While Auralius searched the brewing sky for Spirits of the Lake, and Peter, tiring of Poudini fidgeting in his arms, tied the little dog with his magic rope and led him beside Wolfeá.

And then—so suddenly that it took their breath away—a white light ignited under their feet and paws, as if someone had shot a flare gun inside the ice. Deeper and deeper the light sunk, revealing a treasure of precious stones that twinkled like fallen stars. And beneath them all, there was the round blue door that lay flat on the bottom of the lake. Only now something else was conjured around it, blue flames that danced on the frozen door until they reached its center, where the round, silvery Crystillery lock glittered like a mirror.

"THERE— ON THE LAKE—" a Fate Sealer shrieked, somewhere beyond the blinding white light.

Will flinched back to get away from his Echo, to put out the glow. But the ice blazed on, as if an Echo and his Sound were *still* there, standing over the passage to Olám Shoné.

"Didn't work!" Auralius yelled suddenly.

Will saw that the Prince had fired his copper Incendiary at the thick ice rising high above the door. But only a shallow pool had melted. While far across the moonlit lake, three grotesque figures were whirling toward them at a speed no Sound could match.

"Keep shooting—" shouted the Prince, shoving his crossbow

in Will's hand.

A hail of horizontal ice-arrows shrieked between them. Another volley blasted from Wither Heart's Ice Loom, heading for Peter's face.

"Go—" shouted the Prince.

Will leapt into the melted pool.

A cold blast swallowed him. Like a knife the freezing water seemed to peel the skin off his nose and fingers. Each stroke made the pain worse, but Will swam on, down toward the sunken arrow, his arms sweeping diamonds, rubies and sapphires, until he rearmed the copper Incendiary and fired again. More ice melted above the crystal blue door, more starry gems rained down, but not enough. Then over and over Will shot the weapon, before finally swimming up for air.

He caught sight of Auralius stabbing the hollow eye of a Fate Sealer with his golden dagger. Then Will dove back into that glittering tomb of cold and silence. When his fingers grew too stiff to grab the arrow, he used his chattering teeth. Two more shots and he reached the round door at last and brushed away the treasure of sunken stones, as half his air supply burst out of his mouth in a rush of bubbles.

Then, amazingly, wonderful heat surrounded Will suddenly, as if the blue flames still licking at the door were real fire, underwater fire. His lungs were burning for air, but he lingered and warmed his fingers, then shook out the Royal Shekel from the heel of his glistening white shoe.

The round Crystillery Lock was before him, about the size of his head. Most of it was a mirror, reflecting Will's deathly pale face and blue lips. But at the center was a round cavity that seemed fashioned from a diamond, and its size was identical to the icy coin twinkling between Will's stiff Fingers.

As soon as Will brought the Royal Shekel closer, a magnetic field sucked the coin into the cavity. And then, by itself, the entire Crystillery Lock mirror started to turn clockwise like the dial on a safe.

Already a quarter of a circle was complete when, suddenly, the turning stopped.

With a desperate kick Will catapulted himself back to the surface in a fog of air bubbles.

"Lock's stuck," he shouted, gasping for air and shivering so badly he bit his tongue.

"Safety Measure," shouted Peter, through a blur of gray motion.

The Prince snatched the Incendiary and arrow from Will's frozen grip and tossed them into the shadows. "Catch!" he shouted, and dove into the lake as well.

And now, in the mirror, Will saw his Echo's reflection beside his own—and amazingly the lock turned another quarter of a circle, but only to stop again. His hair drifting before his face like Waterweed, the Prince shook his head and swam back up, hauling Will with him.

"Auralius! Come with us!" he shouted.

Lightheaded and sleepy, Will felt himself pulled down into the icy depths again. He lost all sense of time. Suddenly he was looking in the mirror, seeing his bluish reflection between the Prince and Auralius.

Then, for the third time, the ice-blue coin with the mirror around it turned one more quarter of a circle, only now it kept on turning, turning until a full circle was complete. Bright blue flames suddenly burst around the Royal Shekel. The Prince plucked the coin out again. And a second later, as if someone on the other side was inviting them in—the door to Olám Shoné tore open.

*   *   *

As if a plug had been pulled from a brimming bathtub, the pool of melted water eddied out the open door, sweeping glittering gems, chunks of ice and Will's frozen body down a slanting, grassy path. The Prince and Auralius splashed helplessly beside Will, until they were washed up against the wall of an icy cave, where Will found himself lying flat on his back, spread-eagled and shivering.

"Couldn't close the door," he heard Peter's voice echoing behind them. "Wither Heart— Coming—"

The Prince was on his feet already, dripping over Will. "Stand up, can you?"

Will tried, but nothing moved the way it should. And in a moment Peter was there also, stuffing the Incendiary in his pocket before grabbing Will's ankles with his frozen hands, while the Prince and Auralius each grabbed a wrist.

And then his friends were running for their lives, and Will

was jostled like a sack of potatoes, catching psychedelic glimpses of Wolfeá and Poudini galloping in the lead. Until the lid of the icy cave receded suddenly, and the hum of a distant waterfall thundered free. Then an indigo sky spread over Will like a velvet blanket with a giant full moon shimmering behind a sea of frothy clouds.

"Don't touch that handle," shouted Peter, his words almost lost in the roar of Whirlpool Chasm.

Craning his neck Will saw a metal lever flying past, glinting in the brilliant moonlight. Then he flung his head back to see where the roar of the water was coming from. But Whirlpool Chasm wasn't there. Past Wolfeá and Poudini's galloping shapes, a purple field stretched far and wide, bursts of iridescent blue light flickering across it, shadowy mountains rising behind it. And between the field and mountains, a giant Crystillery rose up to the clouds. Only it wasn't a Crystillery at all, but a clear blue dome encasing a city of glass skyscrapers and gilded spires. A dark chasm protected this land, with only one thin bridge stretching across it like a fragile silver necklace. The Bridge of Knives, thought Will, with a shudder of fear.

And still his friends were running, shaking him like a rattle. Will could hear Wither Heart shrieking behind them, so loud even Whirlpool Chasm couldn't drown the Fate Sealer out. And soon the bridge was just a few feet away, and then before them, and Will twisted in horror to see knives breaking into a wild, churning dance inches from the Prince's see-through feet, slashing the icy floor, appearing and disappearing.

"We'll get cut to pieces," screamed Auralius, backing away, as Peter darted sideways, a blade jutting by his heel.

Wither Heart's shrieks drew nearer. The Prince shouted something to Will. But Will was shouting at the same time, fighting to pull his limbs free from his friends, as an idea exploded in his mind. His foot landed on the bridge. A blade spun toward it, glinting eerily in the moonlight. If Will was wrong, he would end up a cripple for life.

Suddenly, the glinting blade stopped.

So did every other blade. The bridge stood still. Only the river still roared beneath it, dark and writhing. Will caught the Prince staring at him, eyes blazing with triumph.

"You knew!" Will shouted, as they dashed across the bridge, meandering through the motionless knives. "You figured it out by the door, didn't you?"

"Wasn't sure."

The roar of Whirlpool Chasm thundered between them, and far below on their left they could see the black abyss of the giant waterfall.

"Has to be!" Will leapt over a gleaming row of metal teeth. "Two sets of an Echo and his Sound—that's the Primary Safety Measure! Auralius counts as two people. Mixed blood of both races."

Already Wolfeá was reaching the other side. The rest of them weren't far behind. And then Will heard the shriek over the roar of the waterfall. Still running, he twisted back. Wither Heart was in the air, swooping down on the glittering bridge, with Peter below him, aiming the Incendiary at the monstrous creature and the raven flying over the Fate Sealer's flapping head.

"SHOOT!" screamed Will.

But the world was already splintering in a shower of shattered ice, and Will was falling through darkness. The collapsing bridge rattled violently above him, receding fast. Will splashed into the black river like a stone. Icy water poured into his mouth and nose, his limbs flailed madly in the rushing current, his heart beat like a sledgehammer in his frozen chest.

"Invisible— Plants—" someone shouted in the roaring darkness.

Then through the chaos of waves and foam Will spotted tiny dots, like stars fallen from the night sky. He grabbed them and felt something slippery catching him in place, while the black water gushed wildly around him.

And then Will spotted Peter swooshing toward him, yelling frantically, his wet face glistening in the moonlight.

"Peter—" Will screamed, grabbing his friend's sweater.

But the shimmering uniform slipped through Will's fingers. And yet something else thrashed in his hand. The magic rope! He caught it just in time.

"Hold on!" Will shouted, tying his end to an invisible branch.

"Hurry!" shouted Peter, only his head still dangling over the black gulf of Whirlpool Chasm.

Barely seeing for the waves clawing at his face, Will gripped the slimy, invisible plant with his legs and hauled Peter in.

"Poudini!" Peter shouted.

"You two all right?" came a cry behind them.

Will twisted back. Auralius and the Prince were hovering over the moonlit, writhing river, they too suspended on dots of light.

"D'you see Poudini?" Peter shouted back.

The Prince shook his head. "Follow me!" And he leapt away with Auralius, between the clusters of lights floating in the night like frozen fireflies.

"Coming?" Will shouted from the next plant, when Peter didn't jump with him.

"Not without Poudini!"

"Maybe he made it with Wolfeá." Will fought to hold on. His new plant was small, and the raging river was battering his back like a thousand fists.

"What if he didn't?"

"You can't stay here!"

Peter's head disappeared in a dark whirlpool. "Going to die anyway—" he spluttered, barely resurfacing. "Chilling Mist— Remember—?"

And then, not far behind, Wither Heart appeared, leaping in mad pursuit, his sagging skin billowing like an evil squid, though his raven had disappeared.

"You killed my pet," shrieked the Fate Sealer, his Ice Loom glowing in his blustering hand. "Wait for me! I'll kill you for this."

"You killed *my* pet," Peter roared back. "It's all your fault!"

And suddenly the Incendiary was in Peter's hand again, as if by magic, and he pulled the copper arrow back.

"No—" The Prince shouted down the river. "One arrow— Can't lose it— Keep going!" And he leapt on, Auralius behind him.

"What a stupid weapon!" bellowed Peter, finally leaping to Will's side as a wave swallowed him again.

The clusters of light were getting harder to spot in the moonlight. The Prince veered to the left. Wither Heart changed direction too, closing in fast.

"The shore—" the Prince cried out at last.

Past the surging black waves Will saw the solid, still crescent of a dark, pebbled beach. Silver clouds drifted over it as if the land were a sleeping dragon snoring thick smoke. And yet nothing ever looked more inviting, more safe to Will—until he remembered the Heat Rocks.

"Don't jump!" he shouted to the Prince, seeing his Echo swaying like a soaked rag caught in a whirlpool. "Not clouds— Steam! You'll melt—"

"Wait for me!" Wither Heart shrieked behind them. "Why drown? I can rip your heads off!"

Auralius jumped to the Prince's side and hoisted him on his shoulders. Then looking like a hunchback, the Mongrel leapt away from the cluster of hovering lights, plunging with the Prince into the moonlit silver steam shrouding the dark shore. Peter leapt away next. A second later Will followed, landing on the shore of Heat Rocks that glowed faintly at his feet like dying embers.

"COME BACK!" Wither Heart screeched after them, trapped on the river's edge.

*　　*　　*

Auralius was shouting from afar, running with the Prince bobbing on his shoulders, half lost in the clouds of steam silvered by the moon.

"What—?" Will shouted back, feeling sleepy with warmth.

Peter slowly rolled up his magic rope beside Will, water drops sizzling at his feet.

"BEHIND YOU!"

"He's stuck in the river." Will shrugged tiredly, hearing Wither Heart still screeching in frustration. But Auralius kept shouting, and Will gave in and turned around lazily.

And then he saw it.

The dark river was rising like a living crowd. The gushing current was forming into water-people, eddies turning into see-through heads, foam into legs. The waves that rushed past only seconds ago suddenly crawled up the steaming shore, pouring forth like zombies. And the first of them were already clawing at Will and Peter's heels.

"MOVE!" Will snatched Peter's arm, and they darted away into the silvery mist.

"Come back… come back… come back…" the water-people called after them in whispers that rose and fell like the surf. While, over the roar of the waterfall, Wither Heart's screeches twisted into shrieks of terror.

"They're drowning him!" Will realized.

Dark, liquid men were rising in the river, washing over the Fate Sealer and his Ice Loom—until, with a final shriek, Wither Heart was torn from his invisible plant and swept over the black rim of Whirlpool Chasm.

"Gone!" shouted Will with horror.

"We're next!" shouted Peter

On the silvery shore the first wave of zombies chasing Will and Peter began to evaporate on the Heat Rocks. But already a second wave was climbing over the steaming dead, and then a third wave, and a forth, water turning into people who melted into water that turned into people again, in a never-ending march.

"They're not giving up—"

"What's the difference?" shouted Peter, slowing down, losing hope. "Freeze… Drown…"

"Peter! Snap out of it!"

"Poudini's dead—"

"But we're not! The Chilling Mist. Look—! What are we going to do?"

In a few seconds they would hit it, that glistening curtain pouring out of the night sky like a waterfall of rain that wasn't raining down at all, for each raindrop was frozen in midair. The Prince was already standing inside this petrified rain, his shape cut into the still drops as if he had walked through stone and carved a tunnel.

"Stay back!" shouted Auralius, panting for breath on the

480

curtains' shimmering edge.

"Come back… come back… come back…" hissed the surf of water-people.

"What about them?" Will shouted to Auralius.

"Can't come in here. Too cold for Sounds," insisted Auralius, hurling a Heat Rock at the Chilling Mist.

With a soft pop the rock shattered and disappeared.

"Can't stay out here either—" shouted Will. "Peter?" he added desperately. "Think of something."

"Clear a path for us," Peter shouted to the Prince. "Less cold that way."

"Still too cold."

But Peter was already ordering Will to sit down, curl into a ball, and stick his head under his sweater. "Auralius—" he cried next.

"Yes, I'll carry him."

The Mongrel darted forward. Behind him the Prince was already breaking a tunnel all the way through the Chilling Mist.

"No!" Will shouted, as Peter turned back to face the water-people. "They'll drown you— I'm not leaving—"

"You have to—"

"No!"

"You're the Prince's Sound— You're too important— Just *go*! Auralius will come back for me."

Will caught a last glimpse of Peter rushing through the silver mist to intercept the liquid zombies. Then he stuffed Heat Rocks in

481

his lap and pulled his steaming sweater over his head. In a moment, he was bouncing in Auralius' arms, hearing the Mongrel panting with effort, while a cold that felt like a savage animal was digging its claws into Will's skin, bones, spine, skull.

Will shrunk around the Heat Rocks, his frozen breath shattering in his lap. His wet clothes crusted and crackled. The sound of crunching exploded in his ears, and Will hoped it was only Auralius' footsteps.

"I'mmm fffine," Will shivered at last, when he heard the Prince's voice by his ear.

And then Will felt himself falling stiffly to the ground. All the warmth of the Heat Rocks had left him. Just getting his head out of his frosty sweater was a struggle. And by then Auralius was already sprinting through the tunnel broken in the Chilling Mist, toward the water-crowd bending over two flailing, helpless arms.

"Peter—" Will shook and shuddered, trying to get to his feet.

"No!" The Prince threw him back.

"Let me go—"

"You'll die!"

It was no use anyway; Will's legs were shivering convulsively under him. All he could do was watch as Peter drowned on the other side of the Chilling Mist as if trapped in a sinister aquarium. His flailing arms finally gave in and disappeared, just as Auralius plunged into the see-through crowd at long last.

And then came a moment of wonder. The water-people rippled with surprise, and their evil hissing ceased, before they

482

suddenly fell on the steaming shore to bow before Auralius as if he were a king. And in a moment the Heat Rocks melted them all into a cloud of silvery fog.

Will watched as Auralius plunged back into the Chilling Mist with Peter's lifeless body in his arms.

"He'll freeze—" Will yelled helplessly, tearing off his sweater and trying to get up.

"I'll take it!" shouted the Prince. And in a moment Will's Echo was rushing toward Auralius and Peter

In the moonlight, Will could see Peter's dangling head turning to marble. His frozen hair broke and rained down. Even one of Peter's ears shattered before the Prince reached him and wrapped Peter's face in Will's sweater.

Will struggled to his feet, shivering violently.

"Don't do it!" the Prince yelled to him. "He's still alive. We'll need your help saving him. Stay where you are!"

At last, Auralius and the Prince broke through the moonlit tunnel of frozen rain. Will flew at them and helped lower Peter to the ground. Hardly daring to breathe, he pulled off the frosty sweater covering his friend's face. Peter stared back at him, eyes wide open and sightless, like the faces in the Lake of Eternal Ice.

"This'll help—" The Prince tore the black vial from the silver pouch dangling from his neck.

Will shook his head. "Lips are frozen," he said hopelessly. He placed one of his Heat Rocks over Peter's mouth and defrosted an opening. "Peter first," he insisted, when the Prince finished dripping one drop of dark liquid into Auralius' panting mouth, then one into his own and was bending the vial to Will.

Like tears of onyx the healing potion trickled between Peter's marble lips. But nothing happened.

"Give him more," said Will, but the Prince snatched the black vial away.

"No! Too much at once... his blood will burst through his veins. Wait five minutes— Now you drink two drops... you're shivering like mad."

"Let me keep the bottle then," insisted Will, before he obeyed.

A rush of energy trickled down Will's throat with the bitter-tasting medicine. He stopped shivering and noticed for the first time that his Echo's face was scarred with oozing welts.

"Burns," explained the Prince, "from the steam. Potion takes time... Pain's already better."

Still recovering his breath, Auralius stood up to stare at the forty-foot cliff towering at their backs, shimmering white in the moonlight. "Can you hear them?" he asked darkly.

Looking up Will saw enormous black holes dotting the surface of the cliff. Red eyes were blinking inside these dark caves, and a grinding noise poured out of them. "The giant spiders." He shivered in horror.

"Rubbing their pinchers," said Auralius, pulling his golden dagger out. "Getting ready for a midnight snack."

*   *   *

Black heads peeked from the caves in the shimmering cliff. One giant monster slinked out on hairy legs, its pinchers snapping, its roving red eyes searching the moonlit night for prey.

"Have to get him out of here," said Will, stuffing his Heat Rocks under Peter's sweater.

"Who's got the Incendiary?" asked Auralius, shifting his dagger nervously from hand to hand.

"Here—" Will found the weapon curled in Peter's magic rope and tossed both to Auralius.

"No! Don't shoot," said the Prince. "Not yet. What about the rope? Can we climb?"

"With this?" Auralius laughed grimly, holding out the short length of rope. "Maybe to the first cave."

"It's Peter's rope," said Will, shaking his head. "Magic—"

"You mean it's long enough? Good!"

In a flash, Will's Echo snatched the rope and faced the sheer white cliff. What looked like a staircase of spider webs rose from the ground all the way to the sky along the surface of the rock, but the webs were so see-through and delicate they barely showed in the moonlight.

The Prince jumped on the first step in this gauzy staircase.

"By all the flying crystal balls—" Auralius threw his arms up in disbelief. "Are you crazy?"

"Just keep them off me!" said the Prince, already climbing the shimmering parachutes.

Sensing motion in the cobwebs, a giant spider swiveled

suspiciously on its silky string high at the top of the cliff. Each time the Prince shook his hands and feet to loosen the sticky hold of the webs, they tore a little under him, and it looked as if he might fall. But soon the Prince swept past the first cave, and the spider who dwelt there crept out to join the one hanging high above, and the two snapped their pinchers and shrieked furiously.

"Watch out!" shouted Will.

Auralius fired the Incendiary as the spider below the Prince shot up with incredible speed. The copper arrow streaked in the moonlight. In a whirl of dark wisps the spider disappeared into the night, screeching frightfully. Instantly, the second spider spat a silky cord between its pinchers and descended swiftly down.

"What a stupid weapon!" roared Will, staring up at the copper arrow lodged at the entrance to the first cave.

"I'll get it!" shouted Auralius, throwing the Incendiary to Will.

"You're too heavy—"

But Auralius was already climbing the gauzy stairs, ripping through them yet holding on somehow. While all down the shimmering white cliff spiders were suddenly slinking out of their caves, red eyes flashing, the moonlight glinting off their hairy backs. One plunged down toward the Prince, almost knocking him off balance as the Prince fought back with his bare hands, screaming for help.

Desperately, Will hurled a Heat Rock at the spider's face, striking an eye. The monster shrieked in agony but lunged more

486

fiercely at the Prince.

"Catch!" shouted Auralius, finally reaching the copper arrow. He hurled it down to Will and at the same time stabbed a larger spider with his golden knife, sending the monster plummeting off the cliff.

Will jumped clear of the colossal crashing insect, rearmed the Incendiary, and fired.

"Help—" shouted the Prince.

But already the spider was melting above him, and the Prince tossed the arrow back down to Will and climbed on, more spiders chasing after him until, at last, he disappeared over the rim of the shimmering white cliff.

The spiders shrieked furiously but seemed afraid to follow and climbed down their webs again, closing in on Auralius. While more spiders left their caves below and started climbing up. Auralius was trapped between them like a fly. Will shot the spider snapping its pinchers inches from Auralius' head, while Auralius stabbed another and hurled the arrow back down to Will.

Then began a frantic repetition of this battle plan. And as Auralius fought for his life, again and again his feet tore through the delicate webs. Often he seemed about to fall to his death. But, at last, the Prince reappeared over the edge of the cliff high above, and he tossed the rope down and hauled Auralius to safety with surprising strength.

"Now you and Peter!" the Prince shouted down to Will, tossing the rope with a rock tied to its end, to stretch it all the way down.

"Just Peter." Will shouted back. "We're too heavy—"

"No!" shouted Auralius, as his bleeding face appeared over the Prince's shoulder. "Peter can't toss the arrow down. You won't have a weapon to protect him. Both of you! Together. It's the only way."

Will trickled three more drops of healing potion between Peter's marble lips. "Hang in there, Peter," he mumbled desperately.

With the spiders shrieking over him, heading down their webs again, Will stretched on the ground beside his frozen friend, slipping one noose around Peter, another around himself. "All right—" he shouted up at the Prince and Auralius.

A second later Will and Peter were swept in the air.

Spiders spat sticky webs at them, shrieking wildly. Will shot the nearest ones out of their path, each time snatching the arrow through the melting body and the rotting stench of the dying creature. Until finally the edge of the cliff was just above them, and Auralius leaned down and grabbed Peter's frozen shoulders.

"Watch out!" he hollered suddenly, his bleeding face twisting with fear.

Pain shot up Will's leg. A black pincher cut into his ankle. He screamed and writhed as the spider started spitting webs around his foot. Still screaming, Will shot the Incendiary in the creature's face. But the arrow bounced off the scaly forehead and fell away.

"Stab it—" shouted Auralius, throwing his golden dagger to Will.

Will could barely see for the pain ripping through his ankle. He stabbed at the dark mass hovering below him, but the monster kept pulling him down. And Peter's frozen body swayed wildly over Will, smashing into the shimmering cliff until something broke and fell, perhaps the fragment of a sleeve, perhaps a finger.

And then another pincher snapped into Will's thigh. Screaming, he slashed blindly with the knife. The creature shrieked and let go, but another spider cut into Will's hand, and Will lost hold of the Incendiary. In a moment, he knew that the spiders would reach the dagger, and then the creatures would climb over him and slice Peter bit by bit.

Will couldn't let that happen!

"Save Peter!" he shouted to Auralius.

Then Will cut his own noose with the golden dagger.

The last thing Will saw as he plunged to his death, spiders shrieking and tumbling under him, was Peter hauled to safety over the rim of the moonlit cliff, and Auralius shouting something, his face contorted with horror.

After that there was nothing.

The People of Harmoniá

The City of Harmony

Will couldn't hear the spiders shrieking anymore when he blinked his burning eyes open. A foul taste oozed in his mouth, and his body felt sore and heavy. The shimmering giant moon was still there in the indigo sky, but the roar of Whirlpool Chasm had vanished to be replaced by a soft breeze and the tangy smell of apples.

"Where am I?" muttered Will.

A pale figure leaned over him and answered, "Welcome back."

"Peter…" Will gasped. His eyes focused on something furry trying to eat his friend's bandaged head. "Poudini…?" Will gasped again. "He made it?"

"We all did!" Peter grinned, looking as pale as a ghost. "No thanks to this, though—" Peter magicked the copper Incendiary from the dressing covering his ear. "Stupid weapon."

"But it fell out of my hand," slurred Will, his tongue feeling strangely muddy. "*I* fell—"

"On a spider. Auralius says it exploded. Black juice

everywhere. Ugh— You're clean now, though," added Peter, dodging a massive lick from Poudini.

"All right, that's enough," said a deep voice at Will's side. "Stop nauseating my patient, young man. And move over."

By the amber light of a giant fairy fluttering over them, Will noticed a face that looked older than any face Will had ever seen before. More like a tree trunk with features than a man.

"Open wide…" the ancient man spoke again, stuffing Will's mouth with a smoking lump that smelled like apples.

Grease oozed over Will's tongue with slimy mud and something unimaginably worse. He jerked his head back, yanking at the gnarled fingers clamping his mouth shut. His stomach turned. Purple smoke spewed from his nostrils. But the fingers, like an iron mask, simply wouldn't budge.

"Like sucking on a dead hedgehog. Only worse." Peter nodded sympathetically, slapping Will's back as he choked on the smoke. "The dog with no taste buds wouldn't touch it. I had to have three. This one's your sixth… Sorry, Will."

"What— was— that—?" Will spluttered, when the ancient man finally let go.

The revolting lump had melted in Will's mouth, leaving the aftertaste of dead things and, strangely, the fresh scent of apples.

"Think: *Page 1*—road Map!" Peter magicked an iridescent blue lump out of his nostril. Purple smoke curled all around it.

"A Cold Fire Mushroom," whispered Will in amazement. "We made it?"

Peter smiled and pointed sideways. The Prince and Auralius were standing there, each holding an iridescent blue lump and looking infinitely amused when it spewed purple smoke in their faces or zapped them with tiny purple lightning.

"You'll think it delicious in about a hundred years," said the ancient man, closing a smoking bag, no doubt filled with mushrooms.

The amber fairy-light followed him as he joined a group of people standing beside a whole field of iridescent, smoking mushrooms. Both young and old, men and women, some of them were Echoes, some Sounds, and a few looked like Mongrels, half see-through in places. Over each of their heads a unique light hovered like a giant glowworm: a fairy-shaped light, a dragon, a lion, a sword, even a shoe—though no crystal ball. The clothes these strange people wore were also unique, no outfit looking quite like another. And yet every garment seemed woven from Cold Fire Mushrooms, for all the clothes smoked and sizzled with tiny purple lightning bolts just like the field.

"Welcome to the City of Harmoniá," said the tallest person there.

He was dressed in a hooded robe of pure smoke, and over his head a Crystillery-shaped light emitted a silvery glow. Behind him, the great domed city of glass skyscrapers and glided spires rose to the night sky, glittering like a giant jewel box.

"Welcome," he spoke again, "won't you join us?"

Peter helped Will to his feet, which were swathed in smoking

495

blue bandages, as was one of his hands, though the glistening cuff of Will's sweater was trying to clean the bandage off. The Prince and Auralius waited for them, and then all four boys stepped or limped forward together, an apple-scented breeze caressing their faces.

The tall man met them halfway, holding a slightly see-through woman by the hand. Her purple dress lapped at her feet like waves, and a gold light hovered over her head in the shape of a smile. Will couldn't help staring at the two, for both the man, who was a Sound, and the woman, who was an Echo, looked so terribly old that they reminded Will of mummies. And yet the man's eyes sparkled like sapphires and the woman's like emeralds—the most beautiful eyes Will had ever seen.

"I am Fluid Conway," said the ancient man, with a voice that sounded like a young man. "And this is my wife, Illyria. Welcome to our city."

Will stopped still in amazement.

He remembered what Valerie said at the Orphanage library: "*Fluid Conway invented the Crystillery. But the King wanted to execute him and the woman he loved... She was a queen, the beautiful Queen Illyria.*" But didn't it all happen ages ago, wondered Will. How could they still be alive?

Will exchanged a baffled look with Peter, who was mouthing the words "Illyria's Treasure", his blue-green eyes almost popping out of his face with astonishment.

Only the Prince remembered his manners. "We are honored to be here," he said, over Auralius' skeptical mutterings.

496

Fluid Conway smiled, his wrinkled, leathery lips stretching over a perfect set of white teeth. "Your friends have heard of us," he said, amused.

"Of course." The Prince bowed his head gallantly. "Your names are legend in Agám Kaffú. But…"

"Why are we still alive?" asked Illyria, in the voice of a young woman. "We won't be for long. The Cold Fire Mushrooms have kept us alive for over two hundred year. But we are dying. Please, tell us who you are," she added, and the smoky people behind her nodded fervently. "We haven't had visitors from Agám Kaffú in over a century. And a Mongrel among you— How delightful!"

"Why?" demanded Auralius, glaring at Illyria. "What do you do to Mongrels here?"

"We honor them, what else?" answered a girl who stepped out of the welcoming crowd.

She was about Auralius' age and enchantingly beautiful, perhaps because a purple candle traveled over her head, sprinkling her with gold glitter.

"I'm Aurora," she said happily, hugging Auralius in greeting. "Oh, how funny—" She giggled. "You can't control your emotions at all."

"Yes I can." Auralius shook her off.

"No, you can't. Your heads turning invisible."

"No. It's just…" Auralius stammered, "where I come from Mongrels aren't exactly welcome! We're hunted. Like animals."

"Hunted?" Fluid Conway's wrinkled face collapsed in a frown that swallowed his bright eyes. "I am grieved to hear it," he said darkly.

Illyria sighed, Aurora gasped in shock, her ears turning invisible, and the crowd of onlookers murmured so angrily that Will expected them to turn their backs on their guests, return to their city and leave the wild wolves to guard the Cold Fire Mushrooms, as the road map had warned. He glanced at his Echo, wondering what they should do next, when something nuzzled his hand suddenly.

"Wolfeá—"

Will's pet panted up at him, her dark-rimmed yellow eyes glittering with excitement. A few gray wolves stood behind her, two Echoes, a Sound and a Mongrel.

"Your new family..." Will beamed at his wolf. "Then you won't need this anymore," he added, untying the old rope still straggling behind Wolfeá, a single Christmas Firefly stuck in the knot.

Whatever happens next, thought Will, at least his wolf was free!

*   *   *

"Then nothing has changed since I left?" Fluid Conway spoke again. His ancient face was nearly lost in the purple smoke rising from his hood. "The Law of Death? The Fortune Tellers? The Fate Sealers? Everything is just as it was?"

"That's why we had to come here," said the Prince gravely. "I'm Prince William Cleary, heir to the throne of Agám Kaffú. This

498

is my Sound." He gestured at Will.

"We've guessed as much." Illyria smiled serenely, her face a sea of wrinkles. "Even with the bandages, the resemblance between you is clear."

"Resemblance…?" wondered Will, thinking of his red-headed, blimp disguise. "What resemblance?" he asked, wondering if he would ever get used to looking like a walking joke.

"The river—" whispered Peter between them "—washed out your hair color."

"Chilling Mist shrunk you," added Auralius.

Will glanced down at himself in amazement. "I look like me again?"

"I know— A scarecrow." Peter sighed sympathetically.

Will laughed. He looked like himself again, funky hair and all. What a relief!

"And that's why we had to come here," the Prince continued his conversation with Fluid Conway, looking so grave beside Will. He explained who they were and what life was like for Echoes and Sounds in Agám Kaffú. The welcoming party kept sighing their disapproval, and the lights floating over their heads dimmed somberly with every frown.

"Then you still rely on the Fortune Tellers to create your rain, your sky, your sunshine?" said Fluid Conway. The Crystillery light darkened over his smoking hood, and beside it the apple-scented breeze blew out Illyria's smile.

"But once I bring back the Cold Fire Mushrooms, all that will change," said the Prince, holding up the iridescent mushroom sizzling in his see-through hand.

"And you will abolish the Law of Death?" asked Fluid Conway.

"I will! Or die trying... like my father."

The mushroom field spewed purple light behind the Prince's see-through body, as he explained how the true King was murdered then defamed when he was thrown in the Lake of Eternal Ice like a common thief. The story seemed to set Fluid Conway's eyes on fire, and Will guessed why. The starry stones in the lake, now worshiped as sacred gifts of Fortune, had all come from Fluid Conway's Crystilleries, polished by his own hands for the purpose of keeping happy memories alive. But, instead, they were luring men to their death.

"Then Fortune Tellers now murder Kings, as well as innocent Echoes?" said Fluid Conway bitterly. His Crystillery light hardly glowed anymore.

"I don't know who murdered my father," said the Prince. "It could have been the Fortune Tellers, yes. But I think it was my uncle. He always wanted to be king. Now he is."

Fluid Conway sighed and shook his head, smoke shrouding his ancient face. "There is no escaping it," he said darkly. "As long as Echoes continue to believe that Fortune wants them to die when their Sounds die, Agám Kaffú will remain an unhappy land, full of hate and fear."

"I know that," said the Prince.

"*I* know that," spat Auralius.

"Yes, of course."

Fluid Conway nodded sadly at the Mongrel, before turning to look up at the Crystillery dome rising to the night sky behind them. He seemed to read the answer to a riddle there, written in moonlight.

"Illyria and I called our city Harmoniá," he said, taking his wife's wizened hand. "It's a Hebrew name, but it isn't ancient. I'm sure you've guessed the meaning. Here we do not waste time judging each other by how see-through our skin is. We live in harmony. If you come with us," Fluid Conway added graciously, "we will show you our ways. And teach you how to bring peace to your land."

A change came over the Prince and Auralius. All their lives, Will knew, they had heard of Olám Shoné. To be invited inside must feel like a dream. But Will also knew that they hadn't come this far to lose themselves in a fairytale.

"We can't... not tonight," said Will, feeling Wolfeá snuffling his bandaged hand as if she could tell how excited he felt. "The Leader of the Fortune Tellers... Fortis Fortuna," Will explained, "he's waiting for us on the Lake of Eternal Ice. My friends gave up their freedom just to make sure he'd be there. We have to leave. Right away. And—" Will searched for a polite way of asking "—if you will please grant our wish, Mr. Conway... we have to take some Cold Fire Mushrooms back with us."

It happened at last. All the lights floating over the welcoming party went out together. The candle above Aurora's beautiful face

501

started spitting black sparks. Only the moonlight and the iridescent mushrooms still cast a glow around the open field, and the domed city of glass shimmered in the distance.

"You have an arrangement with the Fortune Tellers?" Fluid Conway's voice rose out of his pitch black hood.

"It was my idea," said the Prince. And with a firm voice he explained his plan for clearing his father's name.

"And you trust the word of a Fortune Teller?" The smoke billowed in the dark hood. "How can you be sure Fortis Fortuna will really remove your uncle and place you on the throne?"

"My uncle is a tyrant," said the Prince bitterly. "He wants to destroy the Fortune Tellers. Steal their power for himself. Fortis Fortuna believes I will be different. A perfect King—young and stupid."

"And obedient, no doubt." A gleaming smile appeared in Fluid Conway's hood. A second later, his Crystillery light flickered back on. "A mistake too often made by adults," he added, "confusing youth with folly."

"Or age with wisdom." Illyria smiled also.

The ancient couple laughed, their old cheeks creasing like crumpled paper. The Crystillery light and smile torch burned brightly over their heads again. Soon the whole menagerie of floating lights blazed over the welcoming party as before: a butterfly, a scorpion, a fawn, a thimble, a rainbow of colors and shapes. And then Fluid Conway turned to a young Echo with a carrier pigeon flaming over his head.

"From my private collection," he ordered, "have Aqually send me a black chest!"

"At once, Your Honor!" answered the young man.

His ruff sizzling purple light around his neck, the young man plucked his burning pigeon out of the air. He tapped a message on its stomach, then sent the bird soaring like a burning phoenix, over the iridescent field of smoking mushrooms toward the golden city gate.

"A Carrier Light," the beautiful Aurora explained to Auralius. She was standing beside the Mongrel, smiling at his shyness, which made Auralius' eyes flicker between bright blue and invisible.

"You will have your mushrooms," said Fluid Conway to Will and the Prince. "The chest will arrive soon. The mushrooms in it have roots. You can plant them anywhere, and they will multiply. You will also find instructions and recipes for cures in the chest. I hope you will come see us again. The Bridge of Knives has already repaired itself. Our city will always be open to two sets of an Echo and his Sound. That's how we make sure those who visit us do not bring hate with them."

The ancient Sound exchanged a wrinkled smile with his Echo wife, then he turned to Will and the Prince again.

"The bridge only collapsed under you because you were followed by a Fate Sealer," he explained. "I am sorry about that. If it had not happened in the middle of the night, we would have come to your rescue sooner. Now, tell me—" Fluid Conway's eyes twinkled. "—How did you figure out all our Safety Measures?"

"Your road map… we found it," said Will, glancing at Peter and Auralius. "Translated it."

"Did you, now?" Fluid Conway smiled at his wife again. "And we thought it was lost."

"Then there's only one copy?" asked Peter. In his arms, Poudini was still trying to eat the bandage off Peter's ear.

"Yes, just the one." Fluid Conway nodded, scattering purple smoke with his chin. "And, by the way, keep eating our delicious mushrooms," he added. "Your ear will grow back in no time. Isn't that right, Rippley?"

The ancient doctor nodded sagely from the crowd, his fairy-light fluttering brightly by his ear. "Delicious and nutritious," he declared proudly.

"Delicious…?" Will grinned at Peter. The aftertaste of dead hedgehog still lingered in his mouth.

But Peter stopped listening. Fidgeting and muttering "treasure" to himself, he stared at Illyria with glittering eyes. Suddenly, he blurted out, "You're Queen Illyria, right?"

"Half right." The ancient woman nodded her shriveled, mummy head. "I used to be a Queen. But not anymore. Not for two hundred years. I'm just Illyria."

"But back then," said Peter breathlessly, "you used to… before you stopped being a Queen, I mean… you used to have this amazing treasu—?"

But the burning Carrier Light returned, and Peter had to make room for the tiny bird that came to a landing between Auralius

504

and him, carrying a chest ten times its size.

"All in the handles," explained an old Echo, hopping out of the purple crowd with a peacock light reflecting colorfully in his bald head. "*My* invention," he boasted. "Makes any chest as light as air."

"Lighter, surely," said Fluid Conway, chuckling in his smoking hood.

"Yes, yes, of course— Lighter! Thank you, Your Honor."

"Thank *you*, Fluider."

To Fluider's delighted claps, Auralius plucked the shimmering black chest from the blazing bird's beak with a single finger. Beside him Aurora laughed and invited Auralius to come back to Harmoniá someday, to live free the way Mongrels should. The Prince bowed regally and thanked Fluid Conway and Illyria for their generosity. And Will bowed farewell also, thinking to himself that Valerian's medallion was theirs for sure.

Only Peter still looked thoughtful, staring at Illyria and fidgeting.

"You wanted to ask me something?" said the ancient woman.

Peter nodded so much he bumped heads with Poudini, and the gold smile hovering over Illyria burst out laughing like a real mouth.

"Is it true?" Peter stammered, his pale face turning pink in the middle. "About your treasure being lost?"

"Not exactly…" Illyria joined her light in laughing, and her wrinkles rippled on her cheeks. "Not the treasure. I took it with me

505

here. But... I haven't thought of it in years. The key... the key is lost. Has been for centuries."

"No, it isn't!" said Will and Peter together.

"I mean," added Peter, "if the key's a medallion, we know where it is."

"How exciting!" Illyria's dazzling eyes glittered. She flicked a wise smile at Fluid Conway, then turned back to Will and Peter. "So you have the key, do you?" She paused thoughtfully. "In that case... you'd better have the treasure too."

*   *   *

Happy was too small a word for Will to describe how Peter looked—eyes glittering, mouth grinning, left pinkie swinging a small gold box the size of his shoe—as the four boys retraced their steps up the grassy hill that brought them into this strange land only hours ago.

"So what sort of treasure is it, d'you think?" asked Peter, for the tenth time since stepping off the Bridge of Knives.

The bridge had coated itself in ice again, offering a breathtaking, moonlit passage over the raging river, without a single blade waking beneath their feet. They had looked for Wither Heart dangling over the black fury of Whirlpool Chasm. But it was crazy to think that the Fate Sealer was still alive. And yet it was hard to believe that he was finally gone.

"So what d'you think?" Peter swung the gold box ever higher. "Doesn't weigh much. What sort of treasure is it? Jewelry? Hope it's not jewelry."

"Why?" said Will. "You'd look great in a tiara... Can still see her," he added, casting a final look back. "Hope she'll be okay."

There, between the glass skyscrapers of Harmoniá and the iridescent blue field of smoking mushrooms, Will could see Wolfeá running with her new family of wolves.

"Are you kidding?" Peter clapped Will's shoulder. "She'll be great. For the first time ever."

"Yeah." Will nodded gratefully. "Free at last."

"You coming?" Auralius cried down from the top of the hill.

The Prince was already ahead of the Mongrel, entering the icy cave, swinging the shimmering black chest with the Cold Fire Mushrooms inside it, the proof that would clear his father's name.

"Seemed shorter coming down," said Peter, as Will and he started climbing again. "So what if Valerian gives the medallion to someone else?" Peter asked, this question only for the fifth time.

"For doing what? Going to the moon?" Will grinned.

"You're right." Peter nodded happily. "It's in the bag. So what sort of treasure is it, d'you think?"

"Is he still at it?" said Auralius, waiting at the entrance to the cave. "You don't even have the key yet."

"True," said Peter, unflummoxed. "So what if Valerian gives the medallion to someone else?"

"Can't you hear yourself?" Auralius' eyes disappeared for a second. "You sound like a broken Crystillery. Just bribe Valerian, if you have to."

Auralius bent to pick up a starry diamond and two rubies,

which had washed out of the Lake of Eternal Ice when the blue door burst open that evening.

"Nice," said Peter, trying to grab the gems.

"Get your own—" snapped Auralius.

"Why? Keeping yours for Aurora?"

Grinning, Peter plucked five glittering diamonds out of the grass. Auralius looked away to hide his face, but his head turned so see-through that Will could see the end of the path emerging through it. And soon he could see the round blue door too, with the Prince waiting beside it.

"And I thought blushing was bad. Anyway—" Peter swung his treasure in Will's face "—what sort of treasure is it, d'you think?"

"You'd better hide them," said the Prince, as Auralius scooped up more rubies where the icy cave ended. "Remember the faces in the lake," he warned. "No treasure's worth dying for. All right—" The Prince took a deep breath. "Time to go home."

There was no Crystillery lock on this side of the round blue door, no mirror at the center. The Prince pressed his palm to the middle of the door, following Fluid Conway's parting instructions, which had warned them that the passage will have closed automatically by now. But not locked itself, not to people *leaving* Olám Shoné—not unless Fortune Tellers or Fate Sealers were lurking on the other side, for then the door would not open for anyone.

Soon blue flames appeared around the Prince's hand and the

door moved slightly. Auralius swung it open, and the jagged hole in the lake appeared with a dark stormy sky brewing high above it.

"All clear!" said Peter, swinging his treasure happily.

"No, it isn't," Will realized. "Fortis Fortuna *isn't* waiting for us. The door wouldn't open if he was."

"You're right, by Fortune!" Auralius scowled. "If he's not there... If this was all for nothing..."

"Only one way to find out," said the Prince, as he clutched the shimmering black chest of mushrooms and stepped back into Agám Kaffú.

The Frozen King

The King's Murderer

Fortis Fortuna *was* there, standing on the frozen lake beneath the dark brewing sky, with lightning flashing over him, though no rain fell. He was so see-through and so old he looked like a misty skeleton dressed in shimmering gold, with his human eyes gone, replaced by crystal balls. And just as shimmering were the four male Fortune Tellers standing guard behind him, their clothes blood-red, their bodies muscular, their faces severe in the pale light of the luminous crystal balls topping the icy staffs they were holding.

"Welcome, Fortune's Wards," said Fortis Fortuna, in a quivering voice.

The ancient Fortune Teller's golden cape fluttered in the chill night wind. At his feet the gem-studded ice was brightening as the Prince, Will and Auralius finished climbing out of the lake—two sets of an Echo and his Sound—with Peter in the rear. And by this brightening glow, Will spotted two other shimmering Fortune Tellers, one black, one white, their hands and feet shackled with crystal ball fetters.

"Damian... Deá..." mumbled Will with a heavy heart.

Damian nodded a greeting at Will, the muscles in his dark cheeks pulsing. Deá smiled, but there was no joy in her beautiful, pale face.

Fortis Fortuna continued addressing the Prince alone, ignoring Will and Peter completely as if Sounds were beneath his notice.

"Do my crystal eyes deceive me, young Prince?" He flicked his eerie crystal ball gaze at Auralius. "You defy the decree of your new King? You keep company with a Mongrel instead of torturing him to death?"

Auralius' hand shot to the hilt of his golden dagger. But the Prince stepped in front of the Mongrel and bowed reverently to the Leader of the Fortune Tellers.

"By Fortune's favor," said the Prince humbly, "in defying the King, I stay true to Fortune. No man has the right to decide who will live and who will die, not even the King. Only Fortune has power of life and death over us."

"Hmmm." Fortis Fortuna nodded once in approval, though his crystal ball eyes bore into the Prince as if trying to decipher his soul. "If Fortune rules our fates," he said Shrewdly, "why have you tried to alter yours by going to Olám Shoné?"

"To fulfill my duty by Fortune," said the Prince. "To lay the truth before you, Master of All Fates."

"And if Fortune decides that you shall never be king?"

"I will obey."

Will saw Damian nodding, as if he thought the Prince was

living up to his side of their bargain: Damian would bring Fortis Fortuna to the lake; the Prince would pretend to be young, trusting and obedient.

"He isn't really gonna fall for this, is he?" Peter muttered beside Will.

But Fortis Fortuna, perhaps because he was so accustomed to obedient Fortune Worship from everyone around him, seemed satisfied with the Prince's answers, and a half-smile spread over his skeletal face.

"And what is this thing... shimmering like a Fortune Teller?" Fortis Fortuna gestured at the black chest swinging on the Prince's finger.

"Proof that my father didn't come to the lake to steal the stones."

Dutifully the Prince surrendered the black chest to a blood-red guard who stepped forward silently. Beside Will, Peter fidgeted nervously, his stomach bulging oddly where he hid Illyria's treasure under his sweater, then covered it up by holding Poudini.

"Proof of the true King's innocence?" said Fortis Fortuna, his smile widening until he looked like a grinning skull. "But we have proof already. And from the King's most loyal servant."

Sweeping his taloned hand back, the Leader of the Fortune Tellers stepped aside. And from the shadowy night, a man withdrew into the light of the crystal ball staffs held by the blood-red guards.

"The King did not fall into the lake," said the man, addressing the Prince.

Will recognized the smooth, storyteller voice of Victor Valerian at once.

"We have removed your father's body from the lake," Valerian continued. He waited for the four shimmering guards to step aside until the body of a man was revealed, lying on the ice behind them, eyes wide-open, glassy and bloodshot. "You can see the truth for yourself," added Valerian gravely. "The King did not drown. He was murdered."

The Prince rushed to his father's side. Instantly, the glow of the lake was dimmed under Will and Auralius' feet, as they no longer formed two sets of an Echo and his Sound. Watching the Prince, Will forgot that he was looking at his Echo, and he felt as if he were trapped in a nightmare, watching himself bending by his dead father's body.

"See the deep silver-gray bruising around your father's neck?" said Valerian. His watery Orphanage robe fluttered wildly in the wind as he joined the Prince. "Someone strangled your father. The King did not die trying to steal Fortune's treasure. He was already dead when someone melted the ice and threw him into the lake. Be happy, young Prince, your father's name is cleared," added Valerian gently. "Now you can take the throne and become King yourself."

The Prince's shoulders shuddered when Valerian had said, "Be happy." But with his back to them, no one could see if the Prince was crying or shaking in anger.

Suddenly, the wind blew a cold voice between them.

"And who—? Who but the King's murderer could know all this?" asked a man in a purple wind-swept robe, as he stepped into the light of the crystal ball staffs.

"Drinkwater..." gasped Valerian, his face turning invisible for a moment.

Auralius shot to his father's side like an arrow fired from an Incendiary. The two embraced lovingly, all past wrongs forgiven and forgotten. Then Drinkwater spoke again.

"Thank you, Valerian," he said mockingly, "for that... *medicine*... you gave my wife."

Drinkwater stepped fully into the light of the crystal balls, looking as pale as a corpse. Professor Flower was with him, her pretty, see-through face glowing with emotion. Defying the blustery wind that was almost too much for him, Drinkwater leaned on his wife and son and limped closer.

"Amazing how quickly I got better," he said, glaring at Valerian through his taped glasses. "As soon as I stopped taking your medicine, that is. Poison was it? Or just old-fashioned sleeping draft? Don't bother denying it," added Drinkwater bitterly. "I know what you are, Valerian. A murderer!"

Peter and Will exchanged baffled glances. The Prince looked up from his father in shock. But Drinkwater had eyes for Valerian alone.

"You murdered the King!" said Drinkwater. "You tried to kill me. But worst of all, you killed an innocent boy! Here—" Drinkwater turned sharply to his son, pulling out a Crystillery from his pocket. "Give me your knife, Auralius! We'll show them what Valerian did... How he tried to trick me... make me believe my son was—"

But before Auralius could pass the golden dagger to his father, the knife flew out of his hands and into Fortis Fortuna's boney grip, snatched by a guard who had moved at a speed no Sound, no ordinary Echo even, could match.

"I can prove it!" snarled Drinkwater, shivering in the wind. "Valerian's a murderer!"

"Is he?" Fortis Fortuna chuckled with snide skepticism. "I'll be the judge of that."

Taking his own Crystillery out, one with silver vines twirling around the base of the dome like barbed wire, Fortis Fortuna riffled through the memories of the dagger as through the pages of a book. Finally he stopped when the precious stones inside the Crystillery arranged themselves in a line and, like a pen, drew a sketch of Auralius' face on the waves of blue water.

"What have we here?" Fortis Fortuna blinked his crystal ball eyes suspiciously.

Beside his father and mother Auralius stood stiff and anxious, his head turning invisible with anticipation. At last he would see the Memory that would prove Drinkwater's innocence, prove that his father never sold him to the Fate Sealers. Will and Peter drew near also, with Poudini growling in Peter's arms at the blood-red guards. Even the Prince rose from his father's corpse to stand next to Valerian, who was watching the Crystillery in silence.

An Echo candle appeared inside the blue doom, surrounded by darkness. A boy sat before the small, fake flame, with his body inside the Crystillery but his head sticking out, plunged in shadows. Suddenly a man emerged behind the boy, hooded, gloved and lost in shadows too. Hearing footsteps, the boy snatched up the candle until his face was lit up. Like a drawing made in water, he was a see-through copy of Auralius. Suddenly, the boy screamed. A golden dagger glinted in the candlit Crystillery. And then the shadowy man slashed the see-through throat of the boy who looked just like Auralius.

"My son's Echo," hissed Drinkwater. "The nearly invisible Echo of a Mongrel. And Valerian staged his death."

"That was not Victor Valerian," said Fortis Fortuna, with the voice of a man who never had to say anything twice. Dismissively, he dropped the dagger in Drinkwater's hand and added, "That killer was taller, heavier, shabbier… Nothing like Valerian."

But Will thought to himself that Valerian could be all these things if he wanted to. He could walk in high-heeled boots, stuff a pillow in his belt and trade his aquamarine robe for a beggar's jacket. After all, Will knew all about using a disguise to make yourself look like someone totally different. And yet the fact that Valerian could have done all this didn't mean that he actually had.

"Thank you for your faith in me, Fortis," said Valerian melodically.

Slowly he turned to face Drinkwater, his green eyes looking unnaturally pale in the light of the crystal ball staffs.

"We have known each other for many years, Nicholas," said Valerian, without malice or anger. "True, we have not always seen eye to eye on every issue. But have you ever known me to be a violet man?" Valerian chuckled. "It sounds absurd, even just saying it. I know you have every reason to hate me, Nicholas. Because of me you thought your son was dead. But I was deceived myself."

Valerian pointed at the golden dagger gleaming in Drinkwater's hand and added with a sigh, "The Fate Sealer who sold me this knife lied to me. We all make mistakes, don't we? I made the mistake of believing a Fate Sealer. And you, Nicholas... you made the mistake of running out on your wife when she needed you most."

"No, no... you didn't," Professor Flower whispered to her husband. "By Fortune's grace, you didn't."

"Yes, I did," said Drinkwater, looking suddenly too weak to fight the wind any longer. He leaned even more on his son and wife, his knees wobbling. "The great Valerian." He sighed. "You of all people... How could you trust a Fate Sealer? You never did understand that dealing with evil can only bring evil."

"Evil?" hissed Fortis Fortuna in his withered voice. "A meaningless word! One man's hell is another man's heaven. But, at least..." The Leader of the Fortune Tellers chuckled in Drinkwater's face, and his crystal ball eyes glowed for a second. "At least we agree that senility has confused your judgment, old Sound. Valerian? A murderer? Men like him don't need to murder to get what they want. Now..." Fortis Fortuna turned to the Prince again, "I want to know what the King was really after the night he died."

Greedily, the Leader of the Fortune Tellers reached a boney hand to the black chest resting in the palm of the nearest red guard. He pushed back the lid of Fluid Conway's gift, and a cloud of purple smoke erupted in his eerie face. Then the wind scattered the smoke and with it the tangy scent of apples. And over the chest, little bolts of purple lightning flashed again and again.

Valerian gasped, his green eyes almost glowing like Waterweed. "Cold Fire Mushrooms," he muttered in awe. "So they do exist…"

"I never doubted it," said Fortis Fortuna, his golden cape blustering in the wind. "What puzzles me is why the King risked his life to get them? What do you think?" Fortis Fortuna turned sharply to the Prince, who was crouching by his father once more, looking deep into the King's frozen, blood-shot eyes.

Like bloodied pillars, the four shimmering guards turned their heads in time with their leader, to watch the Prince rise.

"My father…" stammered the Prince. "Fortune forgive me… My father…"

"Yes…?" hissed Fortis Fortuna eagerly.

"My father wanted to give his people a gift," said the Prince, his eyes watering, perhaps from the wind, perhaps from sadness. "The gift of… freedom."

"Freeeedom?" Fortis Fortuna's crystal ball eyes flashed, and his lips shuddered with loathing. "Freedom from what?" he demanded.

"From… you, Master of All Fates," the Prince completed his

confession, with an innocent look in his melancholy eyes.

Will's heart missed a beat. He could hear Peter sighing. Damian's head dropped in despair, and a frozen tear fell out of Deá's eye. Will waited for Fortis Fortuna to erupt in a rage. But the very opposite happened: Honesty disarmed suspicion. The old man's frown fell away.

"Your father wanted to change the world, young Prince," said the Leader of the Fortune Tellers. Lightning flashed over him, adding magnificence to his words. "Fortune punished the King for his arrogance. But you..." Fortis Fortuna studied the Prince with his crystal ball eyes. "You will leave all such matters to your elders, won't you, young Ward of Fortune? Yes..."

Accepting the Prince's nod without hesitation, Fortis Fortuna raised his golden arms and pointed up at the bloody smears of sunrise starting to stain the dark horizon.

"All will soon be Fortune fine again in Agám Kaffú," said the Leader of the Fortune Tellers. "Today—Christmas day—a new age dawns! Happy thirteenth birthday, young Prince. Here is my gift to you. This morning I will send my army of guards to depose the false King. My emissaries will ride to the far reaches of our land, spreading word of Fortune's will. And tonight. At the palace. One hour before midnight—I will crown you King."

*   *   *

The chill wind finally stopped. The giant moon peeked behind the storm clouds. And snow began to fall on the moonlit, frozen lake like white confetti, as if Fortis Fortuna had ordered a celebration. Promising to send escorts for them from the Veiled Village, the Leader of the Fortune Tellers carried away the shimmering chest of mushrooms himself, riding off on a white stallion, flanked by his red guards riding black ones.

Like convicts, Deá and Damian were dragged on foot behind the horses, their crystal ball fetters jangling. By the light of the fading crystal ball staffs, Will watched them bitterly, snowflakes sprinkling his face like tears as he wondered if he would ever see his childhood friends again.

"Very brave," Valerian said softly at Will's side. "But just imagine, if you hadn't made it back from Olám Shoné... their sacrifice would have been wasted."

"But it wouldn't, actually," said Will thoughtfully. He turned to study Valerian through the flurries of snow and added, "Even if we didn't make it back, the true King's name would be cleared. He didn't go to the lake to steal the stones. The King was murdered. And Fortis Fortuna would know all about it... thanks to you."

"It was nothing." Valerian waved his plastic hand dismissively.

"No, I mean... how did you know the King was innocent?" said Will.

Will's gaze shot to the dead reflection of his father stretched on the ice. The Prince was still crouching there, snow gathering on his slumped shoulders. Somehow the Prince had thawed the dead King's eyes and closed them peacefully.

"How did you know the King was strangled?" asked Will,

523

looking up at Valerian again.

"A friend," said Valerian in his beautiful voice. "From the palace... He mentioned—"

But Valerian stopped respectfully as Drinkwater limped over, leaning on his wife and son, his face as white as the frozen lake under their feet.

"We're going to live in Olám Shoné," said Drinkwater tiredly, puffing silvery mist as if just talking was a great strain. And yet he was smiling.

"She promised... Aurora's waiting for us by the Bridge of Knives," explained Auralius.

Will and Peter exchanged grins, and the Mongrel's cheeks turned see-through with embarrassment.

"Then I'll come with you," said the Prince, rising from his father's side.

"To bring more Cold Fire Mushrooms?" guessed Auralius. "No need."

Auralius withdrew a black bundle from his pocket and unwrapped it. A cloud of smoke drifted away from his palm before five iridescent lumps became visible, spewing purple lightning bolts like a storm cloud.

"Keep it," said Auralius, handing the Cold Fire Mushrooms to the Prince.

"And I have something for you," said Drinkwater, gesturing at Will.

The old man fished something out of his pocket. It was a

gold ring with a large pearl glistening at its center like a crystal ball.

"My Safe Passage Ring," said Drinkwater, slipping the ring on Will's thumb. "Yes, yes… for you. You've earned it… No, buts or ifs! I owe you an apology, Mr. Cleary," added Drinkwater with a sigh. "Your courage saved the Royal Shekel. And this kingdom. All I managed to do was end up in bed… half dead to the world."

"A real safe passage ring?" said Will in amazement.

"You can go back home, Will," muttered Peter, looking just as amazed. "And come back."

"Or take anyone you like with you," said Drinkwater, smiling tiredly.

"Well, my dears." Professor Flower beamed at them, her pretty, see-through face glowing. "Can't stand here chatting all night. We have places to go, new people to meet. Isn't that right, Auralius dear?" She winked joyously at her son. "We're done with the Ant Chamber. Done with it for good."

With a farewell wave and a whispered goodbye between the Prince and Drinkwater, the small family of three—a Sound, an Echo and a Mongrel—slipped into the hole in the lake to start a new life in a land where how see-through your skin was didn't really matter.

Will and the Prince were climbing down also, to help Auralius with the self-sealing passage that only opened to two sets of an Echo and his Sound—when they realized that the round blue door on the bottom of the lake had never locked itself again. In fact, it was slightly ajar.

"Lock's all twisted out of shape," realized Auralius, slipping his hand along the gleaming doorjamb. "Totally stuck... I'll tell Aurora," he added shyly. "They'll have to send someone to fix it."

"Must have been stuck before," said Peter, looking down into the hole with Poudini panting happily under his chin. Below Drinkwater and Professor Flower disappeared through the round door, waving goodbye. "That would explain it," added Peter, waving back. "Opened for us before, the door... even with Fortis Fortuna on the other side."

"Yes, that explains it," agreed the Prince, climbing up on the frozen lake again with Will behind him.

Inside the icy hole, Auralius looked up at them one last time. Suddenly, he tossed Peter his golden dagger. "Since you hate Incendiaries so much," he said. Then he slipped away too, calling over his shoulder, "and stop grinning like an idiot!"

"Finally..." came a soft whisper behind Will's back.

Will turned.

Valerian was watching them, smiling brightly, as if he was terribly happy to see a Mongrel set free. And yet something about the old Echo's eyes didn't look like happiness at all. Relief maybe, thought Will, to see the back of Drinkwater.

"Not smoking your pipe tonight," said Will, glad that Valerian wasn't smelling like his father anymore.

Valerian flicked snowflakes out of his face. "Impossible in this weather." He shrugged.

The Prince walked past them to crouch by his dead father again. Will walked over to Valerian with Peter beside him, hugging

Poudini and watching the drifting snow flakes melting on his new weapon.

"If you knew the truth, Professor Valerian," said Will, resuming his interrupted conversation with the old Echo. "If you knew the King was murdered...?"

"Why did I wait until now to speak?" Valerian's voice was enchanting, too beautiful not to be believed. "I only learned the truth tonight. One of my old friends at the palace sent me a carrier pigeon. I came to the lake to see for myself if the King had, indeed, been murdered. And I found Fortis Fortuna here."

"Was this your knife?" Peter held out his golden dagger.

With each melting snowflake, beautiful etchings of crystal balls appeared on the wet blade as if by magic.

"Not this one." Valerian smiled serenely, his voice a lullaby. "One like it. Mine isn't lost."

Suddenly a scream shattered the muffled silence of the moonlit night.

"LIAR!"

Through the flurries swirling in the air, Valerie came flying on her white albatross, her skin glistening like ice, her strangely cropped hair looking like a crown of snow.

"LIAR!" she screamed again, circling low above her uncle. "You *paid* the Fate Sealers— Had me kidnapped— So you could look brave saving me— "

"That's it, she's lost it..." grumbled Peter, as he shoved Will out of the path of the plunging albatross, Poudini barking in his arms.

"Valerie— Valerie—" Valerian called up to his niece, his voice deep and beautiful, even as he ducked under the giant flapping wings.

"*Him*! You wanted to impress *him*—!" Valerie pointed at the Prince, who darted to his feet, snow scattering off his shoulders. "Impress *him*," she screamed again. "So he'll make you Chief Royal Advisor! But they wanted more money. The Fate Sealers wanted more money! Didn't they, didn't they? They wouldn't let me go! So you made a new deal—*Mom* for *me*! You killed her! I sold her ring to buy her letters! I know everything! I wish you were dead!"

"Yep, insane," muttered Peter, "or working for the Fate Sealers. Take your pick."

But Will remembered how Valerie attacked the Fate Sealers with stones that evening. Why would she do that if she was working for Wither Heart?

"My dear child," Valerian pleaded with his niece, darting left and right. "Yes, I freed you from Shadowpain, but not by trading your mother! I bought your freedom with my last remaining ice-gold. But the Fate Sealers wanted more. So they kidnapped her. But, I promise you. Yes! I promise! She is alive! The Fate Sealers will not kill her. She is worth more alive to them than dead."

"LIAR!" screamed Valerie. And as if wielding a sword, she jabbed the hooked beak of her albatross in her uncle's face.

"My child—" Valerian hunched on the frozen lake, his voice still beguilingly mellow. "Your letters— They must be forgeries—"

528

"Not in her handwriting!" screamed the see-through girl.

"Her hand— But not her words! The Fate Sealers forced her to write. I'm sure of it."

Valerian slipped and nearly fell, trying to escape the jabbing beak. His flowing aquamarine robe shimmered like a pool of water around his scurrying feet.

"In Fortune's name, stop this insanity!" He cried out in pain. "My Eyes! Valerie! Not my eyes—"

Will, Peter and the Prince flew forward at the same time to beat the giant albatross back into the moonlit sky. In Peter's arms Poudini barked and bit the bird's webbed feet. The Prince yelled royal commands at Valerie, threatening her with the power of the monarchy and Fortune too. Until, at last, the pale rider relented and flew up, to circle high over her uncle in the falling snow.

Trembling, Valerian pulled a black handkerchief from his pocket. He dabbed at the pale blood trickling down his thin cheekbones, shaking his bald head in shock.

"After everything I did for her," the old Echo stammered. "After I raised her like a father..." And showing the first sign of irritation, Valerian flicked a pesky snowflake off his nose with the end of his handkerchief.

Something glittered against the dark fabric. A gold monogram. The letter M.

"That's—" Will choked in amazement. He had seen that monogram once before. "That's—"

"My father's scarf," snarled the Prince, standing frozen by

the dead King. "He was wearing it— He had it on inside the lake—"

But now the dead King's throat was exposed. The silver-gray bruise of strangulation could clearly be seen, despite the gathering snow which was starting to bury the frozen King where he lay.

"No! We want to see it!" snarled Peter, as Valerian stuffed the long black fabric back in his pocket like a man trying to undo a mistake.

"My handkerchief?" Valerian chuckled. "Whatever for?"

"Not a handkerchief. A scarf!" Will blinked snow out of his eyes, trying to glimpse that golden letter again. "The scarf that killed the King!"

"Is it?" The moonlight set Valerian's green eyes on fire, but his voice was still alluring. "One scarf looks like another."

"Not when it's monogrammed M," said Will. "For monarch."

Suddenly Valerian started to laugh. "Oh, I see," he said, a mocking smile twisting his thin lips. "Yes... M— for monarch."

Valerian pulled the scarf out again and taunted Poudini, who had jumped out of Peter's arms to play at being a pickpocket.

"Yes, you're quite right," said Valerian. "Fortis Fortuna asked me to untie the scarf from the King's neck. We saw the bruising. We were shocked. That's when we realized the King had been murdered. Strangled. I must have slipped the King's scarf in my pocket without realizing."

"LIAR!" shrieked Valerie in the sky.

The beating wings of her albatross swirled the falling snow into a blizzard over her uncle.

"Stay back!" the Prince yelled up at her. "That's a royal command, Valerie Valerian!"

Valerian flicked the snow out of his face again and again, still smiling his mocking smile at them. Will couldn't take his eyes off the golden letter M wafting on the dark scarf. Suddenly the fabric twisted in the wind and the M flipped upside down, turning into a W. And then the scarf folded, slicing the golden monogram in half, and the W became a V. Then two V's side by side.

VV.

Victor Valerian.

The name shot into Will's thoughts like an Incendiary arrow.

"Your initials— Your scarf!" Will shouted his realization.

"What?!" Peter flicked his magic rope out of his sweater. In a second, he lassoed the black scarf out Valerian's hand.

"MURDERER!" shrieked Valerie.

The Prince was too stunned to stop the flying girl this time. In a moment her albatross slapped her uncle's face with its giant wings. Valerian's features started changing into a strange mixture of visible and invisible. A white vein throbbed where his forehead used to be. His pupils dilated where he no longer had eyes.

"You fools!" hissed Valerian's hovering mouth, gleaming in the moonlight like an eerie butterfly.

He slammed his plastic hand into the albatross' head, startling the giant bird away, though only for a moment.

"You stupid, stupid fools!" Valerian hissed again.

"And you're a genius?" Will snatched the scarf from Peter.

"Murdering the King and leaving *this* behind! With your initials!"

"You miss the point entirely," sneered Valerian, his voice finally slipping out of his control.

He punched the albatross again, and the bird screeched and flew up, keeping its distance.

"Of course, I left the scarf behind." Valerian cackled. "I never planned to—"

"To— what?" demanded Will.

Suddenly the old Echo who used to be Chief Royal Advisor to the King turned visible again, shock painted over his treacherous face, wild fury swirling in his bright green eyes.

"You killed my father," snarled the Prince, his face almost invisible with rage.

Will and Peter darted to the Prince's side, Poudini barking before them.

"Like you killed my Mom," screamed Valerie, her bird flapping wildly back in her uncle's direction.

"STAY BACK!" roared Valerian. "BY FORTUNE, STAY BACK OR I'LL SHOOT!" In his human hand Valerian was suddenly holding a blood-red Incendiary adorned with golden, spiraling lines. "And shut that dog up!" he added fiercely, aiming his weapon at Poudini.

Peter snatched up his little dog and clamped his muzzle. Only the beating of the albatross' wings and Poudini's whines could still be heard around them.

"Better," said Valerian. "Much better. You call me a

murderer?" he sneered, his voice almost beautiful again in the silence of the falling snow. "I am not a murderer. Do you hear me, Valerie? I didn't kill your mother. She did that herself—"

"NO!" screamed the girl in the sky.

"Yes! *She* made the deal with the Fate Sealers," said Valerian serenely, as if discussing the weather. "*She* traded herself for you, the crystal clear fool! You think I would ever sacrifice such a beautiful woman—" Valerian's thin lips curled with revulsion "—for a filthy little brat like you?

"And you..." Valerian jerked his gleaming weapon at Will. "You accuse me of murder? Murderers kill for their own benefit. I killed to save a kingdom. That is not murder! The King had dangerous ideas. He was going to set the Echoes free. Take away the power of the Fortune Tellers, destroy the Fate Sealers. In the end, the King even wanted to see the monarchy abolished. He wanted chaos. He called it freedom. I tried to reason with him," added Valerian mockingly. "He wouldn't listen. I followed him to the Lake of Eternal Ice. He laughed at me. He dared to laugh—at *me*! I showed him. I showed— SSSSSSTOP!"

It happened so fast, the moonlight and the snow smeared everything together.

Will saw Poudini leaping out of Peter's arms. The next second a flash of red streaked past the dog's furry head, and Will only realized what happened when Peter crumpled on the snow like a puppet without strings.

Valerian had fired his Incendiary.

Peter's face turned bright red as if a fire was blazing inside him. His Orphanage sweater tried to clean away the blood-red arrow sticking out of his chest. But though Peter didn't melt away like an Echo, he no longer looked alive.

"NO!" shouted Will.

Valerie shrieked and swooped down on her uncle with her bird. But Valerian tore a second arrow from his pocket and aimed his Incendiary up at his niece.

"Drop your weapon!" shouted the Prince, snatching up the copper Incendiary that slid from under Peter's sweater as he fell.

"Ah! Now things are getting interesting." Valerian smiled, his green eyes flashing. "Shoot me, and I shoot her first, you understand? Or... and this is the interesting part—" Valerian flicked his glance to Will. "—Your shoe, click the heel open. Give me the Royal Shekel... and I'll let her live."

Will's insides were screaming with rage. "I don't—"

"You do!" Valerian simulated a yawn. "So don't waste time pretending."

"*I* have the coin," said the Prince. He pulled back the copper arrow to arm the Incendiary he was aiming at Valerian's chest. "How disappointing for you, Valerian," he added bitterly. "Killing my father only to realize that he didn't have the Royal Shekel on him. So much for becoming king yourself."

"You're wasting time," hissed Valerian, keeping careful aim at the albatross circling over him in the falling snow.

"And then my uncle took the throne," said the Prince. "Bad

534

news for you... and your hand."

"My hand?" Valerian shook his plastic limb incredulously. "You think it's funny? *I* gave your uncle the throne! *I* made him King. And he chopped my hand off! Burned my home! Stole everything I owned! Banished me! Destroyed me!"

Suddenly Valerian's human fist collapsed in rage on the trigger of his weapon.

The arrow streaked away from his glinting Incendiary like a shooting star heading up instead of down. In a moment, it hit the albatross in the chest. Valerie screamed. Then the giant bird and the see-through rider dropped out of the snowy dark sky and crashed inches from Peter's frozen body.

Almost at the same time, the copper arrow streaked out of the Prince's hand and flew at Valerian's heart. But then it bounded off the Echo's watery Orphanage robe and dropped in the snow.

"Arrow-proof fabric," sneered Valerian.

He did not even glance at the fallen bodies of his niece and her bird, which lay motionless on the ice so close to him. Smiling cruelly, Valerian took out another red arrow from his flowing robe that seemed to gleam like metal in the moonlight.

"You could have shot my head, young Prince." He snorted in ridicule. "But you went for the obvious. Crystal clear fool. Now—" Valerian aimed his blood-red Incendiary at the Prince, then at Will. "—The Royal Shekel, or I kill you both."

"You'll kill us anyway," said Will bitterly, watching snow starting to bury Valerie and her albatross, as it had already turned

Peter's body into a featureless mound, and Poudini, too, who was lying beside Peter, whimpering helplessly.

"That's a chance I'm willing to take." Valerian chuckled cruelly.

"I'm not!" Will reached in his pocket, pretending to pull something out, then to swallow it. "Now, you," he said to his Echo.

The Prince understood at once and, in a flash, he swallowed the Royal Shekel, which was still in his pocket since he used it to open the door in the lake so many hours ago.

"I'll slice you open for this," roared Valerian, his face suddenly flickering from see-through to invisible in mad succession.

"And if we're lying?" It was Will's turn to chuckle. "If we didn't swallow anything?"

"Or swallowed an ordinary shekel?" said the Prince, snow piling on his head, so still was he. "How will you find the Royal Shekel then, Valerian?"

"Stick to your plan," said Will. "Put the Prince on the throne—with you as Chief Royal Advisor. That's why you had to get rid of Drinkwater, isn't it? The gold dagger *is* yours!"

"Ah... the Mongrel's Echo," said Valerian. A cruel smile stretched over his floating mouth, before the rest of Valerian's face reappeared. "The miserable wretch... But it was a *cunning* idea, making Drinkwater believe his son was dead. Had to be done. I couldn't have the old troublemaker meddling in my plans."

"But Drinkwater didn't stay away," said Will.

"No, the blundering fool!"

"So you left him a note. Sent him to the Ant Chamber. You knew Auralius hated his father enough to kill him."

"Of course, I knew." The green eyes flashed in midair, before Valerian's eye sockets reappeared. "I make it my business to know things."

"But it didn't work out the way you planned!" said Will darkly. "So you gave Professor Flower some... *medicine*. The fatal kind."

"This is getting tedious," snapped Valerian, still switching his aim between Will and the Prince, as if he couldn't make up his mind whom to kill first.

"No, it's getting interesting," said the Prince.

The arrowless Incendiary dangled uselessly in the Prince's see-through hand. While just three feet away, the copper arrow was melting the snow at Valerian's feet. But the Prince didn't dare reach for it.

"Peter was right," said the Prince bitterly. "About my father's letter. It *was* a list. And *you* changed it into a letter."

"Yes," chuckled Valerian, only his teeth gleaming in the moonlight where his mouth was missing. "The magician was right. The bits I added came out darker, the ink was fresh. But none of you believed him... You were all so incredibly stupid. I had to do everything myself. A ringmaster in a circus of morons!

"Who got you started on your quest to clear the King's name?" demanded Valerian resentfully. "I did, that's who! Who brought the road map from the palace library to the Orphanage? I did! Gave it to Abednego as a gift for sheltering Valerie and me from the false King. The vain old fool didn't guess a thing."

"All this time, I've been following you." Valerian's hovering bright eyes flickered to Will's face. "Always invisible. Just had to get rid of the scent of cherry tobacco, and you had no idea I was there... watching your pathetic struggles to get into Auralius' room, avoid Abednego's eyes, avoid the Fate Sealers, avoid Splash Slippery— By Fortune, you were a magnet for disaster! Finally, I had to admit you were too obtuse to translate Mapá on your own. I sent Valerie to you. She had seen the road map in the palace, knew a few of the words. I made sure she took the gravestone book with her. I knew that would start you talking."

Valerian's face was suddenly all visible, a mask of hate.

"When I found that absurd gravestone book in your room," he spat at Will, "I was sure it was important. Spent a whole night poring over it. A waste of time! You dragged it all the way from the Sound realm for *sentimental reasons.*

"But your greatest folly! Really a superb act of blundering idiocy—was taking part in murdering Wither Heart's brother. Yes! I was there! Invisible! I saw what *you* missed—the raven that flew away before Black Heart died... carrying a note for Wither Heart, which *I* had to intercept. A note with full details of everything that happened on the shore. And who was there. Especially a boy who looked like an eggplant sitting on an elephant's backside.

"By Fortune, even your disguise was a complete failure! And now you look like your old self again... and still no great

538

improvement." Valerian laughed, turning to the Prince. "I include you in that compliment, of course, Your Royal Highness."

"Of course," hissed the Prince.

"I guess I should thank you," said Will with disdain, his insides burning. "For keeping the Fate Sealers off—"

"If you had sense, you would thank me—and mean it!" roared Valerian.

"But you failed!" The Prince snapped his head at the hole gaping in the frozen lake behind them. "Wither Heart followed us into Olám Shoné. You never expected to see us again!"

"Fools. Crystal clear fools! Everything was ruined!"

"So *you* went to the lake," said the Prince, his melancholy eyes blazing. "You had to show Fortis Fortuna that my father was murdered. You were going to accuse my uncle, was that the plan? Your word against his? And then... with all the Lords fighting over who should be king... you could try. And if you managed to trace the Royal Shekel—"

"And now I have!" snarled Valerian. "I know you used it to open that passage." He flicked his plastic hand at the gaping hole in the frozen lake. "Why do you think I let you keep the coin? It was no longer safe for me to stroll into the palace with the Royal Shekel and claim the throne. Too much had happened. No, you had to become King. With me as your advisor."

"And after that, you could strangle me too?" said the Prince, looking like a statue with the snow piling over his still body.

"Only if you didn't behave!" said Valerian in frustration.

"Once and for all, violence is always a last resort! You are forcing me to it! Now tell me where the Royal Shekel is. TELL ME!"

Suddenly Valerian rushed forward until his Incendiary was inches from Will's chest.

"Tell me!" he hissed at the Prince. "Or your Sound dies!"

But at that moment, a piercing screech cut the silence of the falling snow.

"DIEEEEEEEE—"

From the corner of his eye Will saw a gray, sagging storm rising from the hole in the lake. A Fate Sealer with one arm missing and holes torn in his see-through chest leapt up on the frozen lake. An Ice Loom glowed eerily in his only hand, and green pupils flickered madly in his hollow eyes. Still screeching, he looked up and spotted them. And Will recognized the scar on the creature's nose.

"Wither Heart!" roared Valerian, a gaping smile hovering under his nose where his chin was missing. "Never thought I'd see you again, old friend! And just in time to witness the execution of your brother's murderer!"

The next second, Valerian fired his Incendiary.

But Will was no longer there. Hurling himself beside Peter, he twisted back as the blood-red arrow flew over his head, then streaked on toward the hole in the lake. Before the Fate Sealer could duck, the arrow pierced the scar on his sagging nose.

Shrieking and writhing, Wither Heart started to melt. White spirals leaked out of his eyes, nostrils, the holes in his chest, filling the night with a terrible stench. Soon the Fate Sealer's sagging mouth unraveled completely, and the last ribbons of drifting, putrid mist billowed away in utter silence.

But the glowing Ice Loom wreaked Wither Heart's final revenge, remaining suspended in the moonlight just long enough to blow a final blast of icy needles before shattering on the frozen ice. The glinting arrows bounced off Valerian's robe and missed the Prince by inches. But Will was struck in his thigh and back.

Instantly webs of ice crept up Will's sweater and down his pants, so fast that Will knew something was wrong. These Ice Loom arrows were special, deadlier than any he had felt before. And within seconds, a wave of bone-chilling cold started turning Will to stone.

"Oh! No you don't!" came a roar from Valerian.

The Prince threw himself at the copper arrow left forgotten in the snow behind Valerian. But the old Echo, green eyes glittering eerily, rearmed his Incendiary once more, his face entirely visible and terrible.

"Back! Get back here!" the old Echo ordered, until the Prince crawled to Will's side again.

Then bending over them, Valerian shifted his aim between the Prince and Will, who couldn't feel his frozen legs anymore. "Eeny, meeny, miny, moe," drawled the Echo wickedly, "who will be the first to go?"

Suddenly Valerian made up his mind! "You're more trouble than your worth, young Prince. Goodbye—"

Before Valerian could fire, however, the blood-red

Incendiary suddenly dropped out of his hand.

The old Echo clutched his chest and fell to his knees. His face contorted with agony and turned invisible. Soon the rest of Valerian's body disappeared, until all that remained of the King's murderer was his collapsing aquamarine robe—and the golden dagger, which Will had plucked from Peter's belt and plunged in the Echo's cold heart.

After that, the cobwebs of ice spreading over Will's body reached his eyes and frosted them. And then the world turned white and disappeared.

Free at Last

A Christmas Coronation

Will glanced frantically around. Instead of the night sky and the giant moon, gleaming walls curved over him as if he were trapped inside a giant crystal ball. The Lake of Eternal Ice was also gone, and Will realized that he was lying comfortably in a snow heap bed, covered with a warm snowflake blanket. A waterfall canopy cascaded from the four bedposts, and where it parted Will could see the watery floor beyond, rippling with rings on a pond as someone walked over to Will's bed.

"Am I really that skinny again?" asked Will, smiling at his Echo.

"How do you feel?" asked the Prince, his voice half lost in the rustle of the flowing canopy.

"Cold. Where am I?"

"My palace... the Seasick Chamber. Our convalescence room. Fortis Fortuna kept his word. He sent an escort of guards for us."

In a flash, Will remembered everything that happened on the Lake of Eternal Ice.

"Peter—" he gasped in horror.

The Prince pointed at another snow heap bed floating on the pond that made up the floor of this strange, watery chamber. And there, past a blue waterfall canopy, Peter was snoring with Poudini curled by his bandaged ear, paws kicking in a dream.

"He's alive…" A wave of relief washed over Will. "He'll be happy to see that—" Will added, spotting Illyria's treasure glittering atop a night stand that seemed coated in icicles.

"All three of you survived, thanks to Auralius' Cold Fire Mushrooms," said the Prince. "But she barely made it." The Prince gestured down the rustling, rippling room.

Will spotted a third snow heap drifting past the Prince's see-through shoulder. The snowflake blanket outlined an invisible sleeper. Only spiky, oddly cropped hair showed against the frosty pillow, as if someone had left their wig behind after rising.

"Her albatross cushioned her fall," said the Prince. "No—" He shook his head. "The bird didn't make it."

"She was rrright about Vvvalerian," said Will, starting to shiver from feeling so chilled to the bone. "Valerian *was* a liar. Wwworse than a liar. And she wasn't working for the Fffate Sssealers…"

"Here—" The Prince handed Will an icy, smoking goblet that smelled like fresh apples. "You'll feel better after."

"Great…" Will sighed but quickly gulped half the Cold Fire Mushroom brew.

The taste of death oozed into Will's stomach, and purple

546

smoke spewed from his nostrils. But wonderful heat spread through Will's body at once. When he stopped coughing the after effects of the potion, the Prince spoke again.

"Thank you for everything you did, Will. You saved my life. And my Kingdom. I still can't believe it… Fortis Fortuna's crowning me in three hours." The Prince glanced at his smoky sundial watch. "Two hours and fifty seven seconds, actually… and I'll be King. Still can't believe it…."

"Nervous?" guessed Will.

The Prince smiled cryptically and pulled out a small white bundle from his pocket. "I have something for you," he said, avoiding Will's question. "The whole Orphanage came down to the Lake of Eternal Ice after you were knocked out… cold."

"Very funny." Will grinned. "So… what happened?"

"Apparently Fortis Fortuna sent them a message from the Veiled Village," said the Prince, his melancholy brown eyes suddenly sparkling. "Everyone at the Orphanage knew about Olám Shoné. About you being my Sound. Even that I was going to be crowned King. Oh yes," added the Prince with a puzzled frown, "there was this boy with glasses… said his name was Genius something. Made me swear to tell you he always knew!"

"Not important." Will shook his head.

"Well, this *is* important."

The Prince unwrapped the white bundle, which wasn't see-through at all. In a moment, he withdrew a large gold coin that dangled on a glittering gold chain.

Will gasped. "We won—?" he said in awe, as the Prince dropped Valerian's medallion in his palm.

"For going to Olám Shoné, that's what Abednego said. It's for you and Peter. Some kind of contest at the Orphanage?" wondered the Prince

Will nodded. "For doing something amazing." He blinked in awe at the gleaming queen staring back at him from the gold coin, surrounded by butterflies and flowers.

"It's the Coin Key to Illyria's Treasure, isn't it?" said the Prince. "Let me know what's in the chest. Oh, yes," he added thoughtfully. "Abednego sent you this Text-A-Face."

The Prince reached in his pocket and pulled out a miniature, watery book with a crystal ball floating on the front.

"Well, I have to go now," said the Prince, a little nervously, handing the tiny book to Will. "Have to get ready for the coronation."

"You'll be great," said Will, smiling reassuringly.

"Thanks. By the way, Nurse Flight came with us from the Orphanage," said the Prince, already walking away, his footsteps spreading rings on the watery floor. "She took care of the three of you on the way here. I'll tell her you're awake. She'll be thrilled."

The Prince stopped by what looked like a fountain splashing against the back wall of the icy, domed room; except that the fountain was shaped like a door, and at its center Will could see a large crystal ball doorknob.

"I'm locking the door behind me," said the Prince, glancing

back at Will. "My uncle, the false King… he's disappeared. The palace guards are hunting for him everywhere. If you need to unlock the door, just turn this knob three times to the right. But don't let anyone in! Nurse Flight has a key."

"Don't worry," said Will, still smiling. "And good luck."

"You too," said the Prince. "With the treasure, I mean. Nothing else should happen to you here. Thanks again for everything, Will. I wouldn't be here if it wasn't for you."

Will chuckled. "Neither would I."

The Prince smiled back, then grabbed the crystal ball doorknob and pulled back the fountain on its hinges. Will caught sight of an ice cube passage beyond, before the door closed again and the doorknob spun for a moment like a giant pearl floating in the middle of the waterfall. Then the crystal ball stopped still, and the Seasick Chamber was locked once more.

Will leaned back against his snowy pillow and looked curiously at the Text-A-Face left to him by Abednego. A crystal ball clasp sealed the tiny book, and when Will pressed it with his finger an eye blinked open to watch him before the watery cover flipped open by itself.

"Whoa—" Will flinched in amazement, for the book contained a three-dimensional miniature of Abednego's head.

Floating up out of the book, the old, wrinkled face stared at Will and spoke in a windy voice.

"Well… So you made it back, did you? It was a close call, by Fortune. I don't intervene in human affairs, you understand. So I didn't stop you. But I didn't help Valerian against you, either. One day, I shall write your story. It is worth capturing in a book. You may have seen my writings in the library? No?" Abednego's miniature blinked with disappointment as Will shook his head, too startled to speak. "Dew Pellucid is my pen name. What? A blank expression? Never heard of me? Well, I will be the Echo who makes you famous one day, young Sound. Remember that!"

And without another word, the head suddenly popped like a soap bubble and disappeared. And, with it, disappeared the watery book too, leaving only Illyria's medallion twinkling in Will's hand beneath the light of the flying crystal balls.

Suddenly, a gasp of wonder echoed behind Will, followed by a happy bark.

"That's not—?"

"You're awake!"

Will beamed at Peter's flabbergasted expression and jumped off his snow heap.

Spreading rings on the shimmering floor, Will rushed over to his friend, though without splashing or sinking for the floor looked like water but felt like stone beneath Will's feet. In a moment, Will reached the icicles night stand by Peter's bed, and he grabbed Illyria's treasure and dropped the little gold box in his friend's lap.

"But how—?" Peter's blue-green eyes looked as big as Cold Fire Mushrooms.

"Won it! For going to Olám Shoné," said Will, grinning so much his cheeks felt funny. "Can you find the lock?"

"Has to be here," said Peter, turning the gold box over and over. But all four sides were as smooth as glass. "Magic..." muttered Peter. "Give me a minute— So what about Valerian," he added, still examining the treasure chest with his magician's fingers. "What happened? Where are we? Where's the Prince?"

Will filled Peter in on all that happened, until he reached the part about—

"Wither Heart?" Peter choked in amazement. He pressed opposing corners of the treasure chest as if expecting something to happen, but kept staring at Will, looking dumbfounded. "He wasn't dead?"

"He is now." Will shuddered, but this time not from the cold.

"Then it wasn't her... following us," said Peter guiltily, glancing at the invisible girl sleeping in the third snow heap bed. "Still weird, though." He grimaced. "I mean, look at that hair on her pillow. And no head... Creepy."

Peter twirled the gold chest on his finger like a basketball, then pressed it to his healthy ear expectantly. Still nothing happened.

"Think it's gonna talk to you?" Will grinned.

"In this place?" Peter flicked the dry waterfall canopy hanging round his snow heap. "Why not?"

But the chest did not speak, and frowning over it Peter pressed one side, then another, in a jumbled order that didn't make any sense to Will.

"You know," said Peter in a moment, his hands still working furiously, "it's kinda weird... about Valerian—"

"What is?" Will frowned.

"Well, Valerian killed the King…" Peter's fingers seemed to play piano on the gleaming chest. "Then he stuck the King in the Lake of Eternal Ice."

"Yeah…?"

"Like a common thief."

Will began to see what Peter was leading up to. "Which defamed the King's name…"

"So why," said Peter, "was Valerian helping us *clear* the King's name all this time? –YES!"

With a soft click a square suddenly opened at the top of the gold chest. And there, just waiting for its embossed mirror image, was Queen Illyria smiling at them.

Without stopping to ask how Peter had done it, Will slipped the medallion in place. Instantly, the Coin Key began to turn by itself, just as it had done on the crystal blue door inside the Lake of Eternal Ice.

"So what sort of treasure is it, d'you think?" Peter managed to ask one last time, before a full circle was complete, and the top of the chest swung open, releasing a cloud of purple smoke and the tangy scent of apples.

At last Will and Peter peered into Illyria's treasure, seeing the famed riches no one had laid eyes on for hundreds of years. But all they saw was a Cold Fire Mushroom spewing angry lightning bolts. And, on either side of it, a useless, ugly object.

"A rusty Incendiary—" grumbled Peter. "And… this? What

is that?" Gingerly he lifted what looked like a crown of rotten leaves. "You've got to be kidding me. That's it? That's Illyria's treasure?"

Growling in agreement, Poudini turned his nose up at the gold chest and started barking across the chamber at the splashing door. Will turned in time to see the crystal ball doorknob spinning. Then Nurse Flight slipped through the fountain doorway, closing it behind her. Her glistening white reflection rippled beneath her tiny feet, as she crossed the room in Will and Peter's direction.

"What's *she* doing here?" wondered Peter, grabbing Poudini to stop him leaping off the bed in a fury of barks.

"Came with us... made sure we got better," explained Will. "What's gotten into Poudini?"

"Dunno..." Peter rolled his eyes—and suddenly his face froze, turning deathly pale.

Will twisted back.

Nurse Flight was still there. Only now she was lying motionless on the liquid floor, and a corpulent, see-through man was writhing out of her mouth, struggling clumsily to put on a gleaming white robe.

"An Echo—" Will shot to his feet.

"He killed her," choked Peter.

"Indeed, I have!" said the Echo, in a shrill voice for someone so plump. "And now," he added gleefully, "now, I'm going to kill you too. One arrow each."

The fat Echo pulled a shiny black Incendiary and two matching arrows from his gleaming pockets, and the arrows seemed to drip pale blood already.

In a flash, Will snatched the rusty Incendiary from Illyria's Treasure. He wondered frantically if the arrow would even release after so many centuries of storage. But the fat Echo was aiming his weapon at Peter, and there was no time to hesitate.

Will fired.

A startling force knocked his hand up in the air. The rusty arrow shot away, entirely off-course. It shattered crystal balls as it streaked across the domed ceiling. And, like frozen tears, the shattered lights rained down on the laughing Echo, while at Will's back Peter screamed—

"NOOOOOOOOOOOOO!"

As if trapped in a recurring nightmare, Will spun around to find his friend collapsing on his snow heap bed. Peter's face turned bright red as if a fire was blazing inside him. In his lap, Poudini whimpered at the dark shiny arrow, which Peter's gleaming Orphanage sweater was trying to clean off his sleeve.

"And now the best part," squealed the Echo, his flabby belly wobbling as he leapt forward, rearming his weapon. "My nephew's Sound, now you die. How delicious."

"Your nephew?" said Will. He threw himself behind Peter's bedside table, icicles shattering under his hands. "You're the false King," yelled Will, catching sight of the rusty arrow by the third snow heap, where Valerie was still sleeping, though turning visible.

"The *only* King!" raged the Echo, his voice turning so squeaky Will could barely make out the words. "*One and only* King, until you meddled. Come out of there, coward!" squealed the King. "Accept your fate, Sound! Face it like a man. Ah! That's better—"

Will leapt across the chamber, liquid rings bursting in the floor under his feet.

"Valerian did you a favor killing the King," shouted Will, his mind racing, trying to figure out a way to reach the rusty arrow without getting killed.

"Valerian?" The fat Echo squeaked like an angry squirrel. "A snake is less poisonous! Or should I say... *was*? I hear you killed good old Victor. At least your life wasn't entirely worthless, Sound. Short life." The false King snickered wickedly. "Show yourself, coward!"

Will crept around the snow heap, then risked a peek.

"Why didn't you kill Valerian yourself?" demanded Will.

"Eeeeee! Stay!" The false King's pale eyes disappeared for a moment as he spotted Will. "Won't shot! I won't shot, till I tell you," he promised. "You'll know everything before you die. Is it a deal?" The false King drew a crystal ball on the air and lowered his crossbow. "Won't shoot! Circle my heart and hope Fortune strikes me down."

"So, why?" said Will, rising slowly to walk toward the rusty arrow—and the false King.

"Better!" squeaked the pudgy man, his paunch wobbling as he teetered on tip-toes excitedly. "I saw him... Valerian. Saw what he did, the murderer! Killed the King, then ran off like the rat that he was. Coward! So I buried my brother in the lake." The see-through

555

eyebrows danced in triumph over the Echo's disappearing eyes. "*I did it! I* defamed the King's name—"

"And kept Valerian alive as a scapegoat?" Will's foot finally scraped the edge of the rusty arrow.

"It's no use." The false King chuckled, raising his shiny black weapon again. "You'll never bend fast enough. Accept your fate, you meddling, useless Sound. You're going to die! And I'm going to enjoy it!"

Out of sheer desperation Will raised the rusty Incendiary to hurl it at the Echo's hand—and suddenly he saw a new arrow gleaming in place of the old. He didn't know how or when it happened, but his weapon was armed again.

In a flash, Will fired.

Once more the rusty arrow streaked away with astonishing force, but this time Will was ready for it, and his aim was true. There was a sparkling explosion as the false King fired also. The two arrows crashed mid-flight. The black one spun back to land at the Echo's feet. The other shot across the liquid floor like the prow of a ship. It disappeared beneath the snow heap where Peter lay motionless, flushed and glistening with sweat, Poudini licking the black arrow stuck in his arm.

Already the false King was rearming his weapon. Will looked down at his own Incendiary. Incredibly another rusty arrow was forming out of thin air. But Will couldn't be sure how many more times his Incendiary could do this. The next arrow had to kill the false King. If Will missed, he would die, and everything would be lost—the Prince would be executed because his Sound was dead, Mongrels will be hunted forever, Sounds would never be safe, the Echoes would never be free… and Will would never get to show his parents that Emmy was alive!

Will took his time aiming his gleaming crossbow. He could see the false King doing the same. Suddenly Will fired—then threw himself on the liquid floor as a black arrow whizzed over his head, missing him by inches.

Violent waves shook the gleaming pond under Will's body, though the floor remained hard to the touch. A scream of terror shattered crystal ball lights high above Will. He twisted back. The false King was melting away, putrid dark smoke pouring out of his wobbling stomach where the rusty arrow had pierced him.

Soon, the fat Echo's arms unraveled, his legs curled away, then his last eye popped like a soap bubble and silence fell.

*   *   *

Will leapt over the floor that looked like a stormy pond. In a moment, he yanked the gleaming black arrow out of his friend's arm—and Peter regained consciousness with a scream.

"Had to do it—" said Will desperately. He dragged Poudini away from the wound spitting blood over Peter's elbow, where the self-cleaning sweater seemed to give up the fight. "Overheats everything it touches, the arrowhead," explained Will. "You're on fire inside! Here— There's some left, Peter—" Will snatched up the goblet of Cold Fire Mushroom brew smoking by his own snow heap. "Come on, drink!" he pleaded, tilting the potion to Peter's burning

557

lips. "You have to, Peter— Do it!"

Purple smoke spewed from Peter's red-hot nostrils. His burning face turned green then ashen. Soon he blinked his blue-green eyes, as if he could see again.

"Last time—" he coughed. "Absolutely the most disgusting thing on the planet."

"How's your arm?" asked Will, watching the wound in Peter's elbow sealing itself.

"Better," admitted Peter. "She's really dead?" he added with a shudder, looking past Will's shoulder. "Nurse Flight... there was an Echo inside her?"

"The false King." Will smeared the last drops of Cold Fire Mushroom brew directly on Peter's wound until it disappeared. "It's okay... he's dead."

"Dead— How? No way!" Peter shook his head in disbelief as Will raised the rusty Incendiary.

"It kept making new arrows," Will explained.

"New? How?"

"Fluid Conway's invention," said a soft voice behind them.

Awake at last, Valerie climbed on Peter's snow heap bed, looking pale and see-through, though she giggled when Poudini started licking her hand. "Where, in Fortune's name, did you get— That's not—?" She suddenly spotted the gold chest.

"Illyria's Treasure." Will smiled back. "We won the medallion. Thanks for helping us on the lake."

Peter scratched his bandaged ear guiltily. "About those

falling Christmas trees…" he began.

But Valerie wasn't listening. Her blue eyes wide with wonder, she lifted the crown of rotten leaves left forgotten in the gold chest and tried to place it on Peter's head.

"Hey— Get off!"

"But it's a Charmed Tiara," said Valerie. "Don't you want to see it working?"

"Working…?" wondered Will.

"You like it so much, you keep it!" Peter slid further down the bed.

"Me?" Valerie giggled. "I don't need it. I can do it anyway. Now, stop fidgeting!"

Jamming Peter against his frosty pillow, Valerie placed the withered garland on his head—and, in a flash, Peter disappeared.

"Fluid Conway's invention." Valerie beamed.

Will blinked in shock, but there was nothing to blink at anymore. Peter was altogether not there.

"What?" asked Peter's voice irritably.

Poudini sniffed the bed nervously.

"How do you feel, Peter?" asked Will, grinning.

"Stupid— Why? Do you want a go?"

"Eh… yeah."

A moment later Peter was visible again, and Will slipped the moist crown on his own head, laughing to see his friend gulping in amazement, looking like someone who had just won the lottery and was busy dying of happiness.

Whenever Will would think back on the next hour, he would remember it as the happiest in his life.

He was walking down a great icy hall inlaid with gold, silver and sapphires. Tall columns glittered everywhere as if sprinkled with diamonds. Snowy Christmas trees graced the far waterfall walls. Flying fairies that seemed carved from blue ice fluttered overhead, looking completely alive. Their voices tinkled like wind chimes, filling the chill air with Christmas carols.

Peter was to Will's left, limping but smiling brightly. Valerie was to his right, grave and pale like a statue, only her blue eyes twinkling too much, as if she was fighting back frozen tears.

All around hundreds of Echoes were assembled, dressed in fine robes of silver, gold and ivory, pearl, pyrite and pellucid fabrics that shimmered and flowed like water. Every eye was watching Will, Peter and Valerie walking through the crowd, down the icy walkway left wide-open for them, stretching to the end of the great, gleaming hall. For there the Prince sat on a throne of diamonds, Fortis Fortuna towering over him, a skeleton dressed in gold holding a crown that seemed made of giant snowflakes.

"Long live Fortune's King!" said the Leader of the Fortune Tellers. His voice quivered as usual, but somehow it carried far and wide, echoing off the diamond columns and the sparkling Christmas trees, as the ancient Echo laid the snowy crown on the Prince's head.

The assembly burst in a great cheer, and hundreds of hands drew crystal balls on the air. Startled, Valerie tripped, but Will

560

caught her and coaxed her on, with Peter still limping at his side. Together they marched forward, three small white figures beneath the glittering domed-ceiling that seemed as high as a cloud.

The newly-crowned King rose, a robe of icicles pouring down his shoulders to the gleaming floor. He raised his arms in the air, and the hall fell silent.

"Come forth, heroes," Will's Echo called to his three friends.

Will knew that it should feel weird to hear his own voice magnified until it shook the waterfall walls, to see his own reflection wearing a crown and addressing hundreds of adults as their sovereign. But in the glittering beauty of the moment none of it seemed strange at all.

Will climbed the crystal steps leading to the diamond throne with Peter and Valerie still at his sides. Then all three kneeled and bowed their heads, as the Master of Ceremonies had instructed them to do beforehand.

The hall fell so silent that Will could hear himself breathing. From the corner of his eye he saw a little girl, see-through and pretty, walking over with a snowflake cushion resting on her little arms. Something golden glinted on the snowy cushion, through Will couldn't see what.

"Friends," he then heard his Echo, his voice reverberating through the hall, "I hereby dub you Knights of Valor, and grant you each a Master Key, to open any door in my Kingdom."

One by one, the King lifted a chained gold key from the snowflake cushion and hung it around each of their necks, beginning

561

with Valerie, then turning to Peter. As he was bending over Will, the young King whispered between them, "They're here. First row. On the right."

Will didn't need to ask who. His mind was flooded with the memory of the crystal ball knocker gleaming on the door of his home back in the Sound realm. On the thumb of his right finger, Will wore the Safe Passage Ring Drinkwater had given him. He wondered if the Safe Passage Ring his parents found inside the crystal ball knocker would look the same.

His heart swelling, Will rose with Peter and Valerie and faced the cheering, sparkling hall. And there—not five feet away from him—stood his sister, Emmy, smiling brightly, with his Mom and Dad at her sides, embracing her between them as if she had never been lost. Will could hardly believe that these were the same sad people he had left behind only two and a half weeks ago. For now the wrinkles of sorrow had left the faces of his parents, and they were smiling without a care in the world. And, in their eyes, glowing brightly at Will, was a look of wonder and pride.

Never Abandon Your Friends

Epilogue

It was two months later, as Will was hurrying down a sparkling, icy corridor in the palace, thinking about Wolfeá and what she must be doing now, that Fortis Fortuna slipped slyly out of a side chamber. The watery floor rippling under his golden feet, the Leader of the Fortune Tellers blocked Will's way, with his red shimmering guards stopping a few feet behind him, their faces beautiful and severe.

"A strange thing happened at the Fortune Teller prison last night," said the ancient Echo, his crystal ball eyes peering eerily at Will.

"Really?" said Will innocently.

Will glanced around, hoping to spot his friends somewhere near. But there was no one else in the gleaming passage.

"Yes, really," said Fortis Fortuna coldly. His bald head looking more like a skull than ever, the Leader of the Fortune Tellers plucked a hovering crystal ball light out of the air and shone it in Will's face. "Your friends," he added bitterly. "The two traitors…"

"You mean Deá and Damian?" Will tried to sound even more

innocent. "Thanks to them the Prince became King—"

"*I* made him King," snarled Fortis Fortuna, the crystal balls suddenly spinning in his sunken eyes. "*I,* Master of All Fates."

"Yeah, that's what I meant." Will shrugged, squinting at the blinding light trapped in the taloned hand before him. "Well, what about those terrible traitors?"

"Escaped." Fortis Fortuna drew the light even closer, as if trying to read Will's soul with his crystal ball sight. "Slipped through my guards. Now how do you think two Echoes could just… vanish?"

"Well… some Echoes can turn invisible."

"Indeed. But not those two."

"You're right, then. Strange. Very strange."

The misty skeleton that was a man tossed his shimmering gold cape back, flicking his captive light free. "That's not the only ssstrange thing," he hissed, his thin nostrils sucking in air suddenly. "Is that apple I'm smelling?"

Will swallowed hard and put on a silly grin. "Delicious and nutritious. Had one for lunch."

"Did you?" The crystal ball eyes swirled hypnotically. "I thought apples grew on trees. Or do my crystal eyes deceive me? Isn't that mud under your fingernails?"

"Oh, that…" Will watched the shimmering red guards watching him with stony faces. "My friend, Peter… not my friend, I mean, his dog," Will rambled, "buried a chew stick in the garden. We had to help him find it."

Fortis Fortuna's skull-like face twisted with disgust. "Then

566

you wouldn't know anything about a secret garden in the palace? Let me finish, By Fortune!" he roared, as Will started shaking his head. "A garden with Cold Fire Mushrooms growing in it, multiplying like rats?"

"Rats? In the palace?"

Fortis Fortuna sighed in exasperation, and the floor rippled suddenly under his shimmering robe. "Children... What was I thinking...?" he spat resentfully. "It's a wonder you ever develop a brain at all."

Then the Leader of the Fortune Tellers swept off down the sparkling icy corridor, his gold robe fluttering magnificently, his shimmering red guards following obediently behind. While Will dashed away in the opposite direction, purple smoke trickling out of the heel of his glistening white shoe.

THE END

Acknowledgements

Only three Sounds read *The Sound and the Echoes* before its publication on Amazon Kindle: Dan Boldo, who contributed many wonderful ideas, read and reread the manuscript a fortunerific number of times, and without whom the story would never have been written or published; Stav Hassidov, whose interest meant a great deal to the author; and Sarah Brunstad, who, as an intern at Anderson Literary Management, rejected the story with a list of suggestions, one of which was incorporated in the Text-A-Face scene.

Two other Sounds read an early partial: Tom Jacobson, who made a few valuable suggestions, and Katie Kotchman, of Don Congdon Associates, whose encouragement and feedback inspired the author to keep polishing the story.

In a period of four years, *The Sound and the Echoes* was rejected by over 180 literary agents.

But thanks to Amazon, the story is now before you, brought to life by the stunning art of Andy Simmons, who was so very generous with his time and talent.

If you enjoyed your visit to the Echo realm, please invite your friends to visit too. It's by word-of-mouth that *The Sound and the Echoes* will become known.

My crystal thanks to you, dear un-pellucid reader!

The Royal Shekel